Also by Tetyana Butler

Adventures of the Little Adoleeseet
Chronicles of Twierks, Book 1

For more information on the books from
series Chronicles of Twierks visit
http://www.Twierks.com

Chronicles of Twierks

Adventure Series
Book 2

The Secrets of Daeya

A Novel

Tetyana Butler

ISBN 978-1-948503-01-3

Printed in the United States of America

Dedicated to the cherished memory of my dear parents,
good-hearted Eugenia Radzikhovskaya
and
the kindest and smartest Yurii Radzikhovskiy.

Acknowledgements

I want to thank Shannon Butler and Kelly Davenport for their help in editing and testing all the twists, turns and adventures that befell the heroes of the book.

I also thank my daughter Olga for her involvement and suggestions.

And, of course, I express my gratitude to great master Brian Kaufman for editing the manuscript.

Contents

Chapter 0. The Very Beginning. Or not the very. Or not the beginning.

Location: Unknown

Ecktoral and Adamant sat in comfortable chairs. A table sat between them. The room *had no doors or windows.* This was a mystery as perplexing as the two mysterious participants of this secret meeting.

"Do you remember the little Adoleeseet Chapa and his pal from Daeya, Davkaleon?" asked Ecktoral.

Adamant nodded and stretched out in the chair. The chair lengthened immediately, adapting to his posture.

"I do," shrugged Adamant. Such a small, weak little Adoleeseet, whom you promised to miraculously turn into an unseen hero and the terror of all enemies of Adolees. Did you invite me tonight to show me what he's capable of?"

"No, today it's not about the Adoleeseet, although he will make a few appearances. You will see, by the way, how he's matured. Today, though, I want to see what his friend Davkaleon is capable of. I prepared excellent adventures for him, but I do not intend to help him. You'll see - he can handle himself."

Chapter 1. At School

Priest Gerklat brought his sons to the city of Assa, the large capital city of Daeya. Today, five of his offspring were going to start their studies far away from their family estate. Their first stop was the School of the High Priests of Daeya. Paradion would study there - not a surprise, because Paradion was smart, cunning, ambitious, and he wanted to be a priest. Paradion shook his father's hand and offered his brothers a brave farewell as he disappeared into an elaborately decorated and spacious entrance hall.

Paradion was impressed by the elegance of his new school. He had not expected school to be more luxurious than his castle at home! The beautiful building was located not far from the central square of Assa. There, Paradion would spend several years studying prayers, rituals, and interpretation of omens. Paradion would become an expert on the will of the Gods—and the laws of Daeya—since the majority of criminal cases were reviewed by the High Priests in the courts of Daeya. Of course, religious violations were not considered criminal actions, but rather, as actions against the divine order. As a result, even the most insignificant offenses could land an offender in the High Priests' Court!

The School of the High Priests of Daeya accepted only a very small number of well-pedigreed and highly intelligent students each year. Each student was assigned a beautifully furnished private room with their very own personal servant. After all, the students would not have enough time to cook, do their laundry, or clean their rooms. No time for that!

Despite the luxurious comforts of the school, the

curriculum and schedules were anything but accommodating. Each room had a small library of specially selected books and detailed daily schedules. The school also had a central priest's library with thousands of runes, manuscripts, papyruses and ancient writings from all of Daeya. Paradion was full of nervous anticipation.

The School of Science was the next stop for Priest Gerklat. Elfid, another of his sons, would be studying there.

The School of Science was brand new and only opened this year, therefore, they didn't even have the detailed program finalized yet. The curriculum for this program was still a point of contention at the council of high priests of Daeya. There had been more and more disparity between the divine predictions and reality. The priests had calculated and checked everything a million times. They recalculated the dates of all the eclipses, giant tides, tsunamis, and hurricanes, and yet their inaccuracies were growing day by day. Even the ordinary people of Daeya were starting to notice the inaccuracies. Jokes were spread about the divine predictors. Some people even switched from their faith in the priests, and starting to believe in the sorceresses of Llill.

The priests retaliated by banning the term *sorceress.* Instead they commanded that people call them witches and only witches.

Labels are important, Priests thought. Sorceresses sometimes can be good and kind, but have you ever heard of or seen a good witch? A witch is a witch in any place in the world. The priests wanted the people of Daeya to associate the sorceresses with the word witch in order to imply that they were all old, evil crones that brought only pain and suffering to the good people of Daeya.

Of course, there was a problem with that. The

sorceresses of Llill (sorry, *witches*) of Llill were beautiful. The people of Daeya did not say so out loud, but many men wouldn't mind marrying a sorceress.

The fact was, the predictions from the "witches" of Llill tended to be more precise than the predictions of the priests. Of course, the priests wanted the people to think that anyone else's predictions were a bunch of lies. When the predictions of the *witches* came true, the priests claimed that the witches were connected with the dark powers, and that the more the people of Daeya believed in the witches, the more their dark power would grow.

But let's return to the school and the arguments about curriculum. The main reason for these arguments was in the level of access to ancient secrets, special runes and manuscripts, as well as divine places and objects in Daeya. The purpose of creating this new school was to prepare future graduates to explain the differences between reality and divine predictions, as well as find ways to eliminate disparity between the two. Everybody understood that if students were not granted access to secret places and documents, they wouldn't be able to give acceptable answers. But if they were granted access to things that had only been available to the highest priests, that would break all the rules and traditions of Daeya. The cost of studying at this school was a small fortune. The complexity of the school's entrance exams left very few eligible students.

What the School of Science lacked in luxury, it made up for in cutting edge technology. Each student lived in a spacious private room. The main library of Assa could be reached directly from the school. Students of the School of Science could get into hidden libraries and secret temples as well. Not to mention their equipment! Such equipment could only be a dream, even for priests. There's was no need to worry about dinners or lunches. Everything would happen according to the schedule and students would be well fed. Just sit, study and don't waste your time on any other endeavors. Only one thing missing - a personal servant for every student.

After all, it was still not the School of High Priests of Daeya.

Leaving Elfid at the school of science, Priest Gerklat went to the military school with his three remaining sons. Davkaleon, Malay and Kvorts waved goodbye to their father and entered the Military School building.

"Have you passed the shooting exam? Flying dragons?" a mysterious voice asked. The boys looked at each other, puzzled.

"No? Then, what are you doing here? Go to the shooting range and come back when you have passed all of the necessary exams!" The boys looked around for direction.

"What? Don't you know where the shooting range is? Interesting, your thick heads didn't even think to check the location of the shooting range before coming to the school!" The voice thundered from somewhere above them.

After looking around, the brothers realized that they weren't the only ones who had no idea about the location of the shooting range. The voice from above was still shouting, talking with someone else—someone they couldn't see.

"Tell me, Harding, where did they find these imbeciles for the school? Where does one find such morons? None of them even tried to find the location of the shooting range, which they have to visit to pass tests before even entering the school."

"Did you send them directions in advance?" asked the other, evidently named Harding.

5

"Do I look like a mailman?"

"Then, how could they know what to do?" Harding seemed more understanding.

"Don't they have their own brains to know that they should check?" answered the cruel voice.

"Have you prepared anything for them? Have you ordered food for them and prepared their dragons?" asked Harding.

"Am I their servant to order food? Maybe I should check all the rooms, wash floors and prepare beds for them?" The first voice was outraged.

The students waited as the exchange continued, confused and open-mouthed.

"How about a schedule or manuals?" Harding did not stop.

"A schedule!? Where can I get a schedule? They called me a couple of days ago and told me that I have to take on all of Haswardian's responsibilities, in addition to my own, with no explanation! They promised to send me more detailed information later. Did they send it? Phah! Of course not."

"So, what have you been doing?" asked Harding.

"I have been coming here every morning on time, reporting my arrival, waiting thirty minutes more, and then retiring to the tavern. It is good that the *Mug and Sword* is located a few steps from the school. I have spent a fortune in that place! It's good for me that the *Mug and Sword* allows those connected to the school to run a tab, because I am out of money. Do you know if there's any hope that the accounts department of the school will refund me this money as an expense? No? What a pity!" He exhaled in anger.

"So, you didn't think to check to see what Haswardian had done in years past to prepare for the new students?

Didn't wonder what instructions and requirements he sent to the students before their arrival?" asked Harding.

"Am I a mind reader? How could I know what they wanted me to do for the students? Haswardian had a lot of other duties and responsibilities aside from these newbies. How am I to know everything without instruction?"

"Didn't you try to go through the papers on his table?"

"What?! Harding, have you seen his table? One year is not long enough to sort through everything." The voices became silent, but not for long.

"Hey! Tell someone downstairs to put this on the door," said the angry voice.

A piece of parchment drifted down from somewhere above. It said, *do not dare to enter the school without test results from the shooting range.* Finally, both voices disappeared.

"Does anybody know the location of that shooting range?" asked Davkaleon, looking at people behind him.

"It's not far from the *Labyrinth of Assa*," said a student that had just entered.

That was simple, thought Davkaleon. Everyone knows the location of the Assa labyrinth. Everyone has visited it at least once in their life.

"I am talking about the military labyrinth of Assa," clarified the student who had just entered.

"Oh," Davkaleon said. After a short discussion, the Gerklat brothers and a dozen of the other newbies went to the shooting range of the military school to pass exams. They arrived at the military labyrinth quickly — just a short distance from the school. Which exams do they have to pass? Just shooting? *That* was no problem for the Gerklat brothers. They'd learned how to shoot when they were just kids.

Chapter 2. Tests, Tests, and More Tests

Several targets of different sizes were set out in a large field. In fact, they were not simply set there, but they were dug deep into the ground.

The smaller the target, the higher the point value. If you hit the largest targets, you will pass, but with less points. If you don't hit any of the targets, you fail. Davkaleon took a heavy spear, swung his arm, aiming to hit the smallest target.

Just as the test began, hurricane force winds blew and took Davkaleon from the ground as if he was a feather. The spear flew from his arms and after flying several yards, it hit the biggest target.

"You passed this test," said an officer, who appeared from nowhere and was marking something in a papyrus scroll.

"I want to try once more," demanded Davkaleon.

"What?! Do you think that we have nothing else better to do than to spend the whole day with you?" the officer said in a resentful voice.

"I can throw a spear much better than that. I was interrupted by the stormy wind," Davkaleon protested.

"Why do you think that there will be no wind next time?" the officer shrugged.

"But there's not any wind right now," Davkaleon insisted.

"Oh, I'm *so* tired of you. Okay, so, you want to shoot once more? Go ahead. But remember, if you fail this time, you will get a zero and you won't be able to enter the school."

The officer raised a horn and trumpeted. Davkaleon felt his stomach turn with anxiety. He took the spear, holding it very tight. Another hurricane wind appeared immediately, trying to pull the spear from his hands. Tall Davkaleon tried not to fall, crouching down and thrusting the spear into the ground. The wind increased every minute. Soon, a genuine hurricane raged around Davkaleon. He couldn't see anything farther than his arm's length! The wind started to calm down in a minute or two, and Davkaleon saw the figure of the officer in the rain, staring at him in disdain.

"So, do we have to wait for you forever?" asked the officer when he saw that Davkaleon was still waiting. The officer trumpeted once more and the wind immediately became stronger. In a minute, the hurricane raged as before.

They're doing that intentionally, Davkaleon thought.

He waited till the moment when the wind started to calm down and it was possible to see the fixed targets to throw the spear with all his power. The wind was still strong, so Davkaleon didn't try to hit the smallest target, though he didn't aim for the biggest one either. The spear pierced the center of the medium target.

"Passed, average level on the second attempt," announced the officer, writing something in his papyrus.

There was no reason to argue, so Davkaleon went away with mixed feelings. On the one hand, it was a very difficult task to hit the medium target with such a strong wind. On the other hand, he was totally disappointed with the officer's attitude.

"Have you noticed that the wind appears and disappears?" Davkaleon asked Malay, who was approaching the test.

His brother nodded and came closer to targets, holding the spear in his hands. The horn trumpeted, and a new hurricane hit Malay.

"Hey, my name is Krilis. I saw how you passed the test.

You are not from a military family, are you?" A young man had approached Davkaleon.

Davkaleon shook his head. Even though he'd been attracted to a military career from his childhood, his grandfather and father weren't military people. To tell the truth, his grandfather was serving as a priest in the army, but that was totally different than serving in the army. Of course, their family had some military ancestors, but that was generations ago.

"I have been watching these tests for a long time," Krilis continued, "and sometimes the wind can be incredibly weak, but in other cases it looks like a hurricane, which they made for you and for the guy who's trying to pass now. My family is not military either. I bet they will make a hurricane for me too."

"So, you are saying that all of the students from military families are welcomed with a soft breeze?" Davkaleon was surprised, because all his life he had lived in the family estate and had been shielded from the ways of Daeya.

"If you want, you can wait and watch yourself," shrugged Krilis. "Do you know how many students were eliminated with this test? However, this is the first year when those who are not from military families have at least some chance to enter this school, so it would be wrong to complain."

"What's so special about this year?" asked Davkaleon.

"What's so special? Don't you know that during the signing of the treaty with the behind-the-mountain savages, the commander-in-chief, along with his deputies, married the daughters of their rulers? They say they've gotten a huge dowry in return. But the rest of the military is dissatisfied. They think the terms of the treaty weren't good enough for Daeya."

10

"Are you saying that the commander of Daeya married for bribe?" Davkaleon was taken aback. Such a thing was monstrous!

"I didn't say that," Krilis reasonably objected, "but everyone knows that the next morning, each of the newlyweds got *felt boots* as an anonymous gift." Krilis smiled.

"I'm not sure what that means. I wonder, what are felt boots?"

Krilis smiled. "They are the favorite shoes of the behind-the-mountains savages. They make the savages look as clumsy as their bears."

For the first time, Davkaleon did not know what to answer. Criticizing the army was certainly new to him. The commander-in-chief of Daeya's army had always seemed to him a hero and the most important person of Daeya in the world, perhaps even more important than the Emperor himself. Anyway, the commander was an important person during war, which was almost constant in Daeya. The Emperor sits surrounded by his guards in complete safety in his Palace, but the commander-in-chief of the army defends Daeya every minute.

Malay joined them, swearing about the hurricane, which appeared during his test. He was relieved that he passed, but disappointed with the results.

"I swear," Malay shouted, "if there was an ordinary wind, I would have hit the smallest target a hundred times in a row, but that hurricane killed all my nerve to hit one of those tiny things."

Kvorts also passed, but he was dissatisfied with his results as well.

The next test was a flight on a dragon. The students needed to fly just ten miles. The brothers were sure that the test wouldn't be a problem — they'd learned how to fly on dragons before they were able to walk! The three brothers called their own dragons, but the military instructor stopped them.

"You have to fly on the dragons that belong to the school. Your flight time has to be less than ten minutes," he explained as he called their names from a list.

Davkaleon was the first to fly among the brothers. When he sat on the dragon, he was thrown up by the angry animal. Though he didn't fall off, people behind him started to laugh.

It was vital to know how to fly a dragon if you lived in Daeya. How else could you reach the most distant places of the wild planet? There were no planes or trains, and if you wanted to use a taxi, he would arrive flying a good old dragon. People learned how to control dragons from their childhood. If you fell off a dragon, you were considered inept, and people would ridicule your helpless soul. Even though Davkaleon managed to stay on the dragon, due to the outburst of laughter, he was very frustrated with the dragon.

"Move back! You are almost sitting on my head," roared the dragon, shaking once again. Davkaleon moved back slightly. Flying on his own dragon, Aleurh, Davkaleon was used to sitting closer to the head. As any person in Daeya, Davkaleon was able to read the minds of others at a distance, but his mind reading skills were average, thus he could only read at very short distance. In the case of dragons, mind reading was both easier and more difficult at the same time. It was easier, because the level of signal was higher, thus it was easy to hear. It was also harder, because the dragon language was significantly different from the Daeyan language. While sitting on Aleurh, he would get as close as possible to the head, to make it easy to give instant commands during various games with his brothers on the family estate of their father.

The instructor blew the horn and the dragon took Davkaleon into the air. At the very same time, a giant bird appeared from the side and tried to hit Davkaleon with its wide-open beak. Taking out his sword, Davkaleon hit the bird in its scary beak. Another bird hit him from behind. He turned around to deal with it, but another one came in to help. Aleurh would have blown fire at one of them and dodged the others, but this dragon wasn't even trying. One of the birds hit him from behind. Swinging his arm with all his power, Davkaleon cut its head off.

"How could you destroy school's property?" roared the dragon, "Do you know how expensive is to grow and train these birds?"

"Train?" Davkaleon was shocked, "Why would one train it to attack people of Daeya?"

"How do you think we can train you, if there are no threats?" the dragon answered angrily.

New birds arrived every minute. Davkaleon took out his second sword. While fighting with both arms, he couldn't see anything in front of him. Unfortunately, there was a giant tree in the way, so the dragon flew sharply up. Davkaleon barely managed to stay on the dragon's back, gripping with his thighs. Fire rocks started to fall from above, so the dragon swooped down, almost shaking Davkaleon off. A fire burst appeared from below and to the sides. The dragon made zigzags to dodge the blasts. Davkaleon's legs were slipping on the side of the dragon. Throwing one of his swords away, Davkaleon caught one wing of the dragon and continued to fight the flocking birds with his second hand.

"You are an idiot! Leave my wing and let me fly," roared the dragon, turning his head to Davkaleon.

"Stop shaking with your wing for at least a second and

let me climb on your back," Davkaleon scowled.

"Stop shaking my wing?" the dragon mocked Davkaleon, "Yes, I'm going to do that right now. A still wing can only fly down. Do I have to fall from the sky just because you can't keep your bum on my back?"

Another burst of fire appeared from below, but the dragon wasn't even trying to fly higher. Why would he do that? Fire brings no harm to dragons. It hurts riders, but this dragon didn't care about that. Davkaleon managed to climb back on the dragon, but that didn't solve the problem of fire. One good thing — the birds flew away, frightened by the flames.

"Fly higher," demanded Davkaleon.

The dragon pretended not to hear, while the fire began to burn Davkaleon.

Swinging with all his power, Davkaleon hit the dragon's back with his sword. His skin was like armor, so the blow did him no damage. The dragon shook, trying to throw his rider off. Davkaleon hit him again. The dragon zigzagged, then flew up and down, bucking like a horse. Davkaleon saw a labyrinth ahead, which was their final destination. Approaching to the labyrinth, the dragon turned upside-down and shook once more. Davkaleon hung on the dragon's wing again, dangling in space.

"How long are you going to hang on me?" the dragon asked spitefully. "Your ten minutes are almost over, and you will fail the test."

Davkaleon looked down, trying to evaluate his situation. If he jumped down, he would definitely break a leg, or even two. If he didn't, he would fail the test. Davkaleon released his hand and started to fall. Suddenly, he saw a shadow and something soft caught Davkaleon. That something was the stomach of his dragon, Aleurh. Flying down, Aleurh gently landed on the ground.

14

Davkaleon hugged his friend, who had just saved him from inevitable broken legs. Davkaleon noticed a wound on Aleurh's head. Davkaleon grabbed his bag with tinctures and other things, all of which were necessary for a military person. He started to clean the injury and applied a bandage. The school dragon landed close to them.

"You tried to kill me!" Davkaleon shouted at the dragon, which shook him all over the test field.

"Silence! Listen to your test results. You passed only because of your dragon. I don't know why he decided to save such a rude person as you. You can use your sword perfectly and you want to study here, and you weren't afraid to jump, but all good things about you end there. You are a chuff, who doesn't know how to deal with dragons, at least not one that is unknown to you. You must treat your own dragon better, because he decided to save you and flew all over the mine field, instead of flying around it. *I give the highest points to your dragon.* And you? You hit me with a sword in flight, which is an idiotic action. I was going to do everything I could to make you fail your test, but when I saw how you cared for your dragon, I changed my mind. I decided to give you a chance. You get the lowest amount of points, but you still pass. At school, you will have to take an additional dragon communication culture class, which will be paid for by you, and you will participate in it during your free time. You will also pay for the dead bird. Starting this evening, you have to spend three days in the school guardhouse for your attempt to attack the chief dragon of the military school."

"The chief dragon of the military school?" Davkaleon was amazed, looking at the dragon.

"Yes, that's my official position. Over the last twenty-five years, you are the first moron to attack your dragon during a test flight."

"But you tried to burn me alive in fire and pretended not to hear me when I ordered you to fly higher!"

"How about asking politely instead of rude orders?"

"I am sorry for my rude actions," Davkaleon said, bowing," but you were the first one to call me an idiot."

"Why were you trying to sit up by my head, instead of just using my back?"

"I am used to sitting close to the head of my dragon Aleurh. It allows us to communicate without wasting time for talking during fighting."

"Are you able to read dragon minds and understand the dragon language?"

"Aleurh taught me the dragon language. I am not the best student, but I can understand the general idea of dragon communication. As for mind reading, I have to be really close to the head. And another thing — during fights with my brothers and their dragons, Aleurh and I don't speak gently and politely. We just give short commands to each other. By the time niceties are completed, the battle could be lost."

"Well, maybe you are not as bad as I thought. I wanted to test you personally after hearing about your characteristics from Aleurh."

"What did he say about me?" Davkaleon was curious.

"He said that you will be the best chief of the army in the entire history of Daeya. I asked him to prove it somehow. He told me how you and he crossed the Valley of Death and returned back home safe. Here are your test results. Bring them back to the school," said the dragon, handing over a piece of papyrus, seemingly produced from thin air.

Chapter 3. Briefing

"You will live in school dorms," the loud voice of Sergeant Croncoross roared. He was a well-built military man, who instructed the newly arrived students. "Each of you arrived with your own dragon. The dragons will stay in the dragon quarters. You will train, compete, fight, learn, perform duties and play cards."

"Awesome!" one of newbies commented.

"Are you happy to participate in patrols?" Sergeant Croncoross said, squinting.

"Patrolling is great, too! You can catch monsters and bring them back for an amazing school dinner. But I am most interested in cards," he answered.

"How long have you played?" the Sergeant asked, nodding approvingly.

"Since childhood," the student answered proudly. "I have three elder brothers, who are studying in the military school. So, they taught me during their holidays."

"What is your family name?"

"Antonis, sir!" the youngest representative of Antonis clan stated.

"That is a military family name," said Sergeant with respect.

The Antonis family was well-known in Daeya. Since the beginning of time, all of the men of the Antonis family had served in the army of Daeya. At least half of all the chiefs of the Daeyan army had the Antonis family name. The Gerklat brothers listened in with great interest. Before that moment, they were sure that their shooting, dragon flying and monster fighting skills would have brought them to the leadership table of the school hierarchy. It seemed that they had totally forgotten about card games. They were able to play some games, but they

17

didn't know that a significant part of their studies at school would involve card games. Their mothers loved to play solitaire, but they were certain that Antonis and the sergeant were discussing totally different games. Elfid's mother, Dallilla, was a witch from Llill (though she called herself a sorceress). During the holy nights of the Big Three Moons, she would read cards. During such nights, a long queue of visitors appeared in front of her home. They brought rich gifts, hoping to learn their future and the future of their relatives, prepared for them by gods. But surely, that was not the kind of cards the military school studied.

Davkaleon focused on Antonis. Since his childhood, Davkaleon dreamed of becoming the chief of the army of Daeya. But "dreaming" is not the right word. He was *sure* that he would become chief of the army of Daeya. And not just when he reached fifty years old. At such an age, people think about comfort and relaxation. Of course, he did not insist on becoming a commander *immediately* after graduation from military school. He could wait a few years. While he was looking at the well-built figure of young Antonis, Davkaleon realized for the first time in his life that he would have serious competitors.

"Which games do you play?" the Sergeant asked Antonis.

"All that are played on school teams!" Antonis answered proudly.

"Imagine, you have a seven, nine and jacks of three suits: clubs, hearts and spades. You are playing *Misère*. You took the eight of diamonds. What will you use as your first card for the following lead?"

"No good lead. Play diamonds," Antonis answered.

"You are on the team!" the Sergeant declared.

Croncoross turned around and asked if anyone else

knew how to play school card games, putting special stress on the word *school*. About half of newbies raised their hands.

"Who has close relatives from military families?" the Sergeant asked.

All those "card lovers" raised their hands once again.

"Great," Croncoross said, nodding. "That means you understand the importance of card games for military people. Now, I have a question for the other newbies. Tell me, why are cards included in the program of the school? Use your brains and show me that you are smart," the Sergeant demanded.

Several boys raised their hands and the Gerklat brothers were among them.

"It allows us to use strategy and act as a team," different voices answered together.

Sergeant Croncoross nodded his head after each answer. Then he took out a deck of cards.

"A deck of cards like this doesn't take a lot of space, and you can always keep it with you. It will help you to pass the time far away from your families. The games push you to use your brain. They teach you both strategy and tactics. You will learn how to make the right decisions in situations when you are faced with a total lack of information. And when your dinner is at stake, you will learn how to play very fast. One or two days without dinner, and all the card rules will magically stick in your head. A couple of weeks in the *breakfast-only* mode, and you will transform from fools into average players. Remember, it's strictly prohibited to use breakfasts as bets. We don't want to endanger your studies just because you die from hunger."

Brave Sergeant Croncoross pointed to a pile of manuscripts, writings and scrolls, piled in one of the corners. "These are your manuals. Take and sort them. Don't wait for someone to do this work for you. We don't have babysitters here."

Sergeant Croncoross took one of the scrolls and rolled it out. The scroll included a description of a game.

"This one is a simple game," the Sergeant explained, "but even this game will show you the difference between playing on your own and playing in a team. Even though it includes a dozen varieties, you will understand its basics in just a couple of evenings. Those who can't understand will be expelled from the school, because we don't need morons here. In a couple of weeks, you will start to learn a real gem in the world of card games, but we'll discuss that later. Now, let's talk about another important part of the school program. I am talking about patrolling."

The Sergeant walked along the line of newbies, looking at the well-built bodies of the newly enrolled students with approval. One can't call the people of Daeya small. Weak people won't survive in the local winds, storms and hurricanes. The new students made the Sergeant happy. All of them were strong and tall. One can rely on such people in a fight.

"So, patrolling. You will participate in patrols from your very first day at the school. You have chosen a military career, so get used to it. A lot of strange creatures have appeared, attacking the people in Daeya these days. Such filth doesn't usually appear in the central regions of Assa. But the people who live in the more distant places can't solve such a problem on their own.

"Please remember, that if the filth is edible, bring it back to the school. The school's management needs to ensure that students are able to find dinner for themselves. The school is obliged to give you a certain amount of food—enough so that you will not lose consciousness when flying on a dragon. If you want to eat meat, you have to find it. Fortunately, Daeya has a lot of monsters and many of them are quite tasty. People will be grateful when students bring home meat to eat. You can't find enough monsters in the city of Assa to sustain the yourselves, but the Valley of Death is perfect for hunting on the weekends."

The sergeant cleared his throat before continuing. "It's not recommended to go there on your own, but if you can find a small group, why not? You can combine both training and team-building while hunting. Both things are necessary in war. In the evenings, you can fry your prey, play cards and prepare yourself for the card tournaments.

"If that sort of life doesn't appeal to you, you are free to go to the priest school or the school of science, which has newly opened this year. There, you don't have to hunt for your own dinner. They will give you enough food to eat. But I'm sure that you are not such idiots as to choose a life of learning of prayers and book studying instead of an exciting military life full of amazing events, fights, hunting and cards." He grinned. "And remember that girls prefer military men. We give them security, and our salary is stable. By the way, the military salary is excellent in Daeya. Rest assured that there are enough monsters and enemies for each of you, so you won't get bored."

The three brothers knew about the patrols, but the advice to go to the Valley of Death for hunting contradicted their mothers' words. Their mothers demanded that they avoid any harmful ventures, at least during their first year in the school. But dinner is a very important thing. If you have to hunt to get it, then you will go to the Valley of Death—this they understood.

"You will participate in patrols in accordance with the schedule. Usually, you will patrol three days a week at six-hour intervals. You will participate more often during national holidays. During the first three months, you will serve as trainees in groups which consist of older students and an officer. After taking the oath, you will become full patrol members and will serve to protect the people of Daeya."

Sergeant Croncoross walked along the line and said, "Now it's time to divide you into very impudent and normally impudent. Half of you were characterized as future chiefs of the army by the tests or according to your dragons. One of you even said that you are going to be the best chief of the army in the history of Daeya. What's the name of the best of the best?" The sergeant stopped to check his papers. "Here we are, Davkaleon. Who's Davkaleon Gerklat?"

Davkaleon stepped forward.

"Congratulations," Sergeant Croncoross grinned. "The future chiefs of the army have to know all sides of the military life, including the guardhouse. You will start your studies by learning the guardhouse. You will spend three days there, starting at eight o'clock in the evening. What did you do to annoy our distinguished dragon Whales to receive such a welcome?"

The line of newbies burst of laughter. Someone had to be a real knucklehead to go to the guardhouse on the first day at school.

"Let's talk about other future chiefs of the army. Who wants to take that position? Take one step forward," Sergeant Croncoross commanded.

Antonis was the first one to make a step. Other people followed his action. Davkaleon was already standing at the front of the line.

"Think twice, before making your final decision," Sergeant Croncoross offered. "All future chiefs of the army are going to patrol more frequently and will be patrolling more dangerous regions. Those who are less ambitions and want to take less risks will clean the school yard and premises more often. After graduation, the first group will be cast into the eye of the military storm, while the second group will be sitting in safe and comfortable offices. So, decide now, which group is for you.

Some people made a step forward, while others made a step backwards. As a result, the number of students in the first and the second row were almost equal.

"Our school has two teams," Sergeant Croncoross continued. "Fighting Dragons and Clever Sages. Future Chiefs, go to the right to join the Fighting Dragons. Office Plankton, go to the left, to the Sages."

Sergeant Croncoross checked his papers once more.

"Who's Krilis?"

Krilis made a step forward.

"Ah, Krilis of the Goodmann family. The Goodmann family has been the cleverest of the Clever Sages," Sergeant Croncoross grinned. "Which team will you join?"

"I will join the Clever Sages," answered Krilis.

"Of course. You were the first to come to the shooting range and the last to pass the test. Have you analyzed everything?" asked Croncoross.

Krilis nodded confidently.

"Perfect. Now you will write a report. Here's a sample from the previous year. You will write it immediately after classes and will bring it to me in the evening. Remember to use calligraphic handwriting and avoid stupid mistakes. You will be our most clever analyzer." The sergeant turned to the other students. "Now, hurry up for your first lesson. It will start in ten minutes."

Chapter 4. A Lesson of Logic

"Does anyone know what happened to Haswardian, the one who dealt with the beginners in previous years?" asked one of the students when most had entered the classroom.

A few people laughed.

"Works every year without a hitch. Everyone is taken in by this prank," smiled Antonis. "The funny thing is, there is not and never was any *Haswardian* at school. They play this trick differently each year, first, in order to immediately weed out those who are accustomed to everything being prepared and presented to them on a silver platter. Second, in order to promote *Mug and Sword*. Do you know how much the owner of the *Mug and Sword* pays the school for that? I assure you, a *lot*. But keep in mind, the place is really cool. I propose to go there today after class and celebrate our enrollment to the school. At the same time, we can get acquainted and play cards."

Davkaleon seriously regretted the fact that he had to go to the guardhouse instead of being in the thick of things. A short military man of middle age entered the classroom. He was short by the standards of Daeya, of course. Imagine—he was actually less than seven feet tall! Despite his small size, he had a thunderous voice.

"Stand up!" demanded the incomer. "This is not a dance school for young girls. You should welcome the teacher by standing."

The class instantly stood, but someone was still whispering about the *Mug and Sword*.

"Quiet!" The military's voice rose up to the ceiling. "You will only speak when you are called upon. Now sit down."

The Gerklat brothers looked at each other. Behavior in the military school was very different from that to which they were accustomed. In the estate of their father, the teachers kept order but also behaved as employees of the family.

"You will call me Mr. Holikus" continued the teacher. "I will teach you logic. First, I want to assess how familiar you are with using logic." He approached the wall-board and wrote something.

"You need to write on your papers the number that corresponds to figure 4. Time allotted is one *second*." said the teacher of logic and stepped aside, giving the opportunity to see the written.

$1 \leftrightarrow 4$
$2 \leftrightarrow 8$
$3 \leftrightarrow 12$
$4 \leftrightarrow ?$

One second passes quickly. Davkaleon barely had time to look at the board and write $4 \leftrightarrow 16$, as Holikus was suddenly standing next to him.

"What team are you on?" asked the teacher in a mocking voice. "Ah, the commander, that is clear. To swing your sword, you don't have to look at the first line, where it is clearly written that 1 corresponds to 4, and then vice versa would be true, no? If 1 corresponds to 4, then 4 must correspond to 1."

They heard laughter in the classroom. Not accustomed to derision, Davkaleon loudly protested. "You could give at least two seconds to have time to look at these ridiculous numbers."

Such arrogance! You think that I will tolerate you calling my lesson ridiculous? Three days in the guardhouse, starting tonight!"

"It can't start tonight" snapped Davkaleon. "I am

already scheduled for the guardhouse. Dragon Whales is the first in line."

The class laughed again.

"You think you are rather smart. Let's get a little more acquainted with you," said Holikus, pulling out the parchment with records of Davkaleon's tests.

"So, there's nothing surprising in the fact that you didn't even glance at the first line. You don't have logic at all, I see."

"Why is that?" Davkaleon was outraged.

"First, stand up when you talk to a teacher. You're in the military school. Get used to discipline. Second, for hitting the first big target you get 10 points, 20 points for the middle one and 30 points for the smallest. Using a score from a second attempt decreased your point value by ten times. You hit the big target on the first attempt. It was not the most brilliant result, but not the worst. Only a third of students in the class hit even the biggest target on the first attempt. If you had even the slightest rudiments of logic, you would have taken the result and immediately proceeded to the second test. But as you are not familiar with logic, you demanded to retake the test. Congratulations! Instead of taking the 10 points from the biggest target, you reduced your points to two for hitting the middle target on the second attempt."

"What a stupid system!" Davkaleon raged. "If I hit a target both times, the results should be added together."

"Just look at this fool! He has barely spent a day at school, and he thinks he can change our scoring system. Didn't you wonder why everyone wasn't taking the test twice? You want to become the commander, and you say that you will be the best of the best commanders that Daeya has ever seen. What a pity to disappoint you!"

"I did not say that! My dragon said that of me." He

26

paused. "But I have to say that I fully agree with him."

The class laughed again.

"You definitely don't suffer from modesty, but you have interrupted me several times. What is the punishment for such a thing?"

"The guardhouse. How many days this time?" asked Davkaleon.

"Three more from me. So, all told, you have nine days, starting tonight, as dear dragon Whales ordered."

While he spoke, the teacher of logic walked between the rows. Looking at the responses of the students, Mr. Holikus shook his head sadly.

"Who is being recruited to this military school? You are supposed to become the officers and defenders of Daeya! And you don't know the word *logic*. You don't have it in your lexicon. Every last one of you wrote $4 \leftrightarrow 16$. No one bothered to look at the first line."

"You didn't give us any time to look at the line!" objected Kvorts, Davkaleon's brother.

"Who's heckling me?" asked Holikus, stopping near Kvorts. "Aha, another son of the priest Gerklat!"

Next to Krilis, Holikus stopped and smiled.

"At last, there is one smart student in this class. What team are you on? The team of Clever Sages? *Great.* This team needs logicians. Not everyone should wave a sword."

Turning to the class, Mr. Holikus began a fiery speech. "You will have other lessons at school. No one will know whether you have to spend five minutes or the whole night to do your homework. You will not have the luxury of time in battles. You will need to command the troops in the future. The lives of Daeya's people will depend on you, and you will need to make your decisions quickly. My goal is to teach you how to do that. One of you asked me to give him more time. Interesting! During battles, is he going to ask

27

the enemy to give him more time?"

The logic teacher stopped in front of Davkaleon.

"Can you imagine how it will look? You will lead a squad into battle. A group of Svargs is rushing at you, and you turn to their leader with a request. *Please,* you will say, *ask your soldiers to stand still for a few moments. My guys intercepted your coded message, but they did not have time to decode it. They are quick, though. A couple of minutes will be enough for them to decipher it.*"

Davkaleon tried to argue. "But you are not a Svarg! You are Daeyat who teaches the other Daeyats."

"And how can I teach you, if you are gabbing instead of studying?"

"Okay, I understand. Let's move on to the next task," Davkaleon nodded.

"Well, thank you for your permission. Did you dictate to your teachers in the estate of your father, the respected priest Gerklat?" There was a definite sarcasm in the voice of Holikus.

But Davkaleon did not recognize his sarcasm, and rushed ahead with great enthusiasm. "Sure! If the captain of the guard is out training with the dragons, what kind of idiot would sit inside and solve tasks? Of course, I was out on maneuvers with my dragon. When the Svargs attacked the last time, did I sit and solve tasks with my teachers?! Of course not! I was out protecting my family and my people. They tried to keep me safe behind the lines of action, but *that* wasn't going to happen. I personally killed two Svargs. If there are not attacks going on and a hurricane is preventing me from training with my dragon, then and only then, I might be willing to work on tasks."

The class laughed again, and the Gerklat brothers nodded approvingly, expressing full solidarity with Davkaleon. The teacher of logic was stunned for a moment before launching into an impassioned monologue in which Mr. Holikus stated that any student who argues and interrupts him would go into the World of Grey Shadows very quickly. Diligent students would get the joy of the Gardens of Paradise. The World of Grey Shadows and joy of the Gardens of Paradise referred to the life after death according the beliefs of Daeya.

"Do we have any chance to make it through your lessons alive?" asked Davkaleon.

The class laughed again. Mr. Holikus shook his head and continued the lesson.

"There is a set of sticks in front of you on the tables. Stack them to get that kind of expression." With these words Mr. Holikus showed a picture of an equation:

$$9+3+2=0$$

"I hope each of you understand that this expression is incorrect. You're required to move only one stick to get the right expression. Give me at least three correct expressions. Those, who get more, will earn their first point. I will give you three minutes."

By shifting sticks, Davkaleon got:

$$9+3-2\neq0$$
$$9-3+2\neq0$$
$$9+3+2>0$$

He thought for a moment and added sticks again. This time he got:

$$9-3+2=8$$

He wanted to add one more expression, but there were

29

not enough sticks in the set. "I have earned my first point and can earn more, but there are not enough sticks here," stated Davkaleon.

"If you do not have enough school sticks, you can gather up them in the dungeon on the way to the guardhouse," the teacher answered angrily. He strode over to look at Davkaleon's equations.

"But you are a cheater!" outraged the teacher of logic, looking at the first three expressions.

"Me? Cheater? Why?!" surprised Davkaleon. "Everything here is correct!"

"The task was to create real expressions like your forth one," the teacher answered.

"What is wrong with the first three? They are correct! If you think they are wrong, then something is wrong with your logic!" Davkaleon's face flushed red.

Mr. Holikus's patience had finally run out. "Guardhouse! Right now!"

"Okay," shrugged Davkaleon, heading out of the Classroom. Near the door Davkaleon stopped and asked, "Where is your stupid guardhouse?"

Rolling his eyes, the logic teacher asked, "Did you even look at the *Military School Code of Conduct*, at least out of curiosity?"

"How could I have looked at it if I had no idea that such a book existed?"

Hopelessly waving his hand, the respected teacher of logic said, "The guardhouse is in the dungeon. Now get out of my lesson."

Chapter 5. Guardhouse

Out of class, Davkaleon had to expend a lot of effort before he got into the dungeon. He appeared in an empty corridor.

"You want to know where the guardhouse is, already? Did you manage to earn the guardhouse at the first lesson on the first day of school?" asked the officer, who Davkaleon bumped into in the dungeon.

"No, at the lesson I earned my second and third sentences to the guardhouse. The first one, I got during the admission tests," explained Davkaleon.

"I really admire you!" The military smiled and whistled. From under the ground a pair of vicious, hairy figures with long arms and long claws on their hands and feet appeared.

"They are goblins," Davkaleon was taken aback.

"Of course. Did you expect that the school staff would guard you?" shrugged the military man.

"Why do I need to be guarded? If I was going to run away, I would have never gone down to the dungeon," said Davkaleon surprised.

"Are you a dispute fan?" grinned the military man.

"That is what the teacher of logic said to me. Dragon Whales thought that I don't know how to deal with dragons, though I grew up with dragons and I have always been very good with them."

"How many days will you spend here?" asked the officer.

"Nine days for now. Oh, no. It seems to be twelve." answered Davkaleon.

"For now? Are you planning on living here while at school? I don't think you'll like it here. Okay, go now. The goblins are waiting for you."

At that very moment, the pair of hairy goblins grabbed Davkaleon's hands, intending to drag him to the cell. If Davkaleon was thinking, then perhaps he would have obeyed. But he did not think and acted on instinct. His instincts told him that if he was being grabbed, he must defend himself. Having escaped from the clutches of the goblins, Davkaleon kicked one of them, and drawing his sword, turned to another one. There was a loud roar and goblins with swords poured in from all sides. Davkaleon grabbed a second sword and struck the nearest goblin. Wielding two swords, he fought off the attackers. The military officer did not interfere. He watched with interest at the action.

"What is this foul evil?" Davkaleon heard Malay's voice.

In the next instant, his brother pulled a pair of swords and crashed into the attackers pursuing his brother Davkaleon. It was much easier to fight the crowd of goblins together. After watching for a few minutes, the military officer ordered the fight to stop. No one paid attention. Pulling out a horn, the officer blew it. A few strong military men descended on the dungeon. After a few minutes of intense grappling, Davkaleon and Malay were disarmed and listening to a heated discussion of their fate.

"Bring them to the military court!" was the first proposal.

"That is impossible. They didn't take the oath. And without an oath they are not military."

"Then a slap to the neck and expel them from the school!"

"We can slap them on the neck, but there is no need to expel them from the school." The first officer, who'd called the goblins in the first place, unexpectedly stood up for the brothers. "Watching them fight was very entertaining. They fight perfectly. The school needs such students. For some reason, our school trains too many logicians-arithmeticians. But they are only able to solve puzzles and have no idea what to do with a sword. I will take these two students on my team."

"What do you want to do about this incident?" asked another officer.

"I will add 10 days to their guardhouse sentence and give them a copy of the *Military School Code of Conduct*. I will let them sit and learn. If, at the end of their sentence, they don't have it memorized, I will add 10 more days. I will continue to do so until they can recite the whole book."

"The whole book? Well, Harding, you're a sadist," said another officer.

"This year, you are our first clients, so you can choose your quarters," said the escort, pointing to a series of empty cells. The guards here are goblins, who are not known for their good temperament. So, be quiet, and act in accordance with the rules."

Their escort threw the brothers a scroll of the rules.

"Read to each other aloud. You will need to pass a test at the end of your sentence. Now choose your cells. The cells in the row near the wall have outlets to the dungeon, but I advise you not to use these. There are a lot of monsters in the dungeon, and encounters with monsters do not lead to good. The remaining cells will protect you from the monsters, but they will not provide you dinner or lunch. So, choose as you prefer—lunch or security. You will go to the lessons and have breakfast. Do not expect more. Immediately after class, you are required to report to the guardhouse. If you fail to do so, you will be expelled."

"I'll take that corner cell near the wall with access to

33

the monsters. They say you can cook the perfect lunch of monsters," said Davkaleon.

"And I will settle in the neighboring cell. By the way, can we have our weapons?" asked Malay.

"As soon as you will serve your time, you will get your weapon," said the escort and went away.

"What are you here for?" Davkaleon asked his brother, as soon as they took nearby cells. The cells were very small. Two brothers wouldn't fit in one cell together. There was a grate between the cells, so it was possible to see each other and talk.

"For the same thing you are," replied Malay "I told the teacher of logic what I thought about his stupid questions, and in response, I got three days as well. Do you want to know the stupid question he asked me?

When the day after tomorrow will be yesterday, today will be as far from the night of the Big Three Moons as the day that was today, when tomorrow was the day before yesterday. What is the day of the week we're talking about?"

"I answered him that today is Monday, so we talk on Monday. And he asks me how this is consistent with the fact that, when the day after tomorrow will be yesterday and today will be as far as, and so on. I told him that I have no idea what should be consistent with what, but today is Monday, so we're talking on Monday and that's all. After a small dispute, he asked my name, and found out that I am Gerklat. He became enraged and screamed something about arrogant egotistical priest's sons, and then sent me to you. He probably felt bad, and wanted not to let you be sad here."

The brothers barely had time to discuss their first

impressions of the school when they heard the peals of laughter. The laughter increased, and several new fellow students appeared in the passage. The third Gerklat brother was among them. Kvorts was laughing with the others.

"Look how these people rejoice the fact that we are in the guardhouse," grinned Davkaleon.

"Do not be greedy, share your good mood. What else did the logician ask you?" asked Malay.

"No problem, listen," laughed Kvorts.

"Musik plessses Pusik. It is required a half of goosik to plesss one Pusik. How many goosiks does one Musik need to plesss four Pusiks?"

"What?! And *that* is called logic?" laughed Malay.

"I'm hungry and I would not refuse that this Musik pleases me with a goosik, whatever it is, instead of Pusik," said Davkaleon. "Isn't it time for us to visit the monsters?"

They heard a noise in the dungeon, and several new offenders appeared in the passage. They were slightly older. Looking around, they realized that there are not enough cells with access to the dungeon for everyone.

"Now, will you just look at those haughty fools. They just arrived at school and took the best cells. What will you have for lunch? There are only two cells near the wall. If you think that two of us will bring lunch for the crowd, forget it. You should have left space for your elders at the wall."

"Why do you think we would expect lunch from you?" the Gerklat brothers protested in unison.

One of the newcomers walked up to the corner cell of Davkaleon and asked angrily "What are you doing in my apartment?"

"Yours has now become mine," shrugged Davkaleon. "You should not be late to the allocation of the best cells."

"Crassius, let him enjoy your cell without lunch," suggested one of the new arrivals.

Crassius gave Davkaleon a hostile look and said, "Who are you? You showed up in the morning, and already started to push for your rights in the afternoon. What family are you from?"

"I am Davkaleon Gerklat, and if you strain your brain a little, you may figure out that I am from the Gerklat family," grinned Davkaleon.

"Ah, that's it! You are the one who is the best of the best," said Crassius mockingly. "You would do better to crawl into a cell in the middle row, cling to the wall and not catch my eye. I'm sick of cocky posers like you. I am Crassius Pompeus and you would do best to stay out of my way."

"And you should better bite your tongue. A mouth should not speak if there is no brain to form the words," parried Davkaleon.

"You are a foolish boy!" roared Crassius, but he couldn't continue. Two vile goblins dragged him away from the cell."Leave me alone, you scum, if you do not want to lose your contract. Do you know who I am?"

The goblins did not stop dragging Crassius away, but they did loosen their grip.

"Choose a cell," one of them said.

Approaching one of the free cells near the wall, Crassius selected one. No one from his group argued, and the door with a heavy lock slammed shut behind him.

"I will go for dinner," announced Davkaleon. "Who will go with me?"

"I will!" startled Kvorts.

"I will," came more voices.

"Well, well, let's see how many of you will run away from just a rustling noise. Not to even mention what you would do if you saw a monster," mocked Crassius.

"Never ever in my life have I run from anything!" Davkaleon shouted. "If you have a problem with me, let's go and sort it out. I promise you that you will forget all about your dinner. You will not need it anymore."

The other students laughed. Apparently, Crassius was a frequent participant in school fights. "Crassius, you should whip this haughty smart-aleck and show him who is boss," said a voice from somewhere in the middle row.

"Of course, I'll put him in his place, but first, I'll see how he runs away from simply hearing an animal growl."

Chuckling contemptuously, Davkaleon stepped into the dungeon. His brothers and a few fellow students followed him. Crassius and his goon followed.

Chapter 6. Hunting

It was almost completely dark in the dungeon. The light flickered intermittently from above. The students worked their way through a maze one turn, another turn, a fork in the path, and then another one. In open space, Davkaleon knew how to navigate by the sun of day and by the moons and the stars at night. But there were no moons, no stars and no sun in the dungeon. Davkaleon chose to turn to the right every time, so that when he came back, turns to the left would lead him back to where he started. The others silently followed him.

"I wonder why it is so quiet? This place seems too silent to be inhabited by monsters," said Davkaleon after they walked through the maze of the dungeon for forty minutes.

No one answered. The silence was oppressive.

"Someone here was talking about the animalistic roars of predators. I don't hear them. Was everything different here before?" asked Davkaleon.

"It was different before," said the companion of Crassius, anxiously looking around.

"So, someone dealt with all the monsters before," concluded Davkaleon.

"Quiet! Freeze! Pompedius, do you hear something?" asked Crassius.

All listened. A dull thrum broke the dead silence. Treading on heavy paws, an animal was sneaking into the labyrinth of the dungeon. Even from a distance, they could hear him wheezing. Everyone grabbed whatever weapons they had managed to get past the goblins. Then, a low, guttural growl cut the formidable silence. Apparently, the beast was very close.

"I think I see it," whispered Malay.

Davkaleon strained to stare through the darkness. A figure of the beast appeared from behind the next turn. The beast was close to the ground. They could see wild power and ferocity throughout his appearance. The beast stirred. It's terrible, burning red fire eyes flashed in the dark. The beast moved forward. Davkaleon was sure that if he had a bow, he could hit the monster in the eye on the first shot. A long bayonet or a lance would help too. But he only had a few knives that were hidden in secret pockets.

"Do you still have a sword?" Davkaleon asked Malay in a whisper.

"No, I have knives only," replied his brother.

"I have one sword," Kvorts whispered.

"Give it to me...or will you hit it?" asked Davkaleon.

"I will hit," Kvorts answered.

"I'm aiming for the left eye, Malay for the right eye and Kvorts for the mouth," commanded Davkaleon.

Three knifes pierced the beast. The beast howled and stood up on its hind legs. Kvorts jumped forward and struck the beast in the neck with the sword, and at the same moment the beast struck with his paw. A glancing blow barely touched Kvorts, knocking the sword out of his hand. Kvorts jumped sideways. Davkaleon and Malay threw more knives. The beast roared and fell to the ground. One of the classmates raised the sword of Kvorts, but he hesitated to attack the beast.

"Let me," demanded Davkaleon, and having grabbed the sword, he jumped onto the beast's back. Swinging, Davkaleon hit with full force. The fierce struggle did not last long, and soon the beast fell silent.

"Dinner is served! Who's got a flint?" asked Davkaleon, wiping his sword on the skin of the animal and returning it to Kvorts.

"What are you going to ignite with the flint?" asked

Crassius mockingly

"Tell me where I can find something to fry our dinner. Be of some small use. Or did you come here to see how we hunt?" Davkaleon said angrily.

"Shut up," roared Crassius pulling a sword. "Do you think you became a hero when it took three of you to kill one unfortunate beast?"

"Give me your sword," Davkaleon asked Kvorts. There was no need to ask—Kvorts was offering him the sword.

"Stop," interrupted the companion of Crassius, coming closer. "You don't want to fight with this incompetent newbie after the officers told us not to do it," said Pompedius.

At the mention of incompetence, Davkaleon hoisted his sword to the ceiling of the dungeon. This would be the last time someone dared to call him incompetent.

"You don't want to attack the nephew of the commander-in-chief of the Daeyan army," Pompedius said to Davkaleon.

"Attack? Who pulled a sword first?" Davkaleon was outraged.

"And you insulted him first, saying that his presence was useless."

"If anything, it ..." began Davkaleon, but Pompedius cut him short and explained that the goblin- guards would trade a flint and something on which they could fry their dinner in exchange for half of the loot.

Reluctantly giving the sword to Kvorts, Davkaleon asked whether all nephews of the Commander-in-Chief took up their swords after the hunt was over, or just this one. The quarrel was ready to break out again with new force. Pompedius intervened, asking Davkaleon whether all the sons of the priest Gerklat stated that they would become the best of the best commander in Daeya's history, or just this one.

"I will!" firmly replied Davkaleon. "What's the point of becoming the Commander-in-Chief if you are not sure that you will be the best of the best?"

"Best of the best? Let's see what you'll do in the tournament," Crassius growled as he put his sword away and headed back toward the guardhouse. He walked confidently. It was obvious that he and his companion were frequent guests at the guardhouse. Davkaleon and his brothers followed them.

Crassius and Pompedius spoke in a whisper, but Davkaleon caught a snatch of the conversation. "I can't stand these new guys. No one in their family has ever fought for Daeya, and yet they are pushing for status, even though they have hardly been at school a day. They are like cockroaches! What is happening? This year, more than half of the students are not from military families."

"Yeah, I noticed," agreed Pompedius, "what is going on?"

Goblins appeared, as if from under the ground. As soon as the team of hunters returned to the guardhouse, the goblins handed them everything they needed to prepare their meal. The pleasant smell of roasted meat reminded everyone that lunch time passed long ago.

"Should we take this time to become acquainted?" asked Davkaleon, once his sharp hunger was appeased. "I am Davkaleon," he began, but never finished.

"Is this the one who is the best of the best?" laughed another one of Crassius companions.

Rumors in military school spread quickly.

"If you like you can call me so," said Davkaleon peacefully.

"Don't you ask for lot of honor?" asked Crassius.

"So, I do not insist *yet*," grinned Davkaleon.

41

"I offer to call you the best of the best insolents," said the companion from the middle row.

The rest of the company of Crassius responded with laughter.

"You know, it's not polite to insult the one who feeds you dinner. That sort of rudeness is not accepted in Daeya. Is your dad one of the Svargs, by chance?" replied Davkaleon, his eyes narrowed.

"What?" The boy's face showed his rage. "You are a Svarg yourself! Wait till get out of here. I'll teach you to be polite."

"You should not hide in the middle cell like a coward. If you sat like a brave man in the line with access to the dungeon, we would come out, limber up and find out which of us is the real Daeyat. We wouldn't need to postpone the politeness lesson," grinned Davkaleon.

"Why, you impudent snot! You and your youngsters stole the best cells!"

"You should not be late to the allocation of the best cells," Davkaleon pointed out. "I booked mine before the start of classes, and you could not tear your butt from the chair, so don't complain."

Dining conversation was interrupted by the appearance of another student.

"Well, a lot of people accumulated here on the first day!" protested the newcomer, when he saw that all the cells near the wall were occupied. The goblins shoved him into the cell in the middle row.

"Which one of you is Davkaleon?" asked the newcomer.

"I am, and what's it to you?"

"I will pull out the guts of your dragon when he leaves the dragon guardhouse, if, of course, he gets out of there alive. That arrogant beast earned 10 days in the guardhouse and put my dragon in there with him. Should

I walk or pay for flights on the school dragons to get around for the next 10 days?" grumbled the newcomer. "You will compensate me for all the damages and, moreover, you'll pay with interest."

"Ha! I will compensate you, of course. Keep your pocket wide open for me, will you? Why did your pathetic lizard latch on to my wonderful Aleurh?"

"Were you there, that you make that accusation?"

"My Aleurh is a gentle and affectionate creature...if you don't touch him, of course. If you hurt him, then don't be surprised if you end up in battle with the best of the best fighting dragons Daeya has ever known."

At the words about the *best of the best*, Davkaleon heard a chorus of laughter in the guardhouse.

"Marcus, how can you be so rude? He's almost the Commander-in-Chief, and you're here with your pretensions," said Crassius.

"Do not worry yourself, Crassius, this is none of your business," snapped Davkaleon. "Who knows where the dragon guardhouse is? And, by the way, do they feed dragons there or do the dragons have to hunt their lunch, like we do?"

"I would tell you, but you asked me to mind my business," said Crassius sarcastically.

"No one feeds dragons there, and there are no paths to the dungeon for monsters—the riders have to feed them, and I am here stuck with you while my dragon is starving because of your stupid beast," said Marcus.

"So, you are saying that my Aleurh will be stuck without food or water while I enjoy your company?" Davkaleon was outraged.

"The best of the best—you got it, finally," snarled Marcus.

"You will not touch my Aleurh, and if you call him a

beast again, you will regret ever being born. You better tell me where the dragon guardhouse is."

"Are you able to get dinner for the dragons or was that story about you and he crossing the Valley of Death together pure bragging?" asked Marcus.

"Of course, I am able to get dinner. Who do you think got this dinner? Okay, okay, not alone...together with my brothers. And I have crossed the Valley of Death with Aleurh, and I was in a battle with Svargs, and I personally killed two Svargs."

"I wonder, who would take you to such a real battle?" Crassius asked contemptuously.

"Kvinsit took me, the captain of guards for my father. He had been training me and Aleurh since childhood. Do you remember the attack on the Watchtowers two months ago? Kvinsit, of course, tried to keep me behind, he promised my father to take me just for training. That was the day when I killed two Svargs."

"The Watchtowers belong to the priest Gerklat. Are you his son?" asked Marcus.

Davkaleon nodded.

"Kvinsit is a distant relative of mine. I'll ask him if it's true," said one of the students.

"Why do you want to wait until you see Kvinsit? Kvinsit gave me a recommendation. It describes my participation in the battle with Svargs. It may be shown to anyone upon request at the school. After imprisonment in the guardhouse, you can go and ask to see it."

"Kvinsit is in the service of your father. Of course, he will write anything your father says," Crassius sneered.

"No, he would *not* have written what was not true," said the relative of Kvinsit.

"I assure you, Crassius, you will have many opportunities to personally observe what I can do," grinned Davkaleon.

"Will you feed my dragon?" asked Marcus in a softer voice.

"I'll talk to my Aleurh first. If it was a fair fight, then I'll feed him. But if Aleurh tells me that he was attacked by a pack of dragons at the head of your scumbag, he can't count to get dinner from my hands."

Chapter 7. Dragon Guardhouse

The dragon guardhouse was in the same dungeon, separated by the goblin settlement. There were four ways to get to the dragon's part of the dungeon, but if you were in the guardhouse, there was only one way.

The first way, the way from the guardhouse, was across the goblin settlement. Going without a guard was not recommended. You'd get lost in their endless caves, and besides, goblins and friendliness were incompatible concepts.

The second way passed through the corridor where the guards were. They would bring you back and add 10-15 days for your escape attempt.

The third way was through the dragon corridor. It started in the dragon part of the school. If Davkaleon was not serving time in the guardhouse, he could go to the dragon wing, pass through the dragon corridor, and explain to the dragon guards that he was carrying food to his dragon. The dragon-guard would then check whether the rider was an offender and whether he was serving time in the guardhouse. For that reason, this way was closed to Davkaleon.

The fourth way was an illegal, pirate sort of way. Its use was officially forbidden, but nevertheless, it was used very often. The dungeon had several exits that led into the city. You leave the dungeon, buy dragon food or go hunting—whatever you prefer. After that, you go back to the dragon part of the dungeon and feed your dragon. Then, you do everything in the reverse order and return to your guardhouse.

After learning about the ways into the dragon dungeon, Davkaleon began to think. If he knew the location of entrances and exits to the city, he would choose the fourth way without a doubt.

But he didn't know them.

"Can I hire a goblin to pass through the goblin settlement?" asked Davkaleon, who had an unspent stock of monthly coins from his father.

"You can, but you don't want to do it," answered Marcus. "Goblins usually work in pairs. You hire one as a guide, and the second runs to report you and receives compensation from the school. The moment you come out of your dragon's cell, they catch you and add 10 days to your sentence. The only plus is that your dragon will be well fed.

"Better to buy a map from the goblins of the exits and entrances, but bear in mind, they will still try to deceive you. They will sell you a map that correctly specifies the nearest exit and then they will immediately report to the school authorities. The other entrances and exits will be marked wrong. You will roam willy-nilly until you have to return the same way. They will be waiting for you near the entrance to the dungeon, of course."

"Where in the city can I buy a map of the dungeon?" asked Davkaleon.

"Turn to any boy who brings food and ale to the *Mug and Sword*, and they will sell one to you. By the way, you will be able to buy dragon food there, if you are too lazy to hunt. One more thing. Your dragon was injured. Buy him dragon meds. And feed my dragon."

Marcus pulled out a few coins, intending to throw them across the passage.

"I do not need your money," said Davkaleon. "Just feed my Aleurh if the need ever rises."

Having borrowed Kvorts's sword, Davkaleon went back into the dungeon in search of a goblin, ready to buy a map. The situation was strange. All his life, he'd known that goblins were enemies, trying to attack Daeya at every opportunity. Sometimes, goblins entered into alliances with Svargs or other enemies, sometimes they attacked lone travelers or stole children from Daeya. Those disappeared without a trace. And here, in the center of Assa, in the most prestigious military school of Daeya, goblins were in the service of the school leadership. How was that possible?

Davkaleon found a goblin with a map near the goblin settlement. The goblin even agreed to bring him to the exit, for an additional fee, of course. The first boy he found who brought food and ale in the *Mug and Sword* sold him a map he could trust. Having bought dragon food, drink and medicine, Davkaleon went to Aleurh. He found his dragon in a deplorable state. A deep wound on the shoulder immediately caught his eye. His paw was broken also, and a wound on his head was bleeding. Aleurh was in jail with his eyes closed.

"Buddy, my dear friend," said Davkaleon.

Aleurh opened one eye and smiled. He moved to the bars that separated him from Davkaleon and slipped a healthy paw between the bars. Davkaleon patted him and asked, "Show me the swine who did this to you, and I swear to the gods, the day when they leave this place will be the last day of their lives."

"I can handle it," replied Aleurh and asked, "Did you bring water?"

"Of course, I brought food and water and medicine, too. Drink, and then I'll deal with your wounds."

Evidently, Aleurh was very thirsty. He drank without stopping.

"Did these scumbags attack you all together?" asked Davkaleon.

Having drained a small keg, brought by Davkaleon,

Aleurh said that the battle had started when each new dragon talked about himself and about his rider. Aleurh told the others about their flight through the Valley of Death, but they did not believe him and he started a fight with the dragon who called him a liar—the dragon of Marcus, Ethandr. In the beginning, the fight was honest. The other dragons made bets. Most of them made a bet on Ethandr, and when Aleurh began to win, they threw stones. Ethandr had gotten it bad as well, for stones flew at both of them. Then, there was a common scuffle. The rider of Ethandr pulled his dragon out of there, and the crowd of dragons, frustrated by their losses, attacked Aleurh.

"I brought enough food. Do you want me to give this to Ethandr?"

"I do. He wanted to fight fair, and he fought back the crowd, until his master pulled him out."

Davkaleon had just finished processing the wound on Aleurh's shoulder with the dragon medicine, when he heard footsteps behind him. Davkaleon turned around and saw two dragons, one of which was the main dragon of the military school.

"Well, well, so you ran away from the guardhouse. Punishment for this offence is 10 days," said Whales, who recognized Davkaleon.

"Curse those days! Shove them to you know where! My Aleurh should see a doctor, so I'm taking him away. I don't care about your school! If you want to kick me out of school, then do it!" yelled Davkaleon.

"You'll be expelled if you don't stop right now," Whales warned him.

"That's fine! I'll cobble together a group of strong boys who know how to fight, along with their loyal dragons. And we can do without your stupid school where you only know how to pose idiotic puzzles and torture the world's best dragon that ever lived in Daeya."

Turning away from Whales, Davkaleon asked Aleurh, "Can you walk to the exit, if you lean on me? At the exit I will hire a cart to take you to the dragon hospital. There you will be cured in a moment."

"You don't have to take him, I called the doctor for him, and he will send him to the school dragon hospital," said Whales. At that moment, the dragon doctor arrived, carrying a small locked chest.

"How about food and drink? Do they feed them there or should I bring it?" asked Davkaleon.

"They are fed and watered there," replied the dragon doctor, opening the lock and starting to examine Aleurh.

"I want to visit him," demanded Davkaleon.

"That may be a problem. You're in the guardhouse, and he is too, by the way."

"I want to see him," said Aleurh firmly. "I can serve out my term when my dragon has recovered. I can serve double or triple time. Or I can move there. Your guardhouse is not as scary as they say it is. Big deal—goblins serve as guards. Am I afraid of goblins? Monsters, hah!"

"The postponement of the guardhouse punishment is not accepted, but I'll give you permission to visit your dragon." Whales interrupted Davkaleon's emotional speech.

Aleurh opened the other eye and said, "three times a day."

"Two times," answered Whales, "before breakfast and after lessons, for 15 minutes."

"Three." Aleurh and Davkaleon spoke together, as if in one voice. Whales frowned.

Davkaleon took a deep breath. "Three. Please, three

times. I need to know that he is all right at the end of the day," asked Davkaleon in his most polite voice.

"You can be polite, if you really need to," chuckled Whales.

The doctor finished examination and Aleurh was sent to the hospital.

"Come with me," said Whales to Davkaleon. Coming out of the dragon guardhouse Whales asked, "Are you and Aleurh blood-brothers?"

"Yes, we are." nodded Davkaleon.

"Was it a real ritual of initiation to be blood-brothers or symbolic one?" asked Whales.

"A real one. Both of my parents belong to the families of Perfects, so a symbolic ritual was not even considered."

"At what age did you and Aleurh become blood-brothers?" asked Whales.

"At age zero," smiled Davkaleon. "We were born on the same day. The ritual was held 5 minutes after my birth. Aleurh was a couple seconds younger."

"That means the blood of your dragon flows in your veins, and your blood is in his veins," clarified Whales.

"Yes, of course, if we can consider the drop of blood that we exchanged."

"Of course, we can! Especially, when this was done immediately after your birth. Can you speak the old Daeyan language?"

"A little bit," said Davkaleon, "I'm not too an eager student, except if the subject applies to military training. I like military science, and I'm ready to practice from morning to evening, and all these ancient languages and legends only distract me."

"Don't say that. There is a lot of truth in the old legends, but a lot of time has passed, and we don't understand everything."

Davkaleon didn't argue, although the words of the dragon Whales didn't convince him.

"Have you ever flown on the other dragons, or only on your Aleurh?" asked Whales.

"I flew on the others sometimes. The captain of the guard in father's estate said that it differs from flying on your own dragon. He argued that it was necessary. I love to fly with Aleurh. In flight and especially during the battle, we are one."

"Here is the flip side," answered dragon Whales. "Blood-brothers are so accustomed to one another and understand each other so well, that it is very hard for them to fly with someone else. Do you remember how furious I was when you sat close to my head? The only rider that was so close to me was my blood-brother. He passed away a long time ago...dragons live longer than humans. I barely restrained my impulse to crush you. I thought you encroached on a place which does not belong to you.

"Many dragons have the memories about their blood-brothers, which have passed on to the other world. Do not stir up their memories. The school has developed a standard procedure of communication between riders and dragons. Do not try to challenge it. It's your business how you will communicate with your Aleurh, but do not interrupt me at the lessons and do not argue with me, or your time at school ends. Is that clear?"

Davkaleon nodded.

"Another thing, I will not assign you extra time, but you need to memorize *Military School Code of Conduct*. And you need to do it quickly, before taking the oath. After the oath, you will go to the military court for such behavior. The oath will be in three months. You are deliberately given time to get used to the school order and discipline. Students at the school come from affluent families, and many of you are accustomed to servants. Military school is a different place. You are given time to decide if a military career is for you or not."

Whales reared back, and what looked like a smile crossed his noble face. "I like the way you treat your dragon. You are not useless and I will be sorry if you get expelled from school."

Chapter 8. Night Monster

"I fed your dragon," Davkaleon told Marcus. "By the way, Aleurh told me that they had a fair battle, at least in the beginning. It was later, when Aleurh started winning, that those who made bets on your dragon started to throw rocks. I don't understand why they sent you to the guardhouse, because you didn't do anything illegal."

"I wanted to hide the fight and pull my dragon back, instead of calling the guards," answered Marcus.

Davkaleon wanted to ask more about the school rules, but he had no chance because a new group of offenders appeared in the guardhouse.

"Where have you been? Classes were over a long time ago." Davkaleon was surprised when he saw his classmates.

"What about the party in the *Mug and Sword?*" someone asked him. "Do you know how many crooks are gathered there?"

"You are a crook yourself!" another card lover said. "Don't try to play the game if you don't know the rules."

"You were intentionally waiting for 9 p.m. to ask your sneaky question about the current time." Still another card lover was indignant and Davkaleon recognized the voice of Krilis.

"What is so sneaky about questioning the time?" Davkaleon asked.

"Don't you know?!" Krilis was angry, "Pritransis asked me what time it was, and I answered, *nine*. Then Antonis said *pass* and Pritransis said *whist*. I asked how one could pass or whist when the game had not been announced yet and we didn't know bids or contracts. That crooked couple immediately said that I had declared nine! I was trying to prove that nine meant 9 p.m., and that I hadn't even opened my cards yet. Then they said that I was playing blind 9 since I hadn't opened my cards and thus, the whists and mountains had to be doubled. I would be a fool to play blind 9! I would not have made such an idiotic move."

Neither Davkaleon, nor his brothers knew the meaning of a *blind 9*. They also knew nothing about playing a *light 9*. They did however, understand that they had to figure out how to play these card games *urgently*. Winning these games could be quite profitable. Players would argue if they needed to play till the end of the game or calculate *as-is*. When they calculated as-is, Davkaleon and his brothers heard numbers which were equal to half the money their dad gave them for one month!

They also needed to learn the *Military School Code of Conduct*, but the brothers immediately decided that Code of Conduct could wait, because they needed to understand the game betting rules first.

"How long do you have stay here in the guardhouse?" Davkaleon asked Malay.

"Three days," answered Malay.

"We need to get a manuscript with the game rules down here."

"I am not sure if that pile of manuscripts we got includes the game that we need now," Malay sighed. Davkaleon already knew where he could get a game rulebook. Someone from the *Mug and Sword* would definitely sell him what he needed.

"Who is Krilis?" A goblin approaching them, roaring insensibly.

Krilis answered and the goblin put an empty roll through the cell and said, "You have thirty minutes to make a full report about what occurred at the *Mug and Sword* this evening." Then, the goblin threw one more roll and demanded, "In the morning you will give me another report, containing information on all of the people in the guardhouse, their reasons for being here and time of detention. You will also identify the most common violations and any other pertinent information. Here's an example for you." The goblin gave him another roll.

"Why me? Why me, again?" Krilis was *mad*.

"They said that you have a high propensity to observe and your brain is working fine. So, start using your brain, now!" the goblin demanded and left.

* * * * *

After such a busy day, Davkaleon fell asleep immediately after stretching his large body on the wooden bench—but he did not sleep for long. He was awakened by a soul-crushing scream.

"A monster! I have a big giant monster in my cage!" someone screamed in the silence of the night.

"How could a big giant monster get to your cage?" Kvorts asked with an angry voice.

"Kill your monster and don't disturb us," someone else advised.

"I can't. I have no weapon!" the weaponless owner of the monster cage whined.

"What are you doing in a military school without weapon?" Davkaleon was surprised.

"I had one, but they took it in the guardhouse."

"Did they take everything? Don't you have a couple of small knifes hidden somewhere?" Davkaleon could not believe what he was hearing.

The silence was interrupted by another scream. "It jumped on me! It's going to eat me now!"

"Is there anybody near?" Davkaleon asked, yawning,

"Come to his cage and crush that tiny monster."

"I'm going," answered Kvorts with an annoyed voice, standing up from his bench.

"Where is the animal? There is no monster in here," Kvorts announced just seconds later.

"He probably ran away when he heard that you are coming to help me with a weapon in your hands." The voice of the unarmed boy sounded timid.

"Well, if you say that he escaped, let it be," Kvorts just grumbled returning to his place.

But when Kvorts had just settled back in his cage, another loud scream shook the entire guardhouse.

"He is under my pillow! I can hear him moving!"

"Where did you find a pillow, you patsy? We are all sleeping on bare benches, but this royal has a pillow! Do you have muslin curtains above your bench? You must be dreaming, right?"

"I made a pillow from my cloak," the scared neighbor explained.

People all around the guardhouse mocked him, recommending a silk bedsheet and a velvet canopy.

"Wear a dragon skin glove, take out your monster from under the pillow and choke him!" Davkaleon advised.

"I don't have the dragon skin glove," the owner of the monster stuttered, clearly shaken.

"Do you have anything? Were you going to a military school or a ballet dance studio?" Davkaleon laughed.

"Hey, Kvorts, can you lend him a knife till the morning? Otherwise, he won't let us sleep," Malay asked.

No way. If you want, you can lend him your knife. Why in the world would I give my knife to such a patsy? Tomorrow he will escape the school and run away to hide in his mother's kitchen and I will lose my knife."

The guardhouse was silent for a while, but it wasn't

long before the screams began again. "It bit me!" the boy cried.

Davkaleon rose from the bench and went to find the monster. The cells were dark, so he tried to find the entrance to the monster chamber by touch. He found a doorway, put his head inside and asked if anyone was there.

"It's me, Kvorts. If you are looking for that crazy nut, use the next entrance. If you're going there, put something in his loud mouth, please, because if I go there, I will choke him."

"Where's your animal?" Davkaleon asked as he entered the monster cage. "I should warn you—if you say he was scared and ran away, I will respect my brothers' request and will choke you right here."

"He's here," the poor fellow said, chattering from fear, "I can feel him."

Davkaleon took a flint out of his enormous pockets and began sparking for light. In a moment, he burst out laughing. A tiny, scared goblin cub sat huddled on the cot with the frightened boy. "What a monster! A big and giant one!" Davkaleon said. "Can we sleep now, or will you scream again that you are being attacked by a giant dragon when a cute little snake enters your room?" Davkaleon reached out an plucked up the cub, stuffing it into his pockets.

"Are there snakes living here, too?" The boy began to shake again.

"Hey, Crassius, isn't it strange that goblins from the security haven't come in here after all of screams and yelling?"

"It is strange," Crassius answered, "It's more than strange."

"Will you kill me?" the small goblin squealed as

Davkaleon left the cage.

"There's no honor in the killing of such a little nonsense like you. You can get out of here, now." He set the cup on the ground and turned to feel his way back to his cell.

"Don't leave me alone," the small goblin begged him.

"Don't leave?" Davkaleon was surprised, "Should I become your nanny, bring you a baby bottle and sing lullabies? No way, maybe you could persuade my sisters to do that, but that's not me."

"There is no need to feed me with the baby bottle. A small part of your breakfast and lunch is enough for me. I can be useful to you, and I can see in the dark. By the way, if you don't change your direction right now, you will stumble into a snagged root."

"Couldn't you have told me that a little sooner?" Davkaleon argued, stumbling into the snag.

"You are walking too fast, and I simply had no chance to tell you," the small goblin said, racing to catch up to Davkaleon.

"Why don't you just return to your home? Don't you remember how to get there? I can take you closer to the goblin village," Davkaleon offered.

"Please, don't," the small goblin said whining, "They will kill me immediately."

"Kill?" Davkaleon didn't believe this, "Who would kill such a tiny goblin cub?"

"Enemies of my father." The goblin cub was very serious.

"And who are those enemies?" Davkaleon asked with interest. He'd suddenly lost his urge to return to sleep. He sat on the ground of the dungeon and listened to the goblin cub tell stories of the goblin community. Before that day, Davkaleon was sure that all goblins were the same—

irreconcilable enemies of the Daeyan people. Now, he realized that the community of goblins consisted of many very different clans. Of course, none of those clans were friends of the people of Daeya.

The little cub explained the huge variety of goblin clans—the clan of gray goblins, a clan of black goblins, a Dark clan, as well as Dwork, Tess, Mooslem and Ish clans. And those were only the big clans. It was simply impossible to count all the small clans, not to mention the mixed ones. The Dark clan was the most powerful. A small paradox existed—even though the Dark clan controlled everything, it was almost impossible to meet with one of them. One couldn't find a village of Dark goblins or see their towns or towers. Nevertheless, Dark goblins were always there when something really important happened. And tribute? Dark goblins collected taxes from all other clans. All important contracts and agreements with other clans were conducted by Dark goblins.

The settlement in the school dungeon belonged to the Gray goblins. The military school had a contractual agreement with the Gray goblins for many years, and the school payed them well. Unfortunately, almost all of the money was taken by Dark goblins. Today had been the first day of the school year, and thus, the first day of the new contract. The Gray goblins demanded that the school pay the money directly to them, without giving any to the Dark ones. That information reached Dark goblins almost immediately, and they decided to attack the settlement of the Gray goblins. The father of the goblin cub was one of the goblins that negotiated the direct payments with the school. The Dark goblins promised to find and kill him and his family. The young goblin cub managed to escape, but it seemed clear that the Dark goblins would kill him if Davkaleon brought him back.

"What is your name?" Davkaleon asked.

"I am Andibraksh," answered the cub.

"Where are you going to live?"

"In your pocket, if you'll have me."

"Are you kidding? Does that mean I will find you in the way anytime I want to take something from my pocket?"

"It will not be for long," Andibraksh answered pathetically, "The Dark goblins will leave soon, and then I will return to my home. They never spend more than a couple of days in one location. I will hide myself here with you. Dark goblins have very good sense of smell, so they will find me easily. But your pocket has so many different scents that I will be unnoticeable here."

"Well, okay... I think that I can stand you for a couple of days."

"You won't regret your decision," the goblin cub promised, "I will give you the best dungeon map."

"Everybody knows that one can't trust goblin maps," Davkaleon grinned, "Such maps contain only one working entrance, where the goblin takes you, but of the others are just tricks."

"What are you saying!?" the goblin cub was shocked, "All goblin maps are very truthful, but each entrance has its own secret, which is not usually shown on the map. But I will give you a map containing all the secrets."

"A map with secrets? That would be very useful," Davkaleon was interested, "Okay, now get into my pocket. I am going to sleep, so don't even try to wake me."

* * * * *

The next morning, Davkaleon woke up and checked on Aleurh. His dragon was looking much better than the day before.

61

"They are good to me here, but I am bored," Aleurh complained. "I sleep a lot because there's nobody to talk with."

"Well, listen to me, I will entertain you for a little bit," Davkaleon offered. Leaning close to Aleurh, he whispered to him about the previous night.

"Is he in your pocket now?" Aleurh asked.

Davkaleon nodded and took the goblin cub out.

"Will you leave him with me?" Aleurh asked, "He will entertain me with his stories about goblins."

"You can stay here," Davkaleon told the cub. "It is safe here and you will be fine."

The goblin cub came out of the Davkaleon's pocket and climbed on Aleurh.

After visiting Aleurh, Davkaleon went to his room. He needed to find some weapons. His resources were limited, because they took his two swords and several knives at the guardhouse. Manuscripts were piled in the corner of the room. Those were the manuals. He simply had no time to sort through them. In fact, Davkaleon desperately needed the card games descriptions, but he couldn't find even one. The scrolls were old and moldy, and the print was too small to read in the dark. That meant he needed to visit the *Mug and Sword*. He needed to go there anyway because he needed to buy a deck of cards as well.

Chapter 9. Lessons of the Second Day

Language teacher Stanglate checked his student's sentences in the Daeyan language class. He walked between their desks, correcting mistakes and writing in his notebook. He paused when he reached Davkaleon.

"You should write *an ocean*. You can't write *an acian*".

"Why not? I saw *an acian* in the manuscripts."

"That is the form of the Old Daeyan language," the teacher explained, "But you are in the class of the *modern* Daeyan language."

"Oh gosh! Now they will give me more days in the guardhouse," Davkaleon thought with displeasure.

"Don't worry. There is no need to add days in the guardhouse. You know both languages and this is amazing," the teacher said, answering Davkaleon's thought.

Davkaleon was shocked to receive a compliment for his knowledge of languages. He did not think that he was very good in languages. To tell the truth, he wasn't even trying to be successful in the languages field. He knew how to read and write and that was more than enough for him. Why would he need more? Was he going to write poems on the battlefield?

"I need to talk with you after class," the teacher said.

The rest of the class was uneventful. The Gerklat brothers were no worse and better than the majority of the students in their group.

When the class was over, Davkaleon approached the teacher.

"You are the son of Arland Gerklat. But who is your mother?" asked Stanglate.

"Arara from the Borlatar family," answered Davkaleon.

"That means both of your parents belong to the ancient

Perfects families of Daeya," the teacher smiled. "Then, I am not surprised that you wrote a beautiful and really Daeyan word *acian*, instead of that stupid modern novelty. Can you tell me, why is this modern *ocean* better than the noble and euphonious *acian*?"

Davkaleon had nothing to say. He didn't want to confess that he knew little in the Old Daeyan language, but the teacher was seemingly reading his mind without problem.

"Don't be shy. These days one hardly knows the language of the first Perfects Daeyats. You can improve your skills. Every Sunday, we perform classes in the True Daeyan Language School. You can only study there if you are invited. I invite you now. Classes start at 10 in the morning. The school is located in a beautiful place on the shore of Saint Lake in the center of Assa. I will send you a map."

"But I have to be in the guardhouse, and they won't let me out," Davkaleon said, trying to avoid the invitation.

"They will let you go. I will deal with it," the teacher answered.

Davkaleon made a giant effort to hide his disappointment in offer of Sunday studies. He even managed several words of gratitude.

His next class was the Fighting, Strategy and Tactics.

"Wars are happening all the time," the round and well-fed instructor Ancake said at the start of class. His appearance made the students think that he had never participated in a war. Mister Ancake rolled to a comfortable chair and continued. "Higher quantity can't guarantee success in a battle. One properly prepared soldier can easily deal with several untrained. And one unpredicted action can totally ruin a well-planned military campaign of your enemy. Today, I am going to tell you

64

about the most unusual battles in our history.

"The first story is the story of *Brayan kosh*. As you know, Brayan people were Daeyats too, but they decided to choose another way. They could belong to the most respected ancient families of Daeya, but they decided to refuse our sacred rules, which were given to Daeyan people by the Gods. They now follow their own fictitious rules. These days, their population has significantly decreased and they prefer to avoid direct battles with the army of Daeya. But just a hundred years ago, they had a much larger army and wars between Daeyats and Brayans occurred frequently. Brayans consider the *kosh* a sacred animal. Just think, how stupid one must be to consider an animal sacred, just because it gives you wool, milk and eggs. They say that one cannot kill a kosh—otherwise, he or she would be cursed. It's not our problem that Brayan people are so foolish. The Commander-in-Chief of the Daeyan Army, Crassius Pompeus, had perfectly exploited this weakness. He gave an order to draw koshes on the shields of the army, and soldiers were accompanied by real koshes. It was a perfect plan, because the Brayans refused to kill the sacred koshes and decided to take a step back. But there was an ambush on their way out, and the majority of them were killed."

The students responded to the story by supporting the actions of the Commander and joking about Brayans and their sacred koshes.

Mister Ancake continued. "The second story is also connected with the name of Commander-in-Chief Crassius Pompeus, but at that time he was not yet a Chief. He was a young officer with a squad of fifty soldiers. He received an order to capture the city of Swaroggrad, which, as you already know, was the favorite place for relaxation of the Swarogg god in ancient times. There is a temple of

Swarogg in the city of Swaroggrad where miracles happen often. But the city was captured by the Brayans and the people of Daeya wanted it back. The Brayans simply had no right to own the temple of Swarogg, because they did not honor the saint rules and laws of the gods! The city of Swaroggrad was not big, yet the squad of 50 soldiers was not enough to capture it. Nobody knows why general Vilaris Antonis decided to use such a small squad to capture the city of Swaroggrad."

"Nobody knows? That's not true and the reason is pretty obvious," said a grinning voice somewhere from the rear. "He wanted to get the wife of Pompeus, so he sent her husband to a place, where one could hardly return."

"What nonsense!" shouted Mister Ancake, and even though he had a lot of pounds of flesh on his little frame, he jumped from his chair. "Who is creating such gossip here?"

"It is not gossip. This information is written in the annals of the Pompeus family."

"It's a lie!" shouted Ancake stomping his feet. "According to the Daeyan laws, if a man dies, a wife has to marry his brother, because her kids need to grow up with their uncle and not with some stranger. All the people of Daeya live in accordance with Daeyan laws for the good of the Daeyan people! Our honored general Vilaris Antonis had no evil intent. And I won't let anyone say bad things about this glorious and mighty Daeyan hero. You will go to the guardhouse for your defamation. What is your name and which family do you belong to?"

"My name is Hilaris Pompeus and I belong to the Pompeus family. I will go to the guardhouse, but Crassius Pompeus had no brother and he was married to the sister of the wife of Vilaris Antonis, so if something would have happened with him, then—"

But Mister Ancake didn't let him finish the speech. He started to knock the table with his fist and demanded the gossiping student to close his mouth immediately, or he would go to the guardhouse. Surprisingly, his loud and energetic knocking transformed into silence at once, and his face was covered with an insinuating smile.

"I am a very kind person and I don't send students to the guardhouse really often, but it's prohibited to defame people," said Mister Ancake with a soft voice. "I understand that one could *misunderstand* the family annals. Our honored Chief, Crassius Pompeus, had almost no time to give us detailed information about those situations. Sometimes, he was writing only short, stiff paragraphs and his descendants could misunderstand some moments of it. Of course, I am not blaming honored descendants of the honored general and not saying that you did something wrong, but you have to be more diplomatic or I will have no other option and I'll have to send you to the guardhouse," Mister Ancake was almost crying in his attempt at sincerity.

"He changed his mind and decided not to send Hilaris to the guardhouse. Interesting, but why?" thought Davkaleon.

"Let's return to our *honored* Crassius Pompeus," Ancake continued, returning to his comfortable chair, "A future great Chief of the Army, who was just Lieutenant Pompeus at that time, brilliantly completed the plan of General Vilaris Antonis. He ordered his deputy to go to the city and tell people that his commander died. Before death, his commander told him to bury him in the cemetery near the temple of Swarogg. If the administration of the city would allow them to carry out the will of the deceased, the army of Daeya promised to leave the city after the funeral and would not try to capture it in the future. Only 50 soldiers planned to participate in the funeral. They had to pay their final respects to their commander. After a long discussion, local administration decided to approve their request. They thought that the number of soldiers was small, and the promise of the Daeyans was too attractive. The administration demanded the soldiers to leave all their weapons before entering the city. In fact, they were weaponless because all of the weapons were in a coffin. Fifty soldiers brought the coffin to the city. Crassius Pompeus was among them. Nobody knew him in the city, and he removed all insignia from his uniform."

"But he broke his promise!" Davkaleon couldn't be silent.

"Why do you think that he broke his promise?" asked Ancake, "They had promised that they would not assault the city after the funeral. *But there was no funeral!*"

Davkaleon was shocked. Growing up on the estate of his father, he thought that the people of Daeya were the most honest and noble people—people who never lied. The teacher considered Davkaleon's silence a sign that he was sufficiently impressed, so he switched to the third story.

"One hundred fifty years ago, Daeya was attacked by an army of enemies from across the mountains. Daeyats called them the *behind-the-mountains people*, because they were living across the mountains that surrounded Daeya. The tips of the mountains were always covered with snow. There was a lake between the mountains, which was covered with ice during the winter. The soldiers of Daeya used blankets of dragon pelts to protect themselves. The ice of the frozen lake was strong enough to freeze moving Daeyats. The commander of the Daeyan army, general Antonis, noticed that their enemies had very heavy armor. Instead of attacking them, he gave an order to step back in the direction of the frozen lake. Daeyats walked across the lake and the behind-the-mountains army came after them, but the ice wasn't strong enough to hold the weight of their heavy armor. The behind-the-mountains army fell under the ice. The few of them who managed to survive met the Army of Daeya, which finished that attack."

The teacher smiled, twiddling his fingers. "I have just told you three different cases of times when the intelligence and ingenuity of the Daeyan commanders saved the lives of thousands of Daeyan warriors. Your manuals contain more information about such cases, and the library of the school has a brilliant collection of such stories. I will give you one week to prepare. During this time, you will write an essay. Your essay has to describe at least three different battles."

When class was over, Davkaleon heard someone say, "Poor Pancake, he almost fell off his chair."

"Are you talking about Ancake?" asked Davkaleon.

"Yeah, Ancake-Pancake. Everybody calls him Pancake, because he's as round as a pancake. Usually he doesn't leave his chair to avoid spending any energy. But today, he jumped, stomped his feet, knocked his fists and immediately became silent when he heard that his detractor was from the Pompeus family."

"Why was he so scared?" another student asked.

"Don't you know that our Commander-in-Chief is seriously ill? They have already called doctors, sorceresses, witches from Llill, and last night, they even called the magician... well you know which one."

Twier...a word clearly appeared in Davkaleon's head. Even though that guy didn't say the *Twierks* word, Davkaleon was sure that they were talking about the *Twierks* magician.

"And what's the connection between the illness of the Commander-in-Chief and fears of Ancake-Pancake?" asked Davkaleon.

"Have you dropped from the moon?"

"He is not from a military family," said another student, thinking that his words were explaining everything.

"Ah, you are Davkaleon, the best from the best," laughed the first guy, "Now listen, and try to absorb some new information. The Commander-in-Chief is ill, and this time it looks very serious. He has two deputies. The first one is from the Antonis family, while the second one is from the Pompeus family. And *nobody* knows who will become our new Commander. Our Pancake doesn't like to argue with the relatives of Commander-in-Chief. By the way, my name is Gaes, and I am from the military clan of Claudis. When you become the *best from the best*, don't forget about the guy who told you about the hidden secrets and taught you how to deal with military tricks. Perhaps you'll find me a warm place," winked the story teller.

"And I am Yulis, also from the Claudis family, and I won't refuse a warm place either," laughed the second boy.

"Are you brothers?" asked Davkaleon.

"We are cousins. All of the men in our family serve in the army. Seven people from our family are currently studying in the school. If we count those from other families, but with mothers from Claudis clan, we could find about twenty of us here. You and your brothers belong to a priest family, am I right? What are you doing in the military school?"

"I am not the biggest fan of prayers," answered Davkaleon, "Since our childhood, my brothers and I have been in love with weapons, fighting and battles. There was a big military squad at the estate of our father. The chief of the guard, Kvinsit, was constantly performing various training sessions. That's what I really liked."

"I read about you. Is it true that you were participating in a battle and killed two Svargs?" asked Gaes.

"Yes, but my dragon Aleurh helped me a lot."

"Well, welcome to our warm company. I think we have to celebrate it, play cards and order a *pintie* for all of us."

"A pintie?" Davkaleon was confused.

"You need to get used to our slang. I will make you a dictionary, so, please, remember my kindness," laughed Yulis.

Chapter 10. Training

The following two classes were training sessions. Davkaleon entered the training area with his head held high. In this field, he was confident because he knew that he would be the best. He simply had no interest in stupid logical paradoxes or linguistic rules. But training and fighting? That was his specialty.

"And what do you think you are doing here?" He heard a familiar voice. "Beginners have to start in the next room, where they are learning how to use a sword. Now, go there!" said Crassius.

"Go there yourself if you need to learn how to fight with a sword. I noticed that you didn't use a sword during our hunt, so maybe you need to take an additional training course," grinned Davkaleon.

"Oh you, tyrant! I will teach you," said Crassius taking out his sword.

Davkaleon took out his sword as well, and heard, "I put three to one on Crassius... does anybody want to make a bet?"

"I want to," said the voice of the Davkaleon's brother. "Put your three hundred against my hundred".

"Three hundred and one hundred in which currency?" someone asked.

"Daeyan sickles, of course," Malay answered.

"Oh gosh, Malay is excited," thought Davkaleon, "He's putting half of his cash up for a bet!"

"I bet four against one on Crassius! Four against one on Crassius!" The audience shouted in anticipation of entertainment.

"Hah, bets are rising! Who wants to bet four to one hundred?"

"I saw Crassius in action. None of the beginners can

defeat a cadet who passed three years of training as in our school," said one of the advanced students.

"I bet four to one on Crassius."

"Well noted!" Kvorts called out, grinning.

"Look at them! I will fight and my brothers will earn money on me!" thought Davkaleon. "I bet one to one on myself. Does anyone accept?" said Davkaleon.

"I do! Five hundred sickles," immediately answered Crassius.

Davkaleon thought that he didn't have five hundred sickles, but he didn't want to make a step back. He nodded, accepting the offer. Students made their bets, negotiating their amounts. Davkaleon and Crassius stood in front of each other holding their swords, surrounded by the crowd. Several voices said that the crowd had to step back in order to give space for the battle.

Someone commanded, "Fight!"

But someone else shouted, "Stop, don't do it here! A coach will come by in a couple of minutes and will send everyone to the guardhouse. In that case, we would have to cancel the battle, and what would we do with all the bets? Let's move to a secret place where nobody can disturb us."

"To the *yew ground* in the dragon forest! Such battles are always performed there, free of disruptions."

All of the students agreed on the yew ground in the dragon forest.

"Let's make it today after the classes," someone offered.

"I can't do it today, because of the guardhouse," Crassius objected.

"Same for me," added Davkaleon.

After a short discussion, they agreed to meet on the first Sunday after they finished their punishment in the guardhouse. Davkaleon had no doubt that he would defeat

Crassius. The chief of the guard in his father's estate, Kvinsit, had trained him for the last five years. Crassius's classmates had useless hopes regarding his supremacy. Furthermore, he had no other choice, because five hundred sickles were simply impossible to find. Even though their father never denied his sons, it was pretty expensive to send five of his descendants to the most prestigious schools of Daeya.

"Why are your swords not in their scabbards? What are you doing here?" came the angry voice of an officer.

Crassius and the other students put their right hands to their chests, immediately throwing them forward, thus greeting the officer. Davkaleon and his brother copied that gesture, but the officer interrupted them, "You don't have to do that, because you haven't taken the oath yet."

"So, what is going on here?" repeated the officer.

"We were arguing over who's sword is better," Crassius lied, without batting an eyelid.

Davkaleon nodded his head, showing his total consent. But such a lie hardly fooled the officer.

"Please note that dueling is strictly prohibited in the school. And Crassius, I will warn you, the beginners are skilled fighters. Otherwise, I wouldn't have invited them to my group. So, don't think that you will have an easy win. Yesterday, they fought with a couple dozen of goblins, and well-equipped goblins couldn't defeat them. It was a pure pleasure to watch that fight."

After those words, Davkaleon recognized the officer, who refused to expel him and Malay from the school. He eyes of some students were full of disappointment. Others who'd made bets were seriously worried.

"Who trained you?" Harding asked.

"Our chief guard, Kvinsit," Davkaleon answered.

"Kvinsit knows his business." The officer noticed with

approval.

Those who'd made bets were even more worried.

"And now, I have a little surprise for all of you." Officer Harding clapped his hands and several people brought a giant cage on wheels into the room. A giant monster with four heads was sitting inside of it.

"I am introducing you to a sea hydra. Usually it lives in the ocean, but sometimes it likes to go hunting on shore. Who can tell me about the unusual abilities of hydras?"

A lot of hands rose up. Everybody knew about the hydra's ability to regenerate their heads and limbs. When you cut off a head, two new heads will regrow immediately. The same principle worked for its limbs.

"Does anybody know how to fight it?" the officer asked.

"You have to cut its heads so fast, that new heads can't grow up," said someone, but Harding skeptically shook his head.

"Its heads grow very fast, and this creature knows how to run. If you are not the winner of the Daeyan running competition and you don't want to run away instead of fighting, you have to try another way. Hydras are scared of fire. If you cut its head and immediately cauterize that place, new heads won't appear. Same works with its extremities. All of you know how to fight holding a sword in each hand. At this time, I challenge you to fight, holding a sword in one hand and a torch in the other. On your right, you will find our exercise equipment. Moving targets will appear in front of you and their speed will constantly increase. You have to cut the target and cauterize the wound before new one appears. At the end of this training you will pass a test, then those who want to fight, will have a chance to meet a real hydra. If nobody wants to fight, then, please tell me, what was your reason for joining the military school? Now, go to your targets and start training."

Davkaleon approached a training machine, which had a circle with targets on it. Several torches were piled near the machine. It was pretty easy to hit those targets and cauterize them, since they were not moving. The officer blew the horn and targets started to move. First, they moved very smooth and slow, and the task was pretty easy. After a couple of rounds, their speed started to increase. Davkaleon was still dealing with them, but when the officer approached, he stopped the machine and showed several places with very light burns.

"You have to cut faster in order to leave more time for the torch. Otherwise, heads and limbs will grow again."

Harding went away while the machine continued its rotation. After about fifteen minutes, they stopped the machines and installed new targets. At that time, the machines were rotating at a crazy speed. The targets were flashing in their eyes. Was there enough time for Davkaleon to burn the place of the cut target? Not really. After another couple of minutes, all of the heads were cut off and the machine stopped. The officer checked all the student's targets, meticulously inspecting wounds of the hewed targets.

"The hydra is safe for today," Harding announced after a couple of minutes. "None of you have passed this test, thus you can't defeat the hydra. With your results, in just ten minutes of beginning the fight, the hydra would have around forty toothed heads instead of four, and ten times more clawed limbs."

Harding made a sign with his hand, and they took the cage with the hydra away.

"Our school gym has such training machines, I recommend that you practice before our next training session. That's all for today. Classes are over."

"Can we practice on those machines, or do we have to go to the guardhouse right now?" Davkaleon asked.

"You can practice," Harding allowed. "But after that, you have to return to your chambers in the guardhouse."

Davkaleon and his brothers went to the school gym.

"I am going to the *Mug and Sword* to find card, maps and rules, then I will check on Aleurh," said Davkaleon after a couple of hours.

"Can you bring us something to eat?" Kvorts requested and Malay seconded the request.

The visit to the *Mug and Sword* brought no adventures. Davkaleon purchased maps, cards, game rules and some food. Thinking again, he bought another deck of cards and game rules to entertain Aleurh and the goblin cub.

Davkaleon was next at the dragon guardhouse, when a small three-headed creature ran from around the corner. Having seen Davkaleon, the creature clung to the wall, and closed his eyes in fear. It trembled and cried. It was probably a cub of hydra. Although, if it had not three heads, Davkaleon would decide that this was a baby dragon. A hydra has no wings, but this animal had wings, however, they were very small, not like dragons have. "Maybe it's a hybrid of a hydra and a dragon," thought Davkaleon. "Can this happen, I wonder?"

After today's training, several people went to hunt for hydra. Perhaps, the poor cub caught the eye of one of them.

"Well, okay. But leave it alone. Why do you chase it? What good is in killing a defenseless cub? It is too small to be a dinner-it is even not enough food for one person. If you consider it a trophy, you'll be a laughingstock. This is nothing like a fair fight with an adult predatory hydra."

A hunter jumped out from around the corner. "Where is it?" the excited pursuer asked Davkaleon.

Davkaleon shrugged his shoulders evasively, and the pursuer rushed on. Davkaleon put the cub in his pocket and went to Aleurh.

When Davkaleon entered his Aleurh's temporary home, Aleurh and Andibraksh were having a funny conversation. Aleurh looked really great—good treatment had improved his state.

"Don't recover so fast," Davkaleon whispered, "This place is much better than the guardhouse. You have a companion and the hospital provides you with food and water. So please, tell the doctor something sad. Let them cure you a little bit longer. I will finish my guardhouse punishment soon and will be able to spend more time with you and give you any food you like." He handed over a present. "Here are some game rules and cards. If you don't know how to play cards at this school, you are considered inept. And I could hardly believe the amount of money they bet with! There's much to be gained by winning." He paused. "Some games require at least three players. I brought you the third one," he said, removing a trembling animal from his pocket.

"Calm down, no one is going to eat you here," said Davkaleon.

"So, you won't cut my heads off?" asked the little animal.

"Why do we have to cut your heads off?" Davkaleon was surprised. "There is no benefit from such training."

"There is no benefit for training, of course," agreed the creature, "but I can be presented as a trophy."

Upon hearing this, Davkaleon and Aleurh burst out laughing.

"You're laughing for nothing. Do you know how many people want to show off?" asked the little animal.

Davkaleon and Aleurh laughed harder.

"There are those who wish to boast buy a dead, adult hydra and add a few heads and the paws of cubs, pretending the battle lasted several hours, heads growing continuously." said Andibraksh.

A fit of laughter of Davkaleon and Aleurh evaporated instantly.

"Calm down, such games don't interest me," said Davkaleon.

"Such swindles occur at school sometimes. Goblins often talk about them," said the little goblin.

"Let him be with me awhile, and then he will be with you till he gets bigger," proposed Aleurh. Davkaleon nodded.

"Do you have a name?" Davkaleon asked.

"No," complained the baby. "The other hydras laughed at me, said that I do not look like a hydra—that I look like a snake. Besides, I have a fire coming out of my mouth like a dragon. And hydras are afraid of fire. But my fire is very small, not like the dragons have."

"Then we will call you Hydragon Snake," suggested Davkaleon.

"Hydragon sounds better," objected Aleurh. "Hydragon Snake is too long name."

"Okay, he will be Hydragon," agreed Davkaleon.

"Later I will tell you about the goblins. I have learned much from my conversations with Andibraksh," promised Aleurh.

Davkaleon's allotted time with Aleurh had passed. It was time to go. After saying goodbye, Davkaleon returned to his brothers. His big bag of food became empty almost immediately.

"Shall we train more, or can we go to the guardhouse?" Davkaleon asked.

"Let's go and play, because yesterday I was feeling like

an idiot when they were discussing cards. 9 p.m.? 9 declared contracts? Blind and light games? I felt clueless. To tell the truth, I even don't remember all of what I heard," Malay answered.

Chapter 11. Card-playing

The brothers returned to the guardhouse and made themselves comfortable in the dungeon next to the entrances of their cells. Having fenced themselves in with burning torches, they fished out a pack of cards and opened the instructions. The game was called *"Preference. Dragon Version"*. The instruction started with the list of rules, a few sounded like they must be jokes.

No money? Do not play!

No lead? Do not whist!

However, right after the rules, there was an in-depth description of the game. A couple of hours passed. The Gerklat brothers had just started to see the meaning of the listed humorous instructions when a voice sliced the air. "Would you just look at these gamblers! They've occupied the best cells with the entrances to the dungeon only to play cards. And who will hunt? People in the cells without access to the dungeon need to be fed, by the way."

As if on cue, the brothers looked back at the speaker. Crassius was sneering, standing next to Pompedius and a few other students.

"Yesterday, we got the food, today it's your turn," Davkaleon answered, dealing out cards.

"I don't remember playing cards yesterday," Crassius answered in a cold voice.

"Well, I don't remember you hunting." Davkaleon kept dealing.

Crassius darted forward, grabbing hold of his sword but Pompedius stopped him. "Your duel has been already scheduled. The bets are on, so everything should be held by the rules and in the presence of witnesses."

Having uttered threats through his teeth to Davkaleon, Crassius and his company went for a hunt.

The brothers were right in the middle of finishing the first Preference card game in their lives when they heard happy voices of homecoming hunters. They came in sight one or two minutes later, carrying their prey.

"Why haven't Goblins shown up?" Pompeus sounded surprised. "What the heck? I haven't seen them since yesterday. Usually, they come around the instant the food is here."

"What will we fry it on?" One of the classmates inquired.

"Perhaps our card players will tear themselves from their pleasant entertainment to take part in making dinner?" Crassius commented.

"Okay, we will," the brothers answered reluctantly taking a break from the game.

But before setting out in search of the needed supplies for the fire, they took a last look into the cells, hoping there would be at least one goblin in the pass.

"I've never thought I would wish this much to see a trashy goblin," Malay noted.

"Where shall we go?" Kvorts asked.

"To the *Mug and Sword*," suggested Davkaleon. "I bet they already know that the goblins have disappeared and we need some wood for the fire and a rotisserie."

"Well, they may be aware of that, but why would they sell wood to us for pennies when they could sell the whole meal?" Kvorts answered.

"We'll make a bargain. One thing is for sure, we'll have to buy something more from them." Davkaleon answered.

In the *Mug and Sword*, everyone knew that goblins had disappeared and that they had taken all of the supplies for cooking meals.

"Pay for six meals, a broiling rack, and seasonings, and you'll get wood for free," the brothers were offered in the tavern.

"How about we pay for the meals now, but we claim them after our guardhouse sentence?"

"That won't do. You know, many our clients are swindlers. You may come to claim your meals and make accusations that the lamb wasn't fat enough and demand a refund."

"Three meals, a broiling rack, seasonings and wood for a fair price," Davkaleon, Malay and Kvorts answered with one voice.

"Five meals, a broiling rack seasonings and wood," came the counter-proposal.

"Three meals, a broiling rack, seasonings, dragon dainties and wood." Davkaleon made one more try, thinking Aleurh would be grateful to him.

"Deal! The wood, broiling rack and seasonings are ready for you. We'll prepare food and dragon dainties now," the waiter from the tavern answered. "You can wait in the closet room on the second floor."

"In the closet room?" The brothers couldn't believe what they'd just heard.

"Yeah. Where else were you going to dine? You cannot eat in the shared hall. Someone may see you, and you are on watch. You cannot eat in the dungeon, because the goblins will rat on you right away."

"But dining in the closet?! No! Gerklat brothers would never eat in a closet under any circumstances. A closet is no place for dinner."

"You don't like the word *closet room*? Just ignore the name. Just think of it as a private dining facility. In fact, it's a small room next to the blue dining room. If our guests dine in the blue room and they want to be served by their personal servants instead of the tavern waiters, we bring the food to the so-called closet room and their servants take it from there. Right now, there are a few people in the blue dining room but the closet room is empty. You'll be comfortable in there."

The waiter explained how to get to the room known as the closet room and promised to bring their food within a few minutes.

The wait was worth it. The food was tasty and the prices were quite reasonable.

It was no surprise that both the teachers and students preferred the *Mug and Sword*. As they dined, there were no sounds coming from the next room. The brothers were finishing their dinner when a quarrel burst out on the other side of the wall.

Some words reached the brothers' ears. The quarrel was escalating, voices becoming louder. The brothers could hear almost everything, but it was difficult to get an understanding of what the screaming was about.

"What is that gibberish?" Malay asked. "I can only understand some words."

"Some way, some temple. The rest is incomprehensible. What language are they speaking?" Kvorts inquired.

"It's an old Daeyan language," Davkaleon answered. "Be quiet." He listened in on the quarrel behind the wall, trying to figure out what it was about. A loud crash sounded beyond the wall. It seemed as if something very heavy had fallen or had been thrown at somebody. Loud screams resumed. Davkaleon could understand more than his brothers—his mother was from an old-Daeyan family and tried to teach her son the old-Daeyan language. Of course, she never used the word "old-Daeyan". She said "true Daeyan" or "perfect." Aside from that, his father had hired a teacher for his offspring. Malay and Kvorts wriggled out of learning the old-Daeyan language on the pretext that their mothers belonged to simple Daeyan families, and for them, old languages were of no benefit. Davkaleon had no such excuse. His mother Arara considered the old-Daeyan language the most important subject for her son and personally made sure her son didn't shirk it. So, throughout the last few years, Davkaleon had to attend lessons with his brother Paradion. Properly speaking, Paradion didn't have to learn the old-Daeyan, but he wanted to become a priest, and Daeyan priests must know the old-Daeyan language. Believe it or not, another one of Davkaleon's brothers, Elfid, joined them too. Considering the fact that Elfid's mother Dallilla was a Llill's witch, no one made Elfid learn the old-Daeyan language. He made that decision for himself. Imagine that! Himself! Davkaleon couldn't wrap his head around Elfid's choice. But from the viewpoint of Davkaleon and other brothers, Elfid was *strange*, not an average Daeyan boy. He didn't like shooting, he didn't like flying on dragons, didn't like playing mock battles. He liked burying himself in Daeyan scrolls, old- Daeyan runes and Llill manuscripts, comparing what they had in common and where there were different. If there was someone who learned the old-Daeyan language well, it was Elfid. As for Davkaleon, he hadn't become an expert of the old- Daeyan language, but he still had some understanding.

Behind the wall, people kept on screaming. The things that Davkaleon could understand sounded more than strange.

"The pass into the rock will disappear soon. I've found a suitable.... He will pass."

Another voice asked: "Is he good?"

The first voice answered: "He is. Maybe not as good as he thinks himself to be, but he's still good."

One more voice got in a word: "You already found one

last year. It will happen again... this time, it won't turn out well..."

The first voice insisted: "He is a blood-brother from the Perfects. He will pass through..."

"They will know," his opponent persisted.

"If not him, then... Twierks..."

Having heard the word *Twierks*, the argument stopped. There were terse whispers ("Shut up! They will pounce on us now!"). The clank and slam of arms sounded. The waiter bounced into the room and hissed at them. "Stay quiet or someone will know you're here. Choke your torches."

The door closed and the lock shut with a snap. The brothers remained in the darkness.

"What were they arguing about behind the other room?" Kvorts whispered.

"I understood only fragments of the argument," Davkaleon answered. "Sounds like the disagreement started in the tavern when somebody said the taboo word. They are probably waiting for the envoys of priests."

Behind the wall, there were voices again, but this time they were very soft and guarded. Then everything fell silent. Ten minutes later. the lock clicked and the door opened. The waiter had returned.

"Leave through the back door quickly. Everything is prepared for you downstairs. The envoys of priests will be here in a few minutes."

When the brothers finally showed up in the dungeon next to their cells, Crassius and his company were there.

"We could grow old waiting for you," Crassius observed. "Where did you hang out for so long?"

"Say *thanks* We managed to bring everything needed for the fire. Patrols are everywhere." Malay omitted the detail about the priest envoys.

Soon, the tasty smell of fried meat spread across the guardhouse. Believe it or not, even with the sweet smells, no goblins came around.

Davkaleon visited Aleurh again and gave him the dragon dainties. Aleurh smiled from ear to ear.

"Where did you manage to get them? You are in the guardhouse." Aleurh asked.

"In the *Mug and Sword*, of course. It's a great place. We'll go there when you recover.

Davkaleon had time left from his allotted minutes, so he told Aleurh that goblins had disappeared from the guardhouse and he and his brothers had to set out in search of wood and a broiling rack. While Davkaleon was telling his story, the baby-goblin settled himself near Davkaleon. Suddenly, he bent over Davkaleon's hand and pierced its sharp teeth into it. Davkaleon scream out in surprise and flung the goblin cub away against the wall.

"Please, forgive me," Andibraksh asked in a guilty voice. "I'm still little and it's difficult for me to restrain myself."

"It's difficult to restrain yourself from what? From biting me?"

"Goblins need a drop of fresh blood or they become weak," the baby-goblin squeaked.

"Is that why you've tried to bite me?" Aleurh became indignant.

"Your skin is too firm for my teeth, I cannot bite it through," the goblin cub complained, shrinking his head into his shoulders.

"Would you look at this little ingrate!" Davkaleon flew into a rage. "Not only I have tolerated you, fed you and gave you drink, now you bite me?" Davkaleon grabbed the baby-goblin by the collar and was about to bounce him but Aleurh intervened on behalf of Andibraksh.

"Leave him alone, I appreciate his company. He has bitten you just a little bit. Do you remember how in childhood I used to hit you with my wing or struck you down to the ground with the lightest of hugs? And you bore it."

"It was you, not him. The last thing I need to bear is a goblin bite." Davkaleon grumbled but still let Andibraksh go.

Chapter 12. Rough-and-Tumble Night

Having returned to his cell, Davkaleon made himself comfortable on the trestle bed. Tired, he fell deep asleep. He woke up because somebody pressed a hand over his mouth. Several goblins took him by his arms and legs and dragged him from his cell. Davkaleon surged and worked a hand free, but the next minute, several claws got into him. He worked himself free again, took a dagger from one of his pockets and stabbed somebody. A howl rang out while somebody else sank his teeth into Davkaleon's arm. He chucked aside a few assaulters and got out another dagger.

Torch light cut the darkness. Davkaleon saw himself surrounded by goblins. Goblins had never been noted for their good looks or friendly manners, but these ones seemed to be the ugliest beasts that he had ever seen. Small narrow eyes shot fire angrily from under bushy, overhanging eyebrows. The goblins were looking at Davkaleon with hatred.

"Where is he?" One of the goblins snarled.

"Who?" Davkaleon didn't understand.

"Don't pretend to be a fool! He was in your cage, we found his scent! What did you do with him?"

A sharp pain fastened on Davkaleon's head, without any apparent source. Where did this pain come from? The pain increased. Davkaleon felt that if he didn't do something right away, the pain would paralyze him. Clenching his teeth, he fired a dagger at one goblin and a second dagger at another. He hurled two more and darted away. The goblins rushed him, wailing as they came. On the flat surface, goblins couldn't keep up with Davkaleon with their short, crooked legs.

The problem was that Davkaleon didn't know where to

run. The darkness was all around him, and it looked like the goblins oriented themselves quite well without light. In addition, the goblins had a keen sense of smell—as the goblin cub had warned him.

As Davkaleon ran, he began to suspect that it was Andibraksh this pack of goblins were interested in.

Davkaleon gave himself a moment to add a bar for the torch. He always had a tinderbox with him. If he had a torch bar in his pocket, he wouldn't have problems. Having moved in circles across the dungeon for long minutes, Davkaleon ended up next to the entrance to a corridor. He forced his way inside and saw light in front of him.

Davkaleon crept forward, not knowing who or what was waiting for him around the next corner. He heard some voices, normal human voices—not goblin wailing. Davkaleon stepped closer and listened. The voices came from men playing cards and discussing the missing goblins. Davkaleon recognized Sergeant Cronkoross's voice. He stood next to the guardhouse entrance.

There was no point in going back to the guardhouse—everyone thought he was in his cell anyway. He could get to his school living quarters through this corridor, get into his room—the one he hadn't slept in yet, thanks to the guardhouse—lock the door and sleep in peace. Davkaleon made his way to the room. He was surprised that the door wasn't locked. He opened it and sneezed.

"Bless you."

The voice was familiar. The candlelight flashed up and Davkaleon saw the little Adoleeseet, Chapa, sitting in the middle of the room.

"ChapiusKloyAlfreyDon, what are you doing here?" Davkaleon asked. He looked around. The room was a mess. Davkaleon had never been known for being neat, but what he saw struck even him. The room looked like a battle site. The table, chairs and bed were upside down. His things had been thrown across the room, and his spare cloak was torn to shreds.

"Morons!" Davkaleon got furious, "Those damn goblins have been here!"

"They have, Chapa answered. "They won't be back."

"Have you met them?"

"Well, yes. Don't you see how pleasantly we conversed?"

"It was *you* who fought with them?" Davkaleon showed surprised.

"Who else?" Chapa answered proudly. "You trained me well to pretend to be the DRAGON of Adolees, so when I opened the door and saw a crowd of the hairy freaks you call goblins, I pretended to be the DRAGON right away. If you could only have seen how they ran! But they made quite a noise, so there were rubbernecks looking out of each room. I pretended to be you, in order to calm everyone down. I poked my head out of the room, said that I had to see out some uninvited guests, wished everyone good night and closed the door." Chapa beamed with pride as he told his story.

"You would have had to wait for me for a long time. I'm here by accident. I am supposed to be in the guardhouse right now. After today's events, it looks like I will have to stay there for a *very* long time."

Chapa rattled of a string of questions. "What is the guardhouse? Why will you have to stay there for a long time? And, most importantly, why haven't you answered my calls?"

"Hold on with your questions. Tell me how long you have been sitting in my room?" Davkaleon asked.

"About ten minutes," Chapa answered.

"That means that the goblins came into my room after

attacking me," Davkaleon stated.

Having gathered all his weapons Davkaleon nodded to the Adoleeseet and turned his steps to the door. "You need to change into a tiny bug and wait in my pocket while I explain what had happened to the guardhouse authorities. Then, I will pass into my cell and will walk into the dungeon. There, I will explain everything to you."

* * * * *

"Where did you come from?" Sergeant Croncoross asked having seen Davkaleon. "You were supposed to be in your cell long time ago. You've been in the guardhouse since last night. Did you run away? Do you know what that means?"

"Yes, yes, I know, it means more days in the guardhouse, but I didn't run away," Davkaleon answered.

Speaking about what had happened, Davkaleon gave an account of the events, passing over the presence of the little Adoleeseet, Chapa. The first part of the story about the goblin attack was laid out in every detail. He fudged the tale a little when it came to returning to his room. According to Davkaleon, he hadn't understood where he was until he got to the school living quarters. At that moment, he thought he needed to take more weapons to fight the vicious goblins. When he opened the door, he saw despicable goblins rifling through his things. In a rage, he kicked them out. To calm down the neighbors, he explained to them he had thrown out the uninvited guests, wished everyone good night, and left for the guardhouse. "I never thought of running away," he said. "Why would I run away, when I've almost come to love my guardhouse cell? It is like my home now." Davkaleon stopped talking and folded his arms.

"Well, you fight well, but it appears to me that you're a master storyteller as well," Sergeant Cronkoross said.

"That tale is good enough for me. Write a report."

Having written exactly what he had told Croncoross, Davkaleon finally found himself back in his cell. He waited for a few minutes, and then slipped into the dungeon where he could talk to Chapa at last.

"I kind of understood what the guardhouse was. What did you do to be cast here?" the Adoleeseet asked.

Davkaleon told him in detail about the enrollment test, about the problems in the Logic lessons and about the fight with the goblin guards.

"We are given the same problems at Logic lessons," Chapa smiled. "Why didn't you answer my calls?"

"I couldn't answer your calls, because I was not left alone, even for a minute. Where do you want to drag me away to this time?" asked Davkaleon.

"I need you to make another trip to the temple with me," Chapa blindsided his friend with this unexpected request.

"You mean the temple in the rock?" Davkaleon was surprised. "Why?"

"We'll start with this temple, but then we'll probably get into another temple. Honestly, I do not know where it is. Sometimes it seems to me that it is in Twie—" Adoleeseet stammered over a single, forbidden word, and then continued. "It seems to me that it is in the place which you cannot talk about in Daeya."

Davkaleon's eyes sparkled.

"You see, I do not know exactly where it is," Chapa confessed. "But I cannot think of where else it *can* be, if all the temples like the temple in the rock obey it.

"Are you sure"? Davkaleon became even more interested.

But the Adoleeseet shook his head again. "No, I'm not sure. And maybe they do not obey it but they send *all* records there, everything from all of the other temples." Chapa tried to explain his idea, but even he wasn't sure of how such a thing would work.

"Then it is not a temple, but rather a supreme depository, to which all depositories are subordinated," Davkaleon suggested.

Interesting theory, but not as intriguing as getting into Twierks. This would be of great interest to Elfid. Davkaleon's brother's dream would be to move to such a place *forever*. Seeing that Davkaleon's interest had cooled a little, Chapa became alarmed and added, "You will see your girl there."

"What girl?" Davkaleon seemed interested.

"What girl? Which girl? Yeah, right, you need to ask. You *know* which one," Chapius smiled slyly. "The one you met in the temple."

"What makes you think that I'll meet her there?" whispered Davkaleon.

"I did not say that you'd meet her there. I said that you'd see her," explained Chapius.

"I may see her in the *record* from the temple." Davkaleon seemed to be disappointed to not see Heather in person.

"Records from the temple show what has been. I mean that you can see what she's doing right *now*." The Adoleeseet winked.

"You are not kidding? How could that be?" Davkaleon's eyes glittered again.

But Chapa said with a sigh, "Honestly speaking, I do not know whether you will see her or not. I am guessing that you may see her. Maybe not her, but her kitten. I'm not sure, though, if you see her kitten, you can see her, too. Right? The kitten will be near her. Where else can he be? In any case, her kitten may be where she is,"

94

Adoleeseet added.

"Chapius, did you get confused at your school? Why on earth are you blowing smoke like this? What does this have to do with a kitten?"

"You see, I really need you to come with me, so I told you about the girl, but I think that you really *can* see the kitten." Chapa grew sad.

"Are you all right? You, spinning this yarn about the girl and about the kitten?"

"Not really. I think you can see the kitten."

"Tell me plainly," Davkaleon scowled. "Why would your stupid depository show me a cat and not a girl?"

"I think that it would be willing to show you the cat but maybe not the girl. Since you were holding a kitten in your arms, a piece of his fleece could remain on your cloak. You remember how fluffy the kitten was? And since you did not keep the girl in your arms, so you do not have any of her hair."

"Fleece? Hair? You think this is a normal explanation?" Davkaleon said with a resentful tone in his voice.

"Don't fly off the handle," Chapa replied peacefully. "I'll explain everything. And will you go with me, even if you are not sure that you will see her?"

"Yes, I will, I will go," Davkaleon waved aside. "Tell me plainly what you know."

Chapius explained that a few days ago, he'd received a private key for access to the school library. "You see, usually Adoleeseets do not need a public key. The key, as it were, is coded in each of us. But sometimes, the embedded code does not work. Then to get into the library, you can use the public key. This basic key is suitable for any Adoleeseet. As for the basic key, you only have to be an Adoleeseet, no additional training or education is required. To achieve higher level keys, you must study,

95

train and pass exams. Starting from your senior course at the university, you can test to gain access to higher level keys. The keys, however, are very costly—so much so that I would never be able to afford them."

"So, what?" Davkaleon interrupted impatiently.

"This is the only school in Adolees which makes personal keys for its students, and the payment for the higher-level keys at this school is expensive."

"Chapius, what is the point of all of this?" asked Davkaleon, who was growing bored hearing about the different keys.

"One moment," Chapius asked. "In many subjects, I'm not the best in the class. However, I'm the *only* student that has ever visited Daeya, not to say the temple in the rock or the depository in it. Besides, I'm the only one who learned how to turn into a dragon at such a young age. My personal key has adjusted to the places I have been and my accomplishments so far. It has given me access to a higher level, higher than I ever dreamed of. There, on this level, I read about what you called the supreme depository. It's called *Scienciya*. All the information from around the world is collected there. There you can also see who was viewing the records of any event and what they did with them. And more, you can *erase* records, if they are the records of yourself. This is exactly what I am interested in, because if I can get access there, then *others also can*. And, having got there, they can see how I deleted the records."

"So, what will they see if the records were deleted?" asked Davkaleon.

Chapa bit his lip "They will see how I erased something and I do not want to attract attention to this at all."

"If it is so, then this mess can go on forever. With each new key, you will erase what you have done with the previous one." Davkaleon objected.

"Probably." Chapa could not argue. "But with each subsequent key, there will be less and less of those who can discover the truth."

"I figured out your keys," Davkaleon nodded. "How is this connected to the girl, and why do you think that I'll be able to see her?"

"There are a lot of ways to find what you need in **Scienciya**. For example, you can give a hair for search, and the depository will find everything related to that hair for you."

"You think I can find the kitten, and then ask your **Scienciya** where exactly this kitten is?" asked Davkaleon.

Chapa nodded his head.

"And how do we to get to this **Scienciya**?" asked Davkaleon.

"I do not know. In my library, I found just one reference that applied. I hope to find more in the depository of the temple."

Davkaleon nodded, thinking. "How soon do you need to get into the depository?"

"Tomorrow night," answered Chapa. "To open the temple doors, I need to show some cause. I read a lot about those who you call mages and sorceresses. Tomorrow, they will celebrate *Walpurgis* night, and I can bring gifts. On another day, I don't know what I could invent to make the temple to open the doors."

"Walpurgis Night? Never heard of it. What in the world is this night?"

"Walpa is the supreme witch or goddess. I was completely confused with your divine titles," Chapa complained. "In general, she is the source of the Life Force. Walpa lives in the luxurious castle of WalpaRaiso with her daughters, the Walpurgs. Every year, Walpa

97

gives her eldest daughter in marriage, and Walpa herself gives birth to a new little Walpurg. The wedding night of the eldest Walpa's daughter is called Walpurgis Night. If you want to ask something of Walpa, make her and her Walpurgs gifts, and then ask for anything you want. You will not find a better time than Walpurgis Night for your requests." explained Chapa.   "I can run away from the guardhouse, although after that I will be adding about ten days duty. But Aleurh is wounded, so I have to hire another dragon. You will have to spend at least five hours in the form of a bug in my pocket," noted Davkaleon.

"It's okay. I will survive," Chapa declared confidently.

"By the way, how did you find your way to my school?" asked Davkaleon.

"You said you would study in a military school in Assa, so I flew to Assa. From there, I took your form and asked passers-by for direction. Before entering the school, I copied your brother Elfid's form and asked how to find you."

"You need to have a rest somewhere. Go to my room. It's empty. And tomorrow, while I'm in my classes, find everything we need to make a mage potion. And visit Elfid—we need a cloak of the Adoleeseet dragon, the adamant dagger and a mask." Davkaleon gave instructions.

"I will visit Elfid," Chapa answered gleefully, "but not to borrow a cloak. I brought such a cloak for you as a gift. Its style is a little bit different—it is more like armor—but it is better. You will be able to use it in battles. I need Elfid's cloak to try to find the kitten's wool on it."

Davkaleon's eyes lit up. "You will gift me this cloak? But Chapius, it's worth a *fortune* here in Daeya. I have to give you an adequate gift in return. What do you want to get from Daeya, which you can't find in Adolees?" asked

Davkaleon.

"I don't know, yet," Chapa laughed. "I would not survive in Daeya without you. And if I see a nice souvenir somewhere on our way, I will let you know."

Chapter 13. The Supreme Depository

"What kind of carnage did you create yesterday?" That was the first question that Davkaleon heard when he entered the classroom in the morning.

"Carnage? What carnage?" Malay was confused. He'd been peacefully sleeping in the guardhouse and hadn't heard anything about what had happened the previous night.

"Haven't you heard? Davkaleon destroyed a whole squad of goblins yesterday! There was a huge ruckus, and then they ran away. The whole school was shaking."

"How many goblins were there, Davkaleon?" asked one of his classmates.

"Do you really think that I was counting them?" asked Davkaleon, who wasn't comfortable with such pressure and questions about the victory, in which he wasn't even involved.

"When did you find time to fight with goblins?" asked Kvorts after entering the classroom. "The whole school is talking only about your fight."

"Those goblins attacked me last night," explained Davkaleon. "I woke up because someone put their hand over my mouth and I couldn't breathe. They dragged me somewhere. I fought with them. But there were a lot of those hairy little beasts, so I had to throw a knife at one and a dagger at another. Then, I realized that I didn't have enough weapons for all of them. So, I ran to my room to get more ammunition, but those freaks were already there. I have no idea what they were trying to find, but they put everything upside-down. That made me incredibly mad, so I threw all of them out of there. I was very polite after that. I wished goodnight to all and went back to the guardhouse to sleep."

"What did they want from you?" asked Malay.

"I really want to know the answer to that question, too. They kept asking me, *where is it?* But I have no idea what *it* is."

The math teacher entered the classroom, ending the questioning. Later, Krilis came to Davkaleon during a break and pulled him aside. "I have no idea what the goblins were trying to find in your room, but you may be interested to know that Crassius Pompeus was living in your room last year."

"Is that the guy who's staying with us in the guardhouse?"

"No," answered Krilis. "The Pompeus family loves that name. They are incredibly proud of it. Several Daeyan commanders had the name Crassius Pompeus, so there are few boys with that name in each generation of their family. The Crassius Pompeus who stayed at your room last year was a newbie last year. He died at the end of the year under very mysterious circumstances, which no one can or will explain. There have been a lot of rumors."

"What mysterious circumstances?" Davkaleon was suddenly interested.

"Waves threw him into the Rock Cliff."

"And why is that mysterious? Many daredevils who try to show off their diving skills jumping from the Rock cliff find their demise this very same way," Davkaleon said, shrugging his shoulders.

"Even the fastest dragon needs at least an hour to fly from the Temple of Assa to the Rock Cliff. But he was seen at the temple within an hour before he was found dead and battered on the cliff. That day was the anniversary of the famous Assa battle and the temple was holding a celebration service. Many people saw him throughout the service and vow that he was there within the hour he was found," Krilis explained.

"Maybe in two hours, but not in one?"

Krilis shook his head. "No, it was just an hour. I read a report and people discussed that case a lot. But that's not everything. Crassius Pompeus, with whom you are having a duel, did everything in his power to get the school to allow him to move into your room. But the school refused all of his requests."

"Do you think that the previous Crassius Pompeus hid something in my room?" asked Davkaleon.

Krilis had no time to answer, because the Daeyan language class had begun. Davkaleon wanted to continue the conversation during the break, but the teacher Stanglate stopped him.

"The whole school already knows that you defeated a squad of goblins. A really nice surprise awaits you. Lieutenant Harding will announce it before the beginning of training. Please, accept my personal congratulations. It's always pleasant to hear about the victories of true Daeyats from families of Perfects."

Training was the last class during that day. After entering the training ground, Lieutenant Harding ordered everybody to line up and solemnly announced that the school was always happy to encourage victorious students, and today was such an occasion. Even though the goblins had an agreement with the school to keep the guardhouse in order, it was strictly prohibited for them to leave the dungeon. Yesterday, they violated the agreement and entered the residential premises of the school. Davkaleon fought with a squad of goblins and kicked them out of the student quarters. To thank him, the school decided to cancel his guardhouse term. Many students looked at Davkaleon with respect.

Not all of them, however. The look that Crassius gave

him was menacing.

Davkaleon paid the dragon that brought them to the caves near Llill. Chapa stretched out on the floor of the cave. Davkaleon began preparing the potion and pondered if he should make a stop at a jewelry store. All women adore jewelry—he was sure that Walpa and Walpurgs were no exception. Besides, he had to buy a gift for Heather. If a magical night was coming, then they would probably meet.

To find a jewelry store in Llill was as easy as shelling peas. Directly on the square in front of the central temple, an apprentice beckoned passers-by to the shop of his master. He promised the best jewelry for every taste and purse. "Talismans, amulets, averters, charms," cried the shill.

Davkaleon requested that they show him something suitable for Walpurgis Night. The owner immediately drew out several boxes revealing a variety of rings, bracelets, brooches and other items, whose purpose remained a complete mystery to Davkaleon. Who knew if this knick-knackery was really suitable for the Walpurgis Night, or if the owner offered them for any occasion? Davkaleon quickly selected a few garnishes and moved others aside.

"Now, I need something unusual," he declared.

Honestly, Davkaleon had no idea what exactly this "unusual" gift should be.

He just wanted the gift to impress Heather, but the shop owner seemed to understand his request.

"Is this girl your bride?" asked the seller.

"No," answered Davkaleon, adding, "not *yet*."

"Are you going to ask for her hand tonight?"

"No," answered Davkaleon, who had not thought that far ahead.

"Then a ring is off the menu," the seller stated. "At what moon cycle was the girl born?"

Davkaleon did not know.

"What color are the eyes of your precious darling?"

"Blue as the sky," answered Davkaleon.

"So, sapphires," the seller said with confidence. "Sapphires are expensive stones, but they protect the wearer from witchcraft and the evil eye. This is the only talisman that is devoted to its owner, and that only to the first owner. Such sapphires are called first-begotten, and they cost more, but they will be a real treat for your favored one."

The seller pulled another box with sapphire jewelry.

"All jewelry in this box has only first-begotten sapphires. Even if the stone is stolen from your girl or she loses it, the sapphire will still remember her and will protect her as before."

"I want these earrings." Davkaleon pointed to a pair that seemed to call to him.

"You have excellent taste! Your girl will be delighted," the seller said, putting the earrings in a beautiful box.

The price of earrings plunged Davkaleon into shock for a moment. In Daeya, Davkaleon could buy a couple of the best quality swords. Having seen the confusion on the face of a potential buyer, the seller immediately continued his sales pitch. "The first-begotten sapphire has one more unusual property—it is able to act as a love potion. If a sapphire is placed in a glass filled with sorcery nectar, cover it with your left hand and imagine the girl you love, and then you will certainly charm your favored one. Go to the tavern next door, tell them that I sent you and you need the divine nectar, and the love of your goddess is guaranteed to you, especially on Walpurgis Night."

Davkaleon took out his purse. Chapa, in the form of a

bug, basted him with his chelas, but Davkaleon paid no attention to him. The bug moved to his collar and buzzed in his ear: "Are you completely out of your mind? Will you really pay that kind of money?" But Davkaleon waved off the annoying buzz and, having got the earrings, went out of the shop.

"Did you hear me? Did you see, finally, how to sell?" The seller turned to his apprentice who froze in the corner.

"Remember, you should *raise* the price and not offer useless discounts, from which we have no profit and only loss."

"Well, but I did not know that a festive night was coming," the apprentice tried to justify himself.

"You, blockhead, these witches have their feasts every night. Use it and profit by it!"

"Davkaleon, how could you believe in what that salesman was telling you?" asked Chapa when they went into the tavern pointed by the jeweler. "He really fed you beans. Put your brain to use. If these sapphires were first-begotten and did not belong to anyone before, how could they find a way to him?"

"Eat your chops silently," snapped Davkaleon removing the dish from the table to the bench, so that no one could see how a tiny bug devoured one chop after another.

Putting the earrings in the glass with the divine nectar, Davkaleon added: "Do you reckon your Scienciya with feline villus sounds more convincing?"

"Seriously? This is the science of Adolees!" Chapa squealed indignantly.

"And this is the magic ritual of Daeya," Davkaleon retorted.

Chapa muttered something and returned to the chops. But the price of the earrings kept nagging at the Adoleeseet, so he asked, "Do you really like this girl so much? You did not even see her face.

"And what for the imagination?" Asked Davkaleon, for a moment coming off the chops.

"And what if your imagination deceived you? She was wearing a mask," Chapius did not stop."

"First, my imagination is not so stupid as to deceive me. Secondly, she was not in a mask, but in a half-mask, and what is more, in a *very narrow* half-mask, so I could see her face perfectly. Third, I met her in the temple of mages—you know what sort of mages. Tell me, what's the point of being a mage if you do not take all the best?" protested Davkaleon.

Chapa paused in his devouring of the chops. "So, she said that she had nothing to do with the mages, or with witches, or rather, with the sorceress."

"Oh, and you listened wide-eyed, and believed every word," Davkaleon laughed. "Elfid told me that nobody appeared in this temple accidentally. So the mages prepared her specially for me."

"Prepared? Specially for you? Are you sure?" The Adoleeseet was astonished.

"Well, perhaps not specifically for me. But they prepared her for someone. Now, it does not matter for who, because I was the one who saw her, which means she was intended for me." Davkaleon folded his arms confidently.

"And what if some mage or his disciple thinks exactly the same?" Chapa would not give up.

"It would be better for him to stop thinking like that," snapped Davkaleon.

"What if she already loves someone?"

"Chapius, do you celebrate the All Fools' Day?" Davkaleon said, resentment in his voice. "Why do you blow smoke? Did you see how she looked at me?"

"How could I see if I was under your cloak?" Chapa asked.

"She was looking very tender," Davkaleon smiled dreamily, and, realizing that the comment about tenderness could be understood as weakness, he added, "Not that I need this tenderness, but sometimes you may want a bit of a change. I do not know about your school, but in mine, if the monster did not attack you and you did not grapple with the goblins, then you may think the day has passed very tenderly."

Shaking the divine nectar just in case, Davkaleon took a sip from the glass. "Wow, this really *is* a drink for the Gods." Davkaleon called out to the innkeeper, ordering a keg.

"What will you do with the keg?" Chapa was surprised.

"What do you mean? I will take it to the temple. To make the Walpa with her Walpurgs happy."

* * * * *

Davkaleon remembered that the temple in the rock must be bypassed three times, then he had to prick himself with an adamant dagger and after that add a few drops of mage potion. To his surprise, the sorcerer's potion was not needed. The temple recognized him and rumbled: "What brought you here?"

"I want to give gifts to Walpurgs," explained Davkaleon.

"Come in," answered the temple, and in a moment, a door appeared before him.

There were already several people in the temple, and it was difficult to enter secretly, as they had on their last visits. Maybe a crowd would gather in the temple later, and no one would pay attention to them as they attended to the task at hand. Based upon the quantity of gifts stacked in the hall, it was common to celebrate Walpurgis Night on a noble scale. Davkaleon solemnly placed his barrel in the middle of the hall.

"Look at you! Who has returned to the temple!"
Davkaleon heard and turned around.

"Is it possible this is Alfreydon himself! Alive and healthy! As you can see, his teacher did not swallow him, and the temple recognized him, so he must have passed initiation. I won! Oh, it will cost everyone five hundred Twierks reals."

Davkaleon recognized three of the mages' disciples whom he had met on the day of initiation.

"What did you bet on?" Davkaleon-Alfreydon asked, approaching the trio.

"Whether you would survive or not, of course," Lenholm laughed. "The whole of Twierks disputed about it. Heh, my friend, Alfreydon, you're a fine fellow to be still alive. I made good money on you, so I'll take care of you. As soon as you find yourself in Twierks, we'll go to the *Tender Monster* to enjoy aira. Which do you prefer? White or black?"

"White? Are you kidding? With such a teacher?" The other two laughed.

"Lenholm, can you imagine a disciple of a dragon who would be fond of white vanilla?"

Davkaleon did not know what this aira was, but he guessed that the white aira somehow was connected with white magic, and black, respectively, with black, sinister sorcerers.

"Vanilla is also sometimes nice as a change of pace," Davkaleon said a phrase, quite innocuous from his point of view, just to support conversation.

"Don't tell me that your teacher supplies exclusively

white aira!" Grilski and Blumendeyl grinned.

"Do you know what the program is today?" asked Davkaleon who did not know how Walpurgis Night was celebrated.

"Everything as usual. Carnival, performance, tournament. Did you come just to have fun or do you want to hack a script?"

"Have fun," answered Davkaleon, who had no idea what the expression "to hack a script" meant.

Davkaleon looked back. The passage, where Heather once disappeared, was open again. Davkaleon made a side step.

"Where are you headed?" Lenholm asked.

"Last time I was here, I saw a beauty that appeared from this passage. Perhaps, I will check up on her."

"Old chap Alfreydon, the little cutie evidently made such an indelible impression on you that you stopped paying attention to the signs. Can't you see that you cannot enter Twierks now? You can only get out," Lenholm laughed.

Davkaleon looked at the signs on the wall. He was not sure about all of the other signs, but one he remembered well—the golden rose surrounded by a curled dragon. He was quite sure that now, the rose had sloped to the other side.

The slope of the rose indicates the entrance and exit, Davkaleon thought. *I should not miss the moment when the rose slopes in the other direction, and then I will be able to enter Twierks.* And, of course, he would certainly find Heather there.

Many visitors gathered in the hall. With this many bodies in the room, you could slip away without attracting attention. Several girls emerged from the passage of Twierks.

"Just a minute," Davkaleon said to the mages, making a feint towards the girls.

"Your teacher must keep you with an iron fist, as to make you rush to the Twierks' witches so quickly." Grilski grinned.

"Not with iron fists, but with dragons. Those are worse." Davkaleon said, moving away from the roaring mages.

"Bear in mind that witches' hands may be more rigid than the paws of your dragon," Davkaleon heard the smirk of grinning Lenholm.

"Beauties, how we missed you here!" Davkaleon flirted while approaching the girls.

"Is that really you yourself, Chapushka-Alfreydon?" One of young witches smiled.

Davkaleon broke into a fabulous smile of his own. The attention of young witches flattered him. Having complimented the girls, Davkaleon circled the column. There were no visitors here, and he quickly drank the potion of mages. It made him dizzy. However, the dizziness and the noise in his head were significantly less than his last time in the temple. Maybe he was beginning to get used to the mage's potion? Davkaleon heard how Chapa said mentally the word "DRAGON" and the name of the secret symbol of Adolees. Davkaleon found himself inside the column. The small space within the column began to expand. Very soon he appeared in the room. Just as before, there were racks along the walls. Neatly packed boxes sat arranged on the shelves. This time, the room was much larger. It seemed that Chapa's new key gave access to more information. Chapius quickly found information he sought about Scienciya. He was right that it was possible to see someone, where they were, and what they were doing. There were many ways to find everything required. And yes, it was possible to use the wool of a kitten. The only thing that remained unexplained was how to get into Scienciya. The depository even showed in detail the actions which should be undertaken to find someone via their hair. Chapa tried to repeat these actions with Fluffy's wool. Alas, neither Fluffy nor its image appeared. The voice assistant explained that for such a search, the displayed actions should be done not in the depository, but right in Scienciya. On the question how to get to this Scienciya, the voice assistant replied that it required a higher-level key. Chapa grew sad.

There was no way around the conundrum. "You'll have to pick up the next key at your school," Davkaleon stated.

* * * * *

"What did he want?" A voice came from the column, as soon as Davkaleon and Chapa left the storage area.

"He was looking for a cat." The second voice answered.

"A cat?! Why did he need a cat?"

"I do not know what he needed it for but I found the cat. And, by the way, it's not a cat, but a small kitten."

"Drop him this kitten during the carnival, we will see what he will do with it," offered the first voice.

* * * * *

Davkaleon returned to Lenholm, Grilski and Blumendeyl.

"Well, did you cherish your deep conversation with the future witches of Twierks?" The trio of mages grinned.

Davkaleon cracked a smile and asked, "Could you tell me how to get from here to Scienciya?"

"Scienciya? I've already heard this word somewhere,

but do not remember where. What's it?" asked Grilski.

"It is the official name of the depository of open scripts in the Twierks library," yawned Lenholm.

"Depository of open scripts? What did you forget there?" Blumendeyl was surprised.

"My teacher challenged me to a puzzle with a script from this depositary," sighed Davkaleon.

"The script for beginners?" Grilski did not understand.

"He said that I can find a clue there. Otherwise, he promised to make a lunch of me," Davkaleon tried to give a conversation a turn.

"How can one find a hint in an open script?" Grilski would not give up.

"It is possible," confidently stated Lenholm. "Sure, if the script you want to hack is based on an open script."

Lenholm, Grilski and Blumendeyl went into a discussion of the matter on which neither Davkaleon nor Chapa had a clue. The only conclusion that Davkaleon made of this conversation was that the unknown Scienciya that was regarded almost as an unattainable source of knowledge in Adolees, considered as the initial step accessible to any newcomer in Twierks.

A pleasant melody came from out of nowhere, and comfortable armchairs appeared by themselves in the hall. Davkaleon and his old fellows settled in their armchairs. Davkaleon himself would have preferred to take a place closer to the stage, but Lenholm, Grilski and Blumendeyl sat down in the seats nearest to them, and Davkaleon did not want to split up the company. In a moment, he realized why the three apprentice mages did not pay the slightest attention to the distance of their chairs from the stage, where it was likely the main events would happen. Either the front rows of armchairs disappeared, or the stage drove right up to him, for Davkaleon found himself in the very first row. He could hardly restrain himself from exclaiming his surprise. The trio of mages sitting next to him chatted gaily, not amazed at all at what had happened. Davkaleon leaned back in his chair, and the chair assumed his shape adjusting to his body and posture.

"Gee!" thought Davkaleon. "Holy mackerel!"

Turning into a small bug, Chapa got out from the cloak and settled down under the Davkaleon's collar. There was no way he was going to sit under the cloak and see nothing. The mage in a purple cloak and a gold turban appeared in the lodge.

"Dear guests, the Twierks' Carnival is about to begin. It will be followed by a performance. Help yourself with any drinks, snacks and anything else you wish. As always, you have only to think about what you would like to receive, and your order will immediately materialize."

The mage clapped his hands and disappeared. The stage disappeared with him. Davkaleon's chair appeared on a neatly trimmed lawn in the shadow of a branchy tree. A small lake with fountains appeared in the middle of the lawn. However, the distance from the chair to the lake was significant.

"Look at that," whispered Chapa delightedly and added, "I want some *avaya* drink."

Davkaleon never heard of avaya drink, but he found a glass in his hand filled with something cool and foaming. Davkaleon looked around. Lenholm, Grilski and Blumendeyl were sitting in their chairs, tables with all sorts of food before each of them. Davkaleon looked up and saw that the ceiling of the temple had also disappeared. Could he be in Twierks now?

A soft melody poured in from somewhere.

The Walpurgis bright night, take me out in flight,
Swirl in wild and delirious dance.
In the splash of star light in sublunary site
Melt me down in ambrosial trance

It's a magical night; it's a sorcery site,
Near miracle mirror in the starring gold glimmer
In this augury night you will come to insight
And before morning dew all will brighten for you.

Walpurgis bright fire takes me higher and higher
Glistens dance in the dark causing everything sparks
This mysterious sign gladdens you like a wine,
Hints you never afraid and believe in your fate

The space between spectators and the lake instantly was filled with dancing girls in light clothes and half-masks. The girls began to spin slowly. The music played faster, and the dancers spun faster. Some of the girls slipped into the waters of the lake. The melody played faster, the girls swirled faster. Faster and faster. The wild, passionate dance fascinated everyone.

Multicolored water jets began to beat from fountains around the lake, the girls flew between the streams. They danced, standing on ... Davkaleon could not determine what the girls were hopping on! Were they flying? Until that moment, Davkaleon had not believed that a witch could fly on a broom, at least he had never seen it. Now, he watched not just flights, he saw mad dances on the brooms. The higher the jets fired, the faster the girls danced. Witches hopped among the colorful fountains above the lake. The first fire burst into flame on the shore, then another, more and more! Someone started singing. The hopping moved closer to the bonfires.

A figure of a girl for a moment appeared among the dancers. Davkaleon jumped up from his chair. Why was he sure it was Heather? The girl was far away, and she was wearing a mask. And the dress was not the one she wore the first time he'd seen her. Davkaleon ran to the place where he'd just seen her, but she'd disappeared.

Black-haired dancers circled around the fire. Davkaleon turned his head back and accidentally touched one of them, but his elbow freely passed through the dancer. The girl went on whirling, without paying the slightest attention at him. Davkaleon stretched his hand to another girl. Not encountering any obstacle on its way, the hand freely passed through the dancer! Golden curls flashed again in some distance. This time Davkaleon even managed to run up to Heather. He called her by name, but the girl did not answer. Davkaleon grabbed her arm, but his hand squeezed the air. Feeling disappointed, Davkaleon made a step back. Fire flamed around him.

Davkaleon looked around, he was standing in the middle of the huge fire, but he did not feel any pain! Coming out of the fire, Davkaleon tried to find Heather again, but the girl disappeared.

"You must get the next key from your school as soon as possible," said Davkaleon to Chapius heading for his armchair.

"Take comfort," the bug buzzed softly from under the collar and moved closer to the glass. "I'll order the best Adoleeseet treats." A table with drinks and snacks appeared close to the chair.

"Try it, it's delicious," the bug buzzed.

A girl approached Davkaleon, cooing. "Alfreydon, let's go dance."

"Let's dance, yeah, right!" Davkaleon thought to himself. "I will have egg on my face dancing with air."

The girl came closer and took his arm by the elbow. A real, live girl! That would have been much better than dancing with the air, but Davkaleon was embarrassed. He'd never learned to dance, and he was not used to looking ridiculous. But the girl understood his confusion. "You will look fine—all you need to do is stand and smile. It's me who'll flitter around you. You will look like the greatest mage and master of the universe in the eyes of all the spectators."

That sounded great. Nobody ever said anything like that to Davkaleon. He rose up and the girl really started spinning around him. Then the music interrupted for a few seconds, and the girl asked, "Did you like it? Then give me a grade here so that I could show it to our main priestess." No doubt, Davkaleon liked it. Why not? He chose the highest score without any hesitation.

"Why can I touch you but I cannot touch the others or the bonfires?" Asked Davkaleon.

"Because I'm here, and they are in Twierks. What you see are just holograms," the girl answered looking at the apprentice of a mage with surprise for not knowing such simple things.

Davkaleon never heard of holograms, but, noticing the surprised glance of the future witch, decided not to question any more. "I have to ask Elfid," he thought.

The girl moved away, and another one sprang toward Davkaleon. Another short dance with a request for a grade was repeated. Davkaleon did not remember how many dances he danced and how many marks he put when Chapa's voice buzzed in his ear. "You should better come back. Your friends laugh at you."

Davkaleon did not like being laughed at, so he headed for his chair.

"Well, could you not resist the honey berries of Llill?" laughed Lenholm.

"Dancing with these honey berries is much better than dry analysis. But are you sure your teacher will pay for your entertainment if you tell him about the pleasure of dancing with girls instead of giving up a ready self-regenerating script?" asked Glilski.

"By the way, what script did you want to find in Scienciya? Maybe it's easier to hack the one based on already written script than to write a new one?" Blumendeyl inquired.

"The teacher did not tell me the name of the script. All simply advised me to find it in Scienciya."

"The value of such council is a big fat zero. There are hundreds of thousands of unprotected scripts in Scienciya! How do you find the right one among them?" Grilski shook his head, as if his friend's teacher was an idiot.

"You know, Alfreydon, unless you write a script for your dragon, you'd better give up your snacks, or he'll turn *you* into a snack," Lenholm said, nodding toward the almost endless table with Adolees delicacies ordered by Chapa.

"Many people will take a gamble on this girl, look how many hunters for white aira run around with her," Blumendeyl nodded toward the dancing girls.

Davkaleon turned his head, but there were many dancers, and it was difficult to understand whom Blumendeyl was talking about.

"I see, Lulliy does not leave her," grimaced Grilski. "Yes, and Villanova turns upon her."

"I'm also looking at her, and I should say that she did not to stir a finger to earn a single ball, so let the idiots bet on her," stated Lenholm.

"What's up with that she did not to stir a finger? Look, how much white aira is around her. She is really cute! There will always be a strong mage hanging around, so I'll include her in my script." Blumendeyl remarked.

"Lenholm, why should she get nervous?" Grilski shrugged his shoulders. "Look, Alfreydon danced with a couple of dozen future witches and gave everyone the highest grade. Isn't that so, Alfreydon?" When Davkaleon nodded, he continued. "Now divide the highest grade in 20, and what you get? Relax, I'll tell you—you'll get zero point zero. And this girl is barely fluttering her eyelashes. Sure, she tells Lulliy and Villanova what a great magical power she feels emanating from them, And, the longer they stay near her, the stronger will be their magic power."

At these words, Lenholm and Blumendeyl smiled, and Grilski continued. "The highest grade from Lulliy is guaranteed to her and from Villanova, too, and others will not stint. Oh, and Gragbrag with his cat is right here. Does anyone know why he schleps the cat around everywhere?"

When they mentioned Gragbrag with the cat, Davkaleon tensed—this was the name Heather pronounced in a conversation with the priestess Mistletoe during their first meeting in the temple.

"I do not know why he schleps the cat around, but I would not call Gragbrag a strong mage," Lenholm said.

"Not so," Grilski disagreed. "He studies at Prann's school, and Prann does not take cookie-pushers to his school."

Prann? What Prann? One of Daeya's Gods? thought Davkaleon, hearing a familiar name. Prann belonged to the pantheon, but unlike other Gods, Prann was a cruel and bloody God, demanding sacrifice. Worse, his priests were not always limited to animals' sacrifice.

The mages' company continued to discuss Gragbrag and Prann. "Sure, it's from the great mind that your vaunted Gragbrag makes a muddle of the *vartereza of agnezita* with *agnezita of vartereza*," Lenholm chuckled.

"Well, when was it! In the classes for beginners you also muddled," retorted Grilski." But no other can compare with the aira from Prann. "After this aira there is nothing that appeals me to black chocolate diluted with white vanilla."

"Prann himself delivers exclusively black aira. This is due to the white aira of the Llill's dolls, he manages to dodge penalties for black aira. We complain about the strict conditions for inclusion in the list of candidates from our school wishing to pass the Mages' exam. Have you seen what Prann demands from his apprentices? And this only for the fact that you'll be included in this list! Whether you pass this exam or not is your problem. In such a way, they need the white aira of the Llill's students," Blumendeyl commented.

"Simple mixing of black and white airas does not

produce real Prann's aira," Grilski shook his head.

"For me, his aira is still too dark." Lenholm did not agree.

"Don't tell that to the clients of the *Tender Monster*. They won't understand you. You know what crazy money the *Tender Monster* makes on aira produced by Prann."

Davkaleon understood only one thing—that if he started asking about aira, his membership in the caste of mages' students would immediately be called into question.

"Take my word for it, this little one will dance in the Walpurgs' performance for sure," continued Grilski, again nodding toward the dancing girls.

"She cannot dance the senior Walpurg, who is given in marriage, as she did not pass the initiation yet," Blumendeyl noted.

"And who says about the senior Walpurg? The role of a young Walpurg, looking in the mages' mirror, is just right for her," Grilski shrugged his shoulders.

"And who will perform the senior Walpurg?" Davkaleon asked, deciding that he'd kept silence for too long, and needed to take part in the conversation.

"Where does your dragon keep you, that you do not know who'll dance the senior Walpurg?" Lenholm, Grilski and Blumendeyl looked at Davkaleon-Alfreydon with astonishment.

Davkaleon felt that it would have been much better if he'd said nothing.

"Tell them in Dragonet," the bug buzzed in Davkaleon's ear.

"Naturally, in Dragonet," Davkaleon said, although he did not have any idea of what that was.

"In Dragonet!? Does your teacher allow you to visit Dragonet?" Davkaleon felt an unconcealed astonishment in his interlocutor's voice. The other two looked at him with sudden, obvious respect.

"Very often," answered Davkaleon. "He does not let me out to Twierks, so do not be surprised that I know much less about Twierks than about Dragonet."

"Can you tell us about Dragonet?" The mages leaned forward, eyes wide open, as well as their mouths.

"I would be happy to, but he strongly forbids me even to mention the word Dragonet. I told you about it only because in the mages' school, you definitely know about Dragonet."

"Sure, we do, but only in the most general terms, like the sorcerer ticket. Is it true that it is stored in Dragonet?"

"Sometimes," answered Davkaleon evasively.

"But it means that you can read the conditions of the tournament in advance!?" Three mages looked at Davkaleon-Alfreydon as if he was a demigod.

"Do you think that my teacher leaves the sorcerer ticket right and left? Maybe you think he also invites me to his secret gatherings?"

"So, secret gatherings of the sorcerer council also take place in Dragonet?" Grilski whispered.

"If I could, I would answer you, but my inner voice already tells me that today I will listen to yet another lecture on the topic of what a delicious roast meat I may turn in," answered Davkaleon.

"If the sorcerer ticket is stored in Dragonet, and the dragon allows his disciples to appear there, then it's clear why he never shows his students to anyone and does not allow them to go to Twierks," Lenholm said.

"Let's do next," Blumendeyl suggested. "We'll arrange for you a wonderful trip around the Twierks, we'll visit your Scienciya, will take you to the *Tender Monster*, treat you with aira, take a walk at the famous Twierks Sabbath, find your Llill's sweetie, create a special script for you with path to her from anywhere in the Universe. You'll be able to meet her in a few seconds from any galaxy. *All these at our expense.* And for this, you have just hint of the date of one event. Actually, no, you do not even need to hint. Make a bet on the Sabbath."

"Sounds like fun," Davkaleon nodded.

"Are you going nuts?" buzzed a bug, but Davkaleon waved off the annoyance.

The bug persisted. "Do refuse! You know what DRAGON will do with you?" Chapa whispered into his ear, but his Daeyan friend pretended to be deaf.

"We'll now make preparations to the event of interest," said Grilski, branching out into a long discourse with Blumendeyl and Lenholm about things which seemed to Davkaleon a full gibberish.

"What is the name of your lovely doll?" Lenholm eventually asked.

"I forgot to ask her name," Davkaleon lied. For some reason he did not want to talk about Heather. Today's short remarks about white and black aira strongly alarmed him, and he was sure Heather had a white aira, although he did not really know what it was.

"No problem. Imagine her," suggested Lenholm.

A mirror appeared on the table instantly and it looked exactly the same as the mirror of Dallilla at the ritual of Isida. Davkaleon felt that beyond his will the image of Heather appeared before his eyes. He strained himself, trying not to let her appear in the mirror, but his will was paralyzed.

Davkaleon recalled that the Adoleeseet had telepathy much stronger than the Daeyats. But what if it's not just telepathy? Davkaleon did not go into scientific speculation on the topic of what or who made him imagine Heather.

Instead, he thought, "Chapius, can you do something?"

Davkaleon did not know exactly what Chapa had done, but the next instant, Heather's image faded at his eyes and instead the image of the dragon began to appear, and immediately it became the image of a huge DRAGON of Adolees.

"Is this your cherry pie?" The trio was taken aback.

"I do not like when somebody putters about my brain," laughed Davkaleon.

"We did it just to help you find her," Blumendeyl protested.

"I'm going for a walk. I sat too long," announced Lenholm.

"Want to prepare a trick to appear in the mirror for young Walpurg?" grinned Grilski.

"No need for me to get up for such a trifle," Lenholm said haughtily.

Davkaleon also decided to walk around and try to find Heather again. From time to time, the girls offered him a dance, but his answer that he had already put several dozen of the highest points extinguished their interest momentarily. The music stopped, and someone announced that the performance had started. As for the numerous Walpurgs, their roles would be performed by the girls who scored the highest grades.

Young dancers fluttered out onto the stage. Davkaleon immediately recognized Heather. She danced well, so he did not pay too much attention to the storyline. The plot seemed to be similar to the legend Chapa told him about the Walpurgis Night. One of the Walpurgs married or was only going to be married, the rest began to dance around a mirror and asked it to show something or someone to each of them. An invisible voice invited the audience to give gifts to the girls and help them persuade the mirror.

Rings, earrings and bracelets flew on the stage. A massive necklace fell to Heather's feet.

"Don't let the necklace reach her," Davkaleon worried.

He worried in vain. None of the gifts fell to any girl. *Magic again,* he thought as he threw the trinkets he'd purchased. The Sapphire earrings stayed in his pocket as he considered how to hand them to Heather.

Then, Davkaleon heard an unusual conversation. Actually, it was difficult to name the conversation as only one interlocutor was speaking. The second mumbled something in response. "Remember, if you fail me again, I'll tear off your tail," someone said.

"Tee-hee," was heard in response.

Davkaleon looked back. Behind the nearest bush, someone was talking to a black cat. Davkaleon was ready to swear that it was the black cat he'd seen in the temple.

"And mind you, don't tell me that you have been prevented again by a tiny kitten", the first voice continued.

The black cat muttered something in response, and his master began to tell it what to do. Davkaleon did not understand all the details, but he understood that the cat was required to change something imperceptibly in the script attached to the mirror. A small white nubbin out of nowhere appeared at Davkaleon's feet. The kitten looked around with scared eyes. It seemed he did not understand how he got there.

"Fluffy!" Davkaleon was ready to burst but he managed to stop himself in time.

At the same moment, the black cat appeared out of the bush and gave a malicious growl. The kitten instinctively jumped up. The next moment, Fluffy was in Davkaleon's hands. Davkaleon was taken aback. The kitten was alive and real.

Why is the kitten real and Heather is not? thought he.

"How long you'll stick out here like a sore thumb? When will you come to the mirror?" The discontented voice of the cat's owner sounded nearby.

Abandoning attempts to reach Fluffy, the black cat rushed to carry out the order of his master. The kitten jumped down onto the grass and rushed after the black cat. Davkaleon followed Fluffy, hoping that the kitten could lead him to Heather, and, at the same time, wondering how such a tiny tot could run so fast. The trained, athletic Davkaleon could hardly keep up with it! The black cat sprang on the stage and ran to the mirror. Fluffy jumped on the cat and then leapt off it, rushing toward Davkaleon, who bent and picked up the kitten. The black cat sank its teeth into his leg, and Davkaleon angrily sent the cat spinning with a kick.

"Hoot, you, idiot, why do you insult my little cat?"

Davkaleon could hear the black cat's owner's voice.

Davkaleon decided to postpone wrangles with the cat's owner until later, because Heather was standing in front of the mirror.

"To the mirror!" The owner of the black cat ordered his pet.

The cat was already behind the mirror when the voice of Lenholm sounded out. "So, my dear Gragbrag, as I see, you want to change the magic script with your cat's help. Don't bother, you 're not able to do it."

"You, rascal! You've already changed everything!" roared Gragbagg.

"This is from Alfreydon," shouted Davkaleon, and threw the box with earrings to Heather.

At the same time, Fluffy jumped off Davkaleon's hands and ran to its mistress. Picking up her kitten, Heather smiled happily.

"You, dolt!" Gragbrag growled and turned something sparkling on Davkaleon.

Davkaleon, in turn, drew a dagger.

"Weapons in the Twierks performance!" A voice rumbled from somewhere above. An invisible force picked Davkaleon up, twisted him and kicked him out. The next moment, Davkaleon found himself in the aisle in front of the temple. His head was buzzing. An unknown centipede clung with all its limbs into the Davkaleon collar. In a few seconds the centipede turned into a familiar bug.

"Wow," it whispered with admiration, "I liked it!"

"Liked? Did you like the fact that they threw us out of the temple?" raged Davkaleon.

"No, I did not like *that*. But the fact that I managed to turn into a centipede is just magnificent. In Adolees, they train the participants of the Big Prize game this way. And to become a participant in this game is the dream of every

Adoleeseet. Let's go into the temple," offered Chapa.

"I wonder how we'll do it? Where do you see the door?"

They stood in front of the temple, but, as usual, there were neither windows nor doors.

"You have the other vial of mages' potion. Have a drink!" suggested Adoleeseet.

"Have a drink!" mimicked Davkaleon, whose head was rustling, and his ears were tingling.

"Davkaleon, I do not know how we can once again get into the temple, except for Walpurgis' Night next year. And if you don't go into the temple, then you'll not get to Twierks. And if you do not get to Twierks, then you'll not meet your girl. Do you want to wait until next year?"

No, Davkaleon did not want to wait until next year, but a few drops of the potion changed nothing. Becoming angry, Davkaleon drank a whole vial. The door did not appear, but the temple uttered in a rumbling voice "For a threat of weapons at the Twierks performance, your entry is forbidden!"

"I did not use weapons, I just only drew it out and then, just in case." Davkaleon tried to persuade the temple.

"Liar! You see, he drew his weapon out just in case," the temple's voice was angry.

"This was my first offense," Davkaleon continued to persuade the temple in his most polite voice.

"If it was not for the first time, then for you the entry would be closed forever. Instead, your entry is prohibited for only one year," the temple stated.

"For a whole year because of a dagger, which I did not even use? And what about Gragbrag? Why did you not throw him out?"

"You ignorant cad! Where did you see the Gragbag's weapon? What's up with you? You muddled a weapon with a simple scripter? All that Gragbrag wanted to do was to

127

use his scripter to change the script, and on Walpurgis Night, nobody forbids you to do it." The temple terminated further objections.

The small bug tugged his collar. Someone was approaching the temple via the passage. Davkaleon took a few steps aside and then tore away to the open door of the temple after a new visitor. Alas, he didn't have a chance to get to the Twierks performance. Davkaleon found himself swirling around in a black cloud, and then he was carried away somewhere. Impenetrable darkness was all around. Davkaleon was twisted slam-bang, his head cracked against something hard. It seemed that the whole body was falling to decay. He must have lost consciousness for a moment, because he did not remember how he landed. He regained consciousness among ruins in an unfamiliar place. He still clutched the adamant dagger in his hand.

High mountains rose above behind the ruins, the valley laid away. The bug was hanging on the Davkaleon's collar grasping it with huge iron teeth. It seems that all the strength of Chapa-bug had focused on growing its teeth, at the first moment it even could not unclench them.

"Where are we?" the Adoleeseet asked, clenching its teeth.

"I was so afraid of losing you that it seems I've bitten through your collar."

It was about the collar of a cloak made from the impenetrable skin of Adoleeseet fighting dragon.

Davkaleon looked back. "I know where we are. We are in the Valley of Death on the ruins of the Black Castle. And I have only a dagger, and all my weapons are left in the cave near Llill."

"What in the world is this castle?" Chapa asked.

"The castle of the mages, and you know which ones. They always told dark stories about it. We need to get out of here as soon as possible—it's not good that I do not have a weapon, I am unarmed."

"But you have me," said Chapius. "I can turn into any weapon."

"And into the sword, too?" specified Davkaleon.

"Into the sword, the spear and even into the axe. I cannot only shoot out flames. But the self-returning spear is also breath-taking!" answered Chapa.

Davkaleon cheered up. Adamant dagger in one hand, Chapa-the-sword in the other? That way, one can cross the Valley of Death. So, they made their way back. Chapa had to turn into a sword or a spear several times, but neither of them was injured badly. Just little scratches. Finally, they even managed to catch a fully edible beast, which had carelessly decided to have them for his dinner.

Chapter 14. The School of True Daeyan Language

On Sunday morning, Davkaleon went to *the School of the old Dayan language* with a heavy heart. He could have used that time to walk around Assa, spend time in the *Mug and Sword,* or go hunting and cooking some wildfowl on fire. One can do so many things on such a nice Sunday! Malay and Kvorts called him to play cards and gave a distinct screw-loose sign when he took a breath and explained what his destination that day was.

"But what can I do if Stanglate wrote about the Sunday school to both of my parents and they ordered me to go there? Mother promised not to give me even one mangy sickle if I try to avoid the school. Dad was even more serious and just sent a letter saying, *if you miss classes, I will box your ears!*"

For the first time in his life, Davkaleon was almost crying, cursing the arrogance of Perfects, as well as their language and his own origin. He opened the map and went to the Sunday class, making deep and heavy sighs.

It was pretty easy to find the way to the Saint lake in the center of Assa. Actually, there was no need to use the map, because he could reach the lake without it. But he could hardly find the way to the sacred Arragorra without the map. The Arragorra was located on the mysterious Buan Island that could appear in virtually any part of Daeya, following its own will and the will of gods. Usually it appeared in the center of the Saint lake of Assa—at least, it stayed there during national sacred Holidays. On any other day, it was appearing and disappearing in the Saint lake, sometimes in the ocean, or even in any other place of Daeya. People said that priests could go to Arragorra to talk with gods, but Davkaleon wasn't quite sure if it was true. His father was told him many times how priests appealed to gods, praying to Gods, but he had never heard that they were actually talking to gods.

Davkaleon checked the map once more when he reached the shores of the Saint lake. The map was pointing to an almost unnoticeable path between giant rocks. Davkaleon went there and faced a pile of rock lumps. An arrow on the map was showing that he had to enter inside. The question was how to do that? Davkaleon went around the pile, but he couldn't find any entrance. In fact, the map was showing one more sign, but Davkaleon didn't remember its meaning. A teacher in the estate of his dad was telling an old Dayan legend about that sign, but Davkaleon totally forgot it. While Davkaleon was thinking what to do, someone tapped him on the shoulder.

"It's nice to meet my own brother in such a strange place," Paradion smiled.

"You!? What have you done to get here?" Davkaleon was surprised, because he couldn't imagine that someone in his right mind would like to study a language, which nobody uses.

Paradion's mother didn't belong to Perfects, thus Paradion could easily avoid studies in the Sunday school.

"Why are you surprised? The Gerklat family belongs to the ancient families of Perfects, so there's no surprise that I want to learn the language of my predecessors."

"Are you doing this voluntarily? On Sunday?" Davkaleon still refused to believe such a thing was possible.

Two Daeyats approached the pile of rocks. One of them was the teacher of the Daeyan language, Stanglate. The second one was bundled up in a hooded cloak, so it was simply impossible to see his face.

Stanglate smiled friendly when he saw Davkaleon. "It's

131

very nice that you decided to come. We really need true Daeyats. And who is that?" asked Stanglate, pointing on Paradion.

"This is my brother, Paradion. He's studying in the school of priests and dreaming to learn the old Daeyan language," answered Davkaleon.

Stanglate broke into a smile, but his companion corrected Davkaleon, "Not the old Daeyan, but the *true* Daeyan language. That's the proper name of the language of the Perfects Daeyats. Only people with dirty blood in their veins call it *old*."

Stanglate and his companion approached rock lumps.

"Do you understand what I'm doing here now?" Paradion whispered.

Stanglate knocked several rocks, one by one. A narrow path appeared in the pile. It was curving, splitting and twisting, thus it was only possible to walk there in single file.

"Have you prepared a speech?" Paradion asked mentally, following his brother.

"A speech?" asked Davkaleon, not believing that he understood the question correctly.

Paradion gave him a prepared introduction instead of giving an answer. Of course, Davkaleon was able to tell about his parents and their families on his own, without any hints or plans. But the speech of Paradion was looking more like a poem than a short introduction. According to Paradion, a long speech about the ancient family of Gerklats, and not less ancient family of Davkaleon's mother Arara Borlatar, should include all their services to Daeya, and had to take at least 15 minutes. After that, the speaker had to introduce another son of priest Gerklat, Paradion, and finish his speech saying that both brothers really appreciated attention and don't want to take more

132

time of such honored people.

"So, do you want me to say all of this?" Davkaleon asked.

"Of course! You are the 100% Perfects, so who else can tell this if not you? Don't be afraid that you can forget something. I memorized all the speech and I will give you a mental hint."

"Have you really written this speech on your own?" Davkaleon asked doubtfully.

Paradion was confused, but he confessed that his father helped.

"Father?! So, my attendance here was your *helpful* action? Did you write to my mother too?" Davkaleon remonstrated.

"Don't be mad, Davkaleon," Paradion asked, "You just can't imagine which level of contempt they show to non-Perfects people in the school of priests. I am slightly protected with my Gerklat name, but this protection is very weak. They ask about my mother's origins every chance they get."

"Tell them that your mother is from a very belligerent Daeyan family and punch someone's jaw as a confirmation. And if they continue to mock you, just take out the sword and gut them. Thanks to Kvinsit, it won't be too difficult for you, because he prepared us really great." Davkaleon gave an advice.

"You can't act like that in the school of priests, Davkaleon. It's strictly prohibited to fight there. They encourage oral duels instead. They support sarcasm and a lot of tricky questions. You are lucky, because two of our brothers are always with you, but I am totally alone. Our beloved cousin is studying with me and I was incredibly happy when I saw him. And what do you think he did? He was waiting for a moment when the official part of a class was over and we switched to the so-called free discussion. We were talking about the differences of the rituals of Perfects and ordinary Daeyats. Our cousin asked if one can consider a child as Perfects if his father is Perfects, but his mother is a witch from Llill, but officially this child is known as a son of a woman from the Perfects family. Then that moron turned around to me and asked my opinion, saying that I had to know a lot about this, because my father had faced such a case in his life."

"What a pity that I didn't crush his skull when he asked me the very same question a few years ago." Davkaleon was sincerely disappointed.

"Can you please visit this school of the old Daeyan language at least for a while? They will accept you there like a beloved son. I really need that," Paradion asked.

Davkaleon agreed. They reached a closed metal door in a few minutes.

"Who are you and why have you come here?" A voice sounded in Davkaleon's head.

Stanglate introduced himself and his companion, adding that they invited Davkaleon and his brother to join the school. The door opened. Several dozens of people were waiting in a beautiful hall. Comfortable chairs were located along the walls. A stage rose near one of the walls. While looking around Davkaleon noticed Crassius Pompeus.

"Oh, he belongs to the Perfects family too?" Davkaleon was upset, because he realized that he would have to meet Crassius every Sunday.

There were other representatives of the Pompeus family in the hall. Several Antonis brothers appeared in a while.

"It looks like half of the military school is here," Davkaleon thought.

"Look, our beloved cousin is here too," said Paradion, while looking at the people in the hall.

Davkaleon turned around. His cousin Rodriguez Gerklat was having a conversation with someone in the corner. Davkaleon firmly decided to go there.

"What do you want from him?" Paradion asked.

"I want to ask about rumors he had created regarding our father, who is the head of the Gerklat family. His claim is related to the estate of our father, which can be transferred to our uncle if the claim is true."

"You can't do this here, Davkaleon. It's not allowed."

"Maybe it's not allowed for priests, but it's perfectly allowed for military people," said Davkaleon, approaching Rodriguez.

But Davkaleon simply had no time to talk with the cousin. Several people went up to the lodge. One of them was Stanglate, who rose his head up in order to welcome people and asked for everyone's attention.

"I see some new people here. It's amazing that you decided to visit us," said Davkaleon's teacher. "At this school, you will learn the true language, which was used by our Gods. You will discover rites and rituals willed by our Gods. We will tell you about the sacred calendar of the Perfects, which was brought to Daeya by the Gods. Today you will have unforgettable impressions, because you will visit the most sacred place of the whole Daeya – Arragorra...because now, we are in Arragorra itself! We will start with an introduction of our new students and then we will walk around the Arragorra and finish our day with a celebration banquet."

Such a plan caused no objections from Davkaleon, since it was different than just sitting and studying a language he would never use.

Davkaleon was the first to introduce himself. Turning

135

around to listen to the speaker, Rodriguez saw Paradion.

"And what are you doing here?" the cousin was really surprised to see Davkaleon's brother.

"I am studying the true Daeyan language, as any future priest does," Paradion answered patiently.

Meanwhile, Davkaleon was still talking. Listing the achievements of the Gerklat and Borlatar families was pretty tiring for the audience. People breathed a sigh of relief when Davkaleon thanked everybody for their attention. Many people started to applaud when they understood that Davkaleon's speech was not only about himself, but about his brother too.

"Do you mean to say that, according to the words of Davkaleon, you are the second son of Arara Borlatar?" Rodriguez asked Paradion derisively.

"Davkaleon hasn't said anything like that," answered Paradion.

"Oh yes, he just hasn't gone into details of your origin," grinned Rodriguez.

Neither Paradion, nor Davkaleon had time to answer him, because Stanglate had introduced another student. Davkaleon was surprised to recognize his own classmate Vikiles, who was staying in the guardhouse and was terrified by the monster in the night, which in fact was the goblin cub Andibraksh.

Finally, Stanglate took the floor once more. "Thank the Gods, we have great weather today. Thus, we can make a stroll around the Divine Arragorra." Stanglate clapped his hands, and a door opened in one of the walls. Davkaleon followed other people and found himself in a fairytale place. He couldn't believe that a clear azure sky, calm blue water, green gardens and windless weather could be a part of Daeya. It was just impossible! And what astonishing flowers were growing in Arragorra! Gardens were mixed with temples. Shady alleys were wriggling among beautiful temples and ancient towers.

"Each temple in Arragorra is devoted to one Daeyan God," Stanglate said, "and today we are going to visit one of them. It's simply impossible to visit all the temples of Arragorra in one day, because there's really a lot of them. We will start with the Main Temple, which was built by Gods themselves. I am sure that you already know this about Arragorra and the Main Temple, as well as about the Daeyan Alatar Rock. Today you will have a chance to see it."

The path to the Main Temple ran between mighty trees alternating with astonishing flowers.

"Please pay attention to the colors of Arragorra flowers," Stanglate's mysterious companion offered. "They are white and yellow. These colors are true Daeyan colors. When Gods created Daeya, they were using exactly these colors. You won't find any red flowers here. The color red was brought by witches. Witches appeared in Daeya and selected Llill as their first place for settlement. Immediately after that, red flowers started to blossom in Llill. Red flowers started to appear all around Daeya and some of them were mixed with true Daeyan plants. But you won't find any witch flowers here in the sacred Arragorra. The Gods of Daeya can't hold them, thus they can't be found here."

The shady alley brought everybody to white mountains blazing in the sunlight. They didn't even have to go uphill to get inside, because the narrow path was twisting right through the mountains. They reached the center of Arragorra in just a few minutes. It was a white plateau, surrounded with white mountains. The majestic Main Temple of Arragorra was rising into the sky right in the center of the plateau. A white hill was located right next to the temple, and it had architecture which was astonishingly similar to the one of the temples.

"Now you are standing next to the Alatar rock," solemnly told the mysterious companion of Stanglate. "It's also called the Daeyan rock or the Rock of gods. The history of Daeya started from it."

Then, he told a story that Davkaleon had heard many times from the teacher in his father's estate. When the Gods put the Alatar at its current place, it was just a small grain of sand. Gods poured divine rains on the grain and it started to grow, transforming into a mountain with a fancy shape. The mountain was growing in height and in breadth, transforming into the plateau surrounded by white mountains, and becoming an island. The Alatar was a divine gift for the people of Daeya. The Main Temple next to the Alatar was built by these Gods.

The very first Daeyans evolved from them. These people were called True Daeyan or Perfects. They created Arragorra, where they built a separate temple for each of the Daeyan Gods. A path, which couldn't be seen by ordinary mortals, connected the Main Temple of Arragorra with the divine city in heaven. At first, Gods visited Arragorra very often. Unfortunately, a split occurred and several Gods chose a different way, followed by some people of Daeya. The true Daeyan language was changing and the Gods decided to leave Daeya. There were four streams with the hallowed water coming from under the rock. Those streams flowed to the north, south, west and east, transforming into rivers and running into the Sacred lake of Assa, filling it with water. One could cure all diseases, if he or she drinks water from under the Alatar. If you touched the Alatar rock and asked the Gods, you would receive the power of a hero.

Davkaleon had heard about Arragorra, the Alatar and

the temple many times. But it was his first time to see that beauty in person.

"Today, according to the tradition of our school, those who have come for the first time will initiate a rite of passage into the *True Daeyan Language School*," Stanglate said. "And the main priest of the Main Temple of Arragorra will hold this rite."

After those words, a priest in totally white clothes came out of the temple. "If you touch the Alatar rock, you will get the power. But it can happen on only one condition—you must prove to the Gods that you deserve to be called Perfects. You have to pass several tests, which won't be easy. If you are ready, please come to me. If not, you have to leave Arragorra now."

Several people took a step forward. The priest waved his hand and a labyrinth appeared from nowhere.

"Please go there," ordered the priest.

Davkaleon was the first to enter the narrow path of the labyrinth. He was more than sure that he would pass that labyrinth easily. He grew up in the estate with a labyrinth for military training. He simply wasn't ready for the thing that happened next. In moments, the narrow path rose sharply uphill, becoming even narrower. Davkaleon's foot hardly fit the path! White walls on either side sloped down to a bottomless abyss. Suddenly, a very strong wind appeared like a hurricane. Davkaleon barely kept his feet. The next minute, a giant black shadow attacked him. Taking out his sword, Davkaleon swung and hit the shadow. The sword passed through it without any obstacle.

The shadow attacked from the front. At that moment, Davkaleon couldn't see his way. He stopped and another shadow attacked him, pushing from behind. At that moment Davkaleon remembered a legend about the

Perfects. Black shadows were his fear, and he had to make them go away. Davkaleon ordered himself to go forward, without paying any attention to the black shadow. The shadow disappeared and the bright, dazzling and sparkling sun appeared in front of him. Davkaleon almost closed his eyes and made a step forward. A step, another one. The sun started to shine less bright, while the path began to descend. Davkaleon found himself next to the exit from the labyrinth. A few more people followed him out, one by one. Suddenly a scream came from the labyrinth.

"Remove him," demanded the priest, waving his hand once more.

The labyrinth disappeared. One poor, shaking guy stood where the labyrinth had been. "You have no right to be in Arragorra. Don't even try to come back here," ordered the priest.

An open door appeared next to the poor fellow. As soon as he entered, the door closed and just disappeared. The priest turned to those who passed the labyrinth and ordered, "Now, touch the Alatar rock."

Davkaleon touched the rock and froze. An unlimited power was filling all his organs. He even closed his eyes for a moment. When he opened eyes, he thought that he had become taller and stronger.

"Hey, try not to hog all the power. Leave something for others," came the voice of his cousin.

"There's enough power for everybody, because it can't be drained," advised the priest.

People who passed the test approached the rock and touched it one by one. Judging by their expressions, they had the very same experience as Davkaleon. Each person stood still, looking at the Alatar with surprise.

The priest clapped his hands and announced "And now

we are going to have the celebration."

Nobody had noticed how someone had been setting tables, bringing cutlery or dishes with food. However, tables with food and drinks were standing in the shadow of giant trees. A nice smell attracted them all. A pair of beautiful carved goblets stood next to each plate. One goblet was small, like the usual goblet used to drink something during meals, but the second one was really big. Some kind of drink was sparking in the smaller goblet, while the second one was empty. Everyone took their places.

"For our new students, the brave Perfects ones, and for the future of Daeya," the priest said his toast.

Everybody raised the goblets with the sparkling drink. A nice, spicy taste slightly burned Davkaleon's mouth.

"You are now drinking the divine Ambrosia, the favorite drink of the Daeyan Gods," explained the priest.

Arragorra looked like a fairytale and the food was just perfect, so Davkaleon forgot about his worries and stopped regretting that he needed to attend classes.

The priest took the floor again.

"Understand, the drink of Gods is not intended to be used just to quench one's thirst. This drink can transform any of your dreams into reality. However, you have to show an unlimited courage to make that happen. Does anyone among the people who passed the test want to try?"

Davkaleon stood up immediately. Several other students followed him.

"Now, take your seats and listen to what the bravest person has to pass," ordered the priest. "Look at the tallest mountain around us. There is a ledge right next to its peak. This ledge looks like a throne. We call it the Throne of Gods. One has to climb on a smooth, sheer cliff to get there. Here, you can just enjoy this sunny and windless weather. But if you try to reach the ledge, you will face a real hurricane. If any brave man has decided to go there, he must take a big goblet and reach the peak. Alatar rock is carved on the goblet. Around it, you can see the figures of Gods of Daeya. For now, your goblets are empty, but one will be filled on its own when one of you reaches the Throne of Gods. The bravest person has to sit on the Throne, tell his will very loud and drink everything from the goblet at once. Then you have to return here. Is there any such brave person?"

Davkaleon felt Paradion take his hand, pulling it down while he shook his head. Davkaleon smiled and stood up once again. He wanted to become the Chief in Command of the Daeyan army—not after many years, but very soon, while he was still young. Who, if not Gods, could help him to do that?

Chapter 15. The Throne of Gods

"Sit down, please. I will tell you more about this goblet later," whispered Paradion and pulled Davkaleon's hand.

But Davkaleon was really stubborn, so he shook his head and took a big and beautiful goblet from the table. It looked as if nobody else wanted to join him.

"My dear cousin, don't you want to accompany me?" asked Davkaleon and grinned.

"You'd better ask your brother," answered Rodriguez with anger.

"I see my brother pretty often, but I haven't seen you for almost a year... maybe I even missed you."

"You won't have time for missing," the priest interrupted them. "So, have you finally decided?"

"Of course!" answered Davkaleon. "Do you have any other advice before I go? Can I ask Gods about anything? Will they make any of my dreams come true?"

"Gods won't make anything instead of you. You can wish anything, but you have to reach it on your own. Gods will give you enough power for fighting and will create specific conditions and obstacles, which you have to overcome in order to reach your dream."

"That's enough fair for me," answered Davkaleon, making a step in the direction of the mountain.

"Wait, I haven't finished my speech," the priest interrupted him. "Please remember, if Gods decide that you ask something that you can't hold or it can harm the people of Daeya, they will kill you with a lightning bolt and you will die. You still have a chance to change your mind."

"I won't even think about it!" Davkaleon remonstrated.

"You have a choice. You can keep your will in secret and try to reach the Throne of Gods. You can also approach the Alatar rock and say it out loud. In that case I will make a prayer near the Alatar rock at the moment when you will ask Gods."

"I have nothing to hide," Davkaleon announced, "I will say it out loud near the Alatar rock".

"One more thing," said the priest, "If you want, you can pass a will of any from the newly accepted students to the Gods. These people will follow you and will wait for you at the foot of the mountain. They received the same power of Alatar as you. They will share their power with you during your climb and return. Please remember, if you promise to pass along their wishes, you will have to make them without any changes. If you use someone's power and you forget his wish or change it, you will die."

"Do I have a right to choose whose help to accept and whose to pass?" asked Davkaleon.

"Yes, you do have such right," answered the priest. "They can share their will to you almost silently near the Alatar rock or they can say it out loud and I will support it with a prayer. Of course, only if you accept to pass their will along."

"Deal," answered Davkaleon and went to the Alatar rock.

When he reached the rock, Davkaleon spoke out loud.

"Gods of Daeya, I want to become the Commander-in-Chief of the Daeyan army when I am 20 years old. I promise to protect Daeya and to be the bravest and the best Commander of Daeya in the history. I beg you to give me a chance to make my dream come true."

"I will support your request and I will ask Gods to help you to become the Commander-in-Chief of the Daeyan army," said the priest.

"That's not what I'm asking for," protested Davkaleon. "I have no doubt that I will become the Commander. I am

144

asking Gods to take this position when I reach *20 years old*."

Davkaleon turned around to see the audience and asked people to approach him if they wanted to help. The first one was Paradion. He decided not to say his will loud and mentally told Davkaleon, "I ask Gods to help me to become the main priest of Daeya. I promise to serve faithfully."

"I will pass your will to the Gods and I will use your power with my pleasure," answered Davkaleon.

The second in line was his cousin Rodriguez. He gave a derisive smile and mentally informed Davkaleon that he wanted to become the head of the Gerklat family when the time would come.

"I am very sorry, my dear cousin, but this place is busy. Any other desires?" answered Davkaleon, answering mentally.

"Well, I have another will. I want to become the main priest of Daeya."

"You can ask Gods yourself about this".

"Thank you for your help, my dear relative," sneered the cousin and went away.

"Anyone else?" asked Davkaleon with interest.

Vikiles approached the Alatar. "I don't know if you agree to pass my wishes, but if you do, I will be grateful for all my life."

"What's your will?" asked Davkaleon.

"I want to ask Gods to become as brave and strong as you and know how to use weapons at the same level as you do."

Davkaleon was speechless for a second.

"You have already received the power of the Alatar. As for weapons, everything depends only on you. Why do you want to waste your chance to get something that you can

145

get on your own? Ask something that requires the help of Gods."

"No," answered Vikiles, "that's exactly what I want to ask from Gods. If they help me, I will reach everything else on my own."

"I will pass along your will," answered Davkaleon.

Another student approached Davkaleon and told that his name was Dolgecate. He asked Gods to help his family to pay out all their debts.

"Why not?" thought Davkaleon and accepted his offer.

The last one was a student from the Science School. "I want to discover all the secrets of the God Prann and become the main priest in his temple."

"No!" answered Davkaleon sharply. Some legends about the bloody god Prann appeared in his mind.

"Why not? Prann will help you too. You won't have time to please Prann because he's a very demanding and moody God. But you need someone related with Prann in order to receive help in your journeys. Prann will help you to become the greatest Commander-in-Chief. You will face only victories and not even one defeat. Accept the cult of Prann and your name will be assured for centuries. Isn't it what you really want?"

Prann was a violent and bloody God and required sacrifices. It seemed that he was included in the pantheon of Daeyan Gods. However, Davkaleon wasn't quite sure about that. One legend was saying that Prann was excluded from the Pantheon, but Davkaleon could be wrong. Probably that was a legend about a different god. On the day when the teacher was telling about Prann, the weather was really amazing and the head of the guard, Kvinsit, carried out training. Thus, Davkaleon was waiting for a chance to escape from the class. The teacher ordered them to write an essay about Prann, but

Davkaleon asked his brother Elfid to write it instead. Why would Davkaleon spend even a second for such nonsense when he needed to participate in Kvinsit's training?

"No," answered Davkaleon once more. "You can ask Gods yourself about this."

"Antonis, why don't you ask the Gods to help you?" Davkaleon heard the laughing voice of Crassius Pompeus. "Just look around! Some strange sons of a priest are trying to become Commanders, and you are just sitting on your chair."

"I don't have to waste time in order to become the Commander. I can manage it on my own," Antonis answered shortly and stiff.

Davkaleon, his brother, and two other students went to the mountain with the Throne of the Gods on the peak. The mountain rose up with its smooth and sheer cliffs. There was no ledge to hold or to put a leg on it. Davkaleon took out a knife and hit the white mountain, which was not extremely solid. Pretty soon, Davkaleon managed to make a hole to put one leg, then another for the second leg. He climbed higher and higher.

The sunny and windless weather changed to fog and gusts of wind. The higher Davkaleon climbed, the stronger the wind whistled and roared. A real hurricane was rumbling around him in a short while. Davkaleon could see nothing. He made new holes by touch. A terrible vortex almost threw him away from the cliff, the knife started to vibrate and Davkaleon realized that he would fall down. Davkaleon had several spare knives and he decided to use them. One more hole, another one. A strong gust of wind took a knife from the cliff and Davkaleon started to slide down, trying to find at least one of holes in the cliff. He was sliding faster and faster. He tried to impale the knife into the sheer cliff. He managed to hang on it for a second, but a hurricane wind threw the knife away and Davkaleon continued to slide downwards. He could hardly see anything around him. Aleurh! His beloved dragon! Davkaleon wanted to see him more than anyone at such a rough moment. Suddenly, Aleurh appeared from nowhere. Davkaleon tried to reach him with his hand, but Aleurh started to fly downwards. Davkaleon was sliding in the same direction. Aleurh stopped, hovering in the air right next to the cliff. Davkaleon prepared to catch the wing of his dragon. His hand just passed through the imaginary Aleurh, but he managed to catch a knife, which he'd impaled a couple of minutes before. Davkaleon pressed himself against the cliff, while holding the knife. After relaxing for a while, Davkaleon found a hole and continued his ascent.

The hurricane calmed down almost immediately. He was almost blinded with the sudden sunlight. Davkaleon stood on a smooth site right next to the peak. That site was the seat of the mountain throne. Davkaleon congratulated himself that he had reached the Throne of Gods and took out the beautiful carved goblet. At the very same moment, the goblet became full of a sparkling drink. Davkaleon sat on the throne, touched Alatar carved on the goblet and repeated his wish out loud.

Davkaleon drank the goblet at once and looked down. He was sitting right above an abyss. The Main Temple where they were having the celebration banquet looked like a small toy castle. He stood up and waived his hand. It was a time to pass the on the wishes of others.

Davkaleon thought that descending would be easier, because he had already prepared holes for hands and feet. But he was wrong—descending was much more difficult than ascending. But he simply had no time for thinking, because gusts of wind were trying to throw him down from the cliff. He was very close to the foot of the mountain when he couldn't hold himself and fell the rest of the way. Fortunately, he wasn't very far from the ground. Paradion, Vikiles and Dolgecate ran to check him.

"Has Aleurh helped you?" asked Paradion. "It was the first idea, which came to my mind when I realized that you were going to fall down."

"Of course, he has, that was a brilliant idea," answered Davkaleon.

The triumphant group was met with applause. However, not everybody was happy to see them. Crassius Pompeus and several others gave them very angry looks. Tables were full of new food and drinks, and everyone continued their celebration. When there was a right moment, Vikiles approached Davkaleon and pulled him aside.

"Do you know that according to a school tradition, duelers are drinking from the *Triss goblets* before the beginning of a duel?"

"No, but why do you ask?" answered Davkaleon carelessly.

"Read about those goblets in the library," said Vikiles.

Chapter 16. The Triss Goblet

"What do you want to tell me about the goblet?" asked Davkaleon when they left Arragorra.

"Let's go my room, I'll show you," said Paradion.

Paradion's room sparkled with cleanliness and order. And why wouldn't it sparkle, since Paradion brought a servant with him? This, despite the fact that the school provided everything necessary in order not to distract the attention of the future priest with housekeeping nonsense. There were dozens of different goblets on the shelves of the goblet board. One of them was amazingly similar to the goblet from which Davkaleon drank sparkling drink on the Throne of Gods. There were a few cages with small animals next to the goblet board. Apparently, they were ear-tailings, named so for its long tails and ears.

"Look what this goblet can do," said Paradion and lifted up the decanter. Having poured some water into a saucer, Paradion put it in one of the cages. The animal drank with pleasure. Paradion raised up the decanter again. This time, he first poured water in the goblet, and then poured it into a saucer. The ear-tailing took a sip and twitched. A few seconds later the animal died.

"This goblet turns any drink into a poison," said Paradion. "The effects can be combated, but the priest in Arragorra did not tell you how to do that, so I tried to stop you."

"How can I deal with it?" Davkaleon was interested

"You should touch Alatar and say a prayer, and then any poison is abated," replied Paradion.

Davkaleon with doubt shook his head, "I didn't say a prayer, and the goblet didn't kill me."

"You had appealed to the Gods. Perhaps that was like a prayer." did not give up Paradion.

The words of his brother didn't convince Davkaleon, but Paradion continued to insist. "Look, there is the same water in the goblet that killed the first ear-tailing." Paradion touched the Alatar which was carved on the goblet and said a quick prayer, and then poured water into a saucer and put in a cage with another ear-tailing. The animal drank the water without the slightest harm.

Davkaleon wasn't convinced. "You touched Alatar on the goblet, and I touched Alatar on the Throne of Gods. Maybe that is the point. Elfid's mother, Dallilla, had a collection of unusual vessels. One day she treated me with different drinks, pouring them from the same vessel. She also appealed with prayers to her Isida, but Elfid later did the same without any prayers."

"Don't say so, Davkaleon, it is blasphemy!" Paradion cried, horrified. "How can you compare the goblet of the sacred Alatar with the witch's vessel?"

"It is not only possible, but necessary," answered Davkaleon. "I want to understand it. And you should, too. Let's go to Elfid. He will have answers."

"It is too late. Moreover, I was never close with Elfid," Paradion said.

"So, become closer with him now. Aren't you interested to know the secret of this goblet?" insisted Davkaleon.

"I can learn all that by myself," frowned Paradion.

"Yes, you can, but how many poor animals will you kill doing so?"

The *School of Science* was not far from them. Shortly thereafter, Davkaleon and Paradion were in the room of a very surprised Elfid. Davkaleon got down to business immediately.

"Look at that goblet. Having poured the water from it, Paradion killed a poor ear-tailing. I was drinking divine ambrosia from the similar goblet on the Throne of Gods in sacred Arragorra and I have survived. Very soon I will have to drink from a Triss goblet in the Grove of Triss.

"On the Throne of Gods in Arragorra? How did you get there?" asked Elfid.

It seemed that the story about Arragorra, Alatar and the Throne of Gods were much more interesting for Elfid than the goblet itself. Having retold the events of the day, Davkaleon returned to the goblet.

"I'm very interested in how to stay alive after drinking from the goblet like this, so give me your advice how to do it.

"Such goblets have many secrets. Before I uncover them, let me treat you with delicious drinks from this curious vessel." With these words, Elfid filled with water a vessel of spherical shape resembling the bud. "Davkaleon, your favorite berry is raspberry. I suggest you enjoy the raspberry drink. It is very tasty." Elfid poured a bright red drink into the cup, put it in front of Davkaleon and turned to Paradion.

"How about you? What do you prefer?"

"Yellow cherry plum," answered Paradion, remembering the statement of a priest of the Main temple of Arragorra that yellow and white are the original colors of Daeya.

"Ok, cherry plum and yellow," Elfid smiled, pouring from the same vessel yellow drink, with the smell of cherry plum.

"As for me, I like tangerine." Drink of intense orange color spilled into Elfid's goblet. "Welcome to the table," Elfid made a gesture of a welcoming host, clearly enjoying the produced effect.

"How did you do that?" asked Paradion.

"Actually, according to ritual, I did wrong. I should say a prayer each time and praise the Gods. My mother, of course, would ask Isida, but the result would be the same." Merry sparks danced in Elfid's eyes. "Personally, I think that there is no need to distract the worshipful Isida and the Gods of Daeya from the important things with such nonsense, so I did it myself."

Davkaleon and Paradion took a sip from their cups. It was delicious.

"So, after all, how did you do that?" asked Paradion again.

"The answer is in vessel's design," said Elfid. "This vessel I made myself when I was trying to figure out how my mother was doing these tricks." Elfid lifted the vessel and pushed in a few places at the bottom, decorated with patterns. A globular bud opened. Inside the expanded bud, there was another bud, slightly smaller. Its outer surface was painted in different colors and covered with red and green circles.

"Pay attention to the wall thickness of the inner vessel," offered Elfid. "The tanks with the powder that turns ordinary water into raspberry, tangerine and other drinks are hidden inside them." Elfid clicked on one of the green circles, a small box of powder moved out. "I click on the inner vessel, so you could see what I am doing. When the outer vessel is closed, I click on the corresponding patterns in the outer vessel." Elfid clicked on the pattern of one of the open petals and a small spike moved out of the petal immediately.

"You haven't changed water in the vessel but you have poured different drinks from it. How did you do this?" asked Paradion.

"It is connected with the design also." Elfid raised the vessel and pressed another combination of patterns. Several separate parts moved from the walls and formed a small bowl that rose up. "This is the bowl where the powder mixes into the liquid and pours from this very spot. It doesn't matter what kind of powder is added to this bowl. It could be a harmless raspberry drink or a deadly poison, as in the case of Paradion's goblet that killed the poor ear-tailing."

"Did you design this vessel by yourself?" asked Paradion.

"I experimented with different designs. I have read in the runes and manuscripts about similar goblets, and I invented this one myself."

"Do priests, warlocks and witches use such vessels, when praising the Gods?" asked Davkaleon.

"If a priest, sorcerer or which have limited finances, they are likely to use reusable vessels, such as this one. All reusable vessels have one common problem. If they are used for foul play or to fain magical power or something like that, the goblets unfortunately contain the *evidence* that could easily reveal the deception. Even if the combination of patterns to reveal the secret is difficult to decode, the vessel could be broken open and all would be revealed. Vessels and other objects used by priests or magicians for something important will be one-time single-use *items* and will be made of materials that will disintegrate after use."But even if the material from which the vessel is made to crumble, residues of powder, either raspberry, tangerine, or the other will remain," said Davkaleon.

"Yes, if someone uses the powder. But in one-time vessels, they try to use something less obvious than powder. If they want to use poison, a goblet of Triss is the best you can find. Triss can be poisonous by itself, so if someone wants to use a goblet as a vessel of poison, he even doesn't need to hide anything.

"I emptied the whole goblet and nothing happened,"

Davkaleon argued.

"Did you notice the color of the *inner* part of the goblet?" asked Elfid.

Davkaleon shook his head negatively, and Elfid continued. "If the color was light, nothing should happen. This Triss was young, and young Triss is not poisonous. However, if the color of the *inner* part of the goblet was dark, as in the goblet of Paradion, it could kill you. Apparently, when you touched Alatar, you activated a mechanism in the vessel similar to the mechanism in my vessel, and you, in fact, drank from a light young Triss. Maybe the goblet was of a different design, and touching the Alatar led to a Triss antidote being added to your drink. Characteristics of Triss are very unusual. Young Triss is harmless. Its wood is light, and slightly yellowish. But with age, the wood darkens and becomes poisonous. Twice-born Triss trees are even more interesting."

"What does *twice-born* mean?" Davkaleon and Paradion asked in unison.

Elfid explained that the trunk of a Triss, upon reaching 1000 years old, becomes hollow. However, the tree continues to grow. New roots sprout and a new trunk begins to grow inside the hollow trunk. Such a tree is called *twice-born*. When a twice-born Triss gets old, it acquires a purplish-red color. A tiny drop of poison from a twice born Triss is able to instantly kill an entire army. After another 1000 years passes, the trunk of the twice-born Triss, in turn, becomes hollow, and again forms new roots and another new trunk grows within it. The tree becomes a thrice-born Triss. They call such Triss, a dragon Triss."

Elfid picked up Paradion's goblet before continuing. "The heart of this goblet is made of old Triss, and it is poisonous, for sure. There are pictures made of young, old and twice-born Triss on the surface of the goblet. If you want, leave the goblet with me, I'll try to uncover its secrets," proposed Elfid.

"The goblets may look alike, but their secrets may be different," said Davkaleon.

"You are right," confirmed Elfid. "If you have to drink from a Triss goblet, it is better to procure your own goblet and drink from it."

"Where is it best to buy Triss goblets?" asked Davkaleon. "I have bought everything from the *Mug and Sword*, but I'm not sure that this is the best place for such a purchase."

"You shouldn't buy a goblet of Triss at the *Mug and Sword*" said Elfid, "Come to me next Saturday. I'll set you up with everything you need."

"I almost forgot, I brought water from the Alatar. Drink as much as you can," Davkaleon suggested to his brother before leaving.

"That's interesting, I've heard a lot about that water. I'll take some for my research and experiments," smiled Elfid.

Elfid flung open the doors of the cupboard to take out another vessel. Several mirrors of different size and shape stood on the shelf. One of them was the very same mirror that had appeared before him while he was speaking with three disciples of Twierks mages in the temple during the carnival at Walpurgis Night. And the very same mirror that Elfid's mother Dallilla had used at the time of the Isida ritual.

"Do you know the secret of this mirror?" asked Davkaleon.

"If you mean the secret of that particular mirror, then of course I do. All of these are my creations," smiled Elfid. "But the secret of this mirror is very simple. If you ask about my mother's mirrors, they all work differently, and I've just barely started to understand them."

"Show me how your mirror works," Davkaleon asked.

"It's a very simple mirror. Let me show you when I invent something more interesting," said Elfid modestly.

"It's okay that it's simple. Let's start with it, and then you can show me another when you make something more complicated," Davkaleon insisted.

Elfid took out a mirror and put it on a stand patterned with figures and signs. On the left side of the stand there was a table, each cell of which contained a sign and a number. On the right side there was explanation what each sign meant.

"This is a mirror of witches, I am forbidden to look in it. And these symbols are witch symbols. I cannot take part in it," announced Paradion, stepping away from the table.

"Paradion, your mother on the *Night of Three Big Moons* always came to Dallilla to receive her fortune and to glance at the witches', ouch! I'm sorry, Elfid—to look at the sorcerous mirror, and brought you there. No big thing, you did not freak out then. Why do you panic now?" Davkaleon stood to look in Elfid's mirror.

"But I had not yet entered the priestly school then. And, besides, my mother always said a prayer before and after visiting Dallilla. And I was forced to do the same thing," replied Paradion in all honesty.

"Then say your prayer now. Who keeps you from doing it?" laughed Davkaleon.

Quickly muttering something, Paradion glanced at the mirror cautiously.

"The idea of such mirrors is to convince you that the deity itself answers your question," Elfid started to explain.

"And how does this happen?" Davkaleon turned to it.

"You think of a question, and the mirror shows you the sign and then you look to see what this sign means."

"How do I know that the sign appears as the answer to my question?" Paradion asked.

"My mirror, of course, is rather simple. But not so simple," Elfid smiled. "You think of a number, handle some operations with it and get the answer in the mirror."

"Can you detail your story?" Asked Davkaleon.

"Think of any number from 10 to 99," proposed Elfid.

"75" said Davkaleon.

"No! You should not tell your number," protested Elfid.

"Ok, I have another number," stated Davkaleon.

"Take from it figures it consists of. For example, the result for 75 will be 63 because $75 - 5 - 7 = 63$."

"What now?" asked Davkaleon.

"Find in the table the number and the corresponding sign. Done?" asked Elfid.

Davkaleon nodded.

"Close your eyes and imagine the sign," continued Elfid.

"Now open your eyes and look in the mirror."

Mirror showed the same sign that Davkaleon saw in the table.

"Now you can read what this sign means," smiled Elfid.

"How did the mirror know it?" Asked Davkaleon looking at the sign in the mirror.

"Don't tell me you did not figure it out. What's up with you?" Elfid was genuinely surprised.

If he'd been alone with Elfid, Davkaleon would interrogate him about the secret of the mirror. But Paradion was in the room as well. Davkaleon did not like to reveal any weakness in the eyes of company. So, he shrugged.

"How about you, Paradion? Want to try?" Elfid asked.

"And you say that the deity has nothing to do with it?" Paradion asked after that the sign appeared in the mirror.

"It's improper to harass the deities for such a trifle request," Elfid smiled.

"Do you accept design requests?" Paradion showed his interest.

"Okay, so, what do you want?" asked Elfid.

"The same mirror, but with divine symbols, and with cutouts of Gods of Daeya on the frame instead of a witch's snake," asked Paradion.

"It can be easily done," Elfid replied, "but do you well understand that this is just a trick, and there is no magic?" Having said goodbye to Elfid, Davkaleon and Paradion went back.

"It's late," said Paradion, "Won't you get in trouble at your school?"

"They'll send me to the guardhouse. Big deal!" shrugged Davkaleon.

But they didn't send Davkaleon there. Upon entering the school, he was faced with his father.

"Come with me, I've arranged that you'll be late," ordered Priest Gerklat to his son, heading for the exit.

Chapter 17. Conversation with Father

They sat in the spacious office of priest Gerklat in Assa.

"Everyone in Assa already knows that you rose up to the Throne of Gods, drank from the Goblet of Alatar, and asked the Gods to help you become commander of the army of Daeya at 20 years old. Tomorrow, everyone in Daeya will know it. On the one hand, it flatters me as your father. On the other hand, you have made so many mistakes in the process, that your chances to live to see your 20th anniversary are very small, *so listen carefully to what I tell you.* But first, answer the question, was there a head on your shoulders when you asked the Gods for this impossible thing?"

"Why is it impossible?" surprised Davkaleon.

"Because, according to the law of Daeya, commanders of the army must be at least 25 years old. The Priest of The Main Temple tried to save the situation, and miss the mention of age. But he hadn't a chance! You immediately intervened and did not let him do it."

"I didn't know about this law, but it does not change anything," replied Davkaleon, "I was told the conditions and I have fulfilled them. Now it is the matter of the Gods to ensure that I could achieve my desire. Big deal, the law can be changed!"

"Davkaleon, you're stubborn and arrogant. And the fact that you fight well, only exacerbates the situation. No wonder I was afraid to send you to study at the military school."

"I'm not stubborn and not arrogant. If I were arrogant, I would name the age of 15, but I *modestly* decided to wait until 20. And I assure you, when I become Commander-in-

Chief, you'll be proud of me."

Priest Gerklat was furious and banged his fist on the table with all his strength.

"You're a haughty and arrogant boaster! The last thing we need here in Daeya is to tolerate a high-handed 15-year-old boy as the commander-in-chief! Listen carefully, and don't dare to interrupt me." Davkaleon opened his mouth to protest, but such a rage flashed in his father's eyes that Davkaleon shut it up prudently.

"No one will change the law because of you. The age of 25 years is indicated in the law, and not accidentally. At this age, the young stupidity just begins to erode out of your head. A child begins to realize that the head is given to think, and not to go on about his desires. For the Council to go to change this law, there must be such circumstances under which the risk would threaten the very existence of Daeya, and you would be the only person able to save the country. As a priest of Daeya, I will do *everything* so that such circumstances never transpire. As you came down from the Throne of Gods unharmed, this can be interpreted as consent from the Gods to help you. Because it is against the law, you will likely find yourself in a situation similar to that in which you were in on the Throne of Gods. Ask the Gods to change the date. If you do not, you are unlikely to meet your 21st year."

Davkaleon disagreed with his father. Big deal, the law! This law is invented by people, and the people could be wrong.

Father continued, "Most of those who rose to the Throne of Gods did not announce publicly what they were asking for. From my point of view, it is correct—there is no need to prematurely disclose your plans. You went on your own way and announced yourself. Now, everybody will wait for you to be at any moment worthy of the level you have asked. You made more errors, and these errors are much more serious."

"What are the errors?" Davkaleon was surprised, still staying in full confidence that he'd acted perfectly.

"First of all, you agreed to convey to the Gods the requests of others. Why? Instead of a single request, the Gods have heard a chorus of requests. If others wanted to ask the Gods about something, they had to do it themselves and not look for those, on whose shoulders they will shift the risk."

"But they helped me during the ascent and descent! Paradion even created the image of Aleurh to support me. He made it so natural that at first, I believed that it, indeed, was my dragon until I realized that Aleurh had no idea where I was or what I was doing."

"It was me who created the image of Aleurh when I saw that you were falling down. Paradion is still too weak for that, although to his credit, he tried with all his strength. As for the other two, they are not counted."

Davkaleon looked at his father with astonishment. He had no idea that his father watched him during his ascent and descent.

"The priests of Daeya can do a lot of things," he said, answering Davkaleon's thoughts, "and don't get me wrong about Paradion. He really tried to create an image of Aleurh, so don't inform him of my intervention. Let him believe that he did it. But let's get back to your errors. Having agreed to pass on some requests, you refused the others. You've made yourself mortal enemies."

"But they asked what could not be fulfilled. One of them asked...." Davkaleon paused, realizing that he had no right to discuss the requests of others.

"I can't say what they asked, but I really couldn't ask

162

the Gods for them."

"That's why you shouldn't have agreed."

"But then I wouldn't be able to transfer the request of Paradion," tried to argue Davkaleon.

"That is right, you wouldn't. It would do a good job for the one who wants to become the highest priest of Daeya. If he had the chance again, he would realize that it is necessary to rely only on himself."

"How do you know what Paradion asked?"

"It is not difficult to guess," chuckled his father.

"What else?" asked Davkaleon, remembering that his father said about multiple errors.

"You have asked the Gods about the request of Dolgecate. Do you know who had loaned money to his family? I had! And I assure you, it is a very big amount. Do I have to forgive the debt?"

"He didn't ask that his family's debt be forgiven! He asked the Gods to help his family to pay off debts. It is quite another matter."

"Why did you refuse the one who wanted to become the high priest of the god Prann?" asked Davkaleon's father.

"Because Prann is a cruel and bloody god who demands sacrifices, and his priests are often not limited to the animal sacrifices! During their savage gatherings, they do human sacrifices!"

"First of all, don't dare say the words *savage gathering* when talking about a meeting of priests. And secondly, do you realize now what it means to consent to transfer the requests of others? You have an enemy in the face of the one you have refused, and, most importantly, you made an enemy in the face of God Prann himself, because he understood perfectly the reason of your refusal."

"So, what? In any case, I don't want to have anything to do with this God!"

"Whether you like it or not, Prann is included in the Pantheon of the Gods of Daeya. He is one of those who participated in the creation of Daeya, and you can't judge if a God's demands are good or bad. As a God of Daeya, he naturally has priests that serve him. If someone wanted to become the high priest of the temple of Prann, you should agree, because if not him, then someone else will still be the high priest of the God Prann."

Davkaleon did not argue, but stubbornly having shaken his head, remained unconvinced. Having finished his lecture, Priest Gerklat smiled.

"I must say, of all my sons, you have always caused the most problems and disturbances, but, nevertheless, I never had to be ashamed of you. Restrain your ego and self-confidence, respect the opinions of others, and I'll be proud to have you as my son."

Davkaleon was taken aback—he hadn't heard such recognition from his father before.

"I talked to the school authorities," continued priest Gerklat. "They surprised me by saying that staying in the guardhouse is not a problem for the future commander. Assuming, that this staying is not permanent, of course. Do not think you can resettle there. According to what they told me, when they choose a new commander, no one expects that he was a saint in his childhood. Your military instructors favor you and your brothers. Your logic teacher is the only one who is displeased with you. Try to establish contact with him, ask some questions, show that you try to understand, even if it is hard for you."

Davkaleon grimaced at the offer. Lessons of logic did not appeal to him.

"You should know one more fact. Few dare to climb to the Throne of Gods, but three years ago, a student from your school did. No one knows what he asked the Gods for, but given the fact that he was from a military family which produced a lot of commanders of Daeya, there is little doubt as to what the request was about. His name is Crassius Pompeus. However, unlike you, his family is very devoted to the God Prann. Be cautious of him."

Having said goodbye to his father, Davkaleon went back to school. First, he went to visit Aleurh.

"Here you are, at last," said Aleurh with an offended voice. "You were so busy sitting on the throne, that you completely forgot about me. You have not come to me at all today."

"You are wrong. I wanted to come to you sooner, but my father met me and took me with him," Davkaleon was not accustomed to complaints from his dragon.

"That is another thing then," Aleurh said, his tone much friendlier now. "Give me the details of your exploits. The whole school is aware of the matter except me."

Davkaleon repeated everything that had happened that day, paying special attention to how, during the ascent, he slipped and almost fell down. He was saved only because he saw Aleurh, or rather his image, though it didn't matter, because exactly where Aleurh stopped moving, Davkaleon stuck his dagger in the wall and it saved him. Aleurh smiled, having completely forgiven Davkaleon for his absence. As the story ended, Davkaleon set a barrel filled with water from the Alatar's rivers before Aleurh.

"You will recover right now. Drink it! Just leave some water for Kvorts and Malay."

The little goblin cub instantly popped up from somewhere and took the biggest drink he possibly could.

"Just try to bite me again, and even the waters of Alatar will not help you," said Davkaleon and wagged his finger.

After sitting a bit longer with his bored dragon, Davkaleon went up to his room. It seemed he was not destined to sleep that night. The door was open, and the room was filled with students. Davkaleon's brothers, Malay and Kvorts, sat on the bed. Vikiles perched near them, retelling what had happened. Other students sat on the floor.

"That is for you," said Davkaleon, pouring the water that remained in the barrel and offering it to brothers.

Frankly speaking, Davkaleon hadn't thought to treat all fellow students with the water of Alatar, but since they all gathered in his room, he decided to make the grand gesture. He always loved to show off in public. "You can divide the rest of the water among yourselves," he suggested to the audience.

It was long after midnight when they were all gone, and Davkaleon stretched out on his bed. Davkaleon fell asleep, barely closing his eyes, but he had not slept long. He woke up because somebody bit his finger. Davkaleon jumped up. Blood was dripping on the floor from his bitten finger.

"Sorry, I came to say goodbye, but could not resist," said the little goblin cub with guilt in his voice.

Indignant, Davkaleon grabbed the little goblin by the scruff of the neck.

"Came to say goodbye, but couldn't resist," he mimicked little Andibraksh. "If you don't stop biting me, I will knock all your teeth out." Having said so, he let the little goblin go.

"I brought you a map of the dungeon. Do you remember, I promised you to give it to you when I was escaping from the dark goblins? Now that the dark goblins are gone, I can go back to my home." said Andibraksh handing him the map.

"And this is the map of Assa," added little goblin. "I brought it for so that you might forgive me for my bites. I can give you great details about the map of the dungeon. I've used each of the mentioned enters and exits. As for the map of Assa, you'll have to figure it out by yourself; I tried only a very small number of the secret passages."

"What do these marks on the map mean?" asked Davkaleon.

"These are the secrets that I know. The rest you'll have to find out for yourself," said the little goblin, handing him the description of marks.

"Andibraksh, we have to go," came the voice of the adult goblin. The goblin stood near the door. Apparently, he was the father of the little goblin.

"Thanks for giving shelter to Andibraksh," said the goblin, turning to Davkaleon.

He seemed familiar and Davkaleon thought that he was one of those goblins with whom he fought with on his first day. But maybe he was not. All goblins looked much the same to Davkaleon. The goblin nodded, and Andibraksh approached him. With so much having happened, Davkaleon didn't want to sleep. Davkaleon spent the rest of the night reading the description of the marks on the maps. Then, Davkaleon went to the dungeons to check and see if he could use the secret entries of the goblins.

Chapter 18. Dragons Master

Davkaleon sorted out the secrets of the dungeon quickly. Over the next few days, he examined all the entrances and exits of the goblins, at least, the ones that were marked on the map. Unfortunately, the map of Assa was more of a mystery. As the little goblin explained, he was not privy to most of the secret tunnels, hidden passages, secret rooms and mazes, and his description of the secret signs of the map was more like a puzzle than a hint. Looking at the map of Assa, Davkaleon noticed a sign near the Triss site in the Dragon's grove. This was the sign that Chapa, in Elfid's room called the Symbol of the DRAGON and the secret symbol of Adolees. Near this sign there was another unfamiliar one, but Davkaleon didn't know its meaning.

Davkaleon didn't know the meaning of the Symbol of DRAGON. Chapa, during a conversation with Elfid, said that he would die on the spot if he revealed what this symbol meant. Having looked at the description of Andibraksh, Davkaleon saw that the other, unfamiliar sign indicated an entrance to the tunnel leading to the Gardens of the Dragon Master. The procedure of getting into the tunnel was described...vaguely. The Dragon's symbol was not mentioned at all in the descriptions of Andibraksh.

Next Saturday, Davkaleon went to visit Elfid.

"This is your goblet," the brother said, nodding at the Triss goblet on the table. The inner part of the goblet was light, so it was made of a young, non-toxic Triss.

"Tell me, why do you have to drink from it in the Triss grove tomorrow?" asked Elfid.

Davkaleon hesitated.

"Is this related to the duel?" insisted Elfid.

"How do you know?" asked Davkaleon, his mouth open.

"They were making bets at our school. They said that two contenders for the role of the future commander were going to compete. Names, however, were not named. After all, duels between students are prohibited. But it was known that both were studying at the military school, both were from the Perfects families, both dreamed of becoming commanders-in-chief, both fight well, both have risen to the Throne of the Gods in Arragorra, and the Gods react favorably to the requests of both. The one, who is older, is called a gamer because of his fascination with the roulette game of Prann. The younger, without false modesty, calls himself the best of the best. With so much that is known, it was easy enough to guess who the participants were.

Davkaleon smiled. Positively, he liked that he was called the best of the best, even in an ironic sense. The irony would not be irony for long. And the duel will be the first step to that.

"Did you bet on me?" he asked his brother.

"No! How could you think so?!"

"Why not?" Davkaleon said, shocked. "Don't you believe in me?"

"First, even though I thought that the *best of the best* was you, I wasn't sure. What if, among the perfect families of our perfect Daeya, there were other perfect ones, eager to find out whose perfection is the most perfect?"

"Our duel is not associated with the fact that we from the Perfects families," shrugged Davkaleon.

"It is surely connected. Throughout the whole history of Daeya, there was not a single commander of Daeya's army who did not belong to the genus of Perfects," said Elfid.

"And secondly?" asked Davkaleon.

"And secondly," said Elfid, "I think it is unethical to make a bet on my brother's life."

"Unethical? Why should it be ethical or unethical? This is an opportunity to replenish your purse, to have something to celebrate my victory. By the way, I have made a bet on myself, but I did it more for publicity than for profit. Malay and Kvorts, they will really make money on me. They quickly realized what was good for their pockets."

"Don't you understand that from the point of view of risk reduction, they now should bet against you?" asked Elfid.

"Against me? They would be sick in the head to bet against me!"

"We are taught the theory of games at school," said Elfid. To make a guaranteed win, you need to make some opposing bets."

"What are the similarities between your games and a fair duel?" raged Davkaleon.

"Do you seriously expect a fair duel on the Triss grove?" asked Elfid.

"Why not?" Once again, Elfid had surprised him.

"First, never believe in honesty if there is a Triss involved, and second, do not believe even in the slightest hint of honesty, if A&Z are involved."

"Who are A&Z?"

"They are bookmakers. There are a lot more them in Daeya, but A&Z are the largest."

"How is our duel connected with the bookmakers' offices?" Davkaleon did not understand.

"In the most direct way," grinned Elfid. "A&Z are associated with anything they can make money on. Before you ascended to the Throne of the Gods, your duel was your private affair, which would not have brought in much money. Just a couple of students of a military school wishing to fight. Big deal! But the duel of the applicants to the Commander-in-Chief, each of whom has the favor of the gods, is a big event. They will make bets on you throughout the whole of Daeya."

"Bets throughout Daeya? Are you sure?" Davkaleon's eyes lit up. This was what he wanted!

"Doesn't it bother you that they mostly make bets against you?"

"That's even better! So, my winnings will make a splash! Everybody in Daeya will speak about it."

"What will you do if you lose?" Elfid said, a serious look on his face.

"Me? Lose? Never! I'll go to these bookmakers and make a bet on myself," added Davkaleon. "By the way, should I say that I make a bet on myself?"

"No," replied Elfid, "no one takes bets on duels between the students of military schools. It is forbidden. Instead, they organize fights of so-called dummies—surrogates for the real combatants—fake fights between people with made up names. They accept bets on the outcome of the matches between them, and the dummy wins which is identified with the real winner of the match."

"How do they do it?" asked Davkaleon.

"With the help of a Triss, of course."

"How do you know?" Davkaleon could not believe what Elfid was telling him.

"And where do you think do they come up with scenarios for the school subject called Game Theory? They are often taken from bets that have occurred in the bookmakers' offices. Listen to the task from my last lesson.

A Clever Noodle made a bet of 100 seekls to D. in the match between P. and D. when betting 4 to 1. After a few days, the Clever Noodle decided to insure against loss and was waiting for the appropriate   bets.

What bets will help the Clever Noodle earn 200 seekls guaranteed, provided that he will put another 100 seekls?

"What bets will help?" asked Davkaleon.

"Here is the solution," Elfid said, handing the piece of paper.

Looking at the paper, Davkaleon disagreed. "Even if these bookmakers will try to affect bets, they will not be able to affect the fight."

"Don't be so sure. Don't forget that the duel will take place in the Triss grove."

"All school duels take place there," protested Davkaleon.

"Are the outcomes all fixed?"

"A&Z don't interfere in these duels. They started to take bets on you immediately after you have ascent to the Throne. Bets were jumping like crazy, but there is not anything unusual in it. I was alarmed in that moment, when someone made a bet that you both would die. I did not like that, and I looked through everything about the Triss in the library. This morning I went for a walk on the Triss site. Let's go, I'll show you one thing."

Dragon's grove was near Assa's border. In the past, it was far outside of the limits of Assa, but Assa has grown and extended, and what was once considered a suburb, has become almost the center. Not the center itself, of course. It would take two hours to reach the dragon's grove on foot. And if you flew on a dragon, then you would get there quite quickly.

Davkaleon took Elfid to Aleurh, and very soon they were all in the Dragon's grove. They found the Triss site very quickly. The glade was surrounded by bushes and trees with fancy twisted trunks.

"At what distance can you communicate with Aleurh?" asked Elfid.

"The closer, the better," replied Davkaleon whose ability to communicate at a distance did not exceed the abilities of an average citizen of Daeya. No wonder that Davkaleon preferred to be close to Aleurh during battles and training. They didn't need even to talk then. One thought about something and the other one heard every word. But at a distance, Davkaleon's power weakened quickly. Aleurh, of course, could hear Davkaleon even at a distance of several hundred yards, and dragons could communicate with each other even at a distance of several thousand yards. Aleurh claimed that he could talk with his mother, Pandra, even while he was in Assa, while his mother was in the Guard Towers.

"Will you be able to hear Aleurh at a distance of 10 yards?" asked Elfid.

Davkaleon grimaced. 10 yards was the limit of his abilities.

"How about a hundred yards?" asked Elfid again.

Davkaleon shook his head. No, at that distance, he could not hear Aleurh.

"I bet 10 seekls that you can," suggested Elfid. "This site is about two hundred yards in width and length. Stand in the middle. Aleurh and I will go to the edge, and I assure you, you'll hear Aleurh perfectly."

Elfid and Aleurh moved to the edge. Davkaleon saw they were whispering about something, but he could not make out the words. Finally, they agreed about something and Elfid waved his hand.

"Andibraksh, what are you doing here?" Davkaleon heard his dragon.

Davkaleon looked back. He did not see the little goblin Andibraksh.

"I won 10 seekls," laughed Elfid, "you have heard your dragon, though he is at the distance of 100 yards from you."

Davkaleon was surprised, and Elfid went on. "I assume that you'll hear Aleurh at two hundred yards also, maybe more."

Elfid was right. Aleurh moved further and further, and Davkaleon still heard him. But most surprisingly, he heard Elfid, although not as good as Aleurh. The thoughts of people of Daeya sounded much quieter than dragons' thoughts. In a few minutes, Aleurh and Elfid landed near Davkaleon.

"Triss groves are very special places. When Aleurh and I are among the Triss, you can hear us. Triss power increases many times, if this is twice-born Triss. These trees are capable of transmitting words and thoughts of those who are near them for long distances. The other twice-born Triss picks up these thoughts and passes them on. Capabilities of a thrice-born Triss are even more unusual. Runes of the witches of Llill say that any three times born Triss is able to preserve the words and thoughts of those who happened to be nearby, even if it happened hundreds of years ago."

"How can I extract these thoughts and how can I find out whom they belonged to?" asked Davkaleon.

Elfid didn't know this yet. But it was said in ancient runes that a fourth born Triss was able to communicate like a rational being. An ancient legend claimed that Triss born more than four times were able to move and navigate. The more times a Triss was born, the more it's limbs and trucks twisted into the body of a dragon. According to the legend, the process repeated again and again until a Triss was completely transformed and became the Dragon Master.

"Does the Dragon Master exist?" surprised Davkaleon.

"There are several legends about him," said Elfid.

"Aleurh, does the Dragon Master exist?" asked Davkaleon.

"Many dragons believe that he does," answered Aleurh.

"And why have you never told me?" surprised Davkaleon.

"Because I know little about him," admitted Aleurh.

Davkaleon took out the goblin's map of Assa with Andibraksh's descriptions and asked if they had heard anything about the tunnel leading to the Gardens of the Dragon Master.

"No, why are you interested in this tunnel?" Elfid asked.

"Because, according to the map, the entrance to this tunnel is located near the Triss site. I thought that it was just a title and that it meant nothing, but if you both say you have heard about the Dragon Master, it is quite possible that the Gardens of the Dragon Master and a tunnel to them also exist."

Elfid carefully read the vague explanation of Andibraksh, but what it could mean? He didn't know either.

"Pay attention to this sign," Davkaleon pointed to the Symbol of the DRAGON. "Do you remember the little Adoleeseet Chapa? He said it was a symbol of the DRAGON and a secret symbol of Adolees. What can this sign mean in the Gardens of the Dragon Master? May the Dragon Master be the DRAGON of Adolees?"

"Unlikely," said Elfid. "Rather, it is more likely a secret entrance to somewhere is associated with Adolees."

"The DRAGON of Adolees is highly respected in the

Temple of the rock in Llill," said Davkaleon. "Maybe it's a secret entrance to the temple."

"Maybe," agreed Elfid.

"Can you find in the runes, how I could get inside?" asked Davkaleon.

"I will tell you about it even without runes," said Elfid.

"You must say in your mind the name of this symbol in the language of Adolees dragons, but I don't advise you to do it. It's dangerous, this symbol is alien and hostile for people of Daeya."

Davkaleon, of course, ignored this warning.

Chapter 19. The Duel

"What terms should we go with?" Kvorts and Malay asked Davkaleon, heading to the place where the duel would be held. The brothers were his seconds, and as tradition demanded, they had to settle the conditions with the foe's seconds. They were very proud of their involvement, and had spent the previous week learning what was allowed and what wasn't in "affairs of honor," which was what duels were called in the military communities.

"Well, you know what I'm capable of." Davkaleon just waved the question away. "Playing the flute and the Old-Daeyan rhetoric are not on the list. So much for choosing weapons and the combat rules. The best way would be if they agreed to fight a duel without any rules at all. This way, I wouldn't have to rack my brain trying to remember what is allowed and what is not. What is most important is that I must not look weak. Don't soften fight conditions under any circumstances, so nobody will dare to say later that Crassius and his seconds offered a real fight when we wanted only a game. If some conditions seem too soft to you, toughen them up. I grabbed a sheet of leather. Write down the terms offered by the foes and those offered by you. After you've arranged the matter, sign it and hang it up for all to see. After today's fight, nobody will dare to make jokes about *the best of the best.*"

"If we and they begin toughening up the conditions, we may end up with a fight to the death," Malay pointed out.

"Awesome! That's exactly what I want!" Davkaleon beamed.

"What if we misunderstand something?" Kvorts started feeling uneasy.

"Don't show that by any means. You aren't going to

discuss the ballroom dancing rules, are you? And no matter what the talk is about, a sword fight, a knife fight or a *whatever fight,* you will sort it out somehow."

Having received their instructions, Kvorts and Malay's only concern was looking strong and confident during the parley.

"A sword fight," Pompedius suggested. He was one of Crassius' seconds.

"And knives too." Malay added.

"Also using spears, axes and any other materials on hand," another of Crassius' seconds suggested.

"A fight using all sorts of weapons." Kvorts confirmed.

The seconds nodded. It looked like they had received the same instructions Davkaleon had given to his brothers.

"A fight according to the Laws of Honor in Assa." Pompedius held out an offer.

Keeping in mind Davkaleon's words about the rules, Malay raised an objection "Why be distracted by rules during the fight? No rules during the fight would be better!"

"A fight by the *Free Rules of the Daeyan Code* will be perfect then. There will be no restrictions," one of Crassius' seconds suggested.

"Sounds good enough for us." Malay and Kvorts agreed.

There was one question left. At what point must the defeat be marked? Pompedius suggested a fight to the first blood.

Malay and Kvorts lined up in opposition: "And what if the first blood flows out of the finger? Will we have to stop the fight over something silly like this? That's child's play!"

Having heard about the blood drop on the finger another of Crassius' seconds went from one extreme to the other.

"A fight to the death. If one duelist falls down dead, the second one will be announced as the winner only if he brings the fight to an end."

"We need a minute to have a quick chat about it," Kvorts said drawing his brother aside. He bent closer to Malay and whispered, "We cannot agree to this. You know Davkaleon, he won't stick a knife into a man while he is down, which means that whatever the outcome is, he won't be announced as the winner."

"We have to ease the rules then, and you know that Davkaleon was dead set against any rule softening," Malay pointed out.

"We'll ease them under a specious excuse, and we'll write the final cut on the leather sheet without specifying who offered what." Kvorts suggested and Malay nodded.

"We are proposing a small correction," Kvorts said, "The duelist is announced as the winner if his foe is killed, or is down unconscious, or calls it quits."

"We could do that," Crassius' seconds agreed, but then we want that to be stated clearly during the announcement of the final fight conditions, that we were offering the fight to the death and you insisted on softening the rules."

"In that case, we are insisting on pointing out that your first suggestion was a fight to the first blood and we turned it down saying it was child's play! As to a fight to the death, it assumes going in for a kill when the foe is already down. The one who does that would inevitably be expelled from the school, since it goes against the Laws of Honor in Assa."

Having consulted one with another, the seconds declared they would go with the announcement of the duel's rules without mentioning the details.

179

"What? You haven't toughened up any of the rules?" Davkaleon boiled over in rage, seeing only the final list of rules for the duel on the leather sheet.

The brothers explained the whole story.

Meanwhile, Crassius Pompeus and his seconds were standing at some distance. Davkaleon could hear their subvocal conversation well.

"They haven't figured it out, have they?" Crassius asked.

"No, they haven't! They were so busy clearing up who toughened what that they didn't pay attention to what kind of heat a fight by *The Free Rules of the Daeyan Code* can bring down to them," his seconds answered.

"And what kind of heat can it bring down to me?" Davkaleon thought carelessly, in full confidence of an easy victory. Having watched Crassius during their practices, Davkaleon was sure that he had found the joint in Crassius' armor. Crassius was brilliant at fighting with his right hand, but his left-hand fighting was not as skilled. Davkaleon was equally great at fighting both with right and left hands, and he was going to take advantage of that.

* * * * *

The waiter from the *Mug and Sword* delivered unopened bottles of "Drink of Strength" which by tradition the duelists and their seconds drank before the duel. It must be said that the waiter brought way more bottles than had been ordered—he knew from experience that spectators would want to join in the drinking as well. Crassius came up to Davkaleon. Each of their seconds held a big box. Pompedius opened his box, unveiling six Triss goblets.

"Choose," Pompedius offered, reaching out the box with the goblets to Davkaleon and his brothers. Davkaleon noticed that the inner part of the three goblets was light color and the other three goblets were dark color inside. Elfid's lecture was of service to him at that moment.

"No, thank you, we will choose from my goblets. They are all the same, made of non-poisonous Triss." Davkaleon opened his box with goblets.

"You choose first, take the light goblets, nobody stops you," Crassius chuckled to himself.

"Hold on a minute," Malay chimed in. "Are you saying that these three dark goblets are made of poisonous Triss?"

"Far from it," Pompedius answered. "You take the goblet in your hand, squeeze the stem, and the dark core disappears and then, there you are, only young non-poisonous Triss is left."

"And you, of course, were going to tell us that in case we choose dark goblets." Kvorts derided.

"No, he was just going to refrain from pointing out that the stem must be squeezed at a certain spot, as well as to say nothing that much the same scenario happens to the light goblets, if we choose the light ones." Davkaleon said.

"Who are you taking us for?" Crassius feigned outrage. "The last thing we need to put up with is your claims that we are trying to poison you."

"You know, you can choose whatever you want from your goblets, but I'm going to choose from my brother's goblets." Kvorts said, taking one of the goblets in Davkaleon's box.

"Like your goblets guarantee no shady secrets," Crassius cracked back.

"Well, nobody is making you drink out of my goblets. You drink from yours and we will drink out of mine."

Davkaleon suggested.

The waiter filled the goblets with fizzy drink.

"To a fair fight." Crassius said drinking up his brew.

"To a fair fight." Davkaleon and the others repeated.

"Now, dragons," one of the opposing seconds said, opening the second box.

There were two huge goblets inside of the box which would be the right size for dragons.

Davkaleon felt his blood ran cold.

"What dragons?" he asked reflexively, anticipating the answer.

"What do you mean what dragons? The ones we are going to fight on." Crassius answered. "On the other hand, you could fight without a dragon if you want. A fight by the Free Rules of the Daeyan Code doesn't forbid it."

Malay and Kvorts turned green. Davkaleon's dragon, Aleurh, was in the dragon guardhouse.

"Take my dragon, he is well prepared and he knows you perfectly," Kvorts said.

"He cannot fight on someone else's dragon. *The Free Rules of the Daeyan Code* dictate fighting on your own dragon or fighting without a dragon."

"There was not a single word spoken about dragons! You are fighting without dragons." Malay tried to argue.

"What do you mean there was not a single word about dragons?" Crassius narrowed his eyes. "Do you know the *Free Rules of the Daeyan Code*? Did you put your signature under the duel rules having no notion of what you were signing for?"

"My brother is not here for listening to your lectures." Davkaleon arrogantly interrupted Crassius' speech.

"Give your dragon a drink and I will change my clothes in the meantime."

"Let's dismiss Aleurh from the guardhouse." Kvorts

suggested.

"One of us will be enough here while another one flies on his dragon to get Aleurh over here."

"You cannot dismiss him, so don't bother Aleurh in vain," Davkaleon snapped at his brothers.

"Of course, I will handle both Crassius and his dragon, but if, just in case, something unexpected happens to me, take care of my Aleurh. Let one of you watch the fight, while the other reads the Daeyan Code. I need to know if I have to defeat only Crassius or both Crassius and his dragon. When you find the answer tell me telepathically."

Davkaleon took out Chapa's present, a cape made of adolgon, the skin from a fighting Adoleeseet dragon. It was good that the cape looked more like armor than a cape—very useful in battle. Setting off to the duel, Davkaleon hesitated, wondering whether to use the Adoleeseet's present or not. The adolgon skin would surely protect him from the blows of the sword and the dragon's fire breathing, but what if someone said that he was hiding behind the cloak? Well, the fight with not only Crassius but also his dragon had changed the balance of strength. Putting on his cape, Davkaleon could hear how dramatically bets had shifted after the word leaked out that he was fighting alone against Crassius and his dragon by the *Free Rules of the Daeyan Code*

"These scumbags shoved the *Free Rules of the Daeyan Code* at us, knowing that Aleurh had been sent to the guardhouse and Davkaleon would fight without his dragon," Kvorts muttered.

"Sure thing! These jerks did this on purpose! We'll have to give them a dose of their own medicine," Malay agreed.

Malay and Kvorts quickly found a copy of the *Free Rules of the Daeyan Code*. The dragon was not allowed to fight on his own. If the dragon-rider fought on the ground, the dragon could not meddle in the fight. But the dragon could fly up to his rider to help him get on. Technically, the dragon was regarded as one more type of weapon which could use his fire breath, teeth, hammer-like paws and his tail with spikes, though he could do so only under the condition that his rider was on him. The sword and knife could not fight by itself during the duel, could it? So, the dragon was not allowed to fight without his rider. Having delivered the message to Davkaleon, Malay and Kvorts started talking to each other.

"We both look like idiots with all these free rules. We agreed on a fight with a dragon knowing that Aleurh was in the guardhouse. Students at school are laughing themselves to death at us! What if they say we set our brother up intentionally?" Malay gnashed his teeth in fury.

"I feel like a gibbering cretin," Kvorts answered. "After reading so many different rules for a whole week, we've missed something of such great importance!"

"Yes, I am surprised too, but those rules...there are so many of them, it may be that we've just forgotten something."

"No! I couldn't have forgotten something like this!" Kvorts disagreed, "I made notes of the most important rules. By the way, where are they?"

Kvorts felt in his pockets and took the notes out. "Here you are! Look! Detailed description of the *Free Rules of the Daeyan Code*! I know I could not have missed something like this."

Malay searched his pockets. Just like Kvorts, he had made notes preparing for his role of the duel seconds. And just like Kvorts's notes, his list had a detailed description of the *Free Rules of the Daeyan Code*.

"Oh, Gods! I've written them too. How could I have

forgotten them?" Malay was looking perplexedly at his notes.

"Now that I think more on it, something is not right. It must have been some kind of delusion. We were *made* to forget the rules. Rumor has it that many funny things can happen around the Triss. The Triss can throw a mirage at you and make you see things which don't exist. As for us, they made us forget things, like we had never read or heard about these free rules."

"Where are they? Does anybody see them?"

Numerous spectators gathered on the Triss glade in the Dragon Grove, trying to see where the duelists had disappeared to. The duel had been going on for more than an hour. Those who had bet that Davkaleon would be defeated within half an hour had lost. Crassius had been wounded several times. Though his injuries were not dangerous, his right hand was hurt and he was much worse at fighting with his left hand. Even a blind man could see that Crassius would lose if he was fighting without his dragon. But the participation of the dragon in the fight had changed everything.

Davkaleon had been lucky so far, though he would never call this "good luck". From his own point of view, he was far and away better than Crassius, and he'd avoided being wounded...so far. Scratches and bruises didn't count, of course. To escape the dragon fire breathing, Davkaleon had to move very quickly. He was jumping and running from one side of the dragon to another, attacking his foes with his spear every now and then. It became worse when the dragon flew up in the air and tried to fry Davkaleon. The adolgon cape was a great shield, but Davkaleon had to twist and turn, not only from the dragon's fire, but also from his sharp-clawed paws and his strong tail with long spikes. The dragon swooped onto

Davkaleon with his ghastly jaws wide open. Davkaleon tossed his spear right into the open jaws. The dragon bellowed with pain and jumped back, Crassius couldn't keep hold on to the saddle and fell to the ground. Davkaleon darted forward and put his sword to Crassius' chest.

"I give up." Crassius said quietly.

Davkaleon put his sword down.

"What are you doing?!" his brothers screamed in horror. Crassius said, "I give up" so quietly that apparently the Gerklat brothers didn't hear him. As soon as Davkaleon put his sword down, Crassius stabbed him with a knife. The knife slipped under the cape and wounded the side, the blood dropped on the ground.

"Liar!" Davkaleon burst into a rage and swung his sword.

The dragon knocked Davkaleon off his feet and rushed to Crassius who jumped onto his back in the next breath.

"This is a violation! The dragon cannot participate in the fight when his rider is on the ground." Malay and Kvorts shouted with one voice.

"He didn't, he just picked me up. And this is permitted." Crassius answered.

"You gave up!" Davkaleon shouted.

"Me? In your dreams maybe!" Crassius snapped, and the infuriated dragon flung himself at Davkaleon. The fight continued. Davkaleon felt himself growing weaker— his wound ached—and it was getting more difficult to escape the dragon. Davkaleon jumped back, pulled out a stone and threw it at Crassius. Crassius slid back and fell off the dragon again. Davkaleon dashed forward and put his knife to Crassius' throat.

"This time you will have to speak loudly to make sure everyone hears you." He announced.

"Don't even dream about it." Crassius hissed.

The next moment, the dragon flew up to the duelists, picked them both up and soared upwards. He let Davkaleon go right away and put Crassius carefully on his back. Having flown a few meters down Davkaleon, struck the ground, bouncing. Malay and Kvorts shouted together about the rules violation.

"My dragon picked me up and your brother clung on me like a leech. Do you think my dragon must carry him around or what?" Crassius argued back.

* * * * *

"Well, well, look at you! How cool-headed you are!" the priest of the main temple of Arragorra said coming into Gerklat's office. "Your son is fighting alone against Pompeus and his dragon and you are sitting here in peace calculating your profit."

"And, of course, it's Davkaleon again? Has he set up another brawl?" the priest Gerklat pried himself away from his numbers.

"What? Don't you know what is going on? Where have you been the last two weeks? Everyone in Daeya has been placing bets on the outcome of the duel between the contenders for the commander, each of whom received the grace from the Gods and you don't know what is happening. When it became known that Davkaleon was fighting without his dragon by the *Free Rules of the Daeyan Code*, people started betting on whether you would intervene in the fight or not and if you intervened, whether you would do that yourself or through somebody else."

"Why is he fighting alone? Where is his dragon?" Gerklat became surprised.

"In the guardhouse."

"What idiot would agree on a fight by the *Free Rules of the Daeyan Code* without a dragon?" Gerklat asked, his face flushing red.

"Your two other sons. They are his seconds." the priest of Arragorra answered.

"Morons!" Priest Gerklat rewarded his sons with a string of unflattering names. "How could they not read the rules ahead of time? When is the duel?"

"Now. It has been going on for already an hour and a half. Davkaleon is wounded, as well as Pompeus."

"Now? Where?" For the first time, Priest Gerklat realized the seriousness of the news.

"They are fighting on the Triss glade in the Dragon Grove."

"On the Triss glade in the Dragon Grove!?" Priest Gerklat gasped, springing up from his seat. "Did someone use Black Magic to make the seconds forget the description of the free rules? Is that why you are here?"

"Sit down! You cannot show up there. It would do Davkaleon an ill turn. Yes, they have used Black Magic, and still are, to make the seconds forget the description of the free rules. Then they made Davkaleon hear his opponent's words about giving up. Davkaleon stopped fighting, put down his weapon and, needless to say, was wounded. I paid attention to what was going on around this duel after I'd seen how bets had been jumping to and fro in A&Z. I took fright when someone had placed a bet that both duelists would be killed. But these are people's concerns, they don't really bother me. A&Z has always played their own games when it smelled like money. What really worries me is that yesterday Pompeus visited the temple of the God Prann in Arragorra, and after that, Prann paid a visit to the Lord of the Dragons. You

189

understand this kind of combination always means Black Magic."

"And you are telling me to stay here quietly without intervening?" Priest Gerklat flared up.

"I am not. I don't like when Black Magic is used. And Dragon Whales doesn't like it either. His blood-brother was killed through the use of Black Magic, and he is still grieving over his death. You can talk about Black Magic to Whales. He will understand you very well."

* * * * *

Aleurh was rushing about the guardhouse. He didn't even know what he'd done to be there. For the very nonsense! He was pushed. Caught off-guard, he lost his footing and bumped up against somebody. That somebody turned out to be the dragon instructor, and Aleurh was sent to the guardhouse for 24 hours. At any other time, that wouldn't have bothered him at all, and he would sleep quietly till the end of his term. But Davkaleon was fighting with Crassius Pompeus. The fact that Aleurh could not see the fight, from his point of view, was simply outrageous.

Dragon Whales showed up in the corridor between the cells. He came up to Aleurh's cell. "Your blood-brother is fighting by *The Free Rules of the Daeyan Code*. It means he is fighting alone against Pompeus and his dragon."

Aleurh threw himself at the bars roaring and flapping.

"I'll let you out. You'll do your time tomorrow," The Chief Dragon of the Military School said. "Keep in mind, they are using Black Magic there. So, don't believe any command you hear from Davkaleon if it sounds the way it taught at school. Use the language you usually speak to your blood-brother. Nobody will understand what you are talking about except you two."

Dragon Whales unlocked the door and Aleurh darted to the Triss glade.

* * * * *

Crassius' dragon flew at Davkaleon again. Even though he wasn't able to shoot flames out of his wounded jaws, his paws and tail were still dangerous. Davkaleon looked around. The spear that he had launched at the dragon to wound his jaws had to be somewhere here. The spear was just a few feet away. Davkaleon ran up to it, took a swing, and tossed the spear at the dragon's throat. Having made a wild howling, the dragon fell down, steamrolling Davkaleon. Having jumped off the dragon Crassius tried to put a sword to his foe's throat. Davkaleon managed to dodge and knock the sword from Crassius' hand, but he was still under the dragon that wasn't in a hurry to release him.

Malay and Kvorts screamed loudly that the dragon had to set Davkaleon free. Crassius picked up his knocked-out sword and with a grin of triumph and strode up to Davkaleon. Taking a wide swing he was about to hit Davkaleon with his sword, but the next moment he was shoved aside. An enraged Aleurh sent Crassius spinning away from Davkaleon with force and rammed at the foe's dragon.

"It's a violation of the rules!" Crassius' second shouted.

"What rules? He is not fighting; he's just trying to pick up his rider. It's not against the rules. Surely you recall the same thing happening a short while ago?" Kvorts and Malay grinned malevolently.

Having pulled Davkaleon from under the dragon, Aleurh sat him with care on his back. "Have a rest. I'm going to fry them up now. And by the way, speak our language," Aleurh thought as he darted at Crassius.

Crassius' dragon rushed to his rider, and having picked him up, took off into the air trying to escape Aleurh's fire. The dragons flew higher and higher. Crassius tossed several knives at Davkaleon, but they bounced away thanks to the cape, leaving Davkaleon unscathed. Aleurh flew up closer to the foes and Davkaleon waved his sword. Crassius ducked the blow, but couldn't keep on the saddle, sliding down. His dragon bolted after him and managed to catch him right before he hit the ground.

Aleurh rushed down, too. Having a sword at the ready, Davkaleon said in his mind, *Swoop onto them and knock down the rider on the ground, I'll finish him off there, and meanwhile, you keep his dragon away from us.* Aleurh did so, and Crassius and Davkaleon ended up on the ground. With his wounded right hand, Crassius barely avoided Davkaleon's attacks, but his dragon was protecting him, despite the fact that he was leaving himself wide open for Aleurh's hits and fire.

"Be ready, I'll wrestle him to the ground now," Aleurh thought, reaching out to Davkaleon. Davkaleon jumped on Crassius, but Crassius' dragon came to the rescue again, having thrown tiny stones into his eyes. Davkaleon closed his eyes for a second and when he opened them, there were two Crassiuses standing in front of him. The next moment, there were already four of them.

"Aleurh, I see four of Crassius!" Davkaleon hoped that Aleurh would give him a clue which of his foes was a real one, but Aleurh saw four of Crassius and four dragons too. All of the four pairs were backing off to the edge of the Triss glade.

Davkaleon rushed for them. Aleurh followed Davkaleon. Keeping in mind the warning from the Dragon

Whales about Black Magic, Aleurh kept a careful eye. Davkaleon overtook one of the Crassius' and hit him with his sword. The sword went through Crassius without doing the slightest harm to him. Davkaleon hit another Crassius but the result was the same. The third one and the forth Crassius' all turned out to be just a delusion. Davkaleon didn't know where the real Crassius was.

In the distance, the four showed themselves again. Davkaleon darted to them. Alas, once more, they were mere delusions. The elusive foes were leading Davkaleon farther and farther from the Triss glade into the heart of the Dragon Grove. They stopped near the Dragon Triss.

Remembering Elfid's story, Davkaleon recognized the many-times born Triss. The tree resembled a dragon, just like Elfid had told him. In the meantime, having circled the tree, Crassius began speaking in a sing-song voice. Most likely, it was the Old-Daeyan language, and Davkaleon could not understand many words. The illusive dragons of illusive Crassius were standing a step aside, howling and signing something along in their dragon language.

"I don't like it, let's get back to the Triss glade," Aleurh said.

Davkaleon agreed with him. He even stopped hitting the air with his sword. The real Crassius jumped on Davkaleon from behind. His sword slithered down the adolgon cape having done no real harm. Davkaleon turned toward him in a flash, but it looked like Crassius didn't have the mind to take up a fight. Instead, he dashed to the dragon Triss. Davkaleon ran after him. Aleurh followed Davkaleon, getting the sense that something bad was going to happen.

Having run up to the dragon Triss, Crassius put his hands on the tree and shouted his appeal to the God

Prann. Davkaleon caught Crassius and waved up his sword, and at that moment the tree stepped back, opening a narrow pass down. Crassius tried to get away. Out of the blue, Crassius' dragon showed up and tried to tear Crassius from Davkaleon. Aleurh lunged at Crassius's dragon. The branches of the dragon Triss stretched toward Crassius and Davkaleon and pushed them down into the narrow pass. The Dragon Triss made a move to the pass in an effort to get back to where it belonged. Having left Crassius' dragon, Aleurh hit the Triss with full force to not let the pass close up. It must be said that the dragon Triss didn't seem to resist, letting Aleurh slip down as well. Crassius' dragon dashed down as well. The dragon Triss got back on its place closing the pass.

Chapter 20. Gardens of the Dragon Master

Malay and Kvorts unsuccessfully tried to shift the Triss. They were joined by their dragons. Dragons of the seconds of Crassius also rushed to help, but the mighty Triss did not yield.

Tangled with each other and holding swords, Davkaleon and his opponent were falling down into the black darkness.

We will inevitably crash, thought Davkaleon, looking into the endless abyss.

To his surprise after a few minutes their falling had slowed, and light appeared at the bottom. More precisely, it was not light but the likeness of twilight, but it was still better than total darkness. The corridor widened. Someone or something had separated Crassius from Davkaleon with force and dropped him on a convenient armchair, floating in the air. As for Davkaleon, he fell into something resembling a large spider web. Davkaleon cautiously looked at the place of his landing, determining that the web could not be torn.

"So you think you can decide yourself whether you will serve the god of Daeya or not," came a mocking voice.

Davkaleon looked around. The speaker was not visible.

"Who are you?" asked Davkaleon.

He anticipated the answer, but wanted to stall for time, hoping to come up with something.

"You know who I am. Do you remember what you said about me? That I'm a cruel and bloody God who demands sacrifices and my priests are often not limited to the animal sacrifices! At their meetings they do human sacrifices!"

"Crassius, did you do this? You understood that you would lose in a fair fight, and decided to resort to black magic?" asked Davkaleon.

Crassius said nothing.

"And by the way, here is your dragon. Great! I haven't had fun with blood-brothers in a long time," came the voice of Prann again.

Aleurh got down to the web next to Davkaleon. Surprisingly, the web resisted the dragon's efforts also.

"Enough talking!" came a second voice that sounded more like a growl. "As you have already understood, you are in *my* world. This is the world of illusion. Here, all is not as it seems. You will see what is not here and you won't see what is here. But it is most interesting, isn't it?"

The web threw Davkaleon up and dropped him down. Then it turned itself on Aleurh and tightly tethered the dragon. Davkaleon stood on the bloody red ground. Aleurh floated in the air, bound at arm's length.

"As you know, it is very difficult to kill a dragon. One of the ways is to shoot it in the eye. This cute dragon-Triss can shoot arrows. Let's see what you can do for your dragon."

A Triss dragon moved to the bound Aleurh and held his paws made of branches close to Aleurh's face. Davkaleon cut the branches with a sword, but new branches regenerated to replace them in a moment. Davkaleon ripped off his adolgon's cape and threw it on Aleurh. The next moment a lot of small branch-arrows flew at Aleurh. Davkaleon grimaced when a few arrows stuck in him.

This is the world of illusions. Everything here is not the same as it seems. The words of the Dragon Lord flashed in his head. But if it is so, then would he be able to create an illusion as well? He would try. Davkaleon imagined the mighty stone Alatar and the streams floating from under it. He tensed, drawing a picture like he remembered it in Arragorra. He even imagined how

196

sprays of water hit him in the face, how he leaned down to streams to drink its water.

"Aleurh, do you see what I have imagined? Do you remember how you drank, when I brought you water of Alatar? Remember the taste and imagine that you're drinking it now!"

Aleurh closed his eyes and moved his mouth as if drinking. He was drinking eagerly, and it seemed to him that the power of Alatar was pouring into him. And then he stiffened, and the web burst first in one place then in another. Davkaleon, too, felt a surge of strength. He jumped on the Dragon Triss and threw it away. Aleurh spread his mighty wings and finally escaped from the nets.

"Sit down!" Aleurh cried to Davkaleon and soared up.

At the same moment, hundreds of arrow–branches flew into them. Dragon-Trisses lined up in the labyrinth, closing the top with branches and forming a narrow corridor. Aleurh was flying in a meandering passage and sharp arrows flew into him and Davkaleon.

"Take the cape!" ordered Aleurh and rushed up.

Dragon branches shot, slashed, and burned. Davkaleon felt the shocks, despite the protection of an adolgon cloak. Aleurh broke through the Triss branches and flew up. There were thickets of dragon Trisses at the bottom— flames were raging at the top. Aleurh was gliding between the inhospitable skies and bloody land of the Dragon Garden. A terrible hurricane came suddenly, tore Davkaleon away and threw him to the ground. Aleurh stayed above.

"Look how they resist! What an aira! It's a real pleasure to watch them." purred the voice of joyful Prann.

Davkaleon recognized a word *aira*, which he heard in the temple in the rock from the mage's apprentices during the Walpurgis Night. So, he was right, the mages were referring to the Daeyan god Prann when speaking about aira. But he did not have time for recollections.

"Yes, there will be an excellent cocktail made of them." roared the Dragon Master.

"Wait on the cocktail, let's have more fun." answered Prann.

At the same moment Davkaleon saw several Aleurh in the sky and several copies of Davkaleon appeared near him. A huge boulder appeared above each of the images of Davkaleon and Aleurh, a barrel hung near it.

"Do you know what this is for?" a voice of Prann sounded. "These are juicers. As you understand, the juice will be squeezed out of you both, and then a wonderful cocktail will be prepared. What a pity you won't be able to try it," Prann laughed. "If you have the desire to continue our fun, you can do that easily. All you have to do is guess who is where."

At the same moment, all of the copies swirled and spun at a furious pace.

"Where are you?" asked Davkaleon, and all his copies mimicked him.

Davkaleon heard the mind voice of Aleurh, "Respond in our way." They had developed a language of their own, a childish mix of Daeyan and dragon languages. It was a useful thing. During children's games, nobody could understand conversations of Davkaleon with Aleurh.

And Davkaleon responded. Not understanding what was being said, the copies were repeating words with a tiny delay. Aleurh rushed to the real Davkaleon and they soared up. Above, above, above. There was a black void at the top.

* * * * *

Davkaleon's father and priest of the main temple of Arragorra appealed to the sacred stone Alatar incessantly.

Visions of what was happening in the Dragon Garden were flashing in front of them in the air.

"How will we get out? A Triss closed the passage there." Aleurh's thought flashed in the mind of Davkaleon. It seemed they'd been flying for a long-long time. But suddenly, light appeared above.

"Close it! What imbecile dared to open the passage?" the indignant voice of Prann sounded.

Davkaleon heard the distant voices of his father and the priest of the Main Temple of Arragorra. They were saying something in a singsong voice in the old-Daeyan language.

"Get out! This is my trophy!" the voice of Prann thundered.

"The devil with them, we have a couple others," roared the Dragon Master.

"I want these!" demanded Prann, but Davkaleon could already discern the faces of his brothers, who were peeking into the dark tunnel.

From below, Crassius and his dragon appeared. "Take Crassius with you," the dragon asked.

"He is the last person we need now," snapped Davkaleon.

"Amuse your favorite Prann, he is bored."

"Take him and I'll close the passage with my body not to let Prann throw you down," the dragon pleaded.

"Gualtus, we'll get out of here together, I with you," came the voice of Crassius.

Davkaleon realized that Crassius was almost crying. His dragon threw his rider up to Aleurh and spread out his wings and legs, pushing up against invisible walls. Could he really protect them from the attacks of Prann and the Dragon Master?

Aleurh sprung from the hole under the Triss, and it

immediately closed.

"Gualtus! No! No! Gualtus!" shouted Crassius, trying to move the Dragon Triss. Tears ran down his face.

Davkaleon's brothers appeared, apparently relieved that Davkaleon was still alive.

"As I understand it, I won," said Davkaleon, but his brothers shook their heads.

"These damned *Free Rules of the Daeyan Code* say that if the fighters disappear for more than half an hour, it is believed that both are dead, and a draw is declared."

"But we are not dead!" shouted the outraged Davkaleon.

"Here are the rules, you can read for yourself," sighed brothers.

"You'll read them in the guardhouse. And to keep you amused, Crassius Pompeus will go with you," said Sergeant Cronkoross, who had quietly approached to greet them. "Duels, you know, are prohibited. As to leaving those who made a bet on you, without a winner? It is a blatant, flagrant crime!"

Chapter 21. Together with Crassius in the Guardhouse

Davkaleon felt like the most miserable Daeyat in all of Daeya. He had never faced such humiliation and injustice in his life. He defeated Crassius, didn't he? That fact was undeniable from his point of view! But according to the *Free Rules of the Daeyan Code*, his success couldn't be scored as a victory. He even saved his rival. He hadn't thrown Crassius from Aleurh, down to his beloved Prann, even though he really wanted to. His own brothers mocked him by eloquently twirling their fingers around their ears when he told how they escaped.

The worst thing was that everybody at the school was calling him "the best of the best" and adding some pretty rough words after that. "The best moron" was the most popular version. People asked him a lot of questions about what happened under the Triss, but they had the very same reaction. "Couldn't you have finished everything in that Dragon Garden in half of an hour? Do you understand how much we lost on you?"

Surprisingly, people showed less contempt for Crassius than for Davkaleon, even though all of them clearly understood that Crassius had asked the God Prann for help, and tried to get rid of Davkaleon using dark forces when he started to lose. People went as far as to show compassion for Crassius, because of his dragon's heroic death.

Davkaleon lay in his corner cell, facing the wall. Crassius wanted to be the first person to choose the cell, but Davkaleon furiously threw him towards the entrance hall. Davkaleon received several additional days in the guardhouse for that little tantrum, but he didn't care. On the cot, Davkaleon fell into a restless sleep. He was startled awake by someone was shaking his shoulder.

Crassius sat next to him, a stricken look on his face.

"Help me to release my dragon," asked Crassius, staring at Davkaleon beseechingly.

Davkaleon was speechless for a moment. "How dare you come here with such a request after all you have done against me? You robbed me of my victory by requesting Prann's intervention! You made a fool of me! You wanted to feed me and my Aleurh to your bloody Prann! You need to face the consequences of your debauchery."

"No!" he said. "I didn't want anything like that. I just asked Prann for help and it's not prohibited, because he's one of the Gods of Daeya. I didn't know what would happen in the Dragon Gardens, or what he would do to help."

"No," said Davkaleon bluntly. "Go and rescue your dragon yourself. By the way, why are you still here? If my Aleurh was captured by Prann, I would have been there already."

"My right arm is injured and I don't stand a change with only my left," Crassius sighed.

"That's why you made a deal with Prann, didn't you? You offered to lure me back in exchange for your dragon. Admit it," Davkaleon chuckled.

"Of course not, I wouldn't do that. Furthermore, Prann is interested only in blood-brothers, not just half of a pair."

"Interested in blood-brothers? So, he wants Aleurh and I together? First, you will bring me there under the pretext that we have to save your dragon, and then you will tell Aleurh about my location while my faithful dragon flies to save me. Do you think that I am a total idiot? That I will allow you to bait such trap? No, thank you! Good night, Crassius." Davkaleon turned to the wall.

"I admit that you won," said Crassius smarmily.

"That's obvious even without your admission. Your

confession won't change the *Free Rules of the Daeyan Code*, so none of those people who made bets on me will get their money."

"I will give you the 500 seekls, which we discussed during our bet."

"What about the other people who made bets on me?" Davkaleon asked derisively. "Will you pay all of them?"

"Of course, not, I don't have that kind of money. Do you know how many people made bets on you? Especially after your dragon appeared!"

"Was it possible to make new bets during the duel?" Davkaleon was surprised.

"Of course! Didn't you know? The people who made bets on a draw made a lot of money. The A&Z is now holding an investigation to determine if they have to pay money to those who made bets of our mutual death. On one hand, we were announced as deceased, while on other hand, we are still alive. Now, they want to take back the funds awarded to winners of the dual death bet. It looks like this case is going to be forwarded to the priest court. One thing is great—your father is a priest, and he won't allow anyone to kill you in order to confirm that the announcement of our deaths was fair."

"So, you are trying to say that some people were making bets on our mutual deaths?" asked Davkaleon, remembering the words Elfid had told him.

"Of course! People made a lot of such bets when your dragon appeared during our fight."

"How do you know this?"

"Both of my seconds were tracking bets during the duel. Weren't your seconds doing the same?" Crassius seemed surprised.

"Why are you sure that your dragon is still alive?" asked Davkaleon, sitting on his bed.

"Prann was interested in you *only* if you were a real blood-brother to your dragon. I went to the school library to learn everything about you in your biography. I told Prann that both of your parents belong to the Perfects families and that you and your dragon had passed a real ritual in accordance with ancient traditions. After that, he gave his consent to help me. He's not interested in my dragon, as a dragon. He needs either you and Aleurh, or my Gualtus and me. I am not asking you to take Aleurh with you."

"That's the last thing I would do!" chuckled Davkaleon.

"I wouldn't ask for your help if I wasn't injured. But if I go there alone, I won't be able to protect myself, and would simply be serving up my dragon and myself on a plate, right into Prann's hands," Crassius said with a shiver.

"Wait until you recover, then you can go and rescue your dragon," Davkaleon shrugged his shoulders.

"I would do that if my dragon was in *any* other place. Any dragon will start to transform into his shadow in the Garden of the Dragon's Lord. In just two weeks' time, it will be too late."

Davkaleon started thinking. His mind was buzzing with bits and pieces of a conversation from the closet room in the *Mug and Sword*, from his journey to the temple in the rock with the little Adoleeseet, to the story that Elfid told him and the unknown signs on the goblin map. "I need some time to think. I will consider going with you," said Davkaleon, reclining on his bed.

"Won't you fall asleep?" Crassius whispered.

"If I do, don't try to wake me up. I will come to you if I decide to help you. Now, get out of my cell," commanded Davkaleon.

While lying on his bed, Davkaleon pondered all he had heard in the temple and tavern, again and again. He remembered pieces of the legends and stories Elfid had told him. Suddenly, he recalled a relevant fragment—one could use the Gardens of the Dragon's Lord to go... but where? To the temple in the rock? But the rock temple is Twier... Davkaleon stopped himself, not willing to pronounce the forbidden word. But if that was true, Davkaleon wanted to discover the mysteries of Twier... Why was it created? How could one get there and who were the wizards of Twier...? What was their purpose? He wanted to seek the answers to all of his questions, but he did not trust Crassius.

On the other hand, Crassius may have some knowledge on the subject. He could use Andibraksh's map to quietly enter the Dragon's Garden and confirm that the map was reliable. But how did Crassius plan to rescue his dragon? Davkaleon took out the map of Andibraksh and thoroughly examined it once again.

"I will help you," Davkaleon said as he entered Crassius's cell, "but I have several terms and those terms are not negotiable. Before talking about terms, I want to understand how you plan to rescue your dragon."

"I know a secret path which leads to the Dragon Lord's Garden," answered Crassius.

"Deal. Now, listen to my terms."

And Davkaleon told him his demands. Crassius had to admit his defeat in public, in front of a number of witnesses. The best option was to admit it during training the next day. While still in front of the witnesses, Crassius had to give 500 seekls to Davkaleon and ask him for help. Davkaleon would ask him to repay money for all of the people, who placed bets on him on the first day.

"Are you out of your mind? Do you realize this amount of money! Where will I get it?" Crassius was horrified.

"It's not worth a fortune. I am talking only about

people who made bets during the *very first day*. I am not interested in those so-called smart people who hedged their bets by betting various outcomes. I ask you to repay my real supporters—not a small amount of money, but not a large fortune either."

"It will to be several thousand together with your five hundred!"

"I haven't finished yet," continued Davkaleon, without paying any attention to Crassius's complaints. "You will pay me 5000 seekls more for rescuing your dragon."

Exhausted, Crassius sat down on his bed from which he had stood up when Davkaleon entered.

"That's over my limit. I can't accumulate such funds even in a year."

"How much time do you need to accumulate it?" asked Davkaleon.

"I need at least two years."

"That's fine. You will write me a promissory note and will make monthly payments. I won't ask for interest, if you pay everything in one year."

"I agree. Is there anything else?" asked Crassius.

"We need to select the day for our journey. Tomorrow during your public declaration, we will agree to rescue your dragon immediately after I finish my term in the guardhouse. Truth be told, we will rescue him earlier, but I don't want to advertise that part. I think that three days will be enough to heal our wounds."

"Deal, but no later than in three days," agreed Crassius.

Chapter 22. Liberation of the Dragon of Crassius

How Crassius managed to get the necessary amount of money in just a few hours was a mystery for Davkaleon. To the great astonishment of the audience, Crassius handed out refunds to everyone who had bet on Davkaleon the first day. The public request for Davkaleon's help surprised everyone even more. The size of the award was amazing. When Crassius presented Davkaleon with a promissory note for the requested sum, the crowd was struck silent.

"A moment," requested the Gerklat brothers.

His brothers crowded in. "Don't you understand that this is a trap?" whispered Malay.

"He has already offered you to Prann in exchange for his dragon.," added Kvorts.

"I understand that, but I got out of there alive once, and I will get out a second time. And, I'll be 5,000 seekls richer."

"But you're hurt," said Malay.

"I am not leaving today. I will serve my time in the guardhouse. My wounds should be healed by then."

The whole school was discussing the incident. Davkaleon felt that the mood in the school had swung in his favor. Emboldened, he entered Crassius's cell and said, "Let's go rescue your dragon."

"Today?" Crassius surprised. "You said that we would go in three days."

"Yes, I said that, but then I decided that three days is too long. Prann and his friend the Dragon Master will be well aware of our plans, and will be waiting, and today, nobody is waiting for us. We will have a better chance of success with the element of surprise."

"Doesn't it bother you that we have fresh wounds?"

Crassius worried.

"My wound is small. As for you—I do not expect a full-fledged fight from you today."

Davkaleon and Crassius went out of the dungeon and hired a dragon that took them to the Triss grove very quickly. Having paid for the ride, they headed inland. A barely noticeable path meandered between Trisses. A few Trisses grew in a small glade. Twice or a thrice born Triss.? Davkaleon couldn't tell. Crassius stood between two trees and took out a dagger, made an incision on the hand. His blood dripped to the earth.

"Do the same," said Crassius, passing a dagger to Davkaleon.

With outstretched hands, Crassius touched the two Trisses simultaneously. A translucent door appeared behind the Triss. Crassius pulled the handle, and the door opened. The door led into a room with a spiral staircase that led downward. Crassius stepped inside. Davkaleon followed him. He was about to close the door, but had no time.

"I won! I told you that this idiot would be persuaded!" came a voice. "Hey, look, they're both here!"

Davkaleon turned around. A few people stood near the Triss trees. The A&Z logo was embroidered on their shirts.

"Hurry!" shouted Crassius, rushing to the stairs.

Davkaleon followed him.

"Wait! Come back!" came a familiar growl. Dragon Whales stood behind. You have escaped from the guardhouse! March yourselves back."

"We will serve our time later. My dragon is dying—"

"Sit on me," ordered Whales, interrupting Crassius.

"You have rigged our arrangement!" Crassius complained as they reentered their cells. "You charged me a promissory note! Any court will find that I owe you! And then you set me up. You never intended to help me!"

"I wonder, when did I have time to organize all of that?" Davkaleon growled. Crassius continued with his accusations, and Davkaleon kicked the bars that separated their cells with anger. "If you don't shut up, you and your dragon and your promissory note will all end up in the same trash pile." Davkaleon continued to rage for another few minutes, and goblins appeared in the passage.

"How many days will I get this time?" asked Davkaleon, slightly reassured by their presence after the verbal clash with Crassius.

Having received an additional three days, Davkaleon stretched out on his trestle and started musing. He had not told anyone about his intention to go to the dragon garden today, Crassius learned about the trip at the last moment. How could the A&Z have known about his excursion?

Aside from the espionage of the A&Z, Davkaleon cared more about another question. Tomorrow, Crassius would begin to accuse him of deliberate fraud with the promissory note. Davkaleon agreed to take part in the liberation of the dragon for the sake of improving his reputation after the ill-fated duel. Of course, it was very interesting to find out what the symbols on the map of Andibraksh meant, but that could wait until his release from the guardhouse. To improve his reputation, he needed to release Crassius's dragon and dismiss the allegations of fraud. Davkaleon decided that he would make another attempt that very night, but without Crassius. Crassius's wounds would not allow him to help. Still, he would say that he had freed the dragon. Davkaleon already knew how to enter the tunnel. Why did he need Crassius? Even better, Davkaleon would be free of the risk that Crassius would betray him in exchange for his dragon.

"How can I get out of this tunnel?" Davkaleon asked when goblin-guards disappeared.

"Why do you need to know?" asked Crassius bitterly.

"My reputation is more valuable to me than your promissory note and the fraud you accuse me of. That doesn't mean I'll help you for free, but that means that tomorrow we will go to release your dragon again, and I want to know in advance all that is required. You could get hurt again, and I'll have to do everything myself."

After a long, reluctant silence, Crassius said, "You should do the same, only three times."

"Should I stab myself with a dagger three times?"

It doesn't matter how many times you stab, but you have to give three drops of your blood." explained Crassius.

Davkaleon lay quietly, pretending to be asleep. This time, he wanted no one to know about his trip. Not even Crassius. He would likely not make it back in time for the beginning of the lessons. They would add a couple more weeks to his sentence in the guardhouse. No matter—the cell felt like home.

After waiting for an hour, Davkaleon stood got up and crept inside the dungeon. He hired a dragon for a second time that day. His first stop was the magic shop of Carducci. "Pay first." demanded the dragon, blocking the entrance, Davkaleon barely jumped to the ground.

"But it's not the end of my flight. I said that I need to get into the Triss grove."

"I remember your order," the dragon sneered, "but many don't come back from this shop. Pay me now, before you enter."

"Okay," agreed Davkaleon. "But I will pay only for the flight to the shop. I don't like the idea of returning to discover that you have disappeared with all my money."

"It is completely useless to accuse me of dishonesty." The dragon was offended.

"You can't be accused of dishonesty, and I can?" opposed Davkaleon.

"I don't mean that you'll disappear intentionally not to pay me. There are various rumors about this shop. Many say that some people who enter might disappear as though they never existed in this world. Others say that some who never entered the place in the first place, miraculously come out."

This made Davkaleon curious. He walked around the building. It was a detached building, set back from the road, hidden by the mighty trees. The front door was decorated with "*Best Buy, Best Purchase and Best Gain*" inscription.

"Where do these visitors disappear?" asked Davkaleon.

"No one knows. There are so many guesses that I could amuse you till morning just retelling them. I don't want to be a chatterbox, so I will not repeat gossip. If you want, go to the *Dragon Tavern*, order a supper with a dragon ale to share with the dragons, and in gratitude, they will entertain you with all sorts of horror stories about this place, until you are bored to tears."

"That is a great suggestion, I will surely do that," thought Davkaleon, paying the dragon and entering the shop of Carducci.

The seller was sitting in the far corner. Davkaleon looked at him with surprise. He was dressed in a crimson cloak with gold embroidery. Long hair trailed below his shoulders. A gold hoop with red and green stones completed his unusual attire. Davkaleon looked around. The shelves were stocked with everything from soup to nuts! Cans, bottles, stones, jewelry, wallets and purses, amulets and talismans, swords, knives, and many more items, the purpose of which Davkaleon could not even imagine. Items were stacked on shelves, stood on the floor and hung from the ceiling. He heard croaking, quacking, mooing and hissing from somewhere in the back. But most of all, Davkaleon was shocked by the internal dimensions of the shop. The building seemed much, much bigger inside than out!

Davkaleon stated his reason for his coming. He expected that the seller would ask questions, but instead the seller stood up from his seat and headed for the door behind him. That was odd, because Davkaleon was ready to swear that a moment ago, there had not been a door there! The seller returned and placed a covered box in front of Davkaleon.

"This costs 500 seekls," he said.

"How much?" Davkaleon was confused by the amount. He had 500 seekls, Crassius had handed it to him today. Did the funny little man know that somehow? Besides, an average family in Daeya lived on 500 seekls a year. A year!

"Before you remove the cover from the cage, insert these plugs in your ears," the seller said, pointing to a small pouch. They have a special filter—you'll hear everything except the singing of the *sirrerne*. If you do not wear the plugs, you will enjoy the sirrerne's singing with the others, and five minutes later, you will doze off, in about ten minutes you will fall asleep, and within an hour it will be impossible to wake you up."

"Then I need the same plugs for my dragon," said Davkaleon.

"That will cost you another 100 seekls." answered the seller calmly.

Davkaleon began to scan the pockets with mounting

horror counting how many he had. A month earlier, his father had given him 200 seekls, and Davkaleon felt like the richest person in Daeya. That feeling vanished when he discovered the card-playing rates at school. Davkaleon pulled 70 seekls from his pockets.

"You must give me a discount after such a purchase," said Davkaleon.

"Usually I don't give a discount for such small amounts. But okay, I'm feeling generous today. You get a 30 seekls discount."

"40 seekls" said Davkaleon firmly. "I have to pay the dragon that is waiting for me."

"Why is this day so depressing? I have only poor buyers today," sighed the seller.

"Wow, poor buyers." thought Davkaleon, taking purchased goods from the counter.

"What are you going to do with the sirrerne after you are through?" asked the seller.

"I don't know, why do you ask?" Davkaleon had not thought that far ahead.

"Bring it to me. I will buy it from you for 100 seekls," offered the seller.

"Just 100? But you sold it for 500! Why not pay me a half."

"First, I sold it to you for 400, because the earplugs were 100 seekls. And secondly, you'll be happy to sell it back to me for 100. Who would buy it besides me? And if you keep it for yourself, then who is going to take care of it, feed, bathe, and play with it? Do you know how many hassles that would be?"

With a sigh, Davkaleon took his purchase with the remaining 10 seekls and left the shop. The dragon brought him to the Dragons' Grove. Following the path, Davkaleon stopped in the appropriate place, pricked himself with a dagger, and touched two Triss trees. Having entered the translucent door, he headed to the spiral staircase. Down, down, down. It seemed the stairs would never end.

Davkaleon had lost track of time when he noticed some shadows at the bottom. After a few minutes, Davkaleon could recognize the outlines of many-born Trisses. The whimsical intertwining of the branches resembled dragons. Inserting the earplugs, and removing the cover from the cage, Davkaleon walked the last few steps. The trees moved slowly. But who knows, maybe, if necessary, they could run very fast. He heard neither Prann nor the Dragon Master. To Davkaleon, it seemed that the dragon trees looked at his sirrerne with affection and were coming closer to it. No one paid attention to Davkaleon. After a few minutes, a few of the dragon-Trisses lay down on the ground. They were followed by several more. Davkaleon realized that it was time to throw the cover on the cage for a few minutes. If Crassius's dragon was here, he would fall asleep too, and what would Davkaleon do with him then? Davkaleon wandered the Dragon Gardens, alternately taking the cover off the box and putting it back.

Davkaleon came across the symbol of DRAGON accidentally. It was on a rock right in front of him. If Davkaleon wanted to investigate the temple in the rock or Twierks, now was his best opportunity.

"I will quickly go there and come back," thought Davkaleon and walked over to the symbol.

He had heard how during the first visit of the temple, the little Adoleeseet, Chapa uttered the name of the DRAGON symbol in the language of dragons of Adolees. Davkaleon tried to repeat the name, but nothing happened. He'd probably pronounced it incorrectly. Davkaleon made a few more attempts, and the result was the same. He remembered that, becoming a dragon, Chapa put his paw to the column. Davkaleon touched the symbol with his palm, but nothing happened.

"Stop, stop, stop," Davkaleon whispered, correcting himself. It was Elfid who had talked about the word dragon. Chapa, for sure, changed it to the word *DRAGON.*"

Davkaleon imagined the Dragon of Adolees, the word 'DRAGON' and dragon Chapa, all at the same time, uttering the password to enter the depository of the temple. Davkaleon touched the symbol again. Which of these had really worked, Davkaleon did not know, but the passage appeared in front of him. Davkaleon went inside the rock.

After a few steps through a narrow corridor, he found himself in a small room with granite walls and ceiling. The floor seemed to be made of granite also. There was a panel with strange symbols on one wall. However, one symbol was familiar. The golden rose, the symbol of Daeya, sat on the panel in front of him.

Davkaleon went out of the granite building and found himself in a secluded place with unfamiliar trees. No other people were around. A small animal jumped out from behind a tree and ran away. Davkaleon had never seen such an animal before—too many legs. The sky looked different too. It felt as if he was no longer in Daeya. Davkaleon went back and approached the panel. If this symbol meant a return to Daeya, then what did the other symbols mean and where was he? Davkaleon went out of the building again and looked around. He heard voices in the distance, Davkaleon stood motionless behind the nearest big tree. Two strangers approached the granite building. They had a heated discussion in a foreign language. It seemed to be the language of Adoleeseets, although Davkaleon was not sure. Continuing their discussion, the strangers stepped in. Davkaleon was almost sure they were Adoleeseets. Did this mean that he was in Adolees? Moving away from the buildings, Davkaleon reached in his pocket to pull out Chapa's gift.

"What color is your sky?" he asked.

Davkaleon was surprised by Chapa's answer. "Do you mean the color right now? Wait, I'll go take a look."

"Can it be different?" asked Davkaleon.

"Of course, it can be! In your Daeya it is also different. I've seen blue, and gray and even pinkish. Why are you interested in my sky?"

"I'm trying to determine where I am now. I have a suspicion that I'm in Adolees, but I'm not sure."

"In Adolees? Are you serious?" Chapa was glad. "How did you get here?" Rather than waiting for replies, he asked Davkaleon to show him what was around him on the screen of his gift.

"I know this place," said Chapa in a few minutes. "Wait for me, I will be there soon."

The concept of "soon" was very relative for Chapa. Nevertheless, half an hour later, Davkaleon saw a small flying dragon.

"So, how did you get here?" asked Chapius, approaching Davkaleon.

Having retold the story of his appearance in Adolees, Davkaleon added that he was in a bit of a hurry. He needed to return to the gardens of Dragon Master. As Davkaleon had guessed, a panel with strange symbols pointed to the transitions to other places, and the Golden Rose was a transition to Daeya. Having touched the rose, Davkaleon whispered the word *Daeya,* and a passage opened in a granite wall.

Triss dragons in the Gardens of the Dragon Master had

begun to wake up, and Davkaleon immediately removed the cover from the cage with the singing sirrerne. Having walked through the gardens, he saw a familiar web in which something was wrapped.

"Gualtus!" called Davkaleon, but the dragon didn't respond. He slept soundly.

Having thrown the cover on the cage, Davkaleon took his sword and began to sever the web. The web started to twitch and tried to attack Davkaleon, but the singing of sirrerne had an effect on the web as well. It attacked sluggishly and seemed to be half asleep. Davkaleon managed to free Gualtus and put earplugs on him, but the dragon was fast asleep, and Davkaleon could not move him. He sat down, trying to wake Gualtus up.

"What the hell is this?" he heard a growl in the distance.

Davkaleon desperately shook Gualtus.

"Wake up! They have caught Crassius," said Davkaleon, bending to Gualtus's ear.

"They have caught him?" replied Gualtus, not opening his eyes. "You yourself showed me that Crassius is asleep, told me stories that he forgot about me, and now you decide to change your song! You have shown me that Crassius stands near the stairs and is about to fall into your trap, then he sleeps sweetly, having forgotten all about me and now you say that he has been caught. Which is it?"

"Gualtus! It is me, Davkaleon. You're dreaming. Open your eyes and look. Crassius hired me to set you free."

Gualtus laughed. Davkaleon could hear the growling of the Dragon Master approaching. Apparently, the song of the sirrerne did not affect him.

"Well, well, well! Look who has decided to pay us a visit! I've missed you, and as it turns out, you have missed me too! Everyone, come around!" growled the Dragon Master.

The Dragon-Trisses woke up, Gualtus also came to. Having looked at Davkaleon, the dragon grinned and flew upward, but Davkaleon was ready for it, and managed to grab a wing.

"Get off me!" screamed the dragon of Crassius, trying to shake him off.

"Beast! Let me ride you. You have a very large wound in your side, and I will plunge a sword into it if you don't let me sit on your back."

Gualtus calmed down for a few seconds, allowing Davkaleon to sit on his back. Very soon Davkaleon understood why Gualtus became so docile. Red flames erupted from the top of the cave. Davkaleon was wrapped in his Adolgon cloak, but he knew that even the skin of an Adolgon would not protect him for long through such a great wall of fire. Davkaleon had already begun to lose consciousness when he heard the voice of Aleurh.

"I brought you the water of Alatar. Do you feel its freshness? Drink."

"I am having delusions," thought Davkaleon, but opened his eyes. He was sitting on Aleurh, and his faithful dragon was racing up the spiral staircase. Crassius's dragon flew right behind them. After a few minutes, the spiral staircase ended. The translucent door was open. Davkaleon saw Crassius, his brothers and several classmates.

"Keep your ungrateful beast." said Davkaleon to Crassius, pointing to Gualtus flying behind. "As thanks for his liberation, your lizard wanted to fry me.

"Why should he thank you?" shrugged Crassius, no longer desperate or conciliatory. "You have done a job, for which I've paid you."

Chapter 23. Chapa's Prompt Note

Davkaleon was lying on the trestle-bed in his cell in the guardhouse. He felt that this time, his punishment had gone differently somehow. Nobody had given him a lecture or had been indignant at his self-willed absence. Nobody extended his term. They hadn't even locked his cell door. Though he wasn't going to break out yet, it was blatant disorder. Malay came to visit him.

"They are going to expel you. They are preparing papers with the detailed description of what has happened, along with an official letter stating that you are out of control." His brother wrung his hands in despair. "Kvorts went to father. Most of the students at school support you. But Crassius' gang is on the lookout as well."

"To hell with all this, let them do that. I'll create my own army. We will join the force somewhere on the border and will do without this stupid school." Davkaleon answered.

Sergeant Croncoross showed up in the passage and announced. "Davkaleon Gerklat? Go and pack your things. You are out of here. You'll get your official school papers tomorrow. They're not ready today." Having come up to the cell, the sergeant added quietly: "Go to your room, stay there silently and keep out of anyone's sight. Not everyone here wants you expelled."

Davkaleon went along the narrow passage between the cells. Kvorts was waiting for him in his room. "Father went to the Council of the Perfects Priests. He is going to present your case as an attempt to eliminate a future competitor from a family of the Perfects. He is going to emphasize that you had ascended to The *Throne of the Gods*, had received the blessing of the Gods, and had gone

219

down on your own to the Dragon Garden to save your foe's dragon. Father told you to pass along a message—button up your mouth and don't even *think* about speaking. He said that he will skin you alive if you boast about how you don't need this stupid school or start beating your drum about you'll make your own troop and join the border forces. I must say that father knows you very well." Kvorts smiled ironically.

* * * * *

Davkaleon sat once again in his father's spacious office. "Most likely, they will let you stay in school, but you will be transferred to the support team. The *Smart-Aleck Sages* or whatever you call it over there."

"No!!!" Davkaleon was truly horrified.

"Do not yell and listen carefully. The fact they are trying to expel or at least humiliate you is the consequence of your public declaration to become the Commander-in-Chief of Daeya's Army when you ascended to *The Throne of the Gods*. You fight so well that I doubt they will ever challenge you from this side. But you have a vulnerable spot—you don't like studying, and they will try to present you as the future Commander-in-Chief who may bring Daeya to ruin because of your stupidity. Or gullibility. It doesn't matter what they call it, they pursue one goal—to demonstrate that you are not suited to be commander."

He took a deep breath before continuing. "Not everyone at school wants your expulsion, but many are pushing for it. I have spoken with everyone that I could today, both in the *Council of the Priests* and at school. The school has agreed to back down and forget about your expulsion, but only providing that you'll be transferred to the other team."

"No." Davkaleon shook his head stubbornly. "No!"

"If you refuse, the school will appeal to the God's court. That means that you would have to pass tests and tasks, most of which will be in field of Logic, in order to gain favor. To save face, the school would prepare tests that would be difficult for even Elfid to pass, given his gift of knowledge. After that, you would either be transferred forcibly to the support team, or you'd be expelled from the school. The school knows your strengths and weaknesses very well. The tests would sting your weak spots. If you agree to be transferred to the support team, it would decrease your chances of becoming the Commander-in-Chief in an instant, but you'll stay at school. Furthermore, when everyone calms down and things get back in order, we could try to transfer you back. If you choose to take the tests, you have practically no chance of passing them."

"Can you help me pass?"

"They will not let me be any part of preparing the questions, and they will make sure that I don't have prior access to them," Priest Gerklat answered.

"That is not what I mean. I want the same tests to be given to Pompeus and me, and they must be conducted in full view of the school and contain not only questions in Logic but also practical tasks. It would be great if they were questions about Adoleeseets. After I chased the Adoleeseet's dragon on my Aleurh, I learned a lot of unusual things about their manners, habits and behavior. Crassius can't even dream of what I could tell him about Adoleeseets."

"On what grounds would we require Pompeus to take the tests? All of his actions were very logical. He had to free his dragon. He couldn't do it himself because his right hand was injured. He didn't try to hide that he'd hired you and paid you 5000 seekls—or at least, he wrote a receipt where he committed himself to pay.

"And you think that *my actions had no logic, right?*"

"Davkaleon, in your actions, I see the traits of a good man. You didn't go in to kill the foe when he was down during your duel. You and your Aleurh spared Crassius and didn't unsaddle him when you were escaping from the Dragon Gardens. You kept your promise to save his dragon. Being your father, I like these qualities in you." His face turned harder. "But this is not about your human qualities, which could be seen as weakness as a Commander-in-Chief. And from this perspective, I don't see your logic. You were wounded because you believed your foe. You took mercy on a foe who had enticed you into the Dragon Gardens. You received the promissory note, but didn't speak of how you would receive the money."

"What do you mean how to receive the money? Did he have to write down how he would come up to me, take money out of his pocket and give it to me?"

"No, of course, not. But if he pays you back one seekl, or even one tiny sheum a month, it will meet the requirements of your receipt, since it doesn't list a time frame as to when the debt must be paid.

"It has! The note says that if he pays down his debt within one year, interest would not be charged. Otherwise, the amount will increase by 10 percent."

"What does it matter that his debt will increase? How long will it take you to get your money? Let's say, if you get one sheum a month? In about 2000, years the debt amount will reach hundreds of thousands of seekls, and in 5000 years you will be a proud holder of the biggest debt in Daeya. Too bad you won't be able to get your money during your lifetime."

"Do you think he planned that?" Davkaleon was stunned.

"I don't know that. I haven't talked to him, and I cannot identify whether he did that on purpose or not. In the next month, as soon as the first payment approaches, you will know," his father answered.

"Doesn't it count that he used Black Magic during our duel?" Davkaleon asked angrily.

"There is no proof that it was him who used Black Magic. He fell into the Dragon Gardens with you," his father objected.

"And nothing happened to him there! He wasn't tortured, and nobody tried to kill him."

"He was running away with you. And his dragon was left there, so it doesn't prove anything either."

"He knew that Prann and the Lord of the Dragons were interested in blood-brothers from among the Perfects. He told me that himself when he asked me to save his dragon." Davkaleon recounted his conversation with Crassius in the cell.

"He only answered Prann's questions, and that is not prohibited," Priest Gerklat sighed, "but I will try to submit the case in a way to maintain the integrity of the proceedings. It will be necessary to compare your answers and actions with his."

"So, nothing can be done to make him pay me?" Davkaleon asked disappointedly.

"If I were you, I would sell this promissory note to the school bankers. They will find a way to make the debtor pay back in full. You will lose half your money in a best-case scenario, but half a loaf is better than none."

"If my test results are better than his, will they leave me alone?" Davkaleon asked.

"To make them leave you alone, your results must be a cut above that," the priest sighed.

After talking to his father, Davkaleon headed off to

Elfid.

"I'll have to do something nice for Elfid," Davkaleon thought on the way. "Because of those few incidents when I had saved him during our childhood, I've been exploiting him for years and years."

"So, you want to use Chapa's gifts?" Elfid asked after Davkaleon had told him about the forthcoming test.

"Of course! If these transmitters can connect me in Daeya with Chapa in Adolees, they must be able to connect you and me. When you hear the question, think of the answer, and I will hear it."

"What if my answer is wrong?" Elfid began to feel uneasy.

"Look, I am not asking you to answer questions about weapons or fighting methods. I'm able to cope with this kind of question myself. And you know the rest better than any of the goons who'll be making up those tests. When it comes to logic, you can knock everybody else out of the ring."

Having returned to his room, Davkaleon got in touch with his Adoleeseet friend.

"Chapius, I'll have to pass a test tomorrow. One of the questions will be about Adoleeseets, but I'll have to name the source where I picked up this knowledge. I cannot name you as my source, but I do want to tell about my visit to Adolees. What place in Adolees can I mention that is not far from the area where we met yesterday where I could have learned all the things you told me about Adoleeseets?"

"*The Adolees Science Museum,*" Chapa answered, "and don't forget to add that Adoleeseets are the most peaceful people that have ever lived in this world!"

"Well, that is something that I definitely shouldn't mention," Davkaleon chuckled.

* * * * *

The test was held the next day. Crassius Pompeus was outraged that he had been made to take the test along with Davkaleon.

"I come from a military family that has been defending Daeya over the course of centuries! Most of Daeya's Commanders-in-Chief come from my family, and you want to put me to the test to verify whether I am fit for the role of Commander along with this total-nobody attention seeker?"

"You both ascended to *The Throne of the Gods* and received the blessing of the Gods. Later, you both broke the school rules, more than once," the official answered.

The test took place in the big Priest Court. Judges sat on a huge stage, hands folded in their laps. Some of them were from the Military School. Davkaleon didn't know the rest. Perhaps they were priests. Davkaleon recognized his least favorite Logic teacher.

"That one will get under my skin—that's for sure," Davkaleon thought with a frown.

There were two tables in front of the stage. One was for Davkaleon, and another one was for Crassius. Spectators sat a good distance from the stage to prevent them from passing answers to the test-takers. Bookmakers were here as well. It looked like Davkaleon and Crassius had become an endless income stream.

"Isn't it time to begin paying me my commission?" Davkaleon asked, passing by the bookmakers from the A&Z Company. They smirked and gave him a knowing nod.

The first question was asked.

You are offered the position of Commander-in-Chief of Daeya. Your starting salary is 10000 seekls a year. You are also offered two pay raise options. The first option— your wages are raised by 1500 seekls once a year. The second option—your wages are raised for 500 seekls each half year. What option is more advantageous? You have three seconds to think it over.

Without a second thought, Davkaleon was about to write "the first one" but he heard Elfid's voice saying "the second one". Davkaleon was amazed, but followed his brother's advice.

To his surprise, Crassius chose the second answer too.

The second question made Davkaleon pause for a moment.

What page Of the Code of the Military Rules are Daeya's holidays listed on?

"They could not expect us to know exactly what page things are written on." Davkaleon thought and wrote: "On the most important one".

Crassius' answer was, "Such page doesn't exist in the Code of the Military Rules."

The test lasted about two hours. Davkaleon understood very well that without Elfid's, clues he would fail.

"What made you think he had problems with Logic? I don't see any problems." Davkaleon heard the judges whispering.

"Regarding the theory, I've prepared him quite well. He's been attending my lessons, after all." The Logic teacher's voice was louder than the others.

The next part of the test was writing an essay on Adoleeseets. They gave half an hour for this part. The test-takers had to list everything known about Daeya's enemies. Davkaleon smiled to himself, because this was what he had wanted and hoped for. Searching his memory for what the little Adoleeseet Chapa had told him during their first meeting, Davkaleon described the existing order of Adoleeseets community, provided the estimated number of Adoleeseets capable of turning into dragons and told about elite troops of fire-breathing dragons. When Davkaleon read his essay, there was silence in the courtroom, and then someone burst out laughing.

"What tales have you read that in?" one judge asked.

"In the Adolees Science Museum," Davkaleon answered. "And if I am allowed, I can explain my answer."

"Oh dear, will you please do that! It's a little frightening when you imagine that someone with this knowledge is to be entrusted with the Army of Daeya."

"I met the Adoleeseet's dragons when they showed up in my father's estate. The guards started in pursuit of them, and I was among the chasers. The Adoleeseet's dragons flew up in different directions. The one I chased flew to the Death Valley, and I crossed that Valley. I'll omit the parts in my story about fights, mirages, and all the rest. On the opposite side of the valley, the Adoleeseet's dragon turned into an Adoleeseet. He came up to the rock where there was an unknown sign and touched it, whereupon a pass opened in the rock. The Adoleeseet went through it and disappeared. Everything happened very fast. By the moment I got to the rock, both the pass and the sign had disappeared. All this time, I had been thinking I'd seen a mirage, but when I ended up in the Dragon Gardens for the first time, I saw the very same sign. I could not quite focus on researching the sign at that time, since I was being chased by the Triss dragons and the Lord of the Dragons had made it public that he was going to make a cocktail of me and my Aleurh. I had my suspicions that it would lead me to Adolees, but I was not so sure about that. I felt I had to check out my assumption since I had seen with my own eyes how Adoleeseets had shown up and then disappeared, and my theory was that it was our lack of knowledge of Adoleeseets' particularities that makes our fighting with them so inefficient. And when my former foe Crassius asked me for help in saving his dragon, I decided that I would go and kill two birds with one stone. I would research the sign and free Crassius' dragon."

It seems that the judges were listening intently.

"To carry out my plan, I had to render the Triss dragons harmless, somehow. I used the money Crassius handed me in recognition of my victory to buy a sirrerne that lulled the Triss dragons to sleep with her singing. I found the sign and managed to get inside the rock. When I came out of it, I found myself in Adoleeseet. I wrapped myself in my cape, so nobody paid attention to me. There were writings in an unknown language everywhere, and I could see Adoleeseets. One of the buildings turned out to be the *Adoleeseet Science Museum*. I saw a lot of Adoleeseets going into it, so I went in too. The signs for the exhibits were in the Adoleeseet language, and I could not understand them, but there was an unfamiliar item near each sign. I saw how one of the visitors dabbed this item against the sign. So, I did the same and right after that, the signs appearing under the exhibit changed to a few different languages. One of them was the Daeyan language. I learned everything I described in my essay in that museum. I spent several hours studying, and then returned to the Dragon Garden and released Crassius's dragon.

There was silence in the courtroom when Davkaleon

finished telling his story.

"This is absolutely ridiculous! Don't even think we'll believe this nonsense!" one of the judges cried.

"Prove you are not lying!" another one called.

An uproar arose in the room. Those present were arguing and screaming. Someone on the stage called for silence. An argument between judges started. A few minutes later, a hush fell over the room, and one judge announced, "If everything you've just told here is confirmed, you'll be able to stay at school on your team. If all this turns out to be a lie, you'll be expelled, and doing military service in any capacity will be off-limits for you."

"How do you want me to confirm my story?" Davkaleon asked.

"You'll go down into the Dragon Gardens one more time, come up to the mysterious sign and enter the rock in the presence of witnesses. You'll be given a task immediately before your disappearance in the rock. If you fulfill your task, you will meet with the *Priests of the Truth*. If they decide you're telling the truth, we will consider that you've confirmed your story."

"No! It's too dangerous!" cried Priest Gerklat.

But Davkaleon interrupted his father.

"I will do it." he stated.

Chapter 24. Journey to Adolees

Davkaleon was back in the Dragon Gardens. This time, there were several priests with him, including his father and a few school teachers. Davkaleon found the sign to the entrance fairly easily. It pointed the way inside the rock.

"This is Adolees money," one of the priests advised. "To prove that your story is true, you'll have to buy a few Adolees toys. It is desirable that there should be a doll among them which looks like an Adoleeseet child or an Adoleeseet dragon. Oh, and, I can't forget, bring back some food. Any type of Adoleeseet food will do."

Davkaleon went inside the rock. Having taken a few steps along the narrow corridor, he ended up in a small room with granite walls and ceiling. On one of the walls, there was a panel with unknown symbols. Chapa was waiting for Davkaleon in the room.

It must be said that Chapa had grown, and the childish nicknames of Chapa and ChapaShka no longer suited him. The name *Chapius* seemed just right. According to Chapius, the granite protected them from being overheard. No one could hear their conversations nor their thoughts from hear.

"What do they want from you?" Chapius asked.

Davkaleon told him about his tasks and got out the Adoleeseet money. "This money is all right, but this coin looks strange," Chapius said. "It may be part of a trick. You have quite a sizeable amount of money here. Just to be safe, do not pay with this coin, to avoid accusations of fraud. You better take out several coins and offer the shop man to choose money himself. After you've bought your toys, we'll go to the restaurant. This restaurant belongs to my sister's friend's father. Once I had a dream about the restaurant and told my sisters. They liked the dream, and created a trio—*ChapaShka's Sisters*. When you leave the restaurant, you can grab some dessert to take with you. By the way, when you're in the restaurant, they chase visitors to make steaks out of them. Stay still and don't run away. It is a part of the show, and any howling people displaying wounds or burns are hired actors."

They came out of the granite facility at the far end of a wild Adolees park. Chapius walked ahead. As they had agreed, Davkaleon acted like he didn't know the little Adoleeseet. Having left the park, Chapius headed toward the side street and entered a small toy shop. The Adoleeseet said something to the seller and stepped away. The seller put a doll in front of Davkaleon which looked like a cute little Adoleeseet with wayward, bluish tinted hair. The toy closely matched with what he had brought to Daeya. The seller pressed a button and the next second the baby-Adoleeseet' face fell, its body elongated, and wings appeared. The baby-Adoleeseet turned into a small dragon.

Davkaleon nodded. Such a toy could have been made only in Adolees. Following his friend's advice, he held out several coins and the seller picked up the needed amount. Pointing at one of the coins, the seller shook his head in disapproval, confirming the assumption that the coin was false. Having left the shop, Davkaleon followed Chapius, who was walking in front of him. Near the entrance to the restaurant, a merry song sounded.

Davkaleon came into the restaurant. *Dragon Kosherat* offered dinner with a show. Visitors settled themselves at the tables. The lights blazed, and Chapa's sisters flew out on the stage. They danced and sang beautifully. On the dining floor, the waiters served appetizers. After a short break, the sisters continued their performance, and the waiters started serving the main dish—well-done steak. Davkaleon enjoyed the tempting aromas. When nearly all the diners had received their steaks, *ChapaShka's Sisters* turned into dragons and singed everyone with fire. Having sprung from their seats, a few visitors scurried for the exits, screaming and holding their burns.

ChapaShka's Sisters returned to their usual shape and went on singing merry songs. The show was ending, and the waiters served the dessert. Chapius must have given them a heads up, because a few minutes later, one of the waiters put a small box in front of Davkaleon, apparently for the dessert. Paying for dinner, again, Davkaleon, took out several coins, one of them was returned to him. It was time to go back to Daeya.

This time, Davkaleon led the way, and Chapius followed at a distance. Davkaleon was already at the entrance to the park when three Adoleeseets approached, wearing uniforms. They demanded something that Davkaleon didn't understand. He was already about to take out a couple of swords, when Chapius approached Davkaleon and three men in uniform who suddenly looked exactly like Davkaleon.

"Well, we are not even allowed to practice turning into the Daeyats?" Chapa said aggrievedly putting on his regular shape.

"I know you," one of the trio said. "You are the one who has been to Daeya. What are you doing here?"

"They gave us a task at school to prepare something unusual for the Transformation lesson. My friend and I decided to portray the Daeyats. I trained myself to do it quite fast, but he needs a whole half-hour to transform."

"Ah, not a true Adoleeseet." One of those three in the uniform waved his hand disgustedly at Davkaleon. "Why are you mixing with him? There are so many true

232

Adoleeseets around, and you've chosen the phony-boloney."

"That is exactly why I've chosen a phony-boloney, because none of the true Adoleeseets want to turn into a Daeyan vandal, and I desperately need a Daeyat to portray a combat in Daeya." Chapius explained.

The three in uniform lost any interest in Davkaleon and after talking with Chapius for a few minutes, they left.

"A Daeyan vandal?!" Davkaleon asked indignantly as soon as he and Chapius went inside the granite room.

"Do not be mad," Chapius sighed. "Here in Adolees, this is how we refer to the Daeyats. If I spoke differently, the patrol would suspect something and would request to show them your identification papers."

"All right then," Davkaleon groused.

* * * * *

"This is a toy baby-Adoleeseet," Davkaleon said, passing the purchased toy to the Daeyan priests. "And now it is transforming into a dragon," Davkaleon added, pressing the hidden button a few minutes later.

"Davkaleon took the box out of his pocket that contained the dessert and several coins that he had left over from his trip. "This coin is false. Nobody wanted to take it," Davkaleon said, pointing at the coin.

"How did you manage to avoid being accused of dealing false money?" one of the priests asked.

"I took out several coins at a time and asked the seller to pick the payment himself." Davkaleon explained.

The priests enquired further about each step Davkaleon had taken, but the toy baby-Adoleeseet–dragon had convinced them. After several exhausting hours of telling stories, repeating the same things again and again, questions and interrogations, one of the priests demanded that Davkaleon describe everything that had happened to him in the reverse sequence, starting from the moment he had returned to Daeya. Davkaleon was surprised, but fulfilled the demand. Then, the priests who managed the Military School and school teachers waved Davkaleon away and then started a discussion. It didn't last long.

"You are staying at the Military School and on your current team," the Military School headmaster announced. "We think you have confirmed your story, but you also will have to write a detailed report."

* * * * *

The whole school gathered at the public reading of the verdict of Davkaleon's fate.

His brothers and his loyal Aleurh were the first ones who came up to him. Krilis was next. "Do you want me to write the report for you?" Krilis asked.

"Of course!" Davkaleon was excited. "Just explain to me why you want to do this?"

"What do you mean why? You are the first Daeyat who has been to Adolees. If I write this report, I will become the first Daeyat who has written about your trip to Adolees!" Krilis answered.

A crowd of students surrounded Davkaleon. From behind, he heard someone ask Crassius a question. "Are you going to pay him back over the next two years?"

"Of course, I am. One sheum a month. The truth of the matter is that it will take more than two years to pay off the debt."

So that's it! I'll show you what is what! Davkaleon thought. He suddenly found himself looking forward to his deal with the school bankers.

"I usually pay 50 percent of the note's face value, but this promissory note will make it difficult to collect your debt, so the most that I can pay you is 10 percent. I offer that because the names of famous Daeyan families appear in the note," the banker said, examining the note that Davkaleon had brought.

Davkaleon was disappointed, and didn't hide his feelings.

"Others wouldn't even give you this much," the banker said. Since your visit to Adolees, you've become famous. Even if I can't collect your debt within a reasonable time, I will be able to sell this paper to collectors after some time. But I'll have to wait until you become the Commander-in-Chief. Otherwise, who would pay this much for a piece of worthless paper?"

Selling the promissory letter to a collector? That was an unexpected turn. Davkaleon had never thought of that himself. If that was possible, the note was worth more than 10 percent.

"30 percent," Davkaleon said firmly.

"12 percent," the banker answered.

They bargained for quite a long time. Davkaleon managed to get the banker to settle on paying 20 percent of the note's face value.

"So, this scumbag will elude payment?" Malay and Kvorts raged after Davkaleon had told them the story about the promissory note.

"Father advised me to sell the note to the school bankers. He said that otherwise, I'd be getting my money back in minuscule amounts for the rest of my life. I'd be lucky to get a measly one sheum a month. I would like to have a school feast on the Oath Day with the money I get from the banker. Just imagine how great it will sound!

Banquet by Davkaleon Gerklat. Everyone will have a great time! It's a shame I'm badly off. I am not sure the 1000 seekls I got from the banker will be enough."

"Or better yet, *Banquet by the Gerklat Brothers.* I still have some money left that I received from Crassius." Malay felt inspired.

"Are you sure you want to spend money feeding and entertaining everyone?" Kvorts had doubts.

"I am! I want to become a Commander-in-Chief. If I want everyone to vote for me, they must know that I am not a cheapskate. They must trust that with me at the helm, everyone will be fed!"

Malay added, "The Commander-in-Chief is supposed to have deputies, and who fits that description better than us?"

"Well, if that's the case, then *Banquet by the Gerklat Brothers* sounds great to me. I got 400 seekls from Crassius too," Kvorts said.

"The total sum is 1700 seekls," Malay summarized. "Will this be enough?"

"Let's go to the *Mug and Sword* and find out." Davkaleon suggested.

"A banquet for the whole school? Brilliant idea!" the waiter declared, calling for the manager right away.

"1700 seekls would be enough for a modest banquet for the whole school. But a banquet by the first Daeyat to visit Adolees and the next Commander-in-Chief of the Daeyan Army should throw a banquet that the whole school would remember for many years to come. And the two next Commander-in-Chief's deputies should support him." the manager of *Mug and Sword* explained confidently.

The Gerklat brothers liked the idea, but liking something didn't make them any richer.

"What are we going to do?" Kvorts asked, looking at his

brothers.

They sat in the dining hall as honored guests while they discussed the arrangements with the manager. They had made up their minds, and didn't want to give up on the idea of a banquet that the whole school would remember for years.

"I am sure that we could find someone to borrow money from," Malay said, voicing everyone's feeling.

"Well, borrowing is not the problem. Payback is the part that can be tricky," Kvorts reasoned. The manager knocked at the door, and in the next breath, showed up in front of the brothers.

"If you have problems with money, I can arrange a meeting with a banker who provide loans for the school. The conditions are quite favorable, especially for you. Who would want to be at odds with future Commander-in-Chief and his deputies? Anyone would be happy to furnish you with the money," the manager claimed in all sincerity.

A banker with money in hand appeared in less than no time.

"It's very simple, he said. "Sign these promissory notes. The terms are fabulous. You won't have any problems paying them back. After the visit to Adolees, you guys can't even imagine how many orders you will have! You will have so much, money you won't know what to do with it!"

The manager from the *Mug and Sword* brought big goblets with fizzy drinks on the house and proposed a toast to the most sumptuous banquet that had ever taken place at school. The brothers drank up, and in no time, they felt a little buzzing behind the ears. The banker and the manager kept talking on and on. Listening to the manager's praises, and directed by the banker, the Gerklat brothers signed their promissory notes.

* * * * *

"Who remembers what we signed yesterday?" Kvorts asked his brothers the next day.

"Did we sign anything?" Malay seemed surprised.

It became clear they had signed something as soon as the brothers came into the classroom for their first lesson. Congratulations and thanks poured in from the very threshold. In every classroom and corridor, there were posters on the walls *Banquet by the Gerklat brothers. Everyone is sure to have a great time!*

Chapter 25. They have gambled and finished badly

Having heard a knock at the door, Davkaleon's father looked up from the papers on the table and snapped his fingers toward the door. The venerated banker and the loan shark-bloodsucker, as he was dubbed by his customers, went into the room and handed the priest a few invoices. Priest Gerklat raised his eyebrows when he looked at the amounts.

"They had a very good time," said Priest Gerklat, placing his seal on the words *for payment.*

Having turned to his secretary, the priest added: "At the nearest day of parental tenderness, remind me to punch the ear of each of these three hooligans of mine. These newly minted cadets have managed to spend a thousand Daeyan seekls on drink and spree! On the eve of the party they were, as I understand it, debating whether to invite partygoers exclusively from Assa. Why would they limit such an affair? Why not invite all of Daeya?"

A few days earlier, his three sons at the military school passed the procedure of *Taking the Oath*, received the title of cadets, and happily went to celebrate a significant event at the *Mug and Sword*, where according to tradition, all the newly minted cadets celebrated such events. Judging by the size of the invoices that their father could see, Davkaleon, Malay and Kvorts had celebrated the event thoroughly and with panache.

Priest Gerklat heard another knock at the door. A second visitor brought the papers from the schools where the offspring of the priest were studying. The first quarter of the school year was over, and the priest wanted to see what he'd paid for. Studying at Daeyan schools was not cheap. Having seen the grade marks of Paradion, who

239

studied at the school of high priests, Gerklat nodded contentedly. Elfid had the highest marks in all subjects.

"How does he manage to do it?" the priest asked himself.

Then, he looked at the grades for the trio at the military school.

"What the hell is this?" he whispered, indignant. "Can't these idiots cope with peasants?"

"They can cope with simple peasants," helpfully answered the one that brought the papers with grades to the priest, "they can't cope with compound peasants and interest."

"Oh, they have problems with compound peasants and interest, haven't they? Now they will not have. The next two weeks the trio will learn well what compound interest is."

* * * * *

"Give me their promissory note," demanded Gerklat, facing the banker. "You'll get your payment from them. Don't forget to accrue compound interest to the sum daily. Young men should understand compound interest, especially if they intend to pay a thousand seekls for a dinner at a tavern."

Gerklat added that banker should report to him the size of their debt on a weekly basis. "The last thing that I need is to become bankrupt because of these imbeciles."

* * * * *

Priest Gerklat's military trio returned to the *Mug and Sword*. They had just returned from a patrol and felt a craving for lamb. The Gerklat brothers intended to enjoy a delicious dinner before returning to school. Within minutes, the innkeeper came to the brothers and asked how they were going to pay for dinner.

"Write a promissory note. You will give it to our banker and get the money," Malay said.

"Your banker informed me that he does not intend to pay your promissory notes," sighed the innkeeper, demanding payment in cash.

The brothers had difficulties with cash. Father had given cash to each of them, but the time had passed when the sum was enough. The money had evaporated instantly upon receipt. The brothers, however, had quickly adapted to writing promissory notes, which their father regularly paid. But the most recent promissory note seemed to be the last straw for the respected priest.

Having rummaged in their pockets, the trio extracted some change from their pockets, but it wasn't even enough for a half of the smallest lamb, not to mention the one they had ordered.

"I'll bring you a plate of porridge, even add a chop to it, but forget about a lamb," the innkeeper said. He clearly didn't want to quarrel with his clients. Over his long life, the innkeeper learned that every cadet goes through rough times, but then a cadet becomes an officer and perhaps a senior officer, and the hard times would disappear. A successful officer would return to the *Mug and Sword* again and again.

Porridge with a chop was, of course, not a lamb, but it was better than nothing. It was already late, and the conversation with the banker would be postponed for tomorrow. The next day began the weekend, so they would have to postpone their conversation even further. On the first working day after the lessons, the brothers went to the banker to find out why he had planted them this pig. They didn't even consider that their father had refused to pay their bills.

"It cannot be!" The brothers sang a chorus of amazement in response to the assertions of the banker that their father had finally put his foot down.

"I told you we had to negotiate with the innkeeper and pay for a few weeks," Kvorts sighed.

"It would have been unlikely to help," said the banker. "Your father got very mad when your grade card made it clear that you had problems with compounded interest."

"So, it was because of the last test! We should have declined the card game the night before the test and read the textbook," sighed Kvorts.

"That could have helped," agreed the banker.

"But we had a good card game! We won! And the total score was in our favor. Now, no one at school will say that we failed because of a lousy test," Davkaleon pointed out.

"And what will you do with this bill?" asked Kvorts.

"Don't panic," shrugged Davkaleon. "There are tons of ads on the bulletin boards in Assa requiring strong guys to work. We'll earn the money."

"What is the interest rate on our debt?" asked Kvorts.

"Only ten percent," replied the banker. "That's a mere trifle. I am not a bloodsucker."

"You see? And you were worried!" Davkaleon clapped his brother on the shoulder.

"Is it per year or per month?" asked Kvorts.

"It is per day," calmly replied the banker.

"What?! So how much do you want per day? A hundred seekls a day for one lousy thousand! You will triple your capital this way!" Kvorts cried.

"As I see, you have problems, and not only with compounded interest. You do not handle with simple interest either," grinned the banker.

"What makes you think so?" Davkaleon asked.

242

"Well, you see, when one of you says I'll triple my capital for a month, he apparently believes that one hundred seekls a day for thirty days will bring me three thousand. But a thousand of them is my loss. So, I won't triple but only double my capital. But in this case, it doesn't matter, because I didn't say that you would pay a hundred seekls a day. I said that you'd pay ten percent per day, and these are different things."

"How much do you want?" squinted Davkaleon.

"If you repaid the debt the same day when you took it, I would have charged you ten percent and this sum would be equal to one hundred seekls. But you did not repay, so on the second day the debt of each of you was equal to one thousand one hundred of seekls, and ten percent is equal to one hundred and ten seekls. On the third day, your debt became equal to one thousand two hundred ten seekls, and ten percent is equal to one hundred twenty-one additional seekls. Today is the fifth day. You owe me one thousand four hundred sixty-four seekls. As I understand you don't have it, by tomorrow, one hundred and forty-six seekls will be added to your debt and your debt will be equal to one thousand six hundred and ten seekls. Here is the table of your debt growth per month at a ten percent rate per day. Please note, I do not consider sheums and round numbers in your favor everywhere. Very few bankers do such a favor to their customers, but I'm an exceptionally kind person and eager to meet my client's needs."

With these words, the banker handed the table to each of the numb brothers.

"Kind person? Do you call robbery kindness?" Davkaleon raged, looking at the table.

Kvorts and Malay kept silence. They seem to be shocked by what they had heard.

243

Of course, I'm a kind person!" the banker's voice sounded completely sincere. "First of all, I always allow customers to return the debt in parts, and this greatly facilitates the payment of interest. Only a few of the bankers agree to such concessions. Secondly, if you'd come to me on the first day and said that you wanted to pay me one hundred seekls for a late payment of the debt, I would have agreed to it. Your debt, in fact, could be a daily updated short-term debt with a simple percent. All you needed was to bring me one hundred seekls every day, and you could continue, *to the end of your life*. Third, you did not pay attention to the fact that I have rounded sheums in your favor. You did not do it in vain. Look at the third day on the table. There should be one hundred thirty-three seekls and ten sheums, but I have not added sheums to the calculations. By the way, I did the same on the fourth day."

"You are kidding," said Malay and his eyes narrowed ominously.

"Not a bit," answered the banker seriously, "here is the table with the numbers, where sheums are added to the calculations. Compare the results in ten years. You know that debtors often do not pay the debt for ten and twenty years and even longer? See the difference with rounding and without it. This is your formula for the different terms, interest and conditions. However, all this can be found in your textbooks. If you opened them instead of playing card games, you would know all that."

"Do you mean that terms and percent can be changed?" asked Kvorts.

"The terms and percent should be negotiated in the beginning. At this late date, there's nothing I can do about them," sighed the banker. "I need to return my money somehow. Repayment of three thousand seekls from my pocket is not a joke. I am a poor man, and it is a lot of money for me."

"Why is it money from your pocket?" asked Malay. "You're the banker, so it should be the money from the bank."

What are you saying?" The banker rolled his eyes in horror and put his hands to his heart. "If I make a payment to the bank that is even one day late, all my property will be seized. I would lose my job and would be naked and bare. And I, incidentally, have a family that I need to feed."

"So, do we have to feed your family now?" said Kvorts, but Malay interrupted him.

"Wait, Kvorts, I want to understand how it works. If we owe you, then what does the bank have to do with it?" asked Malay.

"What does the bank have to do with it? Well, who would give me a license?" asked the banker. "I buy the license from the bank, which in turn buys a license to sell licenses to customers."

"What happens to those debtors who refuse to pay interest?" asked Malay with a frown on his face.

"Then the debtors deal with the bank and believe me, I don't envy them."

"So, what does the bank do? It sells you a license to rip-off, and the rest is your problem?"

"Were you dropped from the moon? The conditions of each transaction are described in detail, the bank receives a percentage of each sheum, seekl and talan that I receive from clients. More accurate to say that the bank gets the majority of the sum, and I get a commission. I have to pay taxes, license, and voluntary donations to the temple from this percentage. Voluntary! Imagine if I tried not to pay! And this, despite the fact that I give the loans out of my pocket, and if the debtor refuses to pay or if he hides, then the cost of searching, capture and persuasion is out of my pocket also."

"I'm almost crying about your unhappy life," Malay mocked.

"Okay, we have learned everything we needed to know. Let's get out of here," suggested Davkaleon, heading to the door.

"How are we going to pay?" asked Kvorts, as soon as the brothers were outside.

"There was a proposal to strangle the banker or to stab him with a sword. Or we could unscrew his head," replied Malay.

"Quit fooling around," said Kvorts. "Who'd have thought it, that father would refuse to pay? You will ask your mother for help. She is from one of the richest families of Daeya. Repayment would be a little thing for her. And Davkaleon won't have trouble paying—his mommy will pay. But my mother doesn't know where to get that kind of money."

"Kvorts, do not try to squeeze a tear out of us," grinned Malay. "The way your Mama can shake money out of our father? The rest of our mothers should take lessons!"

"What else could she do?" Kvorts protested. "She has no other place to get money from. She doesn't have rich parents, like your mothers do. On the contrary, she has to help her relatives."

"If it makes you feel any better, I can assure you that I'm not going to ask my mother for money," intervened Davkaleon. "She would not refuse me. She'll give me money, but in return, she will require me to visit the school of the *History of the Gods of Perfects* in my free time. This is in addition to the school of the old language of Daeya. Did anyone try to brainwash you with their history?"

"And what's so terrible about the history of the *Gods of Perfects?*" Kvorts asked. "You probably don't remember that the teacher at father's estate told us their legends. It was even interesting."

"The legends that the teacher told us in the estate sounded like fairy tales, and it was good entertainment. Those that mother made me study? A real nightmare. The chronology of all kings of Daeya with dates of their birth and ascension to the throne, the story of their deeds and achievements, old laws of Daeya, of course, in the old-Daeyan language, the words of their Gods, kings and priests, of course, again in the old-Daeyan language. And finally, the old Daeyan language itself. Add to that their rituals, traditions and rules, and you'll understand why I always hung around on the street in the morning, far away from my beloved mother. So, I assure you, I will get the money from somewhere, but I won't ask my mother for it. So, let's see what jobs we can do," suggested Davkaleon, heading to the trading square of Assa. Jobs were not a problem. The Bulletin Board near the square was full of announcements. A lot of people wanted to hire strong guys, able to cope with someone or something. The problem was with payment. The proposed payments would only cover a small percentage of what they needed.

Chapter 26. Notes of the Jeweler

Having entered his room, Davkaleon saw a dark goblin sitting on his bed. Davkaleon immediately remembered the story that the little goblin Andibraksh had told about the war with dark goblins.

"Get out of my room!" Davkaleon demanded, hoisting the goblin and dropping him to the floor.

"Don't be angry. I brought you the money so you can pay your debt," said goblin. His voice was as pleasant as goblins were able to muster.

"Why do you worry about my debt?" grinned Davkaleon.

"You need money, and I need your services. For your services, I will pay you very well. You will be able to pay off the banker quickly."

"Ha! I will pay off the banker, and immediately fall into bondage to you."

"Why do you think so? I'll pay you ten thousand seekls, and I'll give you a half right now. No tricks! And my request is quite trivial. All you have to do is bring me a note written by one jeweler," the goblin insisted.

"Where will I get this note?"

"I'll tell you everything, show you a map and explain everything," said the goblin.

"If you know all of this, why don't you get it yourself? Don't you want to keep your ten thousand seekls?" Davkaleon did not believe in goblin generosity.

"I know how to get to the place where the note is hidden, but I can't take it. It is sealed with the sign of the Perfect Dragon of Daeya. Neither I, nor any other goblin can open this sign, so I need you.

"Why do you think I will be able to open it?" surprised Davkaleon.

"Because you belong to the few who are able to do it. Only the Perfects of Daeya, who has gone through a rite of initiation into the blood-brother with a dragon of Daeya, can see the sign of the Perfect Dragon of Daeya.

Davkaleon was suddenly very interested.

"Show me this sign," demanded Davkaleon.

"It is the sign that opened your way to enter Adolees," explained the goblin as he showed him the sign on the map.

The goblin's description of the sign of the "Perfect Dragon of Daeya" caused strong doubt in Davkaleon. It was the sign that Elfid had shown little Chapa in the dungeon of the tower. Next, Davkaleon saw it in the Dragon's Gardens. Elfid and the little Adoleeseet called it the sign of DRAGON.

Davkaleon remembered the explanation of a little Adoleeseet about dragon, Dragon and DRAGON. *It seems that the goblin doesn't understand that this symbol does not refer to the dragon of Daeya.*

"I'll have to think about it. Leave my room now." said Davkaleon, stretching out on his bed.

"I'll leave you a map. Look at it after you rest. It would only take you a few hours, and you would receive ten thousand seekls. Please consider the offer," said the goblin in farewell.

Davkaleon thought the payment would be nice. More than nice, he was desperate for it! He was eager to get rid of the banker, but he really didn't want to deal with a goblin, especially a dark goblin.

Lying on the bed, Davkaleon thought about the sign of DRAGON. He was convinced that the sign had nothing to do with a dragon of Daeya. What is the sign of the DRAGON of Adolees doing in Daeya?

Wondering what to do about the offer from the dark

goblin, Davkaleon dozed off, but not for long. Someone sneezed, and Davkaleon opened his eyes. *My room is turning into a public thoroughfare*, he thought. He wondered if anyone paid attention to a locked door, or did locks on doors mean nothing in Daeya? The face of his uninvited guest seemed familiar to Davkaleon. The man started speaking, and Davkaleon remembered where he had seen him. But this could not be! He'd seen firsthand the death of the seller of magical goods at the meeting with DRAGON of Adolees. Yet, here he was.

"You need money and I need goods. There is high demand for magical artifacts now. The path is dangerous, but I'll pay you well. Here are five thousand seekls. They're yours if you get me what I need."

"We will discuss the price later," interrupted Davkaleon. "Tell me what you need. The stone of Alatar is magical, but I will not get it for you."

"What are you saying?" The seller of magical goods seemed horrified. "I have never mentioned the stone of Alatar! What I need is situated inside the Rock cliff, and it is associated with the *Notes of Piromis.*"

"I have never heard of those. What are these notes?" asked Davkaleon.

"These are the notes of a jewelry maker. There is no master equal to him, and there never has been. He made a few magical items. He worked inside the Rock cliff. He kept detailed records of his work. The records have been encrypted and hidden in a secure location far from the Rock. I am interested in you finding the Notes of Piromis, and then his masterpieces. But for now, I won't speak of that. All I ask now is that you get inside the Rock and find me a small note with numbers."

Davkaleon was interested. It looked as though the dark goblin and the seller of magical goods were after the same thing.

"And how will I get inside?" asked Davkaleon. "Will I dive from high above, as do the swimmers during the competition?" Davkaleon referred to the annual competitions of cliff diving from the Rock, which was an ancient tradition in Daeya. Few had survived this competition, but the winner instantly became a hero in Daeya—his name was revered with honor and glory for a lifetime. Along with this prestige came gifts, a large monetary prize and a Golden Rose—the symbol of Daeya. Davkaleon often dreamed of participating in this competition. He knew that there was a cave at the foot of the Rock cliff. The divers swam inside and rose up to another cave, where they had the opportunity to catch their breath and float up. However, that cave was no secret. Everyone in Daeya knew about that trick.

"There are several ways inside the Rock cliff. Jumping off the cliff is one of them," said the seller.

"I can dive," Davkaleon said confidently, "but so many swimmers visit that cave. If something was hidden there, it would have been found long ago. Why do you think that the hidden note is still there?"

"Because in addition to the two caves at the foot, there are many secret areas inside the rock. I have a map of secret passages. If you agree to help me, I'll give you one."

"You offer me five thousand seekls. Why can't you just hire any athlete who dives? He would deliver the note for a much lower payment." asked Davkaleon.

"The place where the note is hidden is marked with a secret sign. Very few can see this sign. Fewer can open it."

"So, you think that I am capable of this?"

The seller nodded. He didn't name the secret sign nor the sign of the DRAGON of Adolees, nor the sign of the Perfect Dragon of Daeya, but Davkaleon was certain which sign he spoke of.

"Let's talk about the price," said Davkaleon. "You will pay me ten thousand seekls, half now and the other half after I will bring you the note."

"That is a robbery," protested the seller. "What if you die, or don't find what I need?"

"If I die, your money dies with me." said Davkaleon harshly.

"And what if you don't find it?" asked the seller.

"I will keep the first payment. I do not want to stick my neck out for nothing when it is possible that the note had been found a long time ago, and the records of the jeweler had already been read."

They negotiated for a long time, and finally, Davkaleon said, "Bear in mind, you're not the only one who is interested in this note. I had a visit from the goblin who offered ten thousand seekls for it."

"It can't be," gasped the seller. "You went to see about a job on the Bulletin Board of Assa."

"I did. So what? I am not too interested in working with goblins, but I need money, so I can change my mind."

"Okay, deal." gave in the seller. "When are you going to go?"

"After taking a few swimming lessons. I can swim and dive, of course, but I've never tried to dive on the bottom near the Rock." said Davkaleon.

"Here is the map and that is the sign that will lead you to the note of Piromis." the merchant said, handing over the map. "This Sign consists of two characters. One character represents Daeya, and the second represents the dragon of Daeya." explained the seller.

Davkaleon looked at the sign. It was different from the goblin's sign.

After the seller left, Davkaleon compared the two

maps. The paths to the given symbols were different, but they led to one place. Davkaleon, of course, knew about the Golden Rose of Daeya. Surprisingly, though it was the symbol of Daeya, the roses grew only in Arragorra. With winds and hurricanes in Daeya, it would have not survived in any other place in the country. The weather in Arragorra was always calm and sunny with only the gentlest, most pleasant breeze. They say that in the ancient times such weather was everywhere in Daeya. Maybe the roses once bloomed throughout Daeya.

* * * * *

"That's it? He is going to pay you five thousand seekls for such an easy task?" the brothers were in for a surprise when Davkaleon came over to tell them that the next day they would be out of debt.

Davkaleon nodded and patted his plump purse. He could hardly hide his overwhelming pride. He found pleasure feeling himself a hero, who could solve any problem within a few hours.

"So, you want to take swimming lessons to dive to the very bottom just like sportsmen do?" Kvorts asked. "I want to take swimming lessons too. Pay for me now, and I'll square accounts with you as soon as I get some earnings. This is my chance. If I win the competition, I'll become a hero of Daeya. Otherwise, I'll always live in your shadow and I will be referred to as *Davkaleon's brother*."

Davkaleon turned to Malay and asked: "Do you want to take these lessons too?"

"I don't mind taking a few lessons and going with you. Since both the goblin and merchant need this note, somebody may try to take it away from you after you've found it. Kvorts and I will help protect your find. The competitions of Daeya don't really tickle my fancy. If Kvorts is interested in competitions, then full steam ahead! He won't find a rival in me."

"Thank you!" Kvorts brightened up and turned to Davkaleon. "And how about you? Do you want to take part in competitions, too?"

Davkaleon hesitated. He *did* want to. He had been thinking about doing so well before the goblin and merchant's order. He had always wanted to see himself as a winner everywhere in any and every event. But Kvorts was looking at him with pleading eyes and Malay added, "Davkaleon, you've had enough accolades with the *Throne of the Gods* and being the discoverer of the path to Adolees. Leave something to Kvorts."

"All right. I won't participate." Davkaleon sighed.

A smile spread over Kvorts' face.

"And what do you want for yourself?" Davkaleon asked Malay.

"I'm interested in financing the search for wizzy artifacts and selling them, cutting out the middlemen. If both the goblin and the merchant are ready to pay thousands of seekls for a piece of paper, then how much could I get for those magic crafts? As you know, my mother is from one of the richest Daeya's families. If I manage to talk my relatives into investing money in this campaign, we could make good profit from it. Thanks to my military training, I would be able to protect those magical treasures quite well, especially with your help."

The same thoughts had flashed in Davkaleon's head from time to time. Kvorts found the idea appealing too.

"By the way, what are you going to tell the goblin?" Malay asked.

"I'll tell him I've found another way to make money." Davkaleon answered.

"I wouldn't do that. Take the money and make a copy of the note. None of them laid it down as a condition that you have to work exclusively for him," Malay advised.

"And what will I do when they both order the jeweler's manuscripts and then the gems themselves?" Davkaleon asked.

"Well, you'll figure out what to do when they put in their orders. For example, you can read the manuscripts before giving them away and you can lay your hands on that jewelry stuff, and then you'll set up an auction." Malay answered.

* * * * *

"Where did they get so much money?" Priest Gerklat wondered when the banker reported that the priest's sons had completely settled their debt.

"They told me they took the best bite of the plum playing cards. Well, I didn't really believe them." The banker smiled ironically.

"What have those three gotten involved in?" Gerklat mused.

"I don't know what they've got involved in, but I know they have all signed up for Master Gandall's swim classes."

"The best sportsmen's trainer? Have they decided to participate in the Acompetitions of Daeya?"

The news that the Gerklat brothers had signed for Master Gandall's classes spread quickly through the school.

"Have you made up your mind to take part in the competitions of Daeya?" each and every student asked Davkaleon the following day.

"No, not me, Kvorts will. Malay and I are going to take

a few lessons with Kvorts to keep things interesting." Davkaleon answered.

Following Malay's advice, Davkaleon notified the goblin that he would take the job and his wallet was replenished with an additional five thousand seekls. Davkaleon thought it was a good time to check up on Elfid.

"What would you like to have most of all?" Davkaleon asked, drawing out his heavy wallet and carelessly tossing it on the table with a gesture of a generous giver.

"Wow, where did you get all this?" Elfid asked.

"I've been exploiting you for free for a quite long time, it's time to pay my debts," Davkaleon laughed. He told Elfid about the job that he had obtained.

"So, you are going to take payment from both the goblin and the merchant, are you?" Elfid asked.

"I already have!" Davkaleon answered proudly.

"Davkaleon! That's a bad idea. This note may have a secret. For instance, mysterious words may appear when heated. Or some sign may show up when processed with juice of the Triss. Each of your customers is looking to get an original, and you are going to clap on a fake to one of them."

"This had to be specified in advance. None of them mentioned the original," Davkaleon objected.

"But none of them said he needed notes copied from the original paper, right?" Elfid replied.

"Anyway, what do you want? Money? Some rare thing?" Davkaleon tried to drop the subject.

"I'll make a list of things I'd like to have. You can't buy them in regular stalls in Daeya, but you may come across other things I'm interested in during your travels. Just keep in mind that things I need will be costly for you," Elfid smirked.

* * * * *

Two weeks later, the Gerklat brothers dove to the very bottom of the ocean for the first time. Having regained their breath, they came to the surface.

"Tomorrow, I'm finishing my trainings," Malay said. "I will be able to dive to the bottom and then come up, and it doesn't matter how long it will take me, since I'm not going to take part in the competition."

"Well, I will keep on training. I can already dive to the bottom, but Gandall says that if I use the underwater waterfall, it will bring me to the bottom much quicker," Davkaleon pointed out.

Speaking of the underwater waterfall, Davkaleon referred to *Tartrar*. Everyone in Daeya knew about the waterfall Tartrar. The top of the waterfall was 50 meters from the surface of the cliff Rock. However, it was not always so. It depended on the time of day where the waterfall began. During the highest tide, waves rolled over the cliff Rock, and the waterfall began 50 meters from the surface of the rock. During the lowest tide, the waves barely reached the middle of the rock. A thick spray hung over them with white foam. A silvery-white mist enveloped the rock. If viewed from the side, the rock wasn't even visible—just a white swirling haze. Then, the vortices gathered in one place. A funnel appeared on that spot. Against the background of white mist, the funnel was frightening in its black emptiness. The white foam spun faster and faster around the funnel. The vortices rose higher and higher, and then flowed down at a breakneck pace. A black void gaped in the middle, and the Tartrar waterfall streamed down around it.

Naturally, the waterfall Tartrar would take someone to the bottom almost instantly. However, the chances of surviving in this waterfall were not too high. But the rumor among athletes persistently linked the victory in the competition with a jump in the waterfall Tartrar.

The search for the note went smoothly. Davkaleon decided to follow the goblin's map. The note's location was marked by the familiar sign of the DRAGON of Adolees or the Perfect Dragon of Daeya, as goblin had said. This sign didn't let him down in the Dragon Gardens, and it wouldn't fail him this time either. Having gone down into the cave, the brothers found the disguised entrance into the secret room easily, which led into the next one and then into one more.

On one of the walls, Davkaleon saw the sign of the DRAGON, and a few moments later pulled out a small envelope. What surprised Davkaleon was that neither Malay nor Kvorts could see the sign. However, they could see the envelope very well. Perhaps the goblin was right, and the sign of the DRAGON was tied to the Perfects. Malay and Kvorts' mothers didn't belong to the families of Perfects and Davkaleon's brothers could not be considered truly Perfects, even though they belonged to the Gerklat family. Davkaleon and his brother went upstairs. Nobody chased them, and nobody tried to take anything away from them. It must be said that they hadn't stopped their training yet, so neither the goblin nor the merchant expected the note to be obtained so soon. Having said goodbye to his brothers, Davkaleon headed off to Elfid. Inside the envelope, there was a small written note with ragged edges. The note displayed three numbers.

4 5 23

Neither heating, nor processing the note with Triss' juice nor any of Elfid's other tricks and twists brought out any additional secrets.

"You have only one way to find out whether this note has secrets," Elfid said. "Give a copy to each of your customers and keep the original. If either of them comes for the original, it will mean that the note has a secret beyond what is visible on the page."

Davkaleon did as Elfid advised. Sitting in the *Mug and Sword*, Davkaleon and his brothers were enjoying a fantastic roasted lamb. They played cards then discussed what to do with the following weekend, and after that, they went to their rooms. Davkaleon had hardly crossed the threshold when the dark goblin's sharp fangs sank into his throat.

"Where is the second part of the note?" Davkaleon heard the goblin's question in his head.

Having thrown the goblin off, Davkaleon boiled over. "What second part are you talking about? There wasn't any second part in the envelope."

"Well, then the note was in the envelope, you opened it and tore off a part of the note. Where is it? I paid you for the whole note, not just for half of it."

"Get off my back!" The goblin's accusations made Davkaleon really furious.

"Too bad," the goblin answered gloomily, "I was thinking of continuing to work with you but now I'll have to kill you."

"Kill me?" Davkaleon chuckled. It would be interesting to see how a nasty, husky little goblin would manage to kill a nearly adult Daeyat? It was Davkaleon who could easily kill him with a single swing of his sword, or maybe even with a blow from his fist. But the goblin? He was three times smaller than Davkaleon. Yes, the goblin could bite or wound, but definitely not kill.

As he considered these thoughts, the goblin pointed an object at him. Davkaleon heard a loud bang, and felt a severe blow to his chest. The goblin fell down on the floor. Blood spurted out of the wound on the goblin's chest. Davkaleon felt the vibration on his chest—Isida's amulet made by Dallilla. The goblin twitched a few times and went quiet. Davkaleon stared, astonished at the sight of the goblin lying in a pool of blood. What had just happened? Having rolled the dead goblin in a blanket, Davkaleon carried him out of the school. It was late, so nobody saw him move the goblin body to the bottom of a small lake at the end of the Triss wood.

* * * * *

"So, you are saying this object killed the goblin?" Elfid asked when Davkaleon showed him the thing he had taken from the dead goblin's paws.

Elfid took some time to search through his manuscripts and then showed Davkaleon a picture which looked like the thing that had killed the goblin.

"This thing is called a darter," Elfid explained. "The tiny arrow that flew out of it was supposed to kill you, but it ricocheted off of Isida's amulet, killing the goblin. So, thank Isida for her amulet. It saved your life."

Having left Elfid, Davkaleon headed to the nearest armorer's workshop. If weapon-smiths could make big arrows, they must be able to make small ones as well. Davkaleon wanted a sufficient number of these tiny arrows to try out the goblin weapon as soon as possible.

Chapter 27. A Sign of Twierks Magicians

The story of the jeweler's notes wasn't over for Davkaleon yet. The following Sunday, Davkaleon set off for the Old-Daeyan language school with a heavy heart. On his way to school, he wracked his brains, trying to figure out a cover story to wriggle out of classes. He had already tried to shirk school, hoping he would be expelled but his father found out and had a "talk" with him. Priest Gerklat persuaded Davkaleon by monopolizing on his good attitude for his brother. Nobody at school would tolerate his half-breed brother Paradion without Davkaleon's protection. Paradion wouldn't be able to reach the top and become a high priest without learning the Old-Daeyan language. Students often attended Arragorra without expecting games and heroics. Students were required to make *efforts*, be *disciplined* and *grind away* at their studies—the very things that Davkaleon disliked so much. After lessons, Stanglate asked Davkaleon to stay.

"Davkaleon, you can do the Perfects an invaluable favor," the teacher said, once they were alone. "If you do this, you will help all of Daeya. The Perfects will benefit doubly from it, first, because they are Daeyats and second, because the favor will be done thanks to the Perfects' ancient chronicles. You see, there appeared tendencies among modern priests to undermine age-old chronicles and claim that they are just legends and myths."

"So, what do you want me to do?" Davkaleon asked.

Stanglate told him that several Daeyats, including himself, had been working on the chronicles for many years, trying to decipher them. They managed to do that just a year ago. It was stated in the chronicles that there was a jeweler who had been working for many years on an order made by a wizard of Twier...- hush..." The teacher looked around cautiously before continuing. "In some chronicles, he was mentioned as a wizard, but one of the chronicles claimed he was one of the Gods. Whoever he was, he **ordered to create** amazing jewels possessing truly divine powers. A tiny speck of dust was placed inside of each jewel—so tiny that it's impossible to see it, even if you break the jewel."

Davkaleon stared.

"The specks of dust were made by the wizard himself, or maybe even by the God if the last chronicle was deciphered correctly. One of the jewels is the key which opens the way that the Daeyan priests call the *Divine Route*. This route instantly leads to the city of Gods. In the old days, priests made such journeys and had the pleasure of talking to the Gods. Nowadays, the Divine Route is closed and the rituals described in the guidelines cannot open it. And this, despite of the fact that in recent years, there have been more and more deviations from the Gods' predictions in Daeya. Over and over, the priests have counted, verified and recalculated all the dates of eclipses, high tides, tsunamis and hurricanes, but the inaccuracies keep on growing in number. There are a lot of theories as to why the Gods gave up on Daeya, but no one knows with certainty."

Stanglate returned to the story of the jeweler. "The jeweler described all the jewels he had made in great detail. There is a separate entry dedicated to each piece. His entries are stored in the archives with millions of other scrolls, runes and manuscripts from all over the world. Hundreds of lives wouldn't be enough to browse through all the collected materials. However, the jeweler left a hint. He worked inside the Rock cliff, and once, he heard the wizard tell someone the numbers that each jeweler's note would be stored under in the archives. The jeweler wrote down several numbers and added some instructions on how the numbers had to be calculated. This note is in the Rock cliff. I want you to take the trip there and find the jeweler's note. What do you say to that?"

"I'll do it," Davkaleon answered.

Davkaleon already had Piromis the Jeweler's notes and he wondered what kind of instructions the jeweler had left. All Davkaleon had seen on the note was a few numbers. The teacher took a map out of his desk and put it in front of Davkaleon.

"This is the system of secret passages inside the Rock." Stanglate said.

Looking at the map Davkaleon, noticed that it was different from the maps he had gotten from the goblin and the merchant of magical artifacts.

"Only Perfect Daeyats can use these passages—those who have undergone the *true* rites of passage into blood-brothers. Those who underwent the *symbolic* rite couldn't do that. On this map, you can see marked places where you have to give a drop of your blood to open these secret passages. At the very end of the path, you will find the symbol of Daeya the note was sealed with."

Davkaleon could see the Golden Rose on the map for himself.

"So, how will I get into the cliff Rock?" Davkaleon enquired. "Shall I jump from the cliff?"

"You could jump, of course," the teacher answered. "I've heard you are taking lessons from Master Gandall. But there is an easier way to get inside of the cliff. There is a secret passage to the cliff Rock from the temple of Assa. It is marked on the map. You see, up there? Enter the temple, come up to the distant left column. There, you'll see the entrance. Go down the corridor which has statues on its sides, depicting Gods, governors and heroes of Daeya. Prick yourself with a pin or something near any statue of Swarogg, and you'll see the corridor. Walk along it, and you'll find yourself in the cliff Rock."

"You said you deciphered the chronicles last year. Has anyone tried to get the jeweler's note yet?" Davkaleon asked.

"Yes. Last year, one of the school students tried. Just like you, he was from the family of Perfects and like you, he underwent the true rites of passage into blood-brothers. He died before completing the task. We think the cause of his death was that he had undergone the rite of passage when he was five days old, and that was too late. A true rite of passage requires the babe to be born at the same time as the dragon, and the rite must be held immediately after they were born, just as it was with *you*."

"I'll do it." Davkaleon answered saying goodbye to his teacher.

Having left the school, Davkaleon headed to the temple of Assa. Even though the Perfects hadn't offered him any money for the jeweler's note, that didn't bother Davkaleon. The discovery of the secret corridor which led to the cliff Rock from the temple was a reward itself. Having pricked himself near the statue of Swarogg, he ended up in a small windowless room. On the wall, there was a panel with unknown signs. It reminded him of the panel in the granite room in Adolees. However, the signs on the panel in the temple of Assa were different. One of them was like the sign on the Stanglate map. Davkaleon put his hand on the sign. The passage opened in the wall and Davkaleon walked in. Having taken a few steps along the narrow corridor, he found himself in a small room. Apparently, he was inside of the cliff Rock. After he had given a few more drops of blood in several different places, Davkaleon entered the room with the symbol of Daeya. Even though he didn't have to look for the note, since he already had it, Davkaleon still decided to check up on it. To his great surprise, in the cache sat *exactly the same envelope* as the one he had found in the cache with the sign of the DRAGON. Just like that envelope, this one was sealed.

Davkaleon returned to his room, having promised himself that at the earliest opportunity, he would investigate where other signs led from the secret room of the temple of Assa. Having pulled the note out of the envelope, Davkaleon compared it to the note he had obtained earlier.

The first and the second figures were the same, but the third figure was different.

4 5 19

Having taken the merchant's map, Davkaleon decided to visit the cliff Rock one more time. The sign of the Dragon and Rose opened the cache with the third note for him. The first and the second figures looked the same as in the previous notes, but the third figure was different yet again.

4 5 17

The next day Davkaleon gave Stanglate the copied note.

"Is it so small?" the teacher was surprised. Was it like this from the very beginning? You haven't torn anything from it, have you?"

"Of course, I have not!" Davkaleon answered, recalling the goblin's accusations.

"All right, all right, I believe you. But it makes the task more complicated. I hoped to see a full explanation on how to figure out the follow-up numbers. The note doesn't have this instruction, so we'll have to select the next figures ourselves. It will take us more time than I expected. I wonder why it is said in the chronicles that the master jeweler left a detailed explanation?" Stanglate asked pensively.

"Perhaps, he left the explanation in one of those entries whose numbers are given in the note," Davkaleon made a guess.

"No," Stanglate answered, "we had copies of those three entries in a post. They were copied and hidden in Daeya back when the chronicles were being written. They describe the jeweler's story right up to the day he stepped into the cliff Rock and got his first order, but they don't tell anything about the jewels he made. We need the rest of the notes, and for that, we will have to guess the follow-up numbers.

* * * * *

"And you want me to guess the follow-up figures only looking at these numbers, right?" Elfid made sure after listening to Davkaleon's story.

"Yeah. Aren't you at all curious about it?"

"Well, I am, but these numbers are not enough to figure out the next ones." Elfid answered.

"I am sure you can do it. This is not the biggest challenge you've ever faced," Davkaleon smiled.

"The entries are probably placed in the archives. It means the section, room and entry number must be indicated here."

"It's quite simple then." Davkaleon got excited. "The

numbers of sections and rooms are a clear match. All we need to guess is the entries numbers, and that's not the hard part."

"I don't think it's that easy. We have three different last numbers from the notes: **17**, **19** and **23**. What do you think? What is next number?" asked Elfid.

"**29**! I think it should be **17, 19, 23, 29, 37, 47** and so on." answered Davkaleon.

"Or **17, 19, 23, 31, 47, 79**." smiled Elfid.

"Well, that could be," agreed Davkaleon looking at numbers.

"Or **17, 19, 23, 29, 31, 37**" grinned Elfid.

"Why?" surprised Davkaleon. "I don't see any logic to those numbers."

"They are called *prime numbers*, but that doesn't matter." Elfid shook his head and added, "It is unlikely that the one whom the Old-Daeyan manuscripts called a you-know-what wizard would use such obvious progressions. I need time to think it over."

"One more question. Why is the DRAGON of Adolees depicted on the sign of the Perfect Dragon of Daeya?" Davkaleon asked before leaving.

"The correct name of this sign is the sign of the Perfect Dragon or sign of the DRAGON. It can be found everywhere—in Daeya, in Adolees and many other places. Those who passed initiation can see it. Adoleeseets can see this sign without initiation, because it is in their blood."

"Can Llill sorceresses see this sign? Maybe I've got their blood mixed in me?" Davkaleon remembered rumors spread by his cousin.

"Llill sorceresses can see the sign of the Perfect Dragon, but that's irrelevant for you, their blood doesn't flow in your veins. If it did, you couldn't work the way of the Perfect Daeyats. And if someone opened the passage for you intentionally, you would not see the symbol of Daeya."

"How could it happen then?"

"The only reasonable explanation is connected with the potion of magicians, and with Chapa. For a short period of time, you had two full doses of the drink. There was the blood of the little Adoleeseet Chapa in each of these doses and also his blood, form when he took the form of the dragon. If, during your battles, you were both wounded, and the blood of Chapa got on your wounds, all this could lead to the fact that you became able to see the sign of the DRAGON."

"His blood definitely got on me!" said Davkaleon, remembering that during his second journey to the temple in the rock, the temple, having injured them both, threw them on a rock.

"It's clear why you see the DRAGON's sign and why you can open what is sealed with that sign. As for the sign of the Dragon and the Rose, neither the drink of magicians, nor the blood of any usual Adoleeseet will help. To open what is sealed with this sign, you would have to get a drop of blood of a real magician. This is very controversial issue. Is it possible to consider that what happened in the temple during your first journey the initiation? On the one hand, Telatr confirmed the veracity of Chapa. On the other hand, the DRAGON did *not* share his blood with any of you, though he did not kill you. It's more like he postponed his decision. But even if we assume that you have passed the initiation, then you can't see the sign of the Dragon and the Rose without the blood of magicians." Elfid took a piece of leather and wrote on it. "This is the sign of the wizards of Twierks," he explained.

"What? Then why do I see it?" Davkaleon couldn't believe what Elfid had said.

"I have no explanation for this." Elfid made a helpless gesture.

* * * * *

When Davkaleon returned to his room, he found the merchant of the magic there, waiting.

"Have you torn any part from the note?" the merchant asked.

"Why would I tear anything from it?" Davkaleon answered in annoyance. He was getting rather bored with questions that sounded like as an accusation.

"Well, for example, to sell it to me," the merchant answered.

"You've paid me in full and I've given you the whole note. I haven't torn anything from it."

"Tell me in detail how you found it," the merchant demanded.

"I saw a sign on the wall, opened the cache, took out the envelope, made sure there was a note with numbers you'd told me about, and then gave the note to you." Davkaleon listed his moves, omitting Elfid's manipulations with the note.

"So, the note was in an envelope!" the merchant became enthusiastic. "Where is it?"

Davkaleon took the envelope out of his immense pockets and handed it over to the merchant, kicking himself for not hitting upon the idea of exploring the envelope before that. The merchant's eyes shone with joy.

Chapter 28. The Request Of Chapius

Davkaleon entered his room. Elfid sat comfortably on his bed in front of him. At the sight of Davkaleon, Elfid waved his hand in greeting.

"How did you get here?" Davkaleon was shocked.

"I missed you and flew," said Elfid and smiled.

"Less than an hour passed since we parted."

Davkaleon carefully examined his brother. Was this person Elfid or not? He seemed very similar! But Elfid would *never* say that he missed somebody. And he would not use the word *flew.* Elfid did not like to fly on dragons, and he did so only when it was absolutely necessary. It was more likely that Elfid would go on foot to visit Davkaleon. Something was wrong here.

"Your face is so funny when you're surprised!" laughed Elfid, who turned suddenly into Chapius.

"You did well portraying Elfid," Davkaleon smiled and asked, "Where do you want to pull me this time?"

"I need to get to the *Pillentally Cave*," Chapius said, as if nothing had happened.

On hearing Chapius's proposed destination, Davkaleon almost choked. Everyone in Daeya knew that the Pillentally Cave was the scariest place, frightening both children and adults. When someone was suspected of committing a crime, but no one could prove their guilt, they were sent there. This was called sending the accused person to the *Court of the Gods*. The entrance to the cave was located high on a vertical cliff. Huge boulders stood at the bottom, the ocean roared and foamed, and the waves crashed on the rocks. There was a smooth cliff at the top. The rock was so smooth that it seemed polished. The suspect was lowered down to the entrance to the cave on a rope. As soon as he reached the cave, the rope was cut. Guard dragons watched vigilantly, so that no one tried to help. Three days later, a rope was lowered again. If the Gods decided that the suspect was innocent, then he could grab the rope and get to the top. Three days is not a long period, it is possible to survive, but no one *ever* got out of the cave for some reason. Perhaps they were all guilty. In Daeya, they said that there are the *Gates of the End* in the cave—gates that let everyone come in and didn't let anyone come out. And they said that he who enters the gates goes into the *World of Shadows*, and from thence, there is no return. And now, Chapius wanted a stroll in this very cave.

"Why do you need to get to the Pillentally Cave?" asked Davkaleon.

"I don't need the cave itself. I need the *Gates of the End*," Chapius said cheerfully. "They are in this cave. I've read about it in the Depository, although the message was marked as unverified."

"Why do you want these gates?" asked Davkaleon. "If you're so eager to go into the World of Shadows, you can find a dozen more pleasant ways there. The World of Shadows is where all come after finishing their mortal existence, and that's where you're going, if you enter the gates. Bear in mind, these gates will let you enter inside and won't let you get out. So, you'll be stuck there, and you won't come back."

"Are the Gates of the End associated with a legend in Daeya?" asked Chapius.

"Our priests teach us that there are two worlds. This one where we live when we are alive, and the other one where we go after we cease to be alive. That world is also called the World of Shadows." explained Davkaleon.

"You say that a bit allegorically," said Chapius. "Do you

271

believe that there is life after death, and that the place where this life continues is called the World of Shadows?"

"Chapius, shut up!" warned Davkaleon. "Do not invoke bad luck on our heads, and do not say that word."

"What word?" Chapius did not understand. "You're being weird, Davkaleon. When it comes to fighting, you're the bravest person I know. And you're afraid to call a spade a spade? For example, you will not speak the word Twier—"

Chapius did not finish. Having heard part of the forbidden word, Davkaleon jumped as if stung and clamped his mouth. The Adoleeseet twisted around and laughed. "Okay, Okay, I will keep silence. Just tell me one single time clearly and definitely, do you think that you go to the World of Shadows when you die?"

Having raised his arms up and having called the Gods to witness, Davkaleon answered: "Yes!" And then he added that he'd break Chapius's neck if he would not cease disturbing the Lord of the World of Shadows with this discussion. "You see, Chapius, people of my profession fall into the World of Shadows prematurely so often, and you keep reminding the Lord about me by calling his name. I am quite satisfied with life in *this* world. I'm not in a hurry to get to that one." Just in case, he added, "This does not mean, Lord, that I don't respect you. I do a lot. And I understand well that someday I will be in your Kingdom, but let it be later."

"I have figured out your Daeyan ideas about the World of Shadows. Can you explain to me why you believe that the Gates of the End are the gates to the World of Shadows?" asked Chapius.

"And where else could they lead to?" asked Davkaleon, suddenly surprised.

"But that's not logical. Every day, hundreds of people

die in Daeya, and thousands, maybe tens of thousands die during battles. Do they immediately go to the Gates of the End? There's pandemonium there! And what happens to the dragons after they... well, you understand after what I mean." Chapius remembered suddenly that he promised Davkaleon not to say the word death. "Do they also come to the World of Shadows?"

Davkaleon hadn't thought about that before. Frankly speaking, he never thought about the World of Shadows. And Chapius, meanwhile, continued: "Do none of the dragons go to the cave and look inside?"

"They tried, of course. But you're interested not in the cave, but in the Gates of the End, and they are in the depths of the cave. Daeya's dragons are not so stupid to fly into the cave for the sake of idle curiosity."

"If the Gates are in the depths, why do suspected persons flock to them? They could sit near the entrance to the cave and wait until three days pass. No one dies from hunger in three days. Three days later, they would get out and would cease to be considered criminals. Don't you think something is wrong here?"

"Chapius, I won't send Aleurh there, don't even ask me," said Davkaleon, anticipating Chapius's next request.

"I was not going to ask you to send Aleurh there. I am a dragon myself, only I'm from Adolees. I don't even want you to go with me this time. Unless you want to go, that is. But you'll want to! Won't you? You're very interested yourself! Your Aleurh will only bring us to the cave, so no one will see me. He won't need to enter inside and I'll keep you safe in the cave." Chapius looked at Davkaleon with big, honest eyes.

Davkaleon was taken aback. Maybe he was curious, but not enough to go to the Gates of the End. He would always have time to go there. Why should he hurry?

Surprised, Davkaleon did not even respond to the offer of Chapius to be his guard. Still, in all joint campaigns, Davkaleon was the defender of Chapius. However, Chapius had grown and matured. He was not the same little clumsy dragon from Adolees, whom Davkaleon saved in the past.

"Why are you interested in these Gates?" asked Davkaleon.

"This is my homework task for school," explained Chapius.

"Is your task to go to Daeya, enter the Pillentally Cave, find the Gates of the End and enter the World of Shadows?" Davkaleon did not believe it.

"Not exactly. The Depository in Adolees interprets the facts surrounding the Gates of the End quite differently, though, it says that the information is not verified."

"Let's deal with the first part. Are you telling me that schools in Adolees are so insolent that they assign sneaking into Daeya as a homework task?!" raged Davkaleon.

"You know, Davkaleon, that accusation is somehow not fair. When the Daeyan priests gave you the task of sneaking into Adolees, you did not become outraged and didn't say that it was arrogance. You even asked me to help you. And now that I find myself in a similar situation, you speak of it differently."

"And why are you in a similar situation?" asked Davkaleon, instantly cooling down.

"You manipulated things that time when you were assigned an essay about Adoleeseets, and eventually got the task to go to Adolees. And I'm doing much the same now. We were given the task to find unverified information in the Depository and check it out. Frankly speaking, they had something small in mind, like an unknown mutation of a mollusk or checking some of the old recipes. But the winner will get an award that I naturally want to get. So, I began to search in the Depository for something more substantial than a clam or cooking. I came across the Gates of the End. There is much that is not proven about them. According to the Depository of Adolees, the Gates of the End are situated in many places, not just in Adolees. It is very problematic to get to them in Adolees. To enter there, you must be in *Dragon-net.* This means that only the Great DRAGON of Adolees can use them. But I found mention about several other places where there are Gates of the End. One of these places is Daeya. I've never been to the other places, and I have never heard about most of them. So, I came to you. Instead of a warm welcome, you have accused me of arrogance." Chapius finished with resentment in his voice.

"Okay, okay, Chapius, don't be offended. When I asked you for help, I explained at once what my purpose was, and I did not begin with the fact that the priests had sent me to Adolees," replied Davkaleon, feeling guilty. The trip to Adolees really helped him. He'd stayed at school, and on his own team. They forgave him for participating in a prohibited duel and numerous other shenanigans. If Chapius did not help him that time, his education at the military school would be over.

"So, will you go with me?" Chapius said happily.

"What does your Depository say about the Gates of the End?" asked Davkaleon. He didn't want to go to the Gates with Chapius. However, he did feel guilty that he wasn't supporting his friend, but not so guilty as to go to the World of Shadows voluntarily.

"The Depository says very contradictory things. I don't remember all of them." answered Chapius evasively.

"Chapius, don't play me, I know that you took notes.

Read them." demanded Davkaleon.

Reluctantly, Chapius got out his notes. They sounded really vague and weird. The first note said, "The sky is on fire, and fiery hail pours. Pass through the Gates of the End." The second record claimed, "The one who has seen, will not see. The one who has heard, will not hear. The one who has entered, will not enter." Subsequent records did not clarify anything and sounded more than strange. "One will leave, another will come. No one will enter ahead of time. No one will come back."

"Chapius, if I drink a pintie of good ale, I'll write for you a dozen of verses of such nonsense. Listen to me. *The running away person catches up, the catching up person runs away. The Standing person sits, the sitting person stands. The keeping silent person sings, the singing person keeps silence.* And so on. And with ale, I could write a real masterpiece."

"What do you make of it?" asked Chapius, pulling out another note. He began to read.

"The earth was burning, the sky was blazing, and fiery hail was pouring. Those who could not instantly turn into dragons were killed instantly. Those who could turn couldn't breathe in the raging fire. And then HE appeared and chose the strongest and largest dragon. HE stabbed himself with an adamant dagger and sprinkled the chosen dragon with his blood. ChapiusKloyAlfreyDon, you'll be the first Great DRAGON of Adolees, he said. But Adolees no longer exists. It dies in the fire," Dragon answered. "The First Adolees is dying, but the Second will appear. You and those who will follow you, will create it. He swung his wounded arm, and spatters of HIS own blood flew to the fire, and spatters whirled around in a mad whirlwind of fire, and a spinning vortex struck the roaring flames and rushed forward, leaving a winding black corridor."

Chapius took a deep breath before continuing. "Pass through the Gates of the End and lead the others." HE ordered. One after the other the dragons entered the black corridor. And in the end, there was a glimmer of light. A barrage of fire burst into the corridor. With all the forces the dragons rushed to the exit and escaped from the fiery trap. They hovered in the sky, and far away they saw the blue star. The dragons flew for a long time and flaming debris rushed after them." Having read to the end, Chapius set the note down. "What do you think of that?"

"I would say that it is Adolees's version of the legend of the appearance of Adoleeseets in our Daeya. Your Adolees died and you came to us," said Davkaleon. "In Daeya, there is a legend about fiery stones which fell from the sky, and the ground was heaving and shaking, and then the fire dragons came, which turned into Adoleeseets."

"And did you notice the fact that this legend refers to the Gates of the End?" asked Chapius.

"I did. So, what? You came to us, met with our legends and adapted our Gates of the End to what happened with your Adolees. Moreover, it is not your official story, but a legend which you have found in your Depository, and you honestly admitted that your Depository characterizes this writing as unverified."

"You're so stubborn, Davkaleon! What could be easier? Enter your Pillentally Cave, find the Gates of the End, and see what is behind them. That is all!" argued Chapius.

"If the priests of Daeya are right about the World of Shadows, you'll find the Gates of the End, and even enter them, but what good will that do? You will not come back. You won't get the reward for your troubles. And if your legend has even a shred of truth, then according to your own Depository, you will not find these Gates. And even if you stand right next to them, you will not see them. What

277

did you read to me? "The one who has seen, will not see, the one who has heard, will not hear. No one will enter ahead of time."

"See, you're repeating notes from the Depository and do not laugh," Chapius wouldn't give up. "Just think, what would you do if something happened in Daeya, and the only salvation is through these Gates, and you don't even know where they are?" continued the Adoleeseet.

"Chapius, don't bring ruin on Daeya with such assumptions. I will not go to the Gates, and neither should you. What I *can* offer you, is to talk to the dragons of Daeya. There is the Dragon Tavern in Assa. I was told that if a visitor orders a dinner with the dragon ale for the dragons, they can entertain him with all sorts of dragon horror stories as a thanks. I was planning on going there with Aleurh. If you want, I'll go there, and I'll entertain Aleurh at the same time. because my faithful dragon is homesick."

"I want to go there too!" the eyes of Chapius caught fire.

"I don't think that's a good idea. The dragons of Daeya do not like Adoleeseets." Davkaleon shook his head.

"So, I will change my appearance," Chapius insisted.

"You will do it, but they will ask you who you are and where you are from. The dragons fly throughout Daeya. They know it thoroughly, and they will instantly catch you in lies if you say that you're from anywhere in Daeya."

"Then, I'll pretend to be your brother Elfid. You have seen how good I am at imitating him! No one would pester Elfid with questions. Everyone knows that Elfid does not leave his runes and manuscripts."

"And what if Elfid suddenly came there?" suggested Davkaleon, and laughed at his own words. No, Elfid will not go to the Dragon Tavern—it was not a library!

Chapter 29. The Dragon Tavern

Having heard the offer to go to the Dragon Tavern, Aleurh was happy. The trip to the tavern meant a perfect evening with a great dinner and dragon ale, and many interesting dragon stories.

Although sometimes there were fights there...

They sat in the tavern for a few hours. The fifth barrel of ale was on the table. The dragons were in a great mood. They excitedly told different stories about the Pillentally Cave and the Gates of the End.

"Why you are interested in gates?" asked one of the dragons. "Do you want to lure an enemy army there?"

The dragons laughed.

"For me personally, these gates are not too attractive. I like being in this world. But my brother has found a few stories during his studies, and asks whether they are truthful. And I said that it was hard to find better judges than the dragons of Daeya." Davkaleon's flattery seemed to please the slightly tipsy dragons.

"Did anyone witness the disappearance of those who were sent to the cave?" asked Chapius-Elfid.

"You should ask this question to the dragon Whales. Your brother knows him well. After all, Whales is the main dragon of the military school." said one of the dragons.

"Whales? Why did you mention him?" surprised Davkaleon.

"Have you not heard the story of how Whales was appointed the chief dragon of the military school?"

Davkaleon listened with increased interest to what the dragon was telling him. It turns out that many years earlier, Whales and his blood-brother won the military tournament. They won, despite the fact that black magic was used against them. During the ceremony, the blood-brother of Whales was arrested. In court, he was charged that he won because he appealed for help to a black magician. One witness claimed that he saw that Whales and his blood-brother enter the dwelling of a black magician. The witness lied, of course. Whales and his blood-brother were in a very different place at the time, dozens of witnesses swore to it. But the court of priests still decided to send the blood-brother of Whales to the court of the Gods, and he was sent to the Pillentally Cave. Whales tried to save him, and he almost succeeded. He scattered four fighting dragons, as the last of the weaklings, and snatched his blood-brother from the cave. A platoon of fighting dragons answered the sounded alarm. Whales fought off the platoon so they could not reach his blood-brother. His blood-brother was unarmed and could do nothing to help. As to not get in the way, he jumped from the back of Whales to the edge of the cave. Some dragons rushed after him. The blood-brother rushed inside. Whales rushed to protect him. The dragons rushed after Whales and the battle took place deeper into the cave. In a moment, a dense fog appeared from nowhere and enveloped all around them."

The dragon took a drink, and continued his story. "The fog cleared in just a moment, but the blood-brother of Whales had disappeared into it. Whales rushed to look for him. He went alone inside the cave. A few days later, he got out of there, but he never found his blood-brother. He went into the tavern, bought dinner and came back to the cave again. He didn't find his friend, ever. In the court of priests, it was declared that if Whales was able to get out of the cave alive, it meant that neither he nor his blood-brother had anything to do with black magic. However, they tried to arrest Whales for the battle with combat dragons. The leadership of the military school interfered, and it was declared that they needed such a dragon at the school. Whales was faced with a choice—to go to the court, or to accept the offer of school leadership to become the main dragon of the military school. That is how he became chief dragon."

"How do you know this? Were you among those who fought with Whales?" asked Davkaleon.

"No, I did not fight with him, but one who was in the cave and saw it with his own eyes told me this story."

"And did you believe him?" asked one of the dragons. "Didn't you find it odd that Whales went to the cave twice of his own free will? Okay, the first time he did it in the heat of battle. But why did he do it for the second time? He's already spent a few days there, and he didn't find his rider. Why did he go for the second time?"

"You say a *rider,* but I told you he was the blood-brother of Whales. A blood-brother is not just a rider. *He is a part of you.* If you have never had a blood-brother, then you cannot understand it," replied the dragon.

"Aleurh, are you and Davkaleon blood-brothers?" asked one of the dragons. And having received an affirmative answer, he asked, "Do you believe that Whales went into this cave twice?"

"Did he go in a second time searching for his blood-brother? Of course, he did! I would go anywhere for my Davkaleon." replied Aleurh fervently.

One barrel of ale on the table was replaced by another one, and the dragons became more and more talkative.

"It seems that nobody here doubts that the Gates of the End lead to the World of Shadows. I'm not sure of it," said a rather tipsy dragon, and told his story.

"A few years ago, a couple of strangers hired me to take

281

them to a shop of Carducci. There are various rumors about this shop. Many say that people who entered there could disappear as though they never existed in this world. Others say that people who never entered there could come out of it. The customers left the shop of Carducci 20 minutes later, and one of them had a note with numbers in his hands."

"Are you sure this is a real note from the jeweler?" one of the strangers asked another.

"Should be, judging by the description. Three numbers. The bottom edge is uneven," replied the other, "and the parchment is exactly like the parchment that was used in the days of the jeweler."

Having heard about the note of the jeweler, Davkaleon stiffened. Neither the teacher of old-Daeya's language Stanglate, nor Elfid, nor Davkaleon succeeded in solving the mystery of the notes of the jeweler Piromis. The dragon, meanwhile, continued his story.

"His customers said, that they needed to get to another place and they paid in advance."

"Where do you think they wanted me to bring them?" asked the dragon, and answered himself. "To the Pillentally Cave!"

The dragon refused to fly up to the cave, and his customers suggested that he land on a high cliff. They had a long rope and they wanted to go down to the cave using it. One of them pulled out a purse full of money. The dragon had never seen such amounts of money! The crazy customer offered a few hundred seekls to the dragon to hold the rope while they descended to the cave.

"*If you are so eager to get into the World of Shadows, why do you need the rest of the money?" asked the dragon. "Do you think it will be useful in that world?"*

"*Why do you think that we strive to get into the World*

of Shadows?" laughed one of the customers.

"Where, in your opinion, do the Gates of the End lead?" the dragon answered with bewilderment.

"It depends on the key. For example, the one that we have now will lead us to Llill," replied the other. The first customer promised me he would tie a purse with the money to the rope after they descended.

The dragon paused to drink more Dragon Ale. "They both went down into the cave, and, indeed, they started to tie something to the rope. I waited patiently, anticipating an unprecedented award. They waved goodbye and went inside the cave. I picked up the rope with the tied object believing that it was a purse full of money. It was not a purse, it was an explosive package, exploding as soon as I saw what it was. They were not stingy with the gunpowder! I was hit and thrown several yards away. I was surprised that I actually survived. Judging by the stars, I laid stunned for a few hours. One thing pleased me—they could not get out of the cave. And they will be punished for their treachery in the World of Shadows. I could not understand what I had done to deserve such a reward! I realized the answer in a few months, when I brought another customer to the shop of Carducci. *Near the entrance, I saw one of those whom I brought to the Pillentally Cave.* I wanted to kill him on the spot, but then I thought it would be good to find out where the second one was. He didn't recognize me and asked if I was the dragon which had been reserved for the flight to Llill. I had no time to respond when another dragon landed near the shop and announced that he was ordered to fly to Llill. I followed them at a distance and saw how they flew to the rock of Llill. I waited for a long time, but I didn't see them. Then I flew up to the rock. On the rock, I found a dead dragon, and my former customer had vanished. I never saw him again, and I'll never know where he disappeared to off the cliff. There are rumors that the main temple of the witches of Llill is situated inside of this rock. Maybe he got inside somehow. But, anyway, he managed to get out from the Pillentally Cave."

Noise rose in the tavern. It seems that he was the first witness to claim that he had seen someone with his own eyes get out of the cave alive. Was his story true?

"You say you were without memory for a few hours. It's possible that someone came or flew and helped them to get out," suggested one of the dragons.

"Even if it was so, that means that it is possible to get out of the cave," the dragon argued.

"From the cave, maybe, you can, if you stay near the entrance for a short time. But after going through the Gates of the End, it is impossible to come back, and you didn't see whether your clients entered the Gates or waited quietly until someone helped them get out," said another dragon.

"What's the point of this?"

"Maybe they made a bet with someone that they would spend several hours in the cave and nothing would happen," suggested someone.

"Then why did they try to kill me?" the first dragon cried.

"Then how do you explain it?" asked Chapius-Elfid.

"I believe that there was a code in the note that they have used to come back after passing through the Gates of the End."

"Even if that is so, it doesn't explain how they got out of the cave after that. Maybe you just made a mistake, and the one you met was not your former customer. He didn't recognize you," objected someone.

"He didn't recognize me, because for people, all dragons

look alike."

"The same can be said about the dragons. For them all people look alike. That's how you made a mistake."

"And what about the smell? Do you want to say that I could confuse the smell of someone who tried to kill me?" objected the dragon.

He was right. Dragons would *not* confuse the smell.

"Do you remember what the numbers were in the note?" asked Davkaleon.

"No, I don't remember the numbers. I only saw the note in passing. The thing I remember was that there were three digits on the note."

"Davkaleon, I have cracked the code! I've found a hint in the runes," Elfid smiled happily on the threshold of the tavern.

He briskly walked to the desk, behind which Davkaleon, Chapius-Elfid and the dragons sat.

"I am Elfid," he introduced himself. "I apologize for the intrusion, but I need to talk to my brother. It will only take a few minutes, and then you may continue."

Delighted, Elfid did not even pay attention that his twin sat at a table close to Davkaleon. But the dragons paid attention to it.

"Black magic," said one.

"Black magician," added another.

"Which one of them?" asked someone.

"Both of them! We need to invoke the priests, they will find out."

Chapter 30. Priests' Trial

Chapius–Elfid disappeared. He very likely turned into a bite size bug and got away through some tiny crack. But it was too late. Several dozen dragons swore they had seen two Elfids in the tavern. Aleurh, trying to dodge his way out, said that he had drunk too much dragon ale and could not swear whether he had seen two Elfids or he had just seen double. Aleurh even added that by that time, quite a few barrels of ale had been emptied, so the dragon's words should be taken carefully, even though they were surely quite honest. Who knows what you may see after drinking so much ale? But that didn't help. He was asked whether Elfid had been sitting at the same table with him, and Aleurh had to admit that Elfid had been there since the very beginning of their visit to the Dragon Tavern. A dozen other witnesses thumped their chests that they had seen Elfid in the library at that time, and the matter was settled. Elfid was accused of black magic. Besides, they remembered he was a Llill witch's son. Truly speaking, things never went well after accusations of black magic. Though Priest Gerklat was denied the chance to defend his son, he found a brilliant lawyer to defend Elfid.

"Can any of the highly honored priests say an oath that dark wizards are not capable of creating the illusion which will make others see two Elfids or two alike dragons or even two priests?" the lawyer asked. Of course, nobody could swear to that. Black magicians and wizards' abilities went far beyond that little spell.

"And since no one can swear to that, then how can anyone be sure that Elfid is the one we need to blame?" the lawyer argued.

Having carried the debate along the same lines for a

few hours the priest court ruled to send Elfid to the Gods' trial, in other words, to the cave Pillentally.

Despite Priest Gerklat's howls of protest, Elfid was taken away.

"You must send me there along with Elfid!" Davkaleon announced, but nobody paid attention to him.

Before the trial started Priest Gerklat had demanded that Davkaleon sit silent during the entire hearing and keep himself out of all the drama. "I've hired the best lawyer, who has a good grasp of what can and cannot be said in the priest court and how the accused needs to be defended. Stay out of the way and let them do their job."

So, Davkaleon stayed quiet without poking his nose into anything. And what was the use of that? The fact that he was quiet didn't mean he was calm. He was boiling inside because of the blatant injustice. *What does this have to do with Elfid?* In fact, it was Davkaleon who was to blame for all of this. It was he who had agreed that Adoleeseet Chapius would come to the Dragon Tavern imitating Elfid. "You must send me there along with Elfid!" Davkaleon shouted one more time. But again, nobody noticed him.

"Lift me up." Davkaleon demanded, having bent to Aleurh.

"I'll see you tarred first." Aleurh answered indignantly, having clearly understood what Davkaleon was up to.

"Do it! Lift me up! I know what I am doing, I made arrangements with Chapius," Davkaleon lied.

With one eye closed Aleurh bent his head to the side and looked very closely at Davkaleon. "You are lying!" Aleurh decided, adding, "I'm not lifting you up."

Having given up on Aleurh, Davkaleon ran up to the speaker's stand and jumped on it. Half of the priests were already at the door. Having taken the goblin's weapon out of his pocket and pointed it up, Davkaleon made a shot. There was a sound loud enough to wake the dead. In the hall everyone froze.

"You must send me there along with Elfid," Davkaleon shouted. "It's not Elfid's fault that someone used him for illusions. Elfid is not a warrior. He has never been in a real battle before and has never learnt how to fight. If some kind of a monster lives in this cave, Elfid won't be able to fight it. He has no chance without me. Elfid is smart. Would he really perform anything like this on himself if he wanted to practice Black Magic? When I fought the duel against Pompeus and then ended up in the Gardens of the Dragons' Lord, I saw a few of me and a few Aleurh. Do you think I was practicing Black Magic too? No! Those were Prann and the Dragons' Lord having fun. But if you are accusing Elfid, these accusations can be pressed against me. I don't want people to whisper behind my back that I am rubbing elbows with dark forces. I have never done that! Neither has Elfid! And if you are sending him to the cave, send me along with him. I am not afraid of the Gods' trial. I am guilty of nothing. But there might be some monster alongside the Gods' trial in the cave. And if I am right, I'll be able to protect both myself and Elfid."

"That's sacrilege to argue that the Gods' trial depends on some kind of a monster," somebody shouted.

"I don't know whether such a statement is sacrilege, but the fact that he has put himself on the speaker's stand in the priests' court and has set off the explosion is definitely sacrilege," a second one added.

"He asked to be sent to the Gods' trial. So, let's send him indeed, and let it be the way the Gods decide!"

That was how Davkaleon found himself in the Pillentally Cave. His loyal dragon had lunged at those who were trying to cut the rope, but standing at the edge had shouted, "Aleurh, I will be waiting for you in three days. Bring a barrel of ale with you! We are going to celebrate Elfid's and my release!"

* * * * *

"Welcome. It is about time that you decided to join us. We were getting tired of waiting for you."

Davkaleon turned as he heard the greeting. Two Elfids smiled at him.

"I've won. You owe me ten seekls," one of them said.

"Where can I get your ten seekls *here*?" the second one answered. "When we get out of here, I will pay you."

"Making the bet, you didn't think about where you'd get the ten seekls. Then, when it came to paying, you all of a sudden remembered you have no money," the first one sneered.

"Well, I am not refusing to pay, I am saying I will pay when we get out of here," the second one answered.

It seemed like the two Elfids were having fun without worrying about being stuck in the cave.

"Davkaleon, let's make a bet," one of the Elfids offered.

"What bet?" Davkaleon asked mechanically.

"If you guess which of us is the real Elfid, each of us will pay you ten seekls. If you are wrong, you pay us."

"Of course. The real Elfid is the one who keeps silence, and you are an awful chatterbox, Chapius." Davkaleon answered.

"Thanks to me, you got into such an awesome place. Aren't you having a good time?" Chapius frowned.

"What have you placed a bet on?" Davkaleon asked without responding to Chapius' question.

"Elfid thought you would show up after it got dark. I insisted you wouldn't make it that long and would come down more while the sun was still high." Chapius answered. "By the way, have you brought anything to eat and drink? You know, I've gotten kind of hungry."

"You've gotten kind of hungry?" Davkaleon mocked him.

"You wanted to get into the cave, didn't you? Congratulations! You have your wish! Have you forgotten food and drink was not included in the package?"

"You haven't brought anything at all?" Chapius asked with disappointment. "Elfid, do you think we will find a dinner inside this gateway?"

"I am not sure about the dinner, but we may find a couple of monsters."

"Are you both sure that after we have passed this Gateway we will not enter the World of Shadows?" Davkaleon was just a little worried.

"I don't know where we'll enter, but I don't think it'll be the World of Shadows. On the other hand, I'm not so confident we'll have to go through the Gates of the End at all. According to what is said in the runes and manuscripts, the Gateway is closed up till a certain time," the real Elfid answered.

"In the tavern you said you had broken the code," Davkaleon reminded him.

"Yes, I had. You were curious about the numbers in the jeweler's note. I think they are tied together with the cave Pillentally. Have you ever heard anything about different numeral systems?" Elfid asked.

Davkaleon had heard some such thing, but he didn't want to clutter his mind with such nonsense. His arithmetic teacher spoke about the binary system. Having listened to him for a few minutes, Davkaleon and his brothers decided they'd have no use of that, and had a wonderful time playing cards. Could anyone tell him why someone might need such nonsense and what for? Was the binary system for somebody so lazy that they couldn't memorize ten figures? If seven enemies approach you from the right and five more from the left, that makes a total of 12 enemies. End of story! No other numeral systems needed here. You have to pull out your sword and fight rather than converting your enemies into different numeral systems as though that will make their number smaller.

In the meantime, Elfid continued his story. "As long as I saw only one note, the figures didn't tell me anything. Even when I was looking at the three notes at the same time, I didn't figure it out right away. It all made sense when I was in the library and I discovered that goblins use the octal system of counting among themselves. Why does it have to be the octal system? Who knows? Maybe, because each of their limbs only has four fingers. The Daeyats use the decimal numeral system, and you know that wizards use the duodecimal numeral system. Look at the numbers in all three notes.

4 5 23 in the note you found using the goblin's map.
4 5 17 in the note you got by way of the map you had received from the merchant of the magic items.
4 5 19 in the note meant for the True Daeyats.

"The numbers 4 and 5 remain constant in all three numeral systems. As for the numbers 23, 17 and 19, that is the same number written in the octal, duodecimal and decimal systems. Hence, these notes contain the same numbers, just written in different numeral system."

Davkaleon listened to Elfid with amazement.

"We use these systems, too, along with the hexadecimal and vigesimall number systems. And, of course, the tridecimal system, but that is used only for the DRAGON numeral system. I haven't figured out what it is needed for yet, though," Chapius added.

The DRAGON numeral system sounded fascinating, but Elfid and Davkaleon didn't want to divert their attention at the moment.

"There's more to come," Elfid continued. "Until the moment when the merchant of magic items showed his interest in the envelope, I hadn't paid attention to the envelopes at all. And I should have. After you had told me about that, I examined the remaining two envelopes. At first glance, there was nothing special about them. But that's only at first glance. As you know, my mother is a Llill's sorcerer. In the Llill's manuscripts, I found a clue and discovered one more number. Look here."

Elfid took out one of the envelopes, and having pricked himself, he dripped a bit of his blood on the inner side of the envelope. The barely visible number 241 appeared on the envelope. A few seconds later, it faded and then it disappeared without a trace. Elfid took the second envelope and dripped a drop of his blood on the inner side of the envelope. This time nothing happened.

"Speaking honestly, I didn't really expect that my blood would make the number show up on the envelope meant for the True Daeyats. But you belong to the families of Daeya's Perfects in every way. What is more, you and your dragon are blood-brothers. In your case, it must work. I'd bet my shirt on the number being 337."

Elfid was right. After Davkaleon had dropped a bit of his blood on the envelope, the number 337 showed. However, only he could see it. Neither Chapius nor Elfid could see the number.

"Can you see it? I didn't expect that even the envelope would be made so that only True Daeyats would be able to see the number."

"241 and 337 are the same numbers in different numeral systems," Davkaleon said in wonder. "But it means that I have given the merchant of the magic items the envelope which is not intended for him. And, by the way, the numbers in the note were written in the goblin system: 23 instead of 17."

"I warned you not to do that, but you wanted to get payment from both of them." Elfid answered.

"He won't be able to use these numbers, will he?" Davkaleon felt twinges of conscience. There he goes, clever guy! Look how successfully he has started his business. One client is dead and the second one is duped!

"I cannot predict whether he can use the goblin numbers or not. The fact is that the octal system is related not only to goblins. It is used by many others. I find it quite doubtful that the jeweler Piromis, provided that he belonged to the human race, cared about leaving his instructions to goblins. Most likely, he had left his guidance notes for someone else, but goblins found that out. I don't think that a goblin having dropped his blood on the envelope would see the number."

"Why do you think these numbers are related to the Pillentally Cave?" Davkaleon asked.

"Because the ancient scrolls state that in Daeya, there are several places that are connected to each other by means of some secret roads. These roads are also called *Gods' paths*. Each of these places has its own code. The place located in the cliff Rock is marked with the number 4 and the one located in the cave Pillentally has the code 5. I suppose the maps you received from the goblin and the merchant had the ways to the place marked with the code 4. You could have gotten from there to the cave Pillentally. But it's not important now, since you are in the cave anyway. And all you have to do now is find the place where you can use the next code."

"Alright, let's go find this place," Davkaleon said, and took a few steps deeper into the cave.

As if out of nowhere, a thick mist appeared and blanketed everything around. It vanished quite fast, but Davkaleon vanished along with it.

Chapter 31. Pillentally Cave

The mist had cleared. Davkaleon was alone, Elfid and Chapius had disappeared. When his eyes adjusted to the gloom, he saw he was in the room with uneven walls and ceiling. The floor was uneven as well. Apparently, Davkaleon was inside the cave. Numerous corridors led in different directions from the room. Davkaleon didn't know which one of them led to the exit from the cave if, of course, it really was the Pillentally Cave. He went around the room having no clue what corridor he had to choose or whether he *should* choose.

Maybe it was better to stay where he was. He remembered that once in the Dragon Tavern, he had heard a dragon telling the story of how Whales had looked for his blood-brother. His loyal Aleurh would certainly be looking for him. So, if he stayed in this room, Aleurh would have a chance of finding him. Davkaleon hunkered down in the middle of the room reasoning out what to do. His peace and quiet didn't last long. Five minutes later, the uneven floor tossed him up. Davkaleon sprang to his feet. The floor in the cave continued to toss him up. Surprisingly, the floor in the corridors remained absolutely still. It felt like the cave was hinting that he had been sitting long enough and it was time to go somewhere.

"I'm not going anywhere!" Davkaleon shouted, intending to stay in the cave.

The floor tossed him up so furiously that Davkaleon hit the stone ceiling. Now the walls and the ceiling joined the wild dance.

"All right, calm down, I'll go now. Just let me choose which way to go." Davkaleon said reluctantly, not really expecting the cave would settle itself. To his surprise, the mad dance stopped, though the floor continued a soft swing.

Davkaleon went around the room one more time, examining the entrances into the numerous corridors. They all looked the same. The floor tossed him up once more. Davkaleon stumbled and hit again, and a drop of blood fell to the floor. Davkaleon stood in front of one of the corridors at this time. A barely-visible number flashed above the corridor and disappeared. Maybe, his eyes were playing tricks on him? Davkaleon squeezed his small wound and another drop of blood fell on the floor. Number 16 showed up once again and then disappeared. Davkaleon remembered the numbers in the note. Number 16 wasn't among them. Davkaleon went to the next corridor. Neither the first blood drop nor the second one made any difference. Nothing happened in the following few corridors. Davkaleon was about to return to the first corridor when number 23 floated above another corridor. Davkaleon remembered this number. The fact that it was the goblin number made him pause. He had given the envelope with the matching number to the merchant of the magic items.

Instead, Davkaleon went to the next corridor. A drop of blood did its thing and he saw the familiar number 19. Davkaleon took a step inside. Scarcely had he entered the corridor when the exit disappeared behind him. A blank wall stood behind him. Ahead in the distance, there was a barely discernible glimmer of light. Davkaleon walked along the corridor. As he moved forward, new blank walls arose behind him, which meant the way back was cut off.

Looks like after all I have entered the Gates of the End, Davkaleon thought. There is no going back and my faithful Aleurh won't be able to find me, just like dragon

Whales couldn't find his blood-brother.

After another blank wall had risen, and Davkaleon found himself in a deadlock. The corridor ended and the blind, uneven walls towered around him on all sides. Davkaleon was in a small room without any windows or doors and without the slightest hint of an entrance or an exit. There was a small overhang in the wall. Just in case, Davkaleon dropped some blood on the overhang, and right then, numbers from 0 to 9 appeared.

"If I don't get it right, I guess the ceiling will flatten me out," Davkaleon whispered.

The numbers began fading away. Davkaleon pressed three numbers in the order they were written on the envelope – 337. The numbers became invisible and there appeared an envelope on the overhang. Davkaleon drew out a note of the envelope. There was no doubt that he now had the missing part of the first note. On the tissue-thin parchment, he saw a few unknown signs and several numbers. Davkaleon did not know what they meant.

512 4913 5832

Keeping in mind that the note had been placed in the envelope for a definite purpose, Davkaleon dropped a little bit of his blood on the envelope. The number 37 appeared and then melted away. Davkaleon dropped a bit of blood on the overhang one more time. Same as last time, he saw numbers from 0 to 9. Having concluded the enveloped had given him a clue, Davkaleon pressed the number 37. The first few seconds nothing happened, and it felt like he was being encouraged to think again—the floor tossed him up to the ceiling. Having fallen back down, Davkaleon saw that the walls and ceiling were shrinking. In the next few seconds, he would be smashed.

"Okay, okay, I was wrong! Please, stop it. Give me one more chance," he told the room.

The walls and the ceiling froze. Not knowing what to do, Davkaleon pressed numbers 337 again. To his amazement, one more envelope appeared on the overhang. The note he drew out of the envelope looked like the previous one. And just as had happened before, after a drop of blood, the number 37 became visible and then disappeared. Davkaleon repeated his action for the third time, and became the proud owner of three similar envelopes with notes.

"And what now? How do I get out of here?"

Just in case, Davkaleon dripped a drop of his blood on the floor. That helped. The wall disappeared. He was back in the cave with a lot of corridors leading different directions. Great! He had obtained the note—or rather, notes—and he could quietly wait for Aleurh. His loyal dragon would surely fly in after him.

But what if he couldn't find him? What if the mist which had brought Davkaleon there wouldn't do the same for Aleurh? He found that he had no time to consider the question.

Goblins came spilling out of every corridor. So many of them! The whole place crawled with dark, disgusting goblins. Davkaleon had a weapon, he even managed to take it out, but goblins were all over him, hanging from his arms and sitting on his shoulders. One of them even got hung up in his hair. Several goblins tried to rifle through his pockets. Davkaleon threw them off, but dozens of others rushed to take their place. Davkaleon hacked several goblins with his sword.

"We don't want to kill you!" one cried, suddenly less interested in fighting. "We need the thing you had to get for us. You were paid for it! Give it to us!"

"You haven't paid anything for this note," Davkaleon objected unwilling to show the goblins the numbers that were destined for the Daeyats. "I gave you the note I found in the cliff Rock using your map. We made *no* agreement about Pillentally Cave."

"You gave us the note, but you kept the envelope. We can't get the second part of the message without the envelope," the goblins answered back.

"We've been smooth-talking him enough! Let's take away what is rightfully ours and grind him to dust for duping us," another goblin demanded.

"Grind him to dust?" the first goblin mocked. "Look at you idiots! How smart you are! And who will get the second part of the note for us? Maybe you will? Go ahead! Go and get it!"

"We can shut him up in the corridor and keep him there until he brings us our note!"

Davkaleon realized he couldn't meet their demands, since the merchant of the magical items had the goblin's envelope. He might have converted the number 337 into the goblin octal system, but when the teacher had been explaining how to do that, Davkaleon had been playing cards, and Elfid was not there.

"We need his blood to make the corridor unveil its secrets!"

"Then, what's the problem? He is here, isn't he? We don't have to kill him—we may still need him. But we can make him bleed!"

As one, the goblins flung themselves at Davkaleon.

Davkaleon brought his sword into play, but it felt like the goblins were everywhere and their numbers were countless. They shoved Davkaleon to the ground and plunged their fangs into him. His blood flowed like water on the floor.

"That's enough!" one of the goblins growled. "Don't you dare get drunk on his blood! We need him to be strong enough to walk down the corridor."

Davkaleon felt his head was spinning. Everything waved before his eyes, but having gone mad, the goblins didn't rush to let him go.

"So, what's the big deal if he doesn't have strength to walk down the corridor? We'll carry him!" another goblin answered.

Davkaleon felt the goblins pick him up and drag him along the corridor. And then, there sounded a terrifying roar and an enormous dragon appeared in the corridor.

"Who dares to enter my domain?" Davkaleon heard.

The dragon opened up his frightening jaws and let out a breath of fire. Having dropped Davkaleon, the goblins ran off at once. Free of the goblins, Davkaleon found himself in front of the huge Adolees DRAGON. His ears buzzed because of his blood loss. Davkaleon felt too weak to run away from the DRAGON, to say nothing of fighting him.

"It worked out! I did it!" Davkaleon heard a familiar voice.

Delighted, Chapius jumped with happy laughter in front of Davkaleon.

"You've already done that before," Davkaleon answered recalling their first journey together.

"Before, I could pretend to be an Adolees DRAGON. Today, I've managed to breathe fire for the first time! You have no idea what that means to me! Now I can join the forces of *Fire Breathing Dragons*! That is what every Adoleeseet dreams of!" Chapius jumped even higher, applauding for himself.

"And what name should I honor you with now?" Davkaleon asked. "Maybe, it's time to search the memory for your real name?"

"Oh dear! No, no!" Chapius looked scared. "We can't disturb the DRAGON! He *knows* when his name passes someone's lips."

Elfid came up to them. As it turned out, when the mist had wrapped everything around and Davkaleon had disappeared, Chapius rushed after him. Dragons fly faster than they run so, Chapius had turned into a dragon. He tried to draw Davkaleon out of the mist, but failed. Flying round the cave, he remembered a dragon telling the story about dragon Whales' missing blood-brother. That story had something in common with Davkaleon's disappearance. In both cases, there was a mist and the flying dragons couldn't locate those who had disappeared. Chapius returned to Elfid and shared his theory.

"Perhaps, the cave doesn't turn its attention to the flying dragons. Maybe, it responds to the weight of a walker. This time, I won't fly! I will walk! Are you coming with me or will you be waiting for us here?"

Elfid hesitated. He had always wanted to take part in Davkaleon's adventures, but his height and body build made this impossible, at least in Daeya. He looked at Chapius. The little Adoleeseet had grown a lot in the time since their last meeting, but he still was smaller than Elfid. And he was going to go inside the cave alone.

Elfid stood up. "Let's go," he said, even though he was trembling inside.

They took a few steps forward. Thick mist folded everything around, it whirled and twirled them for a few moments and then tossed them into the room awash with goblins.

* * * * *

"Don't you dare get drunk on his blood!" Elfid and Chapius saw goblins pick up Davkaleon and drag him into the corridor.

"It's my call now," Chapius said. "Sit still as a mouse and wait for me here." Chapius turned into a tiny bug and vanished into the corridor where goblins dragged Davkaleon.

"Who dares enter my domain?" he growled taking the shape of a huge Adolees DRAGON.

* * * * *

"So, you are saying there was a new envelope every time?" Elfid and Chapius were surprised, listening to Davkaleon's story.

"Since we happen to be here, it would do us well to get the notes from the goblin and merchant's corridors," Elfid said.

It was a good idea. Quite soon, they had all the notes in their hands. The unexpected thing was that the numbers and symbols on all the notes were the same, except for the number in the circle.

"This will make sense if these figures are the manuscript numbers," Elfid said. "Nobody will count the manuscripts by hand. Everyone will look at the numbers as at the pictures in the manuscripts. The symbols mark the way to the secret library then. I have never seen the last three symbols before, but I know that the step-pyramid is the *Temple of Stall*. The eye means a *City of Gods*. The ancient runes insist that the path to the City of

302

Gods lies through the temple of Stall. Unfortunately, the temple was ruined. I don't know what numbers in the circle mean. As soon as we get out of here, I'll search through the manuscripts and runes to find a clue. Maybe, there is a way to get to the City of Gods other than through the Temple of Stall."

"It is time to get out of here," Davkaleon said. "The new envelopes show the number 37. Maybe it is the number of the corridor to the exit," Davkaleon said.

"The goblins raced into that corridor." Elfid pointed at one of the corridors.

"I don't feel like seeing them at all." Davkaleon seemed hesitant.

"I can fly up and check what is going on out there." Chapius suggested.

"I don't think so. Let's stay together. If necessary, you can impersonate your DRAGON," Davkaleon answered.

Davkaleon approached the corridors and dripped a drop of blood near each of them. The number 37 flashed above one passage.

"The number 37 was on every envelope, which means we should go this way."

They entered the corridor. Once they stepped inside, a blank wall arose behind them and the exit disappeared. They went along the corridor, the wall moved after them. Minutes later, they reached a dead end. Davkaleon dripped one more drop of his blood and on the wall and a panel with numbers appeared.

"I assume that if we press the number '3' we will find ourselves in the temple of Assa." Elfid said. "There are several places in Daeya that are connected by secret routes. Each of these places has its own code number. The complete list of codes was lost long ago, but we know that the temple of Assa has code number 3. The cliff rock has code number 4, and Pillentally Cave's code number is 5. They say that the temple of Llill has code number 6, but no one is certain."

"We can try all these numbers and then we'll know for sure!" Davkaleon's eyes were shining.

"It is a dangerous experiment," Elfid said, shaking his head. "Many of these places were destroyed, and the secret passages to them were damaged also. We were told at school that there were brave men who wanted to try such experiments. They're all gone. But even if the passages are preserved, what will you do if you find yourself in the waters of Tartrar? According to rumors, Tartrar also has its own code number."

Davkaleon pressed the number 3.

The next moment, something twirled and whirled them around, everything was covered with black mist. When the mist had cleared, they were in a small room without windows. There was a panel on the wall with unknown signs. Davkaleon could have sworn it was the same room in the *Temple of Assa* from which he had set off for the jeweler's note using Stanglate's map. Several minutes later, they were standing on the square in front of the Temple of Assa. Having shrunk into a little tiny bug, Chapius made himself comfortable in one of Davkaleon enormous pockets.

"First of all, let's go and set Dad's mind to ease." Elfid said, heading for Priest Gerklat's office.

Chapter 32. Back in the Pillentally Cave

"Where is Aleurh?" asked Davkaleon after the tenth or twentieth time he had told the story of what happened in the cave.

He'd told his story, minus a few details of course. He omitted the part about the jeweler's note, so the story was quite short and came down to the fact that the fog that had appeared from nowhere thrown them in a place with many corridors. One of the corridors led them to the panel with the sign of the Perfects of Daeya. Having clicked on this sign, they found themselves in the temple of Assa. Davkaleon did not fail to add gratitude to the Gods of Daeya for helping him and his brother to get out of the Pillentally Cave. The story ended with an exclamation that the court of the Gods had happened! The Gods had made their decision! So, to him and Elfid's pleasure, all charges against them were dropped!

But where was Aleurh?"

"Aleurh is in the Pillentally Cave," Malay said.

Davkaleon's heart sank when he heard what had happened. Aleurh, of course, heard Davkaleon's screaming about a barrel of ale and meeting in three days. But he did not want to wait three days, and immediately rushed for Davkaleon to the cave. Guard dragons stood in his way. Four against one and yet, what could they do? Aleurh wounded two, nearly killed the third, threw away the fourth one and rushed into the cave. The platoon of dragons which flew on alert found neither Aleurh, nor Davkaleon with Elfid near the entrance to the cave, and nobody ordered them to fly inside the cave. What for? The Court of the Gods was in session. It's rude to disturb the Gods.

"I will go to the cave," said Davkaleon, rising from his seat.

"Let's buy some food at first, I'm starving," squeaked Chapius, having moved from the pocket of Davkaleon by his collar.

"Okay, let's go to the *Mug and Sword*," agreed Davkaleon. Eating the food that they brought to the Pillentally Cave, they discussed how to find Aleurh.

"I think I have to go without you to look for Aleurh," said Chapius. "It seems like the cave doesn't pay attention to the flying dragons. It seems to me that it responds to the weight of moving subjects. Your dragon was likely flying while he was looking for you. It is unlikely Aleurh was taken to the room where the fog threw all of us. It's hard for me to carry you on my back, and if you go, the fog will surely take you to a place where Aleurh isn't likely to be."

That sounded logical, but Davkaleon felt uncomfortable sending the little Adoleeseet alone. Of course, Chapius had grown up and was able to spew fire, but he was still a very small dragon. Would he be able to stand up for himself if he is attacked? Wondering what to do, Davkaleon watched in amazement as Chapius ate the second lamb. Davkaleon was sure he had brought enough food for a couple of lunches. But he was wrong! Chapius with his appetite, didn't leave a crumb!

"Don't look at me like that! Do you know how much energy I lose during my transformations? A lot!" the Adoleeseet protested, having noticed Davkaleon's surprised look. "I need to get some rest, and then I'll fly to look for Aleurh," said Chapius, stretching out on the floor and instantly closing his eyes.

Looking at Chapius, Davkaleon remembered that Adoleeseets had amazing powers of telepathy. And dragons of Daeya were much more capable to communicate at a distance than the people of Daeya. Maybe Chapius and Aleurh would be able to hear each other. A half hour later, Chapius opened his eyes and said that he was ready to go on his quest.

"Try calling him mentally," suggested Davkaleon. "Maybe he will hear you."

Chapius nodded and called Aleurh. Initially, there was silence in response, and then Chapius tensed harder and called again. After a few minutes the Adoleeseet jumped happily.

"He asks for you to call him." explained Chapius.

Davkaleon tried, though he didn't expect Aleurh to hear him.

"Call him so, as you called him in childhood," Chapius said, repeating what Aleurh had told him.

Davkaleon called.

"He hears you!"

Within minutes, Aleurh arrived. Tenderness is not common in Daeya, especially among the male population. In the dragon culture, it was not acceptable at all. But joyful Aleurh was overcome by emotion as he flew at Davkaleon, knocked him down and happily licked him, gently purring something to himself.

"I wanted to be sure that it was really you that accompanied Chapius," explained Aleurh. "The goblins tried to attack me. I have dispersed them, of course. Then they tried to lure me into a trap. I do not understand what they wanted from me."

"If they caught you, they would have leverage to force me into giving them a note I had found in the cave." Explained Davkaleon.

* * * * *

It was a busy day. Having said goodbye to Chapius, Davkaleon looked into the office of Stanglate, although he was not sure he could reach the teacher of the old-Daeya's language so late. To his surprise, the teacher was in the office, and the old-Daeyan manuscripts were in front of him on the table. Davkaleon told him about what had happened in the cave, omitting some details, and he handed a note to the teacher. To his surprise, hardly having looked at the signs on the note, the teacher groaned from frustration.

"I've never seen the last two signs, but I know what the step pyramid means. This is the Temple of Stall. Once, it was possible to get into the City of the Gods from there. But the temple has been destroyed. It was destroyed in those days, when Daeya was inhabited only by true Daeyats and they talked to each other in the true Daeyan language. Then, some of the Daeyats rebelled against the divine authority, destroying the Temple of Stall and the way to the City of the Gods disappeared. That is when things started to change and the disparities between events and the divine predictions began."

Explaining this, Stanglate almost cried. It seemed that he believed that the notes of Piromis the Jeweler were lost forever. Davkaleon said goodbye and went to see Elfid. Davkaleon was confident that Elfid could find anything in the manuscripts. Of course, he caught Elfid reading runes and manuscripts. There were ancient papyruses with mysterious signs on the table. Most of them were unfamiliar to Davkaleon, but one caught his eye. It was an unknown sign from the notes that were found in the cave.

"These are the signs of the places you can get from the City of the Gods," explained Elfid. "The sign shown on the note led to the *Temple of Attl*. I've never heard of this temple, and I don't think that it is located in Daeya."

Having stretched out on the bed, Davkaleon immediately fell asleep. He did not sleep for long before someone vigorously shook his shoulders. Having opened his eyes, Davkaleon saw goblins.

"Get your paws off me!" Davkaleon became angry and grabbed for his weapon.

"We are not going to attack you," said a relatively peaceful goblin. "We want to offer you money for the second note. You have it anyway, so give it to us and we will pay you."

"Oh, no! I'm fed up with doing business with you. You see, you are extremely *friendly* customers." Sarcasm was clear in Davkaleon's voice.

"And you're not the most *honest* contractor. We paid you in full, and you didn't give us the envelope. Moreover, you gave the envelope to another client. And, by the way, our courier has not returned. Where is he? What did you do to him?"

"Your courier tried to kill me, so he got what deserved," muttered Davkaleon. Davkaleon almost agreed that the goblins assessments were at least partially right, but he didn't want to admit it.

"Give us our note. We brought the money and will not hold a grudge with you for giving our envelope to the competitor," proposed a goblin as he put a heavy purse in front of Davkaleon.

Davkaleon tossed and caught the purse from hand to hand as he thought. The purse weighed a lot.

"And why not?" thought Davkaleon. "In any case, Daeyats cannot use the path specified in the note. Maybe the goblins know of another way."

"Okay," muttered Davkaleon. "You can have your note."

He reached into his pockets. There were no notes there. Not even one.

"You've taken the notes while I slept!" Davkaleon raged.

"What do you mean *have taken*? We didn't touch them!" roared the goblins. "And why would we pay you if we had it?"

The question was logical, but how could Davkaleon explain the disappearance of the notes? "In order to make me go somewhere else?" suggested Davkaleon.

"But we do not hide that we want to supply you with constant orders and pay for them well. Are you against such orders?" asked the goblins.

Davkaleon did not object to getting orders. He silently searched his pockets again. He didn't find any notes. There had been five notes. He'd given one to Stanglate and one to Elfid. Where were the other three? The enraged goblins headed for the exit.

"You forgot your purse," reminded Davkaleon.

"That is payment for our note," said the last goblin, leaving the room and closing the door behind him.

Davkaleon sat on the bed, recounting each of his steps. One note, he gave to Elfid in the Pillentally Cave. He gave another one to Stanglate in his office. The other notes were in his pocket at this time. After his visit to Stanglate he didn't touch them. If the goblins didn't take the notes, where are they?

The door opened, and the merchant of magical goods entered the room.

"Won't somebody pay attention to the fact that the door is locked? You could knock on the door for decency before barging in!" Davkaleon raged.

Honestly, the indignation of Davkaleon was a little ostentatious. He felt that the merchant, as well as the goblins, would demand his notes. He would give the note, if he had it, but he didn't. So, the appearance of this uninvited guest without knocking was just a pretext to get rid of him.

But the merchant was not just going to retreat. "I did not get anything from you for my money! You gave me the one note and the other envelope. I barely survived in the Pillentally Cave when I tried to use them," wailed the merchant.

"Come to me tomorrow night. I want to sleep now." said Davkaleon, pointedly lying down on the bed. Closing his eyes, he decided to go to the Pillentally Cave for the third time tomorrow and to get an ill-fated note one more time.

* * * * *

"Where could these notes have disappeared to?" said Kvorts, surprised after Davkaleon told the brothers what had happened.

"It does not matter where they are, if Davkaleon can get a dozen of these notes." said Malay. "I am more surprised by another thing. Why did the goblins leave the purse with money after they found out that the note disappeared?"

Their first lesson that day was Daeyan language. Upon entering the class, Stanglate came up to Davkaleon and quietly asked him if he took the note when he left the teacher's office yesterday. "I ask just in case," explained the teacher, "I remember putting the note in the table, but this morning I didn't find it there."

For the remainder of the lesson, Davkaleon couldn't stop thinking about what had happened to the notes. After the lesson, Malay asked, "How much money was in the goblin's purse?"

"I do not know. Probably, five thousand. They did not say. And yesterday I was too tired to count the money. And I have not time today."

"You don't know how much?" gasped Malay. "Count it immediately."

Having taken out the purse, Davkaleon wondered why it was so light. The answer was obvious. The purse was empty.

"I know what the goblins have planned," said Malay. "While you were sleeping, they stole the notes. All notes. And now they want to force you to give them back what they have paid you, and even more. They could say that there was five, ten, or even twenty thousand in the purse. They will declare that they had paid you, and you did not execute the order. I heard about such cases from my relatives on my mother's side. They are related to financiers and bankers, they told me many stories about such cases of fraud."

"How could the goblins do that? We did not have a written contract, so it is my word against theirs. But the case won't come to that. They do not have rights to appeal to the criminal court of Daeya. No one will hear the complaints of goblins. Not even the court of priests." Davkaleon shrugged.

"They will appeal to the arbitration court," said Malay, "and that's not good for you. The rumors will spread that you have taken the money and did not execute the order. The best case for you is to get these notes as fast as possible and hand them over. Let them choke."

"Davkaleon Gerklat!" came a thunderous voice. "You should come to the executive's office!"

Chapter 33. Arbitration Tribunal

A few goblins and the merchant of magical goods sat in the high executives' office at the military school.

"We paid him thirty thousand seekls, and we got nothing in return," the goblins complained.

"Thirty thousand?!" Davkaleon sputtered. "You paid me ten thousand and not a sheum more."

"That was the first payment. Yesterday we left you a purse with twenty thousand." the goblins said in one voice.

"What?" Davkaleon pulled out his purse, preparing to throw it to the goblins. At the last second, he froze in disbelief. The purse was heavy again—tightly packed with something.

"Who asked you for the twenty-thousand seekls? Not me! On the contrary, I pointed to your purse and asked you to take it with you. I said that I didn't want to do business with you."

"But you haven't completed your first contract!" the goblin protested. "Moreover, you gave the envelope to our competitor."

"I gave you the jeweler's note. You did not request the envelope. Our agreement was the note only."

"But you gave our note and the envelope to another customer!" the goblin cried.

"Do you deny that I gave you your note? How did you find the Pillentally Cave? You learned about it from the note! That's why you were waiting for me there! You wanted, by the way, to kill me, but then you realized that you could not get the second note without me, and changed your tactics. I never agreed to get the second note for you."

"We demand an arbitration tribunal!" said the goblin, turning to the executives of the school.

"Myself as well," said the merchant of magical goods who'd been silent before that moment. "I gave Davkaleon the map and told him how to get the jeweler's note. I paid 10 thousand seekls, and in the end, I have a note that was intended for goblins."

"Very well," said one of the executives from the school. "Sign your petition to the arbitration tribunal."

The goblins and the merchant immediately signed the document.

"Now, you sign," said one of the executives to Davkaleon.

"And why should I? I did not appeal to the court. They want a hearing. Let them do it," said Davkaleon.

"You are accused of dishonesty. That is not compatible with you staying at school. Either the arbitration tribunal will decide who, what and whom ought to do what, and you will immediately comply with the decision of the tribunal, or you will leave the school."

The case took an unpleasant turn. Davkaleon signed what they wanted.

"Fine," said the administrator. "You all agree with the terms of the school arbitration tribunal. This means that the school gets 50 percent of the disputed amount. The goblins wanted to get back 30,000 seekls. The school will get 15,000. That is, 7,500 from goblins and 7,500 from Davkaleon Gerklat. The dear merchant of magical goods wanted to get back 10,000 seekls. The school will get 5,000, including 2,500 from the merchant and 2,500 from Davkaleon. Pay, please."

The goblins and the merchant immediately paid the money. Davkaleon was taken aback by the unexpected request, but then he remembered that the purse of the goblins was full again. Pulling the purse from his pocket, he vividly described what he thought about the goblins and their magical purses.

Of course, the purse was empty.

"We don't know what you did with our money." the goblins calmly commented on the flowery speech of Davkaleon.

"If you have no money, we will provide a credit to you," came the school's offer.

It was not true that Davkaleon had no money at all, but he had much less than he needed to pay. The first 10,000 that he had received from the Goblin and the merchant, he'd spent to cover their debt to the banker and, of course, for a small dinner to celebrate getting out of debt. And he did not remember where he spent the half of the next 10,000. Swimming lessons cost a lot, and he had to enlarge his weapon set, but still, it was a mystery to Davkaleon how he managed to spend so much money in only a few days.

Then he remembered Saturday's card game. A good game. Interesting, but very expensive. He would just have to borrow several thousand from the banker.

The familiar figure of the loan shark appeared at the door.

"What is your percentage for the day?" asked Davkaleon.

"Only 10 percent. I am not a bloodsucker," replied the banker.

"I want a daily updated short-term loan with simple interest," demanded Davkaleon who remembered well his first meeting with the banker.

"If that is the case, then I must charge12 percent," said the banker.

"10.5 percent."

"11 percent and we have a deal," the banker offered.

Waving his hand, Davkaleon signed the I.O.U. The

tribunal began immediately. The goblins and merchant demanded their money back. Davkaleon stated that he was willing to provide the merchant and goblins all the notes with all the envelopes no later than the following night. He promised the merchant to provide the note from the Pillentally Cave for free as compensation for what had happened with the note from the Rock cliff.

"Fine. It will be arranged." said someone from the school leadership. "But let's meet in a week, instead. We are very busy for the next few days. So, we'll meet in a week at seven o'clock in the evening," summarized the arbitrators.

"They get a kickback from the banker," thought Davkaleon. "In a week, I'll have to pay the bloodsucker much, much more."

After school, Davkaleon went to Elfid. He could not wait to find out if Elfid kept the note or if it disappeared as well.

"Did you come here to say that all of the notes are gone?" Elfid asked, peering over the mountains of runes and manuscripts. "After my note disappeared literally before my eyes, I found something interesting. Read silently, please, as it concerns you know whom," warned Elfid.

The manuscript concerned the magicians of *Twierks*, so Elfid's warning was very helpful.

"Do they allow you to read this in your school?" Davkaleon was surprised, accustomed to the fact that the word *Twierks* was strictly forbidden in Daeya.

"We have an ongoing controversy at our school about what we can read and what we cannot, where we can go and where we cannot. But in the end, we have permission to do all that we ask, though they require a detailed explanation of why we are doing it and where we will practice it."

"I wonder, how do the magicians do it? I mean, how do they make envelopes with notes appear when someone clicks the correct numbers, and disappear in a few hours?"

"I wonder as well," smiled Elfid.

Davkaleon again looked at the manuscript of Elfid and said, "I think I know where to get the money to pay off the banker".

"You have a strange hobby, Davkaleon. You earn money in order to immediately hand it over to your lender."

* * * * *

Once again, Davkaleon found himself in the Pillentally Cave. This time, he was with his faithful Aleurh. However, this was not his last visit. He visited the cave the next evening and the next, and then another one. He wanted to know in how many hours, minutes and seconds the notes would disappear. Davkaleon was angry at the goblins, and wanted to pay them back in their own coin.

* * * * *

The time for tribunal approached. Davkaleon sorted envelopes with notes for the goblins into his numerous pockets. *This note will disappear in an hour, and this one will disappear five minutes after the first, and this one ten minutes later.* It was a pity that he had only 36 pockets. The tribunal could not last more than three hours. And if it did, well, he was ready to decline his earnings—he had one last note that would be good for five hours in the last pocket.

"I brought the envelopes with the notes," reported Davkaleon upon entering the room. "But before giving them to you I would like to clarify the procedure."

"You put the envelopes with the notes on the table," the arbitrator explained. "Next to them, you put 2,500 seekls for the distinguished merchant of magical goods and 7,500 seekls for the goblins. The merchant of magical goods and the goblins, in turn, put in 2,500 and 7,500 seekls. We examine the envelopes. If they're all fine, we pass them on to the merchant and the goblins, and you take all the money from the table. If something is not in order, the merchant and the goblins take all the money. In this case, you'll have to give them back what they paid you before. If someone doesn't have money, our respectable banker will gladly supply the necessary amount on account."

The procedure was clear. The additional 10,000 seekls was a surprise, but Davkaleon was ready for it. Malay had visited his relatives—true experts of the arbitration tribunals—and told Davkaleon what he should be ready for. The additional money actually fit within Davkaleon's plan. After all, he could write the IOU quickly or slowly, adjusting the time remaining until the disappearance of each subsequent note.

"Where is our dear banker?" asked Davkaleon.

The banker appeared instantly, as if waiting for this moment. Having written the IOU, Davkaleon put the envelopes on a table and walked to the window, away from the arbitrators. From there, he watched as the moneylender, the merchant and the goblins lay out their money. Having considered the notes, the arbitrators put them in envelopes and announced that the goblins and the merchant could take them, and Davkaleon could take all the money from the table.

The court of arbitration was over. The merchant and the goblins left the room. Davkaleon payed off the banker, and as the shark counted his money, they heard a heartbreaking cry from the goblins. The door swung open, and the enraged goblins burst into the room.

"Where's the note? Where'd you put it?" the goblins cried, attacking Davkaleon.

"What more do you want of me? Didn't you see that I put your note on the table along with the envelope, and did not touch it again?" Davkaleon spoke as if utterly confused. He was not very good at lying, but everyone saw that he had not come to the table.

"Look for the note in the envelope instead of accusing me of stealing it," suggested Davkaleon.

"In the envelope?! Do you think that we didn't think to look in the envelope? Here it is! Look for in the envelope yourself!"

One of the goblins held out his paw. There was nothing in it.

"Where is the envelope?!" yelled the goblin. "It was just here!"

"So, you have lost the envelope! Or was that also me?" asked Davkaleon.

"You have planned this!" screamed the goblins.

But this was just too much for the school leadership. The last thing they wanted was to let the goblins disgrace the school, slandering their student. Moreover, a *highly respected* student. The goblins were thrown out of the office.

However, Davkaleon had no doubt that he would meet them again very soon. Having entered his room, he saw them. The dark goblins met him in grim silence.

"How much do you want?" asked one of them.

"You called the price yourself," replied Davkaleon with a smile.

"Have a conscience! Do you know how much we have lost because of you?" the goblins raged.

"And I have lost so much because of you. Why did you give me your idiot's purse, and then appeal to the arbitration tribunal? I still have to pay the moneylender! Do you know that with all of your kindness, I'm in debt again?"

"Will everything be fair this time? Will you give neither the envelope nor our note to someone else?"

"Everything will be fair," promised Davkaleon. "How could I know the first time that the numbers in the notes were different? And *no one* spoke to me about the envelope."

"And was it hard to guess that you should deal with one client?" asked the goblin.

"No one demanded that I worked exclusively for him, and no one signed an exclusive contract with me, so stop your empty accusations. Tomorrow night at the banker's office, you will receive your order. You will give him the money, and he will pay me. He will ask for a huge percentage for this, of course, but at least I will get something. Otherwise, I will owe you."

When he approached the banker, Davkaleon was astounded at the shark's offer. "Only 20 percent?" Davkaleon was amazed having heard the banker's offer. "You must at least pay me 40 percent."

"I can't," the banker said sadly. "I would love to, since you're my favorite client. A permanent client, I might ad. I always give my favorites a discount, but to deal with money from the goblins is a source of continuous loss. You yourself know it. No matter how I plan the details, appeal to Gods, no matter what prayers and spells I can utter and no matter what rituals I hold, I still can lose everything."

"Okay, give me 20 percent," agreed Davkaleon.

In the end, the banker assumed the entire risk, so there was no need to be greedy. After paying the moneylender, he would even have a couple of hundred seekls for himself. Of course, it was not the 20,000 seekls he had hoped for, but it was better than nothing.

* * * * *

"Swine! You lied to us again!" came the warm greeting from the goblins, as Davkaleon entered his room.

"Are you at it again? What is wrong this time?" Davkaleon was taken aback.

"What is wrong? The Temple of Stall was destroyed a long time ago! What is the meaning of the note, if we are unable to use it?"

"Has the Temple of the Stall been destroyed? Really?! And this, of course, is my fault again?" Davkaleon pretended a great fury. His face grew red, and he shook.

"You knew that the note mentioned the Temple of Stall and you didn't tell us about it! What did we pay you for?"

"Contact the Arbitration Tribunal again, because I am out of money," Davkaleon advised them.

"You'd be better not to quarrel with us," said the dark goblin.

"I am not quarreling with you. The argument is all on one side! You tried to kill me and throw me a purse with disappearing money. What do you want from me today?"

"Give us our purse." asked the goblins.

"I won't!" said Davkaleon. "You said yourself that it was a payment for the note when you gave it to me. The note is yours, so we're even."

"Why do you need the purse?" asked the goblin. "Sell it to us. We will pay you 100 seekls."

One hundred seekls for an empty purse? Something wasn't right about that. The goblins were not that generous to just throw away money.

"I won't give it to you! I want to keep it in memory of doing business with you," replied Davkaleon.

"Two hundred seekls?" suggested the goblins.

"Do you need to pay someone, but ran out of all your fraudulent purses?" asked Davkaleon.

The goblins did not have time to answer. A knock at the door, and Elfid appeared on the threshold. Davkaleon carefully examined him, wondering if it was, in fact, his brother or perhaps Chapius. Dissatisfied, the goblins left the room, and Davkaleon listened with interest to what Elfid had to say.

"I brought you copies of the first three manuscripts of the jeweler. The manuscripts have the image of the sign from the jeweler's note. However, I don't know how this will help you. The sign leads to *Attl*. I've never heard about Attl, and I don't think it is in Daeya. The manuscripts do not tell exactly where this unknown Attl is located, or how to get there."

He shrugged before continuing. "Also, I expected the manuscripts would have numbers from the second note—

512, 4913, 5832.

They don't. The manuscript covers have numbers, but these numbers are different. They are

826, 5072, 6097.

I don't know how to explain it."

That was interesting! After all the efforts spent on getting the notes of the jeweler, Davkaleon was curious what was written in these notes that everyone in Daeya was hunting them. Elfid handed Davkaleon three manuscripts.

"Let's go to the *Mug and the Sword*," suggested Davkaleon. "My treat."

After dinner with Elfid, Davkaleon came back to his room and opened the first manuscript.

These are the records of the jeweler Piromis, the son of the jeweler Piromis, carved in the cliff rock, where he was transferred by the powerful magician of the Temple, and where he resided for seven long years, making jewels by the order of the powerful magician who filled them by his magical powers.

Davkaleon laid back on his bed, alone at last, a smile on his face, immersed in his reading.

Epilogue

"What do you think about him?" Ecktoral asked his companion.

"He is brave, cheeky, cocky, boastful, and moderately smart. It may work well for him to guide the army of Daeya. For the Twierks, it won't work," Adamant said, shaking his head.

"Why do you attack my protégé?" grinned Ecktoral.

"He does not like to learn. Weapons, fighting, battle training? He's good at those. But for Twierks, this is not enough. For Twierks, his brother Elfid would be a better fit."

"Elfid is not a leader. Elfid has no equal in sitting alone, solving riddles and puzzles, but he cannot lead an army. They won't believe in him and won't follow him. Twierks needs a charismatic leader, able to inspire and ignite," objected Ecktoral.

"Your Davkaleon can inspire and ignite. The question is, where he will lead to and what will he make his troops do? The leader of bison, you know, drags the whole herd, even when he races toward the abyss. Davkaleon fights well, and he does not hide behind the backs of others, but for Twierks *this is not enough*. Even a simple sequence puts him at a standstill. He runs to Elfid for advice in the case of any problem. Can you imagine the level of physics and mathematics that he will need to learn, at least in general terms, to understand what happens in Twierks? When will he do it? He's not a child. Making your Davkaleon the leader of the army in Twierks is about the same as relying on a Neanderthal from the stone age. A little wash, a comb, and explanation that a laser gun is not a truncheon, and boom, he is the next commander of the space forces? It is a good idea to train a commander that no one is expecting, and Daeya is perfect for this. No one would bet on a Daeyat. But how will you make your Davkaleon forget about fights, battles and, among other things, about the cards—which he is fond of—and make him read textbooks? And not just Daeyan textbooks!" argued Adamant. He pointed to the glass of the foaming beverage on the table and the glass soared up and slowly floated to his hand.

"I will not only make him do it. He himself will *burn* with the desire to understand," answered Ecktoral.

"Don't count on that. If you think that your girl Heather, or whatever her name is, will be of great help in bending him, I hate to disappoint you. She will not."

"Of course, she will. No doubt she will!" Ecktoral smiled slyly.

"She may draw him in, but that is where it will end!" Adamant grunted. "She will lure him with her good looks and sweet voice, but you are wrong to think that Davkaleon will immediately sit down and begin studying geometry and algebra at her suggestion. Do you think that he will be so committed to his studies that he'll not be able to fall asleep without a logarithm? Ensure that he will give up on his training and soak himself in quantum physics? For her, your Davkaleon will show up in Twierks...I don't argue that. But you will not make him want to hit the books. If she tries to put pressure on him, he will pack all of his textbooks and send them to Elfid as a gift. After that, he will immediately fall head over heels in love with any other pretty that comes along."

"Oh, Adamant, you don't believe in romance, but it is the strongest stimulator," smiled Ecktoral.

"And you think this girl Heather is such a great inspiration?"

"Yes, I do. Davkaleon will aim for Twierks even

without her. But with her, he will aim to get there even more. He will get to the most dangerous places in all of Twierks even without her, but with her he will get there even faster. His brain works well without her, but with her, he would rather die than admit that he does not understand something or is incapable of doing so."

"Why did you choose Davkaleon over all other Daeyats?"

"I didn't choose him. In fact, he caught my eye by accident. I first had my sights on the little Adoleeseet, Chapa. It turned out, that he had been chosen by many, most likely for the same reason. In fact, there were those in Adolees who wanted to eliminate him so that he could not become stronger. If you remember, he was supposed to die at the stadium, but he survived. I observed it, but I have not intervened, so no one can reproach us for changing events."

After another sip, he continued. "He escaped from the guards at the stadium. That was the first surprise. Nobody knew that he was able to turn into a dragon, but he could, and he got away from the guards. It was decided to send him to Daeya. He had zero chance to get out of there alive, but he did so, to everyone's surprise. And everything, or almost everything, happened without my intervention. I had the intention to make a small hurricane to hide him in a safe place and let him take a breath as hurricanes in Daeya happen almost daily, but even this was not necessary, for Davkaleon helped him. As for Davkaleon, when he gets into trouble—which he gets into it all the time—he does not blame anyone, does not complain and gets out of it by himself. And he studies at this very minute."

"If you believe in him so much, what are you going to do about his education?" asked Adamant. "He is useless in

326

Twierks with his current knowledge and understanding."

"I am working on that. Let him learn at his school for a while, be tempered and matured, be addicted to adventures, and then, I will send him to one very interesting place. There, he will quickly make up for lost time."

"If you pin so much hope on the girl, then you can't draw attention to her. She has already appeared in the scripts of many magicians and their disciples during Walpurgis night," said Adamant.

"Yes, she has appeared. It is impossible to get away from this, unfortunately. I need a beautiful girl with a strong white aira, who is at least a little capable of navigating in Twierks. Such girl will always attract attention. But so far, no one connects her with the upcoming tournament, and no one makes bets on her. Although, they insert her in the scripts, just in case."

"That's bad. Your Davkaleon will attract attention to himself ahead of time."

"He hasn't done so yet. Besides, he is not a magician. He is not even an apprentice. He is just a tweener now. He doesn't realize that he has got the blood not only of Chapa, but the blood of DRAGON himself. That is why he sees the sign of Adolees, and the sign of the Dragon and the Rose."

Adamant tapped his chin. "Why does your Heather wear a mask all the time? Have you not made her your final choice yet?"

"She wears a mask in order to warm up his interest and create mystery. I made my choice long ago, and I have been preparing everything. It has all been carefully calculated. However, I'll tell you more next time."

TO BE CONTINUED...

www.ingramcontent.com/pod-product-compliance
Lightning Source LLC
Chambersburg PA
CBHW070539260626

47161CB00002B/450